BURIED SECRETS

"What is it you want me to see?" she called out.

Aaron pointed with the light, deeper into the passageway. "There," he said.

Hesitantly she stepped forward and looked around the corner. Ten feet in, the beam bounced off a wall of silt—then lowered to the ground to illuminate an old tennis shoe.

Roni inched her way down the passage, her own beam playing along the silt. The closer she got, the more apprehensive she became. Silt. Cave-in. Somewhere in time this passage had become weak, releasing a couple of tons of sandy earth to close a portion of the tunnel.

She wrapped her fingers around the yellowed canvas shoe and lifted. She felt resistance as the silt higher on the mound began to funnel down. Frightened, the shoe clutched in her hand, Roni pulled back and fell against the rough wall. Something inside the shoe rattled. Bones, tiny bones spilled from the shoe onto her lap . . .

NIGHT PASSAGE

NIGHT PASSAGE

CAROL DAVIS LUCE

ZEBRA BOOKS
KENSINGTON PUBLISHING CORP.

ZEBRA BOOKS are published by

Kensington Publishing Corp.
850 Third Avenue
New York, NY 10022

First Printing: June, 1995

Printed in the United States of America

Dedicated to the loving memory of
Joyce Faith Farrell

Dedicated to the memory of
Ryan Maloy

Acknowledgments

I wish to thank Rob Cohen, Richard Curtis, and Tracy Bernstein.

Special thanks to these people in business who made certain this and other novels of mine were available and highly visible: Greg Sheppard, Richard Carlson, Steve Hunter, Ray Cheeseman, Lance Larson, Michael Engelmann, Toni Reetz, Chris Whitney, Myrtle Henry, Diane Martinez, Dan Earl, Kathie Nyberg, Jeff Cultice, Jim and Sheryl Lane.

I owe thanks to my good friends, family, and patient readers: Kay Fahey, Michele Luce, Renée Luce, Margaret Falk, Patricia Wallace Estrada, Cathy Pierce, Barbara Land, Sara Wood, Harry Davis I, Harry Davis II, Alan Christian, Irene Gunter, Mike and Patti Specchio.

My thanks to Edward Cope, Arlene Kramer, Crystal McCay, and Carol Mick of Mines and Geology for their time and information.

One

Eagleton, Nevada
Sunday, Midnight

Between the dark and the daylight,
When the night is beginning to lower,
Comes a pause in the day's occupations,
That is known as the children's hour.

I hear in the chamber above me
The patter of little feet;
The sound of a door that is opened,
And voices soft and sweet . . .

—"The Children's Hour," H. W. Longfellow

The grandfather clock struck the hour, midnight, the deep chimes drowning out the sounds of the wind rustling the trees, rattling the windows. Caroline Holt's glance went from the leather bound volume of *Best Loved Poems* spread open on her lap to the ceiling of the old house. No patter of little feet, no door opening, no voices soft and sweet. Tonight her son, Aaron, worked quietly two floors above in the attic. Soon she would go up and shoo him off to bed.

She placed her hand over her abdomen, thinking back twelve years, remembering her excitement at the first gentle flutter she'd felt. The miracle of new life. A child of their own. Aaron.

She opened another leather bound volume, lifted the pen tucked in the crease, and began to write.

My darling Richard, how I wish you were here to guide me. In the past month I've learned something I did not want to know, and I've done something that cannot be undone. I must tell someone before it's too late. I'm afraid for Aaron, for myself. If only you were here to help us, to tell us what to do.

With icy, trembling fingers she lifted the glass from the lamptable and sipped at the brandy. Pressing the glass to her chest, Caroline leaned back against the chair and closed her eyes. "In the round-tower of my heart," she whispered softly to the husband she had lost twenty years earlier in Vietnam, ". . . I keep you forever . . ."

Minutes later in the dining room she refilled her glass, lifted the phone, and dialed. An answering machine on the other line clicked on. Caroline had left a message earlier—no point in leaving another. She hung up, carried the glass of brandy through the house, and, somewhat unsteady on her feet, climbed the stairs to the second floor.

* * *

As he moved through the dark passageway beneath the streets of Eagleton he listened to the echoes, to the hollow underground sounds of scurrying creatures, dripping water, and his own heavy breathing. The insipid beam from a penlight danced several feet in front of him. Long shadows crawled up the walls, growing and stretching as he neared the ladder to the trapdoor that led into the house of a woman he once loved.

How long since he had come in this way, passion and exhilaration rushing through his veins like fire and ice, the world outside unreal, nonexistent? He felt exhilaration now, passion as well, but tonight both were different. For a long time he had thought about this. Exactly how he would do it.

He took the gloves from his pocket and worked his fingers into them. Then he climbed the ladder, opened the trapdoor, and pulled himself up into the tiny basement.

Silently, quickly, his footsteps muted by the gusting wind outside, he made his way through the large house to the dining room. Satisfied that a good measure of the brandy in the decanter had been reduced and that she and the boy had turned in for the night—the lights had gone out over an hour ago—he continued up to the second floor to her bedroom.

At the open door he paused, directed the beam of light at the foot of the bed, and let it slowly glide along her slender length to her face—pale, lovely, relaxed in sleep. If she sensed the light from beneath her eyelids, there was no indication.

Holding the light on her face, he entered and went

directly to the nightstand that had once, years ago, held her so-called shrine. All that remained of that ridiculous display was the wedding photo and the pocketknife. He stared at the photo, feeling a flash of pure hatred. He wanted to smash it. Wanted her to witness it, to see and feel her pain, let her see and know his pain.

Instead he lifted an empty glass by its stem and tipped it. A bead of amber-colored liquid, clouded with a powdery sediment, rolled at the bottom. He replaced the glass and lifted the pocketknife. In the moonlight the metal plate on one side glinted. It was too dark to read, but he knew what was engraved there. *R. Holt.* He pulled out the smaller, sharper blade and turned back to the bed. Caroline Holt slept on her back, her arms at her sides. He gently lifted a limp hand and pressed his lips to her palm.

Her face in sleep was beautiful, serene. She had always been beautiful; even now with her illness, with dark smudges and tiny lines around her eyes, she was lovely. He felt the crushing ache pushing all rational thoughts away. She had done this to him, had forced him to kill. If he didn't stop her, she would destroy him.

He raised his mouth from the soft flesh of her hand. He pressed the tip of the blade into the pale skin of her wrist and made several superficial cuts. Two tiny beads of blood formed and ran down her arm to the hollow of her elbow. Her hand lay limp in his. He sighed and pulled the blade away. He fit the knife's handle in her right hand, then wrapping her fingers around it he drew the blade across the left wrist. For an instant the opening glowed bone-white, then blood welled up and began to pour out. Fascinated, he watched. He repeated the process with the right, not going as deep, until both slim wrists were open, the blood flowing freely. He let the knife fall from her fingers onto the white quilt.

Her arm jerked upward, surprising him. A stream of blood darkened the front of his shirt and flew across the framed picture that stood on the nightstand. He took hold of both arms and gently pushed them down to her sides, securing them. Her eyelids fluttered, then opened wide to stare with surprise into his. Her direct gaze jolted him. He nearly released her. A moment later her lids lowered halfway to stare vacantly ahead. He felt a strong resistance in her body, an instinctive will to survive. His heart throbbed in his chest. He waited, his insides churning, until there were no more struggles, until her face turned ashen and her skin grew cold and clammy.

Finally releasing her, he lifted the framed wedding picture and carefully placed it facedown on her chest. He took the glass, went downstairs, rinsed out both glass and decanter in the kitchen sink, and returned them to the dining room. Back in the kitchen he lifted the stove top, blew out the pilot light, and turned on a burner. He listened for the hiss of escaping gas before making his final retreat to the tunnel beneath the house.

Long Beach, California
Sunday, 1:22 AM

Roni Mayfield struggled with her luggage, shifting the totebag, laptop computer, and a week's mail around to free a hand to unlock and open her front door. She used her foot to close the door and her elbow to switch on the entry light and was immediately enveloped by bright light and stale air. The rapid invasion of mustiness always amazed her. She had been gone less than a week, yet the small house smelled of mildew as if it had been closed up for months. The bedsheets, she knew, would feel cold and damp—a small price to pay for living at the edge of paradise.

She piled her luggage in the entry, crossed the living room to the glass slider, and opened it all the way. The night was mild. The rhythm of crashing waves filled the house with a familiar, soothing sound, like fine music. Tonight the sea was fluorescent. Beautiful. Haunting. She loved it like this with the waves glowing an eerie greenish-white, the microscopic shells, pebbles, and foam sparkling like jewels beneath a late-night full moon.

This was the ultimate pleasure—coming home. The traveling didn't get to her as long as she had a home base, and home was on the Pacific Ocean with her own stretch of beach ... that is, if she didn't mind sharing it with thousands of others from June to October. Unless the grunion were running, nights on the beach were usually quiet, free of surf and sand worshipers. Tonight the beach was deserted.

She stepped out onto the deck of the robin's-egg-blue bungalow with its white gingerbread trim, leaned against the doorframe, and inhaled deeply of the salty air. That very afternoon she had filled her lungs with the dusty, parched air of the desert.

It all came back in a rush: three highly emotional, drama-filled days spent in the hills overlooking a nameless ghost town on the California/Nevada border. In the center of a barbed-wire barricade, thirty-five feet down into an abandoned mine shaft, seven-

year-old Dennis Stemmer clung to a makeshift plat-
form of rotting boards wedged precariously across
the narrow opening of the shaft. Where at any
moment the boards could give way and send the boy
plummeting a hundred feet below to certain death.
As the first agonizing, though hopeful, hours
stretched into days, Roni knew with a profound sense
of dread what the child was going through. Years ago
as a young girl in another Nevada town, she'd survived
a similar experience and she had only to close her
eyes to relive the ordeal. For seventy-two hours she'd
known Dennis's pain, his fear of death and darkness,
his complete aloneness.

On assignment for *Tempo Magazine*, Roni had been
the first major media journalist on the scene. Her
prospector father, working a claim in the area, had
contacted her within an hour of the accident. At first
the boy had been lucid and quite brave, calling to
them. But after the third freezing night, in a great
deal of pain from several broken bones, terrified each
time a board beneath him shifted or groaned, his
bravado and strength had finally dissolved. At the
end no more words or soft whimpering could be
heard from the shaft. With the deadly silence Roni's
faith dissolved as well.

Then, suddenly, into the bright morning light, a
small, limp form, streaked with dirt and blood was
lifted out, then cradled in his parent's arms as para-
medics worked feverishly to revive him.

The following morning at the hospital in Bishop,
where Roni spent a sleepless night in the waiting
room, Dennis's condition was upgraded to stable,
then to good. When it came time to leave, the parting
had been emotional. Those long days of hovering

impotently around the shaft with life or death hanging in the balance had bound her to the family. Remembering little Dennis's brave smile when they said goodbye made her smile too.

At twenty-eight, single, a journalist for six years, those were the stories Roni liked to cover. The ones with happy endings.

It was late and she was exhausted, yet the need to unwind before turning in, especially after an out-of-town assignment, was an old habit she couldn't break. She would check her mail and phone messages, then change into sweats and take a midnight stroll on the beach.

The next few minutes were spent sorting mail. Halfway through she came across an envelope, its stationery strangely familiar, as was the handwriting. No return address, but she wasn't surprised to see the postmark—Eagleton, Nevada.

Eagleton. A town she thought of often. A part of her past that was never far from her mind. Although it was only one of a dozen towns her family had touched down in during her father's years as a commercial miner, Eagleton was the most memorable. Memories, bittersweet, of Frank Scolli, Larry Glazer, his brother James, but most of all, Caroline Holt. Happy days— before it had gone sour.

Roni felt her heart flutter softly as a wave of nostalgia washed over her. She carefully opened the flap, not wanting to destroy the delicate, rose-tinted envelope. Two questions raced through her mind. How long had it been? And why now?

The matching sheet of paper revealed the distinctive penmanship of the letter writer along with a trace of her scent. Roni smiled, caressing the translucent paper. The first time she'd laid eyes on Caroline had been the day Roni, going door to door, had sold her this very stationery.

Dear Roni,

You must be wondering why on earth I'm writing to you after all these years. Voices from the past have a way of resurfacing, stirring memories, some pleasant, some not so pleasant. I wish I could say this letter is merely one friend greeting another, but the truth is I need your help. Aaron and I need your help. Aaron is my son, a very special boy, and my one and only reason for living.

Something has happened recently to compel me to write you. The fact that I hired an investigator to find you should convince you of the seriousness of my situation. Dearest Roni, I don't know who else to turn to. I don't know who I can trust in this town.

Will you help?

A loving friend,
Caroline

P.S. It is much too complicated to go into in a letter. Please call as soon as you receive this.

Below the signature was a telephone number. There was no address, but Eagleton was small enough that a letter addressed to a certain party in care of general delivery would find its way.

Roni hurried to the phone in the bedroom. Caroline contacting her after twelve years! Caroline with a son. Caroline asking for her help. Although she would be past forty now, Roni still visualized a lovely woman in her late twenties.

Perhaps it was the late hour, or her exhaustion, or

hearing from someone who at one time had been like a second mother to her, or a combination of everything, but Roni felt a profound and grave sense of dread.

On the nightstand the blinking answering machine indicated messages waiting. Ignoring them, she dialed Caroline's number and, as she waited, pacing the room anxiously, she realized it was well past midnight. Surely she would be asleep. Everyone in Eagleton would be asleep. Four rings in, too late to hang up now.

Continuing to pace, Roni mentally ran through her schedule for the next week. She had several assignments, but nothing she couldn't get out of if she chose to drive to Eagleton. *Caroline*. A gentle, benevolent woman who had taken a lonely young girl under her wing during the four years Roni's family lived in town now needed her and there was no question that she would go.

"Pick up. Pick up," she muttered, each ring intensifying her sense of urgency. She hung up, dialed again, more carefully this time. While it rang she pressed a button to retrieve her messages, hearing without really listening. Her sister was checking in. Her boss needed to talk to her—pronto. A carpet cleaning company and a local charity soliciting. Her sister again. A woman's voice, speaking too fast, the words slurred, rambled on about something crazy.

Roni slammed down the ringing phone and hit the stop button on the machine. *Caroline?*

She backed up the tape and started it again. "Roni, it's . . . it's Caroline Holt. I need your help. I'm—oh, this sounds so crazy but . . . but I'm afraid . . . very much afraid for Aaron and myself. I've done something unwise, something incredibly foolhardy. Roni, I feel that you're the only one I can count on. Please call me. Please." It clicked off. Roni had no idea when the message had been recorded.

She tried Caroline's number again, letting it ring on and on before giving in and calling the sheriff's office in Eagleton. She spoke to a Deputy Deming, explaining the reason for her call.

"You say she left a message on your answering machine?" the deputy said.

"Yes. She sounded upset . . . distraught. I wonder if someone could drive to her house and check on her."

Silence.

"Officer . . . ?"

"It's after one here, ma'am."

"Yes, I know. Please . . ."

A sigh. "Yeah, okay. Sheriff Lubben's patrolling. I'll get him on the radio."

She gave him her number and asked him to get back to her as soon as he could. She hung up, changed into sweats, and went to brew a pot of coffee.

The ringing startled Roni out of a deep sleep. Curled up in the wingback, her arm asleep under her, she groped for the cordless phone on the endtable.

"Ms. Mayfield?" a man asked.

She glanced at her watch. Four-twenty. Three hours since she'd placed her call to Officer Deming. "Yes. Yes. Officer Deming?"

"Ms. Mayfield, I'm sorry to have to be the one to pass along the bad news. I've just come from the Holt place. It seems you were right to be concerned. The place was full of propane gas. The boy's okay. A little groggy, but okay. If we hadn't got there when we did . . .''

"And Caroline?"

He cleared his throat. "I'm afraid we didn't reach her in time. Before turning on the gas, Mrs. Holt took a knife to her own wrists this evening. She's dead."

TWO

Nevada, Monday

James Glazer secured the buck by its hind legs, tossed the rope over the tree branch, then hoisted it upward until the four-pronged antlers cleared the ground. With a branch he propped open the deer's chest cavity. The sight of the blood as it began to drain through the nose and mouth onto the grainy earth made him think, strangely enough, of Caroline Holt. The last time he'd seen the widow was yesterday when he'd gone to her big house on the hill. He'd stood by silently and watched as the sheriff and doctor wheeled her out on a mortician's gurney, a blood-soaked sheet covering her body.

The shock of her death had hastened his hunting expedition. He needed the time alone to sort things out and think. Hunting and the open outdoors cleared his mind like nothing else could.

An accomplished hunter, James killed for food,

taking only what he needed. That morning he brought down the large buck a half-mile from camp. The arrowhead had entered the broad chest, nicking the aorta, and the animal had managed to bolt, causing James a moment of trepidation before it faltered and dropped dead several hundred feet away.

Years ago as an overly-exuberant novice on his first bow hunt, he had shot in haste. The gut-shot buck ran. James followed the blood trail for hours only to lose track of it in the rugged mountains. Knowing that the animal would no doubt die a slow, agonizing death, a meal for scavengers, he vowed never again to release his arrow unless he was as confident of a kill shot as he could be.

He straightened, arched his back in a stretch, and stared across the great expanse of valley to the opposite mountain range, its once-pristine contours altered by tailings and roads. Just off the narrow highway several miles to the north, more signs of civilization intruded. A mining commune of trailers peppered the desert flats. Along an unpaved road leading into the foothills, plumes of dust from mining vehicles rose here and there. A golden eagle soared overhead, a thick snake twisting in its talons. James watched until it became a mere speck in the cloudy, ashen sky.

He would spend one more night on the mountain, then break camp and return to Eagleton. In a few days, depending on the weather, he'd dress out the deer and distribute it like he did every year. With Caroline Holt gone, James decided to deliver fresh cuts of steak to the boy and his soon-to-arrive house guest.

He thought of Caroline again. *Suicide?* No.

Three

With mixed pride and envy, Roni watched her sister, older by two years, stride toward her table at the oceanfront restaurant in Long Beach. Women as well as men tracked her across the room. She wore a cool, three-piece designer suit of navy blue and white with crisp nautical lines. Her long, blond hair was caught in a bow at the nape of her neck. She was a reverse picture of Roni—Jolie had taken after their mother. Roni's olive coloring, dark hair and eyes came from their father. And for as long as Roni could remember, she'd wished she'd been born fair like Jolie.

Jolie swept down on her, sank into a chair, and without a greeting, started in. "Christ, beach bums and tourists. For the last three miles I was stuck behind a bunch of rubbernecks moving at a snail's pace. Why can't we meet in my neighborhood? Burbank has nice eateries, too, you know."

"It also has tourists," Roni reminded. "Does Burbank have an ocean with a stunning view of the *Queen Mary?*"

Her sister took a moment to take in the panorama before pursing her lips and arching her eyebrows in a sign of acquiescence. "You get points for the preferred seating." Jolie was a director for a film casting company in Hollywood. With a generous expense account, she was accustomed to special treatment, at least in her own neck of the woods. She leased a penthouse in the heart of Burbank and was presently living with and supporting a gorgeous two-bit actor who, according to Jolie, was about to get his first real break.

The waiter appeared, a tall Latin with green eyes. Jolie brazenly sized him up before giving him her drink order. The man squirmed, not unhappily, under her candid scrutiny.

When he went to get their drinks, Roni said, "I wish you wouldn't do that."

"What?" Jolie asked innocently.

"Turn our waiter into a drooling lapdog. He won't leave us alone now. I had something important to tell you and I'd hoped we could talk without being constantly interrupted."

A look of intrigue brightened Jolie's face. "Gossip?"

Roni shook her head. "First things first. I talked to Mom this morning and she didn't sound good. Is she okay? She's not slipping again, is she?" When they first moved to California, after the divorce, after Jolie had moved out, Irene Mayfield had had a mental breakdown. The responsibility for her care had fallen on seventeen-year-old Roni. Although she'd made a full recovery and was working as a waitress in the

neighboring town and living with two other wait-
resses, Roni worried about a relapse.

"Oh, no, nothing like that. It's her feet. They're
gone."

"Damn. I told her a million times that you and I
would chip in for the surgery, but she's too stubborn
to take the time off. What can we do? Knock her over
the head, hogtie her, and admit her against her will?"

"We might have to. I think she just likes to have
something to bitch about."

The waiter returned with their drinks, a Long
Island iced tea for Roni and a champagne spritzer
for Jolie. They ordered lunch, crab cakes and an
avocado salad.

"I'm leaving town for a little while."

"So what else is new?"

"This is personal. I'm going to Nevada—"

"Nevada? Where in Nevada?" She pronounced it
Ne-*vah*-da. The correct way, the way no Nevadan
would ever say it. "Vegas?"

"Eagleton."

It took a moment to register. "Eagleton? Good
God, are you crazy? Have you been frying your brain
with acid?"

"Nobody does acid anymore."

"Oh? You'd be surprised. Acid is making a big
comeback—but to hell with that. What's in
Eagleton?"

Roni told her about Caroline Holt's letter, message,
and subsequent death. "The sheriff and his deputy
seem to think she killed herself and tried to take her
son with her."

"And you don't?"

"No. Why the letter? Why the call for help? She
was afraid of something . . . or someone. She wanted

my help. She had a baby since we moved away. A boy. She was afraid for him, too."

"How'd she supposedly do it?"

"Cut her wrists. Turned on the oven or something. It's a miracle the boy didn't die of gas poisoning or the place didn't just blow sky high."

"Honey . . ." Jolie paused, studying her sister for a long moment. She covered Roni's hand with her own. "I was about to say 'Don't make it your problem.' But you're going to make it your problem, aren't you?"

"I have to, Jol. At one time Caroline and I were very close."

"I remember. And oh, brother, was Mom ever unhappy about that. But then Mom wasn't happy about anything in those days."

"If the tables were turned, Caroline would do everything she could for me. She asked for my help—"

"But she's dead now. It's too late to help."

"No, it's not. She asked me to help the boy, too. He's there, without a mother . . . without anyone."

"But, Sis—oh, never mind, I know you've made up your mind. So, okay, give me a little background. What have you found out so far?"

"I contacted Caroline's attorney. The boy . . . Aaron, is eleven. There are no known living relatives—"

"Wait a minute. Wait just one minute, back up." Jolie stared intently at Roni. "If he's eleven, then he's . . . jeez, he must be Frank what's-his-name's kid."

"Scolli. That's what the attorney implied."

"Then he has relatives in town. The whole Scolli clan."

Roni shook her head. "They won't admit or even consider the possibility that their son raped her.

There was never really any proof. Even Caroline doesn't know for sure what happened that day."

"But Frank ran away?"

"Yes."

"Frank was one of your best friends. What do you think?"

"I can't believe it, either. He was really sweet. But at sixteen, with raging hormones and the body of a man . . . and he did break into the house . . ."

"He hits the road and the widow has a baby within the appropriate amount of time. The plot thickens."

"So, as I was saying . . . no known relatives. Mr. Granville told me Caroline was concerned about Aaron and his future should anything happen to her. They were going to discuss a suitable guardian for him, but she died before anything could be decided."

"What will happen to him?"

"I don't know."

"Honey, you're not thinking about taking on this woman's kid, are you?" She leaned forward.

"I hadn't really thought about it that much. But, hell, eleven's a great age. They can feed themselves, run errands, screen your calls. I like kids. I'm almost thirty. Forgive me for saying this but my so-called biological clock is tick-tick-ticking."

"Oh, brother, give me a break. Today, with estrogen therapy, grandmothers are having babies." She gave Roni a sober look. "Sis, I know you have some sort of misdirected guilt or responsibility for what happened that day, but that's not reason enough to become involved in their lives. Not after all these years."

"It's more complicated than that. I owe Caroline. Those first few years in Eagleton she was the most important person in my life besides you and the folks.

You were always so popular, busy with your horde of friends. Every new town we moved to, you immediately fit in. It wasn't as easy for me. Mom and Dad worked all day and fought all night. For four years Caroline was my mentor, my salvation. I have to find out what happened to her. The rest I'll take as it comes. And if the boy and I . . ." Roni paused, clearing her throat.

"What?"

"Nothing. He's probably loved by everyone in the town. If he's half as sweet as his mother, somebody will want to take him in."

"Let me remind you that you have a job that requires a lot of traveling. Eleven is too young to leave at home alone."

"Okay, okay. Let's drop the subject."

The waiter brought their lunch. As they ate, he hovered around the table, refilling water glasses, bringing bread even though the bread in front of them had gone untouched. After he asked for the third time if everything was all right, Jolie smiled sweetly and told him they could use a little privacy. He quickly disappeared.

"You're not going to be welcome there, Roni, the big city journalist rushing in crying 'Foul play.' Small towns have their own way of doing things. They don't appreciate outsiders butting in. Do you think this sheriff will be thrilled to hear your theory?"

"I don't give a damn what he or anyone else in town thinks."

Jolie sighed. "When?"

"Tomorrow. I've already cleared it with the magazine. I got two weeks. That should be enough."

"Look, maybe I can take a couple days, go with you . . . ?"

"Thanks, Jol, but I need to do this on my own."

"Sure. I understand."

They engaged in small talk for the rest of the meal, catching each other up on jobs and relationships. After the plates were cleared away Jolie brought the subject back to Eagleton.

"Have you kept in touch with anyone in Dogpatch? Any contact whatsoever?" Jolie always referred to mining towns as Dogpatch; dogs of all sizes and breeds, most of them yellow, roamed the streets in substantial numbers.

"I tried early on, with no luck." Aside from Caroline, her two best friends had been boys, Larry Glazer and Frank Scolli. Roni's family had left Eagleton several weeks after the incident to go to another town in another state. They lived there only a short time before her mother, no longer able to stomach the nomad life, packed up the girls and moved to California where she found a waitress job and filed for divorce on the same day. Once they were settled in their new surroundings, Roni had written to Frank, hoping he had returned home, and she also wrote to Larry. Neither wrote back. She wrote a dozen letters to Caroline, yet never mailed one of them.

"The town has some good people in it. People I'd like to see again."

"So where are you staying?" The waiter brought the check. Jolie snatched it up, handing him a credit card.

"Mr. Granville—he's the attorney who's the trustee to Aaron and the estate—invited me to stay at Caroline's. Aaron's too young to be alone and from what I understand he won't leave the house. The lawyer thought I might be of some comfort to him."

"Did she mention you in her will?"

"As a matter of fact, she did. She left me her doll collection."

"That's it?"

Roni nodded. "It's quite a collection."

Four

Tuesday

The view from the highway had changed little in the past hundred miles or so. In Roni's mesmerized state, the miles and hours rolled past. The rich browns and yellows of the high desert, like broad sepia strokes on a vast canvas, became as monotonous as the drone of the tires on her four-year-old Chevy convertible. Traveling on Highway 50, the Interstate tagged "the loneliest road in America," Roni had lost radio reception fifty miles out of the last sizable town.

She was delighted to spot any sign of life on the open range dotted with juniper bushes, pinyon trees, and red rocks. Earlier she saw herds of cattle, wild horses, and burros. Now only hawks, eagles, and magpies soared overhead or perched on posts, an occasional jackrabbit darted across the road. Dust devils sprouted here and there, dancing aimlessly over the coarse sand.

She had been on the road since four-thirty that morning. An early-morning phone call from her father had ended her night's sleep. She'd sent word to him via his post office box in Tonopah informing him of her plans to go to Eagleton. Like her sister, he had tried to persuade her not to go. Even using the same argument as Jolie. He warned her she wouldn't be welcome in a small town that had been touched by a scandal in which she and her friends had been directly involved. Her final words had been: "Dad, I'll be there at least a week. You're less than two hours away. Drop in." Knowing her father as well as she did, Roni was certain he'd take her up on the offer.

Unlike the bent and grizzled prospector of old with his grubstake-laden burro, Thomas Mayfield, handsome and clean-cut, had taken to the hills with the latest in mining technology. Many times over the years, usually when the pressures of her job got too demanding, Roni took off to join him. There was nothing like the sound of a rushing river, the dredge motors sputtering, and gravel crunching under her boots. Nothing like the feel of icy water sloshing over her hands as she swirled gravel and sediment around in a gold pan searching for that first flash of glitter. Or the sharp smell of pine and sage or camp coffee brewing on an open fire. She smiled at the memories. She loved camping, especially near water. Oceans, lakes, rivers. Water gave her energy, renewed vitality; it drew her in like leaves in a whirlpool. Eagleton, she remembered, had very little water.

It was now three in the afternoon. Driving fast, a watchful eye on the rearview mirror for highway patrol, munching on Fritos from the bag, she pushed it, feeling an urgency to get there, to meet the unknown head-on.

Though she hadn't planned to stay long, she brought along her laptop computer—which over the years had become an extension of herself—printer, tape recorder, answering machine, VCR, and a small, black-and-white portable TV. Two suitcases with warm, casual clothes—she remembered how winters came early in the high desert—and a dark skirt and blazer for Caroline's memorial service. As an afterthought she grabbed a pillow and down comforter from her bed. On the seat beside her were the football and rollerblades she'd bought for Aaron.

As the landscape whizzed by she tried to remember the history of Eagleton: a once-prosperous gold and silver boomtown, a summer home to the golden eagle, an American frontier initially comprised of Welsh, Cornish, Italian, German, and Irish mining immigrants. Some settled, others moved on. Long gone were the charcoal burners, the mule train, the smelter and refinery. Gone was the Chinatown, complete with opium den, that once existed in an elaborate network of tunnels beneath its bustling main streets. Eagleton had escaped the hapless fate of many mining towns that became ghost towns reduced to weathered wood and crumbling foundations. With its population of 2000, the town's melting pot of miners, ranchers, seasonal hunters, and tourists occasionally reached a vigorous boil with the resurgence of a new mine operation.

As Roni neared the foothills, a gusty northerly wind rocked the car. Thunderclouds, black and swollen with moisture, multiplied overhead. She tried the radio again and got static. She realized she hadn't passed anyone on the highway in either direction for nearly an hour. Just then the deafening roar of a low-flying jet on maneuvers out of the Fallon Naval Air Station rudely brought her back to civilization.

The gray sky began to spit, spotting the dusty, bug-splattered windshield. It stopped as quickly as it started.

A sign flashed by on the right, SALTZMAN MINE 20 MILES. An arrow pointed south. A new mine? Her father had worked at the Goldline Mine north of town.

She found herself tensing as she neared her destination. What sort of reception would she receive in Eagleton? Aside from Caroline, Frank's family had been the closest to her. The Scollis owned several businesses in town: Al's Tavern, Al's RV and Mobile Home Park, and Al's Mini-storage. She remembered how the good-natured Mr. Scolli often let his two eldest sons and their friends ride through town on his old Dodge pickup, clinging to the outside of the stakebed. And Mrs. Scolli, Anna, who used to pinch Roni's arm and call her Bony, had made Roni the official taster of her homemade lemon ice each Saturday morning at the tavern.

She wondered if Larry was still in town. Larry had lived with his father and big brother, James, both miners like her father. Roni smiled, thinking of James. *Lord, but she'd had a terrific crush on that one.* They were probably long gone. Gold mines came and went, and the miners with them.

Would any of the others remember her? Her favorite teacher, Mrs. Anderson, or Dr. Burke with his ropes of red licorice? Miss McCartney, the tiny, turban-headed fixture in the ticket booth of the Majestic Theater—looking like a mechanical gypsy in a carnival's fortune teller booth—would have to be over a hundred if she still lived. And, of course, there was the sheriff . . .

Roni felt a coldness in her stomach. Sheriff Hank Lubben's size, his deep voice, his uninhibited power and, she remembered now, a certain look in his eyes, had intimidated her beyond words.

An almost forgotten conversation drifted back to her. The day after Frank ran away, Roni had sat alone on a bench outside of the sheriff's private office waiting her turn to be questioned—*interrogated* was more like it. Larry sat on her left, eyes downcast, refusing to speak to her. On the other side of the thick mahogany door the heavily accented voice of Alonso Scolli filtered out. ". . . Lies! . . . My boy is no rapist. Maybe he go into the house—a childish prank—but he don't rape nobody. He don't run off, neither. The boy has a future here. Here with his family . . ." That conversation had taken place twelve years ago. Aaron Holt was eleven. The numbers did indeed add up.

Startled back to the present by the sudden appearance of a sand twister that momentarily obstructed her view and rocked the car violently, she fought the steering wheel and jammed her foot down on the brake. Then it was gone, swirling along the sandy shoulder alongside her before abruptly veering off.

She resumed her speed, again taking stock of things around her. A farm to her left, a scattering of trailers to her right, the town straight ahead. Roni approached Eagleton, staring at the giant letter "E" that marked a hill on the far side of town.

From above, like a scene on an inspirational card, luminous rays of light fanned out of the storm clouds and pointed down into the little town. An omen?

Five

Roni reduced her speed and entered the town of Eagleton, taking in first one side of the street, then the other. Nothing had really changed. Here and there a few businesses had closed. The padlock on the door of the Majestic Theater, its ticket booth window soaped opaque, bode ill for Miss McCartney. Many of the original structures had been restored or given a facelift. Coombs's Market and the Eagle Cafe had new signs. The two-story brick courthouse had received a fresh coat of white trim. To the left of the courthouse, on a salmon-colored building, hung a shingle with the name FADIUS GRANVILLE, ESQ. Roni drove on by.

At the end of the next block, she turned right, then three blocks up she turned left onto Juniper Street. Only a handful of houses stood on the south side overlooking the town. As she approached Holt house, she saw that the two neighboring houses were vacant, boarded up, with weatherworn signs of KEEP OUT and FOR SALE in the yards.

At one side of the Holt property Roni braked, the car idling quietly. Through the leaves of the surrounding trees she stared up at the tall, gray structure. The scalloped gables, turrets, and odd-shaped windows gave the three-story Victorian house both an ornamental and sinister facade. This house, built a hundred years ago by Orson Holt, great-grandfather to Caroline's husband, was by far the oldest and largest in Eagleton, surviving not one but two fires that raged through the town during the days of the big mining boom. The Holts, one of the wealthiest families in town, had owned a large brewery on Sage, three saloons on Main, and a sizable chunk of two gold mines north of town.

Because of its imposing size and archaic style, the house had seemed ugly and frightening to the other kids, but not to Roni. Solely because it was Caroline's home, Roni thought it quixotic and awe-inspiring.

Yet now, twelve years later, in need of paint and landscaping, it looked depressing and malevolent. Cheat grass, pigweed, and great creeping bushes of wild yellow rose had overtaken the beautiful yard. Wrought-iron bars covered the downstairs windows. The words HELL HOUSE were scrawled in red spray paint across the peeling wood on the south side of the house.

Through the grimy, bug-flecked windshield, Roni's gaze traveled from one dark window to the next. At the attic window she thought she saw something move. She quickly leaned forward to get a better look. If there had been something there, it was gone now.

Half an hour later at a table near the front of the Eagle Cafe, Roni wiped her hands on a mound of napkins and, with a sigh, pushed the colossal, half-eaten hamburger away. From the Holt house she had gone to the attorney's office to find the door locked. A clock sign in the window read BACK AT 4:00.

She leaned to the side, sipped water, and stared out the window at two yellow dogs across the street strolling shoulder to shoulder down the sidewalk. The larger of the two wore a blue bandana around his neck. *Dogpatch.* She smiled, remembering her sister's words.

The town seemed familiar, yet alien. It hadn't changed much, but she had. As a kid she had cared little for the authenticity of these small towns. Cared little about their history or their founders. She cared now.

It was a town of two or three blocks. She spotted the courthouse, Granville's law office, the senior citizen center, and the Eagleton Press Building. Down the street on the same side as the Eagle Cafe was the bank, Al's Tavern, and the post office. Across the highway, midway in town, the Exxon station sat adjacent to the Pioneer Motel where most of the contract miners, geologists, and surveyors stayed. If memory served her, the library and opera house were two blocks up on Main.

Foot traffic past the cafe was brisk: farmers, miners, tourists, hunters, and those who owned or worked in the local businesses. Roni tried to sort them out by dress, posture, and attitude.

She glanced at her watch. Five after four. Of the dozen tables in the oblong room only one other was occupied. A young couple with three children, road map spread open over the remains of lunch, fanny pack at each hip, indicated tourists. Seeing the children reminded her of Aaron Holt. She wondered who had been taking care of him since his mother's death two days ago.

In the adjoining barroom Roni made out the shadowy outline of someone sitting deep in the corner. She sensed he was watching her, had been watching her the entire time, and she felt a slight tightness along her shoulder blades.

The young waitress, wearing tight Wranglers and a T-shirt, her long, sunstreaked hair in a ponytail, crossed the diner to Roni. "That gonna be it?"

"Yes."

"Headed into Utah?"

"No. Just up the street."

Curiosity and a flash of wariness glinted in the woman's dark eyes.

"I'll be staying at the Holt house for a while."

The waitress seemed to assess Roni in a single sweep. She peeled the check from her pad and gingerly laid it on the tabletop, directly over a ring of water. "Do come again."

As Roni paid her bill the door opened and a man she knew stepped in. The man had changed very little—his reddish-blond hair a little less burnish, the flesh on his face a little looser and the freckles paler, his belly a little more rounded, but she would have recognized him anywhere.

"Dr. Burke?" she said, walking toward him.

He stared at her blankly, his eyes narrowing, before recognition kicked in. His smile was slow, then he was gushing with enthusiasm. "My, my, little Roni Mayfield. Good Lord, look at you. All grown up and prettier than I ever imagined you could be. What in the world brings you to Eagleton?"

"Caroline Holt's death."

His grin dissolved. "Such a fine lady. Probably the

finest lady, aside from my Charlotte, that is, in the whole town. We're all going to miss her.''

Roni nodded. "How is Mrs. Burke?"

"She's hardy and robust, as usual. She'll be pleased to know you're in town. Where are you, at the hotel?"

"Mr. Granville has invited me to stay at Caroline's."

He frowned. "At the Holt house?"

"Yes, why?"

"Well, it's just—I can't believe Faddle would encourage . . .''

"What?"

"Roni, go to the hotel. I'm afraid the house . . . well, it isn't as nice as you remember it."

"I know. I drove by. It's all right, I won't be here long."

"Well, I can't very well tell you what to do, now can I, but if it's fond memories you want, memories of Caroline and the way she was back then, I suggest you stay away from that place."

"Thank you for your concern, Doctor, but memories are not what brought me back."

"Oh?"

She glanced at her watch. Four-fifteen. "I'd better go. I have an appointment with Mr. Granville. Dr. Burke, I'd like to talk to you about Caroline and how she died. Can we get together soon?"

"Of course. But—"

She opened the door. "See you in a day or two."

She left him standing in the cafe entry, a disconcerted expression on his face.

Six

Roni sat in the wooden chair on the other side of Fadius Granville's antique cherrywood desk. Faddle, as he insisted she call him, was a large-boned, rednecked man in his late fifties. A deep tan changed abruptly to pale flesh on his upper arms and forehead where shirtsleeves and hat had provided a certain protection from the sun. In her mine-brat days, Roni had seen many men with those telltale markings— men working the heavy excavating equipment, cutting away at the mountain in the blistering sun. Mr. Granville was no typical pencil pusher, shut away poring over depositions and case histories. He spent a good deal of time outdoors. Today he wore a short-sleeved button-down shirt with a walnut-sized gold nugget bolo tie, indigo jeans, and an expensive pair of western snakeskin boots. On his pinkie finger, between worn, scarred knuckles, glittered a yellow gold ring with a two-carat diamond.

"Mr. Granville—Faddle," she amended when he

opened his mouth to correct her. "Do you really think Caroline killed herself?"

He hesitated a moment. "I only know what I was told. And I was told that she took her own life and tried to take Aaron right along with her."

"But do you believe it?"

"Aw, Roni, it don't matter what you or I believe. I know you came all this way looking for answers. And that's okay. Maybe you'll get 'em, and then again, maybe you won't."

Roni dug into her purse and brought out a small tape recorder. "I want you to listen to this and then tell me what you think."

A flip of a switch and Caroline's voice filled the room. ". . . I need your help. I'm—oh, this sounds so crazy but . . . I'm afraid . . . very much afraid for Aaron and myself. I've done something unwise, something incredibly foolhardy. Roni, I feel that you're the only one I can count on. Please call me. Please."

Roni looked up at the lawyer. Some color had left his tanned face, his bright blue eyes suddenly seeming dull and unreadable.

She handed him Caroline's letter. He slipped on a pair of reading glasses and, with the utmost care, unfolded the paper. When he finished reading, she said, "What could have happened recently to compel her to write to me after twelve years?"

His expression became blank, yet within the depth of his eyes something stirred, a blending of emotions, none of which Roni could read. He pressed his lips together and shook his head. "I would only be guessing . . ."

"Go on. I'm open to anything at this point."

"Well, as you know, Caroline is—*was*—a very private and complex woman. She had tremendous inner strength, but it was no secret her health was poor. Heart disease, complications from rheumatic fever as a youngster. You may recall how frail she was back when. The added ordeal of giving birth didn't help matters. Over the years she just sort of . . . slowly withered, like a fragile flower."

Strange he should use that analogy. Caroline had always seemed so delicate, easily bruised, like the smooth white petals of a gardenia. Dead at forty-two. Much too young.

"Was she in a lot of pain?"

"Possibly. The doc could tell you better."

"Are you saying the sheriff and the doctor came to the conclusion that she committed suicide to end her suffering? And that she planned to take her only child with her rather than leave him here alone?"

"It wouldn't be the first time. If you think about it, the phone message coulda been a dying plea. She's about to cut her wrists, the gas is on, and she suddenly has a change of heart, wants someone to save them."

"Someone over five hundred miles away?"

"Your call to the law at that particular time probably saved Aaron's life."

There was a remote possibility he was right. But somehow Roni just didn't buy it. That message could have been on the machine for days.

"Does Aaron know about me? Does he know his mother tried to reach me?"

"He knows now. I mentioned it the morning she died. Told him you were coming and that you'd be staying at the house."

She leaned forward. "And?"

"Nothing. Aaron don't communicate a whole lot."

"What, in your opinion, are his feelings about sharing space with a stranger?"

He rose and strolled to the window to gaze out. "Aaron is well aware that as a minor, by law, he's got to have a caretaker, be it temporary or permanent. As trustee of the estate, responsibility falls on my shoulders."

"What are the choices?"

"Well, there's Hazel Anderson. She's close to the family. And, of course, there's me."

"Would you be willing to take him in, be his guardian?" Roni asked.

"I might. It's not out of the question. I've got an invalid momma to consider first, but I'd sure as hell hate to see him fostered out."

Roni nodded. "Where is he now?"

"At home. Sheriff Lubben is seeing to him. Hazel Anderson would've been happy to stay with him, but unfortunately she took off for Flagstaff to attend the birth of her daughter's baby a week before Caroline died. She's due back soon though."

"You mean for the most part he's been there alone? In that huge house by himself . . . all night?"

"Not really. I talked Mrs. Wiggins into staying the two nights."

"Mrs. Wiggins? She's a neighbor, isn't she? The old one who's hard of hearing?"

"Eighty-eight and stone deaf. Beggars can't be choosers. She came at bedtime and left at dawn. An' like I said, the sheriff looked in. You gotta understand that Aaron don't mind being alone. He's, ah . . . well, he's different than most young folks."

"Different? How?"

"He's a loner."

"No friends?"

He perched on the windowsill. "None that I know of."

"What about school? No friends there?"

"When Caroline's health became chronic, Aaron refused to leave her alone during the day. Hazel tutored him."

"Is he a problem child?"

That same enigmatic look behind a vacant gaze. He shook his head. "He's illegitimate, Roni . . . a bastard. I don't mean to sound harsh or discriminating, but the truth is he was conceived under rather disreputable conditions. He's the illegitimate son of a woman who the town never quite understood. Guess you'd say he had three strikes against him before he even cleared the chute."

"That doesn't answer my question."

"He's shy. Real shy." He cleared his throat, pushed away from the window, and walked behind her chair. "He don't come out of the house much. At least not much in the daylight."

Roni twisted around, staring up at him in disbelief. "What?"

The attorney returned her stare, then he laughed. A loud, genuine laugh, obviously amused. "No, no, nothing freaky like a vampire. He likes the night. Sounds peculiar, I know, but some of us are morning folk and others are night folk. He's of the night variety."

"What does he do out at night?"

"Gathers things."

"What sort of things?"

"Don't know exactly. Pieces of this and that. No one ever bothered to find out. You're a journalist, an investigative reporter, right? Bet you can find out real quick."

She opened her mouth to speak but was cut off.

"Lord, look at the time," he said abruptly, lifting

a ring of keys from his desk. "I know you have a million questions, but there's still lots to do and I have legal business out to the mine before I can call it a day. We'll just get you settled in and we'll talk again real soon."

In her own car she followed the lawyer's vintage black Cadillac to the large house on Juniper Street. Storm clouds roiled, forming an ominous backdrop for the already-menacing-looking house. The sky had begun to spit again. The wind whipped at her hair and clothes as she followed Faddle Granville up the rickety front steps. Several front windows were cracked, but they held. In twelve years it had become dilapidated—a once-grand house that Caroline had kept with pride now seemed to droop in want and disrepair. The only saving grace was the pristine beauty of the large yellow roses growing wild everywhere.

"It was such a magnificent old house," she said, looking around in dismay.

"Fixed up, a little paint here and there, and it can look just as you remember it."

He pushed open the door and gestured for her to enter. She stepped across the threshold and felt her stomach knot. The entry was dark and cold and smelled of ancient tombs, old and musty.

Faddle bustled on through and into the house proper, chattering all the while. She heard creaky window sashes lifting and dust took to the air from disturbed curtains.

"Aaron!" Faddle called. "Young man, come meet Miss Mayfield."

Roni gingerly stepped into what she remembered was the main parlor—a large room with antique furniture, fringed area rugs, and cabbage rose wallpaper, now faded and dingy. As if in a trance, she moved into the music room. A layer of dust dulled the shiny wood of all the furniture except for the baby grand piano. It glowed. Of course, Caroline would have thought it sacrilegious to treat the instrument with anything but respect. The house could fall apart around her, but the piano would be dust-free and tuned. An intoxicating whiff of brandy and gardenia teased her senses. A figment of her imagination, she told herself, since the musty odor was far more potent.

Footsteps on the stairs. Aaron? Roni's palms felt clammy. She realized she was uneasy about meeting him. Would he look like Frank? Who was this boy who nobody seemed to know?

He was probably wondering the same about her. Who was this woman who had come uninvited into his house? And what exactly was she doing there?

Roni couldn't answer that. She had made a snap decision to come, to try to find out why Caroline had wanted her help. And now that she was dead, Roni's determination had only become greater. In the past she always trusted her ability to make on-the-spot decisions, and for the most part they were accurate. No reason to believe it would be different now.

She heard a knocking from the second floor and the attorney's voice calling to Aaron. Faddle had gone up to get the boy.

She moved out of the shadows toward the light of the kitchen.

The long table was cluttered with grocery bags, tin cans, food wrappers, and a cat or two. She was surprised to see the sink free of dishes until she realized that what food had been consumed had been eaten straight from the can or package. Open bags of chips and cookies, discarded apple cores and orange rinds littered the counter and tabletop. A cat lapped at an empty can of Dennison Chili, another at a can of Chef Boyardee Beef Ravioli.

She peered into one of three grocery bags on the table and saw more canned meals and junk food.

"Bachelor food."

Roni jumped, whirling around. She hadn't heard Faddle enter the kitchen. She had to swallow to respond. "The sheriff plan the menu?"

"I'm told he brought cooked meals from the cafe the first day, but they went untouched. I s'pose the boy is used to doing for himself. Has he been eating?"

"What? Oh . . ." She tipped over an empty can. "Looks like it. Unless cats can open cans and use utensils. Where is he?"

"In his room. Guess he's not ready for company. But don't you worry, he'll come out."

When, she wondered. After sundown, when all night creatures meld quietly into the night?

"Well, I have to go. Call me or Sheriff Lubben if there're any problems. Shouldn't be, though. I appreciate you staying here with the youngster instead of at the hotel. This is a bad time for him. About the only person in the world he loved and could relate to has died. This house is his sanctuary, his life. He may be a little standoffish at first. Just give him some time, won't you?"

She nodded and walked him to the front door.

He looked sheepish. "I'm sorry the place isn't spick-and-span, but I'm an old bachelor and my momma's an invalid, so . . ."

"It's okay. I'll straighten up. It'll give me a chance to reacquaint myself with the house."

"Now you just make yourself at home. Take Caroline's room. It's the only other room with a bed in the house besides Aaron's.''

He was halfway down the steps when Roni asked, ''By the way, where is Caroline now? I'd like to pay my respects before the funeral?''

''Funeral?''

''Funeral service. Memorial. Aren't you handling the arrangements?''

His pale brow furrowed. ''She was buried this morning. There was no service.''

Several minutes later she stood at the open front door staring absently at the black Cadillac as it pulled away. She watched it cruise down the narrow lane, turn the corner, and disappear. The landscape grayed even more, became bleaker. The chilling wind was relentless. The town below looked deserted. Roni closed the door to shut out the grim sight. She turned. With her back against the cool oval window the walls of the dark entry hall seemed to slowly press in on her.

What the hell was the hurry to get Caroline in the ground?

''Aaron?'' Roni stood at the door the lawyer had told her was Aaron's. Tapping lightly, she called softly again, ''Aaron, it's Roni Mayfield. Can we talk? Get acquainted, maybe?''

She put her ear to the door. No response. No movement or sounds, no TV or radio. She thought she heard the sound of soft sniffing. Was he crying?

''Aaron?''

With a sigh of resignation, she turned and left.

The master bedroom stood at the far end of the hall, on the other side of the stairway. Two other rooms occupied the second floor. One seemed to be a catchall room, closed off for years. The other was a nursery. It was exactly as she remembered it. The nursery had been a part of the house when Roni lived in Eagleton. Caroline's great longing for children had prompted her to fix up a nursery within months of Richard Holt's departure to Vietnam.

Roni entered the master bedroom and what she saw brought a lump to her throat and a sense of loss. It wasn't at all like she remembered it.

She closed her eyes, visualizing the way it was, recalling the first time she'd entered Caroline's sanctuary one sunny spring day.

It had been almost magical. The room was bright with sunlight, made brighter by the white crocheted bedspread, sheer white chiffon curtains and canopy, the white and gold striped wallpaper. The hardwood floor shiny with a resin glossiness. A white area rug flanked each side of the high four-poster bed. On one side of the room, all in white frames, was a wall of family portraits—stern faces and stiff backs, relatives of Caroline and Richard, all dead and departed years ago. On the Queen Anne dresser, above a long scarf of Irish linen and lace, sat a mirrored tray with one perfume bottle and one crystal atomizer. The perfume, *Laureli*, filled the room with the scent of sweet gardenias. A handpainted china bowl contained a slim gold wrist watch, an infant's ring, gold and pearl ear studs, and a fine chain bracelet with a cat charm. Enormous vases of wild roses graced each end of the dresser. Cat figures abounded, made of ceramic, fabric, glazed and glass finishes, pewter, wood, and stone. But that which had held the most fascination for a young girl had been the doll collection.

In neat rows along two white wicker shelves sat at least twenty dolls in assorted sizes: tiny infant dolls clothed in flaxen crocheted dresses and bonnets with tatting and ribbons; child dolls in taffeta or eyelet, hats of straw or felt; and the adult dolls—smaller in size, yet more intricate in design—were dressed in satin and velvet adorned with tiny jewels. On porcelain heads, beneath various shades of hair—much of it real—their handpainted eyes had a life-like sparkle. One doll even looked like Roni and Caroline had named it after her.

Each and every time she entered this room she had stood in awe of its ethereal beauty, its pureness which mirrored her conception of Caroline. To be allowed in such a special place made her feel special, too. Inside this room she had shed her tomboy ways and had become gentle and feminine—like Caroline.

Now, standing in the doorway, she noted that the immense room was as dreary as the rest of the house. Gone was the special glow. Old fashioned window shades sealed out the daylight and a layer of dust gave the room the overall appearance of an antique photograph. The canopy was gone, the bed stripped to the mattress, a folded crazy quilt and goosedown pillow at the foot. Mrs. Wiggins?

Roni crossed to the two windows and lifted the shades. Ashen light, making the room no less dismal, filtered in through dirty windows latticed by a vine-choked trellis. Leaf shadows danced on the walls.

Roni flicked on the overhead fixture. Anemic light from a low-watt bulb did little to brighten the room—she made a mental note to buy 100-watt bulbs. The dolls stared back at her with dull eyes, as though saddened by the conditions they were now forced to endure.

Looking at the dolls brought back another memory—she and Caroline had been sitting in the windowseat downstairs working embroidery thread into fabric caught in hoops, when out of the blue Caroline had said: *Roni, when I die I want you to have my doll collection.* Caroline had kept her word.

Roni sank down on the edge of the mattress, wrapped her arms around the bedposter, and leaned her head against it. Through misty eyes she stared at the nightstand and the photograph on top. The Holt wedding photograph. She lifted it, blinked back tears, and gazed at the loving couple. Mrs. Richard Holt, formerly Miss Caroline Stanford, with her handsome, serviceman groom. They had met at a barbecue in her hometown of Charleston, South Carolina, and within six months fell madly in love, married, and migrated from the lush, sultry garden of the South to the arid high desert of the West; a young gentlewoman of magnolias and mint juleps transported to a town of sagebrush and beer. Raised by an ancient grandmother after the boating death of her parents, the sheltered girl harbored a Cinderella dream of a charming prince whisking her off to his fairyland kingdom. Richard had been that prince and Eagleton—unlikely as it was—his kingdom. Less than three weeks after returning to his ancestral home on Juniper Street, her airman husband went off to Vietnam to serve his country. Eight months later he was declared a casualty of war.

For years Caroline kept an array of things personal to him and dear to her on the nightstand—the wedding photo, a packet of letters, a gold watch, aftershave, and an engraved pocketknife, a shrine of sorts to his loving memory. It was all gone now, except for the photograph.

Roni leaned closer. Dust covered the nightstand, yet the photo was clean, dust-free. Also dust-free was a cigar-shaped area alongside the frame. Something had been removed. There was a trail of rust-colored specks near the photograph. Roni scratched at one. Dried blood?

She had the feeling she was being watched. She put down the picture and twisted around. The slanted gold eyes of the black cat on the bed watched her warily.

"Where'd you come from?" Roni said quietly, rubbing at the goosebumps on her arms.

The cat yawned and rolled over on its back. Another cat, this one a tortoiseshell, jumped up and joined the black one, licking its face before settling down beside him.

She moved around the room, opening the door to the tiny closet and the tall wardrobe, looking but not touching. The perfume in the bottle had evaporated, leaving an ugly brown residue. Her eyes burned, not from tears of sadness this time, but from the gritty air.

On her way downstairs, she paused at the landing and debated whether to try once again to speak to Aaron. His closed door spoke louder than words. *Give him time*, she told herself, turning away. *He has to come out sooner or later.*

In his patio a half-mile away from the Holt house, James Glazer briskly cut and trimmed the large buck lying atop the redwood table. It would be dark soon and he hoped to finish while there was still enough natural light. With a boning knife, he deftly cut the last of the filets from the carcass, removing the fat that gave it most of its gamey taste, then wrapped the fresh venison in freezer paper.

Red Dog sat at the end of the table, waiting, his tongue quickly lapping at the saliva that escaped his mouth. Only now and then would James allow Red a scrap of meat. He didn't want the dog, who was half coyote, to acquire a taste for wild game.

As dusk gave way to night, he carried the last armload of packages inside and deposited them in the freezer. Tomorrow he would divide it, as he'd done for the past two seasons, and deliver it to others in town.

After scrubbing and hosing down the tabletop and patio, he turned off all the lights inside and out, twisted off the cap on a long neck bottle of Bud, and eased himself into the macrame hammock in the patio. The hammock was handmade by Molly McCracken. Her husband Andy, injured on the job at the mine last spring, would hobble on crutches for another two months. Two years ago Effie Perkins's husband had been crushed to death by a loader, leaving her a widow with four youngsters. Most of the venison would go to these two families. And to show their appreciation, Effie put up brandy fruitcake and homemade wine for James; Molly knitted, mended, and at the moment labored over a heavy quilt to warm him on the freezing winter nights.

Red trotted over, licked James's hand, and rested his head on his chest. His gold eyes gazed at his master affectionately.

"Good boy," James said, patting his head. "I love you, too, guy, but you've got killer breath tonight so put it down somewhere, huh?"

Red nudged him under the chin with a cold, brick-red nose, putting the hammock in motion before plopping down beneath James.

James reached into his shirt pocket and pulled out a slim cigar. He struck a wooden match along the concrete, waited for the flare to subside, then put it to the cigar, drawing until it was lit.

He smoked, sipped beer, and thought about the return of Roni Mayfield to Eagleton. That afternoon he had sat on the end stool in the dark interior of the bar and watched her having lunch in the adjoining cafe. He rarely frequented the bar in the early afternoon, but today he'd made an exception. He wanted to observe his brother's friend without detection.

With obvious admiration he had watched the pretty brunette tackle an infamous Eagle burger. There was only one way to eat the monster—unabashedly, with juice dripping everywhere, and that's how she had approached it. He liked that. She looked to be a woman accustomed to eating in a restaurant alone, accustomed to eating on the go.

He sighed, swallowed down half the beer, fit the cigar into the corner of his mouth, then swung off the hammock. Red jumped up, his tail twitching in anticipation. The night was mild, milder than the day had been.

"Wanna walk?"

Red whined and spun around, his bushy reddish tail fanning the air. He ran ahead, favoring his bad foreleg, jumping like an excited puppy.

James walked a block to Main, crossed the highway, and climbed the three blocks to Juniper Street. Red tried to anticipate his master's direction by running ahead, and James had to call him back repeatedly.

James headed in a direction Red had not been before—at least not with him. The last few times James had come, he'd deliberately left Red at home.

When they had passed the two boarded-up houses, James stopped and took stock. With both houses vacant, the nearest neighbor resided a block away on the opposite side of the street, and as neighbors go, Stephanie Wiggins was deaf and notoriously unneighborly. The structures on Sage—the street between Main and Juniper—were commercial businesses, closed tight after five.

The wind came up again, sudden, strong. Red lifted his head and sniffed the air. James cut along the side of the house until he could see through the foliage of tall elms surrounding the Holt house. He stopped. A light shone in the attic window. No surprise there— it usually did. He could see that window from his own place on the other side of the highway. The kitchen light was on, but from this angle he couldn't see inside. The rest of the house was dark. James wondered if a light burned in the upstairs master bedroom.

He had gone halfway around the house, weaving through trees and wild roses with Red at his heels, when he realized that what he had in mind—looking in a window—could very likely be construed as an invasion of privacy. If caught he'd be considered a Peeping Tom.

Whistling softly for Red, James backtracked to the road.

He decided to walk home down Country Lane, a seldom-used gravel road lined with cedar trees and the Holt Ditch, a drainage trench that ran parallel to the road. With the wind pressing at his back, his head lowered, he walked fast.

Halfway to the main highway, James heard a car turn from Juniper Street onto Country Lane. He turned his head into the powerful wind and watched the car coming toward him at a steady speed. Bright headlights blinked on, blinding him. James raised his hand to shield his eyes. The car seemed to increase its speed, heading straight at him. James frowned, veering to the side of the road. Surely the idiot could see him standing here, he told himself, with those brights lighting up everything for a square block. Suddenly the car was upon him and James, without thinking, was diving headfirst down the embankment. He rolled twice and ended up in the dry ditch. Leaping to his feet, he charged up the embankment to the road in time to see taillights disappear over the hill, heading toward town.

For three hours Roni had killed time by straightening the kitchen and washing and drying linen for the bed. Things from her car were piled on the kitchen floor. Until she had a chance to meet Aaron and talk with him, she didn't feel comfortable simply moving in and taking over. After all, it was his house and she had come uninvited.

The wind continued to howl. Something at the back of the house, a loose shutter or board, banged incessantly, but Roni lacked enthusiasm to investigate. She had turned on every functioning light on the ground floor. The cats—so far she had counted four, though she suspected there were more—moved silently from room to room, watching.

At nine sharp Mrs. Wiggins, wearing a long sweater over a nightgown and yellow rubber galoshes, walked in the kitchen door. After several attempts to communicate with the elderly lady through sign language, Roni got the message across that she would be staying with Aaron. Roni ran upstairs, grabbed the quilt and pillow, and brought it down for the woman. When Roni offered to drive her back home, the old lady laughed as though she'd heard the best joke of the day. Then just as abruptly she turned grave, and with eyes milky with cataracts, she stared hard at Roni and said: "Take him out of this town." And then she smiled and went out the door, humming as she moved down the driveway.

The kitchen was directly beneath the master bedroom. At ten o'clock the ceiling overhead creaked. Roni looked upward and wondered if Aaron had ventured out.

Climbing the stairs, the freshly laundered bedding in her arms, Roni called out to Aaron again. Over the wailing wind and the banging at the back of the house, she heard a door close softly. Shadows twisted and vaulted. The banging, whatever it was, seemed closest to the master bedroom. Sleeping in there would be impossible. Tonight she would leave the second floor to Aaron.

Twenty minutes later, after a shower, Roni went back downstairs. She locked the doors and windows and switched off all but two small lamps at the front of the house. She claimed her pillow and comforter from the pile by the back door and, on the kitchen floor, in the airiest room in the house, using a folded area rug as a mat, she made up her bed for the night.

Lying on her back in a long cotton shirt, she stared upward at the twisting leaf shadows. The ceiling overhead creaked again. She squeezed her eyes shut, her thoughts alternating between Caroline and the now-motherless boy upstairs, and waited for sleep.

Seven

Wednesday

Roni tossed and turned throughout the night. The strangeness of her surroundings, the consistent bark of a dog, the hourly chime from the grandfather clock, and the wind howling, then dying down to an eerie silence, kept deep sleep at bay.

The house made its own sounds. As old as it was, it appeared to still be settling. Sometime in the early morning Roni detected, through a light slumber, the metallic sound of the kitchen doorknob jiggling.

Aaron? Was it Aaron returning from a night of gathering whatever it was he gathered? Although she had hoped to meet him under more auspicious circumstances, she decided that she'd settle for what she could get. They had to talk. If he wanted her out of the house, then she would move to the hotel. But no one, not Aaron, not the sheriff, could force her to leave town until she was ready.

She gripped the comforter, held her breath, and listened.

The door opened wide and a huge shape, silhouetted against the graying sky, filled the opening. Three steps inside and it stopped. Her eyes strained to see. Could this full-grown person towering over her be a kid of eleven? She opened her mouth to speak his name, but all that came out was a rush of air.

The silhouette lifted an arm; paper rustled. The head bent and she heard a raspy sound moments before the brilliant flare of a match forced her to blink and look away, but not before Roni saw the hard, craggy features of a man in his late forties. He lit a cigarette and shook out the match.

She jerked upward into a sitting position. "Who the hell are you?" she whispered hoarsely.

He reached out. Roni recoiled. This time the bright light from the overhead bulb momentarily blinded her.

She moaned, then squinted. Hovering over her was a big, barrel-chested man in a khaki uniform. She knew him. Remembered him from way back when. There was no mistaking the coarse, pockmarked face, the thick black hair combed straight back in a style favored by state prisoners and ex-cons, the cold glare of his dark eyes. That same feeling of dread and intimidation engulfed her. Sheriff Lubben. She pulled the comforter up.

"Roni Mayfield, ain't it?" he said, dragging on the cigarette. Smoke curled around his nostrils and eyes. He squinted at her through the smoke. A cat that had been sleeping at Roni's feet rose slowly and, skirting the table, made for the open door, a wary eye on the man.

She wrapped the comforter around her nightshirt

and struggled to her feet. "What are you doing here in the middle of the night?" she asked.

"What're you doin' down there on the floor?" When she didn't answer, he said. "I came by to check on things."

"This late?"

"It's early. After five. My day starts early. Why you here?"

It suddenly dawned on her that he had seen her car in the driveway, knew she was here, and yet he'd just let himself in. The thought of him prowling the house in the middle of the night while she was asleep gave her the creeps.

"I'm here by Caroline's invitation," she said quietly, hoping her voice sounded more self-assured than she felt.

"Caroline's dead. She killed herself."

"Maybe. But somehow I'm not real satisfied with that theory. And you, Sheriff, are one of the people I want to talk to, but not at five in morning in my bare feet and nightgown."

"Faddle let you in?"

"Yeah. He thought someone should be with Aaron."

"That's touchin'. How long you plannin' to stay?"

"I don't know. As long as it takes. But while I'm here, I think it would be a good idea if you'd knock and wait for me or Aaron to let you in. Faddle said you had a house key for me."

He glanced at her extended hand, turned, and crossed to the sink to flip his cigarette ash. "You're pretty damn bossy for someone who don't belong here."

Feeling ridiculous with her hand in the air, she dropped it.

The tortoiseshell cat jumped on the table and put its nose inside a grocery bag. The sheriff strode across the room, shoved the cat off the table with the back of his hand, then rummaged through the bag. He came up with a box of Yellow Zonkers and tore into it. He propped the cigarette on the edge of the table, lifted the box, and shook caramel corn into his mouth. Pieces dropped to the floor. Brushing crumbs from his shirt, he opened the refrigerator, pried the top off a full milk container, and drank from it. "Guess the kid don't like milk. I thought kids needed milk for healthy bones and teeth."

With a feeling of helplessness, Roni stood in the starkly lit kitchen and watched the man help himself to whatever he wanted. She felt a hot resentment at his incredible gall. Although technically the food was his, supplied by him for Aaron, he had no right waltzing in and taking what he wanted, when he wanted it. But who was going to stop him? He was the sheriff and unless things had changed he was the only law in town.

How was it possible for a woman as kind and gentle as Caroline to be friendly with this crude, overbearing man? Had she a choice? According to the attorney, when Caroline's progressive illness had pretty much confined her to the house, the sheriff took care of her needs. Remembering back, the sheriff had always been there for her, his police cruiser appearing on her end of town more often than not. Caroline had never owned a car, had never learned to drive. When she needed something moved or fetched, it was the sheriff who was Johnny-on-the-spot.

He shook out another mouthful of Zonkers, tossed the box into the bag and, chewing with his mouth open, turned to her. "There really ain't no reason for you to hang around. She killed herself. She was buried. End of story."

"Look, Sheriff, I'm not here to cause problems. I came because Caroline needed me and I won't stay a day longer than necessary. Okay?"

Putting his broad back to her, he moved to the other bag and peered inside.

"I understand you bought those groceries. I'll be picking up a few things today, so feel free to take what's left with you."

"What'dya think of him?"

"Who?"

"The night owl . . . Aaron?"

"I haven't met him yet."

"No shit. He won't come out?"

"Well . . ."

Before she knew what he was doing the sheriff was out of the room.

When she heard him on the staircase, taking the steps two at a time, she realized what he intended to do. She tried to go after him, but tripped on the comforter that was wrapped around her, falling to her knees. She swore. She rose, hiked it up off the floor, secured it around her, and was about to go after him again when she heard footsteps coming back down. A moment later he appeared in the doorway, gripping a confused, sleepy-eyed boy by an upper arm.

The boy was in his underwear—briefs and T-shirt. His thin, bare legs trembled.

Roni was shocked at his size. He was eleven, but looked eight. His face, puffy from sleep, was cherubic. Such a tiny thing. Too small and fragile to be on his own. Hardly more than a baby. She wanted to reach out to him, to protect him.

The boy blinked, trying to see in the bright kitchen light. When his eyes met hers, his pale face and chest flushed a deep sanguine. He quickly looked away.

"Sheriff Lubben," she said in a hoarse voice, "what do you think you're doing?"

"Makin' introductions?" Lubben said with mock innocence. "Aaron Holt, this here's Roni Mayfield. Her and your momma was real tight at one time. She says she's come to look after you for a bit. Maybe she'll stay till the state decides what to do with you. Maybe she'll take you back to California with her."

At the appalled look on Aaron's face at those last words, Roni quickly said to the sheriff, "Let him go. Jesus, why are you doing this?" She took a step forward. "Aaron, I'm sorry, I had no idea he was going haul you out of bed and bring you down." She reached out to him.

The boy looked her in the eye, his gaze filled with pain and uncertainty. He backed away from her touch and jerked his arm free of the sheriff. Then he turned abruptly and ran into a dining room chair. Both fell to the floor. Looking back once more, his face glowing scarlet, he scrambled to his feet and rushed off.

At a loss for words, Roni could only glare at the sheriff. She couldn't have met Aaron under more adverse circumstances. Was the man a complete sadist or just incredibly stupid?

"Well now, that didn't go too well, did it?" Lubben shrugged, righted the chair, then brushed past her. "Well, I tried. Got work to do. See ya."

He sauntered out the door, leaving it open.

She stood, her back stiff, her hand tightly grasping the ends of the comforter to her chest as she twisted her head to stare after him.

She released the comforter and kicked it aside.

Then with enough force to throw her off balance she slammed the door shut, strode to the table, and with trembling fingers, lifted the smoldering cigarette butt and angrily flung it into the sink.

"Aaron, please open the door," Roni said, tapping lightly on his bedroom door. "Look, don't pay any attention to what the sheriff said. I'm not here to take you away. This is your home and I respect that."

She waited, then in a soft voice she added, "Aaron, I'm so sorry about your mother. She was a super lady. She . . . we—well, listen, I'm here if you want to talk about her or . . . or, y'know, about how you feel." She stared at the floor and waited. She wanted to tell him she knew how he felt, but she didn't know, not really. She'd never lost anyone that close to her. She took a ragged breath. "Okay, look, I thought I'd run to the store for some *real* food. If there's anything you want or need . . ."

"Just leave me alone, okay?" a tiny voice said. "No one asked you to come here."

"Aaron?"

Inside the room voices, from a radio or TV, discouraged any more conversation. She turned and left.

She stepped into the shower. A needle spray of hot water eased the sore muscles of her shoulders made stiff by sleeping on the floor. She washed her hair, filthy from the dust of the house. At least she didn't have allergies like so many people nowadays. Frank Scolli had had asthma, so acute he'd worn a medical alert bracelet, the bulge of the ever-present atomizer in his shirt pocket. *Frank.* She closed her eyes and saw the boyish face on a man's body. Over the years she had thought of him often. His large frame and deep voice had most of the kids terrified of him. But only a few, Roni and Larry, knew how sweet-natured he was. Which was why she found it so hard to believe that Frank had raped Caroline Holt.

With her eyes squeezed tightly shut she turned off the water, pushed back the plastic shower curtain, stepped from the claw-footed tub, found the towel, and pressed it against her face. She quickly dried off, then with the towel poised to wipe the steam from the mirror, she froze.

Written across the face of the steamy mirror were the words: GET OUT WHILE YOU CAN.

Roni clutched the towel to her body and spun around, searching the large bathroom.

She was alone.

She twisted back to glare at the mirror. The steam was dissipating, the words running together, becoming distorted. Within seconds they were gone.

Roni drove up the winding road to the city cemetery. She left the car and carefully picked her way through an unattended portion of the old graveyard, bright with orange and lavender wildflowers and overrun with yellow roses. She strained to read the inscriptions on marble and granite headstones of towering winged angels inside ornate wrought-iron enclosures.

Over the first hill she found a mound that looked to be the most recently disturbed. There was no headstone, only a marker with Caroline's name and the date of her birth and death.

She picked a bouquet of yellow roses, Caroline's favorite. She knelt, placed the roses at the head of the faded rectangle of grass and, not good at this sort of thing, offered an ineffectual prayer. Finally she said, "Caroline, I'm sorry I was too late. It seems that I just can't do anything right where it concerns you. Please forgive me."

In the regional office of the Goldenrod Mining Corporation on Main Street, James Glazer leaned over the large map spread out on the table in front of him. As an exploration geologist, it was his job to scout for new deposits. Having discovered the present deposit of in-place gold at the Saltzman Mine and following the theory that gold deposits tend to cluster, he was in the process of determining the next claim block for exploration. He and Sandy Watson, Goldenrod's other geologist, had two years to complete the exploration program and 50,000 acres in which to explore.

James dropped a file on Sandy's desk. "Feasibility reports. Have a look at them, will you?"

The phone rang. Sandy answered, then covered the mouthpiece and looked up at James. "For you, Jamey boy. Female."

James felt a stir of excitement. Could it be? A few minutes ago he'd seen her drive into town. He went into his office and lifted the receiver. "James Glazer."

"Hi, Jim, it's me, Linda."

A mixed bag of disappointment and pleasure. Linda Shaw was a visiting psychologist from Elko and a good friend. "Linda, hello. Are you calling from town?"

"Yes, I'm here at Doc's," Linda said. "It's been a while. Buy you lunch?"

"If I can get dinner."

"You're on."

* * *

Roni walked down Main to the Eagle Cafe. Through the plate glass windows she saw the cafe was crowded. Mine workers, both men and women, fingers wrapped around coffee mugs, large thermoses at their feet, took up every seat. She went in and made her way to the counter at the back.

Roni smiled at the waitress and asked for coffee.

The waitress picked up an order and moved off into the dining room. After several minutes it became obvious the waitress, taking orders and clearing tables, was going to let Roni stand there, absorbing the curious stares of the crowded diner, until she was damn good and ready to wait on her.

Several locals were filling thermoses and Styrofoam cups with coffee from a service bar in the corner. Roni went to the bar, poured a large Styrofoam cup of coffee, capped it, took a dollar bill from her pocket, and strode back to the counter where she tossed it down. "Keep the change."

As she headed for the door she heard the waitress say to a customer: "City folks . . . no patience."

Faddle Granville stood in the doorway, grinning. "Atta girl, don't take no sass from any of them." He put his Stetson back on, took an arm, and walked out with her. "Come, let's walk."

"But . . . you were going in. What about your breakfast?"

"They serve it all day."

Roni stopped to admire a tan and reddish-brown dog sitting at the door of the cafe.

"That's Red," Faddle said. "Different, don't you think?"

She agreed. "What is he?"

"Half coyote for certain, the other half probably a mix of German shepherd and mutt."

"Is it—is he friendly?"

"Oh, sure, gentle as a kitten." Faddle patted the dog on the head. The busy tail briskly swept back and forth, clearing debris from the sidewalk. "However, he is something of a rapscallion in town. He's a randy ol' boy that no fence or wall can keep in—or out. When a bitch goes into heat, Red's the first to know and the first to show."

As they walked, Roni sipped her coffee and Faddle nodded at passersby. A tall, big-boned man stepped out of Al's Tavern and nearly ran into her.

The man apologized, smiling nervously, and tried to go around them.

Faddle blocked his way. "Not so fast there. Son, you remember Roni Mayfield, don't you?"

The man stood stiffly, arms at his sides, his hands opening and closing unconsciously. He nodded.

"Dean." Roni needed no prompting. Frank Scolli's older brother, Dean. Although he was much older than she—James's age—the family resemblance was strong. Except for the receding hair and twenty additional pounds, he looked the same.

He tipped his head in greeting, shoved his hands in the back pocket of his jeans, and looked exceedingly uneasy.

She wanted to ask about Frank but felt the time wasn't appropriate. Instead, she asked, "Your mom and dad, are they well?"

"They're getting by."

"I'd like to say hi to your mother. Would I find her in the tavern or the house?"

"She, ah ... she don't socialize much since Frank ..." his words trailed off. "Look, I gotta run. See you."

Roni turned to stare after him.

With a hand at her elbow Faddle urged her on. "Dean don't usually have much to say. Nowadays he lets his malt and hops do his talking for him." Then he asked, "So how are things going at the house?"

Although she was the outsider, Roni felt she could trust this man who had been born and raised here. She told him about her early morning episode with Sheriff Lubben.

"He's crass, Roni, I'll say that. Too many years in a hick town toting a gun and a badge can do that to a person. But he ain't all bad. The less head-buttin' the two of you get into the better off you are."

She agreed. The sun slid in and out of the clouds, making Roni sorry she hadn't worn her sunglasses.

"Someone wants me out of here?" she said softly.

"Pardon?"

"There was a message on the bathroom mirror this morning. It said, 'Get out while you can.'"

"Aaron," he said flatly.

"Maybe."

"Who else?"

She shrugged.

"My, my, my. Nary a dull moment. A writer's paradise. If you find yourself with lemons, little gal, make lemonade."

"Faddle, I didn't come here to write about Eagleton or anyone else in this town."

"No, 'course you didn't. But you have a writer's overactive imagination. That's a compliment, gal, so don't look so offended. I wish I had half your imagination. You'll see, Aaron will be the culprit—"

"Should I lock away the rat poison and cleaver?"

"If I thought you was in any kind of danger I wouldn't have allowed you anywhere near him or that house."

"I don't want to intrude in his life."

"You're not intruding. Aaron's confused right now. He'll come around, I promise you, and what he's gonna need most is a soft, sympathetic shoulder."

"He's been a shut-in all his life?"

"Good grief, no. In the beginning he played outdoors like the others. But he was always a frail little mite, couldn't defend himself when the bigger boys called him names . . . *bastard* and such. You know how cruel children can be. As I said before, he's a loner. It don't bother him to keep to himself."

"Like Boo Radley in *To Kill a Mockingbird?*"

He smiled. "Not quite. There was one friend he was real tight with, a boy a few years older. He lived in the neighboring house. This boy's mother came in once a week to clean and wash for Caroline. The father was one of the contract mine employees. They lived here 'bout four years and moved on a couple years ago. It's only been since then that he's really withdrawn."

"Faddle, tell me everything you know about Caroline's death and what led up to it."

They had reached the courthouse. He took Roni's upper arm and steered her through the double doors of the courthouse. "How 'bout a tour?"

She held back. "I'd rather talk. I can't leave Eagleton until I get some answers and I don't have a whole lot of time."

"Reacquaint yourself with the townfolks. Hazel Anderson, who was the closest female to Caroline, will be back any day, and she'll fill you in. Talk to

Doc, Father Roberts, and, when his ruffled feathers
have settled down, the sheriff. It won't take more
than two, three days to find out everything you need.
You got my solemn word on that."

"Good. Let's start with you."

"Fire away."

"Caroline hired an investigator to locate me. Was
that you?"

"Nope. My duties were, and still are, for that matter, strictly financial. Estate, business, and legal
affairs."

They walked side by side, peering into the court
chambers and offices while he defined his role as
Caroline's attorney. He talked of a government pen-
sion, interest-bearing trust funds, a mortgage-free
house, and shares in several defunct mines north of
town.

He guided her up the wide staircase where they
stopped to look out the window.

"Check out the town," he said, gesturing with that
workworn hand, pinkie ring glittering, at Main Street
below. "Eagleton is a mighty interesting place. The
local color, the opera house, courthouse, street tunnels, and all those abandoned mines. Fascinating."

Something he just said sparked a memory. It was
gone before she could grasp it.

Roni leaned close to the window and looked down.
On the sidewalk below she saw a couple standing at
the corner. The woman was striking. Her clothes—
jeans, pullover blouse, and linen jacket—though simple in design, were chic and obviously expensive; a
week's paycheck for a mine worker, the jacket two
paychecks. Her shiny blond hair, pampered with con-
ditioners and regular trims, was cut in a short, stylish
wedge. She was doing something to the man's collar.

The man—Roni's pulse accelerated. It couldn't be. Not here in the same town at the same time. Not after all these years. She felt her cheeks and chest grow warm.

Larry Glazer's older brother, James. The hazel eyes, the strong chin, the high forehead. She could almost see the tiny crater at his temple where a childhood case of chicken pox had scarred him, almost hear the slight Aussie accent.

He tilted his head and stared up at her without any sign of recognition. Maybe it isn't him, she told herself. It's someone who only looks like him. She was so eager to see a friendly face, a face from the past, a face that belonged to one of the mining families, that she was jumping to conclusions. It couldn't be the same man she'd had a mad crush on twelve years ago. An image of him then, at twenty, came to mind. She felt her stomach roll.

"Faddle, that man on the corner, do you know him?"

Faddle had started down the hall to the main courtroom. "Ummm? Where?" By the time he joined her at the window the couple was gone.

"Someone you thought you knew?" Faddle asked.

"Maybe." She turned her head to look out the window again.

Eight

After leaving the courthouse and Faddle, Roni went shopping.

She sat on a three-legged stool at the rear of Coombs's market, inhaling the distinct odors of aged meat, ripening fruit, and fresh vegetables and finished lacing up a pair of trail boots. She tested the fit of the boots, deciding to wear them.

Glassy-eyed deer and elk, stuffed and mounted, stared at her from high on the planked walls all around the market as she set about getting groceries. Later, at the register, the store proprietors, Peggy and Henry, were friendly and helpful, but somewhat aloof as they rang up her purchases. Other patrons in the cluttered country store eyed her curiously. No one knew better than Roni that residents of small towns were naturally suspicious of newcomers, and this newcomer also happened to be a writer. These people voraciously guarded their privacy. She'd been the newcomer in enough dinky towns to know you had

to earn their trust and friendship. Of course there
had always been other kids like herself—displaced
miner's kids. They had bonded almost instantly,
rarely mingling with the town natives.

After leaving the market she stopped at the post
office and informed the postmistress, Abby Cromwell,
who smelled of Ben-Gay and a fresh permanent, that
she might be receiving mail via General Delivery and
left her name and phone number.

Before heading back to the house, Roni made
a slight detour, driving farther up the hill to the
end of the road. She parked at the edge of a copse
of junipers above the Holt house, got out, and
walked into the trees until she came to a spot with
a clear view of the Holt property. She sat Indian-
fashion on the moss-covered ground and stared at
the house.

She hadn't realized just how hard returning to
Eagleton would be. So many memories, names, and
faces. Bittersweet memories. Four of her most formidable years had been spent here. Yet she had never
wanted to relive them. Especially not that day in
August when she saw Caroline for the last time.

All summer, two days a week, though she suspected
she possessed absolutely no musical talent, Roni took
piano lessons, something she would have dreaded
with a passion if the teacher had been anyone but
Caroline. That morning a gardenia-scented Caroline
had sat demurely at the piano, wearing the cat brooch
Roni had made for her from plaster of Paris in the
Beaver Park ceramic workshop, her long slender fingers creating magic on the keyboard as only she
could—a reminder that the piano was not an instrument of torture, and that beautiful sounds could and
did emerge from it if properly coaxed. After the lesson

that day Roni said goodbye, not knowing it would be for the last time.

She closed her eyes and allowed her mind to go back through the years.

It was a scorcher of a day. Fifteen-year-old Roni Mayfield hugged the grocery bag to her chest, a chest that over the summer had finally filled a bra without help from the tissue box, and walked along the edge of the road. She walked slow, in no hurry to get where she was headed. At the end of Al's RV and Mobile Home Park, on a concrete pad beneath a large cottonwood tree, the Mayfields' trailer sat at a slight tilt, collecting clusters of fluffy cottonwood seeds and bird droppings the size of fried eggs deposited by the red-headed buzzard that roosted on the top branch.

The ground around the trailer was wet, which meant her mother had recently hosed down the aluminum siding to cool it off. Mid-August in a high desert town. Even with all the windows open and a fan in each room, the interior would be hot enough to soften the candles atop the rented upright piano.

Roni blew at the thick bangs hanging into her eyes. Through the shimmering waves of heat rising from the sticky asphalt, she watched with growing interest as Floyd Budner, owner of the Eagle Trading Center, bounced toward her in his old Dodge delivery truck. When he passed he honked and waved.

She waved back, then went on waving to clear the dust his truck had stirred up, now a suffocating cloud around her. She wondered what had brought Floyd out to their place today. Maybe her dad had finally bought those metal detectors and the gold dredge he'd been promising her for months now.

The thought of the two of them heading into the hills, using the detectors to uncover coins and such and the dredge to suck in the river's hoard of gold flakes and nuggets, sent a wave of exhilaration through her.

Roni loved the outdoors, loved anything to do with it. As a bona fide tomboy she could climb, swim, fish, hunt, and handle bugs and snakes with the best of the fellas, and she seemed determined to live up to her somewhat masculine given name—she shuddered when she thought of the name her mother had wanted to saddle her with. *Veronica*. Her father had balked, saying it was too stuffy, too old-fashioned. Lucky for her they'd compromised on "Roni."

The name Jolie—a French name meaning pretty— fit her sister perfectly. Prissy, ladylike Jolie hated camping, hated being more than an arm's length from civilization, electricity, and a hot shower. Ditto for her mother. The only time Roni felt truly feminine was when she was with Caroline Holt.

As Roni neared the trailer she heard voices raised in anger. It was her parents' day off and lately, this was how they spent it. Anymore, her mother seemed to hate everything. Each day found her more bitchy than the day before. Her father made an effort to remain sweet and soft-spoken, bowing to his wife's moods, trying hard to sidestep her tirades. She hated the cramped quarters, the heat and dust, the locals, the entire town, had in fact hated the last two towns they'd lived in.

Roni's stomach knotted. She wanted to turn around, away from the constant bickering, away from her mother's irrational hostility, and return to Caroline's house. If it weren't for her father, she might never go home.

Tom Mayfield charged out the door of the trailer and headed for their old Ford pickup.

"Dad!"

He paused at the open door, waiting.

"Where you going?" she asked when she reached him.

"I don't know . . . into town." His movements were jerky, agitated. Confrontations unnerved him. He dug into his pants pocket and brought out a penny, which he began to roll between his fingers.

"Can I go with you?"

" 'Fraid not, pal. Your mom's got stuff for you to do."

Roni stared curiously at the penny in his hand. "Where's the nugget?"

"What?" He looked at the penny. "Oh, I . . . ah, I guess I misplaced it."

"Oh, Dad, no." Her father had carried a gold nugget in the shape of a teardrop for as long as Roni could remember. A nugget scooped out of the Feather River the year she was born. It was his good luck token. He was forever pulling it from his pocket and rolling it through his fingers.

"Ah, it'll turn up. Don't fret," he said, squeezing the back of her neck.

Her mother's voice, harsh, insistent, called from inside. "Roni, is that you? Where the hell've you been? Get in here."

Her dad tousled her hair and jumped into the truck.

Roni went inside and dumped the groceries on the Formica table, knocking over a candle.

"They sell you the cigarettes?" Irene called out from the bathroom.

"They always do." Roni twisted the cap off a cream soda, saw the candle and, puzzled, turned around to stare at the bare space under the window. "Mom, where's the piano?"

No answer.

"Mom?"

"Floyd took it back."

"Why?"

"The damn thing took up half our living area, that's why."

"But—Mom, how'm I supposed to practice?"

"That's the beauty of it. You don't have to. I called the widow and told her you quit." Her mother took a defiant stance in the bathroom doorway and looked at her. "You and musical instruments got nothing in common. If you gotta play something, why don't you make it something small like a mouth organ."

"The lessons were free. Mom . . . I—dammit, you could've discussed it with me first," Roni said, trying to control her rising anger. "I mean, I think I'm old enough to make my own decisions."

"Who paid the rent on the piano? Who has to listen to those endless, godawful scales? Believe me, I'm doing you a favor."

"What did she say? Was she upset?"

Her mother shrugged, disappearing back into the bathroom. "I don't know. What do I care? Toss me my Kools."

Roni slammed the soda down on the table. As she headed for the door, her mother leaned through the doorway and called out, "Hey, where do you think you're going?"

"To talk to her."

"There's nothing to talk about. I made it perfectly clear."

"Mom, you don't understand. She's not like other people, she's lonely, sensitive—"

"Stay away from there. You're always with her. You're never home. I work all goddamn day and you're with her. She's trying to steal you away."

"That's not true. She'd never do anything like that."

"A lot you know. You're *my* daughter, not hers. She can't have you. She's nothing but a . . . a conniving home-wrecker."

"You're nuts!"

Irene charged out of the bathroom and slapped Roni hard across the face.

Roni rushed out of the trailer. As she ran down the dusty road, she heard her mother calling her name.

Twenty minutes later, walking alongside her best friend Larry Glazer, who had detected her mood and had the good sense to keep quiet, Roni's mind was somewhere back at the trailer arguing with her mother. She was still upset—upset that her mother had sent the piano back. Upset that her mother was jealous of the widow. Upset that her mother had slapped her—she could still feel the heat on her cheek. If her mother could be just a little bit nicer, maybe, just maybe, Roni would want to spend more time at home.

She sighed sharply. When she was twelve her family had moved to Eagleton. Her father, a miner, and her mother, a cook at Al's Tavern, worked long, exhausting days. Roni and the widow had been drawn to each other through loneliness, filling a mutual void. Fascinated by Caroline's gentleness, her artistic and musical talents, and her overall female mystique, Roni spent many hours with her at the big house— inside working on crafts and outside tending the flower and vegetable gardens. Caroline always wore a floppy, wide-brimmed straw hat just like a character out of *Gone with the Wind.*

Well dammit, her mother could scream and carry on all she wanted, but Roni had no intention of staying away from Caroline.

They were in the copse of trees above the Holt place. Roni glanced down at the house at the same moment she stepped into a chuck hole. She stumbled, scraping an ankle bone.

"Ow, shit."

"Have a nice trip, Grace?" Larry said.

Ignoring his attempt at humor, she leaned down to inspect her ankle. At fifteen she thought herself gangly and awkward. And she must be, for Larry and Frank teased her often enough and Frank's mother was forever wrapping her fingers around Roni's upper arm and saying: "So, so bony. Oh, too bony, Roni," inspiring Larry to nickname her "Bony Maroni."

Roni felt Larry's eyes on her. She looked up and caught him staring at her. He smiled. His smile made her stomach twist. Sometimes he looked so much like his older brother, James. She loved James, and had for years, although he had no idea she was alive. Twenty-year-olds hardly took notice of lowly sophomores.

She stood. "What's Frank doing up here?"

"He headed into the trees with his binoculars. That means Frankie's gone a-spying."

Frank, Larry, and Roni were best friends. Larry was a mine brat like her. He, his brother, and their father came from Australia when the boys were young. Frank was a town local. The locals and brats rarely hobnobbed. Frank had made an exception by saving Roni's life her first week in Eagleton. While exploring in a mine shaft in the hills behind the RV park, she had fallen into a winze—a shaft sunk into a tunnel. Hours later, hearing her cries for help, Frank had come along and pulled her out. She owed Frank.

"Who's he spying on?" she asked.

"That's what we're gonna find out."

Roni searched the branches of the junipers, catching a reflected flash. Twenty yards away she saw Frank, large for his sixteen years, standing in the "Y" of a tree, binoculars to his eyes.

Roni nudged Larry and pointed.

Frank, completely engrossed, never heard them approach. He shrieked like a girl when Larry grabbed his ankle.

"You shitface," Frank said, jumping to the ground and twisting Larry's T-shirt in his large fist. "I could've fallen."

Roni separated them. Frank, too easygoing to stay mad, quickly backed off. He turned back to the house and lifted the binoculars again.

"What's so interesting about Caroline's house?" Roni asked.

"Her." Frank lowered his voice. "You gotta promise you won't blab this. My ol' man'll kill me if he finds out I've been peeping on her. Promise?"

Larry nodded eagerly.

"The widda's making it with some guy."

"You're lying," Roni spat out.

"Oh, yeah? You shoulda seen her. She had her hair down. It's real long, comes clear down to her waist. I saw her roaming around upstairs like Lady Godiva."

"So what?" Roni said. "It's her house—she can dance the fandango naked in all the rooms if she wants to."

"She wasn't fandangoing alone."

Frank had to be lying, Roni told herself. Caroline Holt had no one to let down her hair for. The war had been over for nearly five years, yet she still waited faithfully for her airman husband.

"No shit," Larry said. "So who's she making it with? Is he there now?"

"I don't know," Frank said. "It was a couple months ago when I saw her running around in the buff. But tonight I swear I caught a glimpse of a man in the upstairs window."

Larry lifted the binoculars and focused on the house.

"Knock it off," Roni said, grabbing the binoculars. Frank started down the hill.

"Hey, where you going?" Larry asked, following.

"Signal if anyone comes," Frank said. "I wanna sneak in and see who this guy is."

"Are you crazy?" Larry said. "You'll get caught."

"Not if you signal me." He poked a finger at Larry's chest. "If anybody shows up, throw gravel at the house or start yelling. I'll hear it and split. Larry, I'm counting on you, y'hear?" He turned to go.

"Frank, *don't.* Leave her alone." Roni grabbed at him. She couldn't allow anyone to hurt or scare Caroline.

"What about your asthma?" Larry said. "With all those cats you'll be wheezing the minute you get inside."

Frank glanced at his medical bracelet. He pulled his breath inhaler from his pocket, gave it a couple of mock pumps, then grinned, winked, and hurried off.

"Frank . . . NO!"

Larry grabbed Roni and held her, twisting and kicking, until Frank had disappeared around the front of the house. "Go on home, Bony Maroni. You'll get in trouble here. I'll take care of it. I'll get him out. I promise." He turned her, gave her a gentle push, then took off running toward the house. Moments later she watched him climb the trellis to the second story and peer through the vines of wild rose into one of the windows.

A tremendous roaring sound filled Roni's head as she rushed down the hill. Loyalty for her friends kept her from screaming her head off, yet she had to do something to get them away from there.

The doors were locked. On the veranda at the side of the house she located an open window. She climbed in and found herself in the library. Quickly she moved across the room to a doorway that led into the brighter music room. Two tabby cats appeared from nowhere and began to rub against her legs, meowing. "Caroline!" Roni screamed out. "Caroline!"

Footsteps trod overhead.

She froze, staring upward. Caroline? Frank?

The cats continued to meow, yet over the insistent mewling, she heard soft cries. A woman's voice?

Something thumped on the floor above her. Heavy footsteps clamored overhead. The sharp crack of wood splintering merged with a strangled scream. Roni's heart leapt into her throat. Her feet refused to move.

Suddenly her shoulder was gripped. A scream escaped her as she was pulled backward against a tall, firm body.

"Where's Larry?" a husky voice said in her ear.

Roni swiveled to look into the hazel eyes of Larry's brother.

The footsteps overhead moved rapidly toward the staircase.

"C'mon!" James said harshly, pulling her through both rooms to the window. He climbed out, lifting her with him. When they jumped the porch balustrade, she caught her chin on the handrail but scarcely noticed. With a firm grip on her hand, he forced her to keep up with him as he ran up the hill to the trees. Once inside the shelter of junipers, he stopped and twisted her around to face him.

"Larry—was he with you?"

Her lungs in agony, she could only nod.

"Inside the house?"

"Outside . . . trellis."

"Who else was there?"

"Fr . . . Frank."

James turned to leave.

"Where're you going?" she asked.

"Back to get Larry. You damn fool kids—"

James's words were cut off by the sight of Larry tearing across the vacant lot behind the widow's house to disappear down a steep ravine.

James stared solemnly after him, a set expression on his face. "I'll catch up to him at home." He turned and looked at Roni, his hazel eyes searching her face.

Her cheeks flushed under his intense scrutiny. He reached out and touched her chin. Blood covered the end of his finger.

"That's going to leave a scar," he said quietly. "Go home and take care of it."

He left her standing in the dark canopy of trees, shivering.

* * *

That was twelve years ago. It seemed like a lifetime, yet the memory was still sharp, painful. She couldn't face Caroline after that. She was ashamed, ashamed to have been a part of whatever it was that happened that day. A short time later she and her family moved away—*ran away?*

She had let Caroline down then—she wouldn't let her down this time. Although it was too late to help Caroline, there was still Aaron.

She rose slowly, drew a deep breath, and brushed the moss and leaves from her jeans. To her left, at the highest point of the hill along the treeline, something sparkled—the glint of sun on glass. She immediately associated it with the past. Here on the hill. Binoculars. *Frank up in a tree with his binoculars.*

Staring upward for many long moments, she saw only trees and shadows, no movement, then just as she looked away it happened again. From the corner of her eye she saw a flicker of light. Not wanting to be seen, Roni carefully stooped down in a squatting position. She waited, watched. Long minutes later, her legs cramping, she was rewarded by a full-circled reflection. No doubt about it, someone was up there spying down on the house just as Frank had done. The windows on this side were the kitchen, music room, upstairs bath, and Caroline's bedroom.

Who would be so interested in what went on at the Holt house to hide in the trees and spy? Other kids like Roni, Frank, and Larry? Aaron? Or the person or persons whom Caroline had feared?

She had come here for answers, so here and now was the place to start, she told herself as she began creeping silently toward the reflection. A hundred feet closer and she was able to make out a figure dressed in camouflage clothing—pants, shirt, and cap—partially hidden behind a large tree.

Roni inched forward, adrenaline pumping. The figure moved off. Not wanting to lose sight of him, she quickened her pace, keeping him in view between the trees, certain he had not yet spotted her. Suddenly, an explosion of boisterous activity and sound erupted outward and upward from a juniper bush in front of her. Startled, she cried out as a covey of chukar, wings beating the air, swooped around her and disappeared down the hill.

Turning back to the man she was pursuing, Roni was momentarily blinded by a circular reflection. She stopped abruptly. Not two circles of light as she'd have expected from a pair of binoculars, but only one. The lens of a scope? Then she heard the sharp metallic sound of a rifle bolt slamming home.

Frozen to the spot like a frightened rabbit, her heart pounding visibly beneath her shirt, she stared at the reflection trained directly at her. Someone with a rifle had her in their sights. A pitiful mewl came from her throat. The muscles in her legs loosened enough to allow her to back up. She wanted to turn and run, but couldn't. For some insane reason she felt that if she stared him down he wouldn't pull the trigger. Her feet unsteady on the sloping, broken ground, the reflection continued to follow her as she backed away, holding her a prisoner in its blinding circle. Through the scope the rifleman could surely see the fear and indecision on her face. She imagined the bullet ripping through her forehead, directly between her eyes. Would she hear the shot? Would she feel it?

Her foot sank into an animal hole. She fell backward, the fall breaking the hypnotic connection. She quickly scrambled to her feet and ran. Crashing through the trees, she didn't slow down until she reached her car. It took several clumsy attempts before she managed to open the door and climb inside.

With an eye to the trees, her shaking hands jangling the keys, she started the engine, swung a tight "U," and drove away. Dirt and gravel sprayed up behind the car, obliterating anything back there in a cloud of dust.

Nine

Safely back inside the house sometime later, Roni began to entertain the notion that she'd grossly over-reacted to the situation above the house. There was little doubt someone had trained a rifle on her, but the critical question was whether or not he intended to fire. She rather doubted it. He had used the scope as one would use binoculars, the blinding reflection assuring his anonymity. A poacher, hoping to scare her off? Well, it worked and she had the scrapes and bruises and probably a few new gray hairs to prove it.

Although her nerves had settled considerably, she wasn't about to put off installing the two safety chains at the front and back door. In the market, when she asked where the locks were kept, Peggy Coombs had given her a curious look before pointing out the dusty packages on a shelf of household odds and ends. As she installed the chain lock on the back door, she told herself the sheriff would have no trouble breaking the lock, but at least he couldn't sneak in without her knowing.

The kitchen, with its wraparound windows, was the only room in the house that didn't give her the feeling the walls were closing in on her, and she was reluctant to leave it. How different this house seemed without Caroline. Years ago, her presence had filled every room with a dreamlike aura. Now all the rooms were merely rooms, dark and depressing.

One of the cats, the gray tabby, entered the kitchen. It crossed the linoleum, leaving a trail of bloody footprints.

Roni went to it, knelt down, lifted the front paw, and caught a glimpse of a gash in the pad before the paw was pulled away. She tried to lift the cat to get a better look, but it resisted. She tried again. It squirmed, refusing to allow her to hold it or even to look at the wound. "C'mon, kitty, lemme see it. Kitty, kitty." It twisted, mewling mournfully.

Suddenly, small, pale hands were lifting the squirming cat out of her arms. The tabby stopped resisting and went limp in the boy's thin arms. Kneeling, Aaron held the cat in his lap, scratched its head, and stroked the fur for several minutes before lifting the paw to inspect the cut. The cat purred, nuzzling his arm.

Roni, also kneeling, watched him. Once again she was shocked at his size. Caroline had been tiny, but Frank, even as a teenager, had been tall and big-boned, quite mature for his age.

"Is it serious?" she asked, looking back at the bloody paw.

He shook his head, refusing to meet her eyes. "She'll clean it up herself."

"You're very good with animals. Cats are usually

pretty independent, but she turned to putty in your hands."

"She trusts me."

Not knowing what more to say regarding the cat, she went to a universal subject. "Would you like something to eat? Have you had lunch?"

"I'm not hungry." He scratched the cat under her chin, released her, crossed the room, opened a drawer, took out a package of thumbtacks, and was out of the room before she could think of anything more to say.

Roni spent the afternoon cleaning the master bedroom. Everything she touched seemed to trigger a memory or image, fleeting yet profound, of Caroline. As she worked she repeatedly glanced at the door, expecting to see Aaron standing there. She listened for sounds of him moving around, sounds of a radio, TV, running water, toilet flushing, but heard nothing. Give him time, she told herself.

She made up the bed. Her muscles balked at the thought of another night on the kitchen floor. She cleared a drawer and a small space in the wardrobe for her few things.

At dusk she made a fire in the bedroom fireplace, using the last of the wood. When she went to stoke the logs, she noticed that among the fireplace tools, the poker was missing. She used the shovel instead.

She took the brass wood carrier outside to the shed. Just inside the door was a stack of dry pine. After opening the shed door wide to let in the light, Roni entered and filled the carrier with wood. As she turned to leave she saw the mattress leaning against the opposite wall.

She advanced slowly, looking it over. Toward the top and to one side she saw a dark brown stain several feet in diameter. She lightly touched the dry, crusty spot. Blood. Had Aaron seen the blood-soaked mattress? She felt a renewed wave of pity for the boy.

As Roni turned to leave, her foot struck something hard at the bottom of the mattress. She stooped down, ran her fingers over the corner, and felt the outline of a hard object wedged there. She pulled on the cording until she found an opening, reached inside, and extracted a leather bound book.

She quickly backed out the door to see more clearly in the waning light. The inside page was inscribed in the tiny, curlicue handwriting of Caroline Holt. Her diary.

Roni looked up at the attic window. A figure stood in the oval frame staring down at her. She clutched the book to her chest guiltily, protectively.

Aaron. The sharp angle of the window, however, and the dirty glass obstructed her view. He could see her much more clearly than she could see him. His sudden presence at this particular time unnerved her.

She lifted a leaden arm and waved.

The figure disappeared from the window.

Aaron had stepped back from the window, out of her line of vision, though he could still see her. He wondered what she'd found in the shed that she had clutched so protectively to her chest when she saw him.

He continued to watch her until she returned to the house.

She was a lot younger than his mother and Mrs.

Anderson and she was pretty like his mother. She seemed nice, too. But he couldn't think that way. He didn't want to like her. He wasn't going anywhere with her. Especially not as far away as the California coast. He wasn't. Period.

He sat on the floor, crossed his legs in front of him, pulled out a blade on his Swiss Army knife, and made an incision down the middle of the bean-sized object in his fingers. Carefully he scraped the moist, pulpy insides away until only the soft, furry skin remained. He took another one and did the same. In the room below him, his mother's room, he heard her moving around. The blade slipped, nicking his finger.

Roni pushed the chicken back into the oven and closed the door. She wasn't much of a cook but it didn't take a culinary expert to roast a whole chicken. Some seasoning, a quick basting with barbecue or soy sauce with butter and—*voilà!*

Good smells filled the house and the cats, five of them now, stayed close to Roni, rubbing against her legs. As she stood at the sink cutting tomatoes and mushrooms for the green salad, playing along with the contestants on "Jeopardy," she wondered what in God's name a housebound eleven-year-old did all day for entertainment?

Ten minutes later Roni climbed the stairs. At the closed door of his room she said, "Aaron, dinner is on the table. I don't usually cook so you really should take advantage of it." She tapped with her fingertips. "Hey, look, if you'd rather eat in your room that's okay with me. Why don't you just come down and make up a plate. What do you say?"

She waited. Silence. She turned the knob. It twisted easily in her fingers. Not expecting the door to be unlocked, Roni jerked her hand away as if burned.

Above her she heard a soft hissing sound. Aaron was still in the attic. What did he do there all afternoon?

She stared at the ceiling, apprehension tightening the back of her throat. She could holler that dinner was ready, or she could leave a plate for him in the refrigerator, or she could climb that dark, narrow staircase to . . . to . . . what?

She suddenly laughed at herself. He wasn't Frankenstein in a laboratory creating unspeakable things, for heaven's sake. He was just a kid doing something in an attic.

She breathed deeply, tucked a strand of hair behind her ear, and wiped her damp hands on her faded jeans as she made her way to the dark, closed-in stairway. She climbed the narrow steps to the top. The attic door was slightly ajar; pale light framed the opening, spilling out on the wall an inch or so.

Roni tried to swallow, found it difficult. Shadows moved in the light under the door and she heard soft hissing and clicking sounds. The tips of her fingers touched the dry, peeling paint on the door. She pushed slowly and heard a hinge squeal like a scream an instant before he appeared at the door, his body blocking the opening.

"You can't come in here. Nobody can come in unless I say so. This is my private place." The door closed softly in her face.

Ten

After Aaron had closed the attic door, Roni ate dinner alone at the kitchen table while working at her computer. She made up a plate for Aaron, cleared everything away, and returned to the computer. An hour later, distracted by a pinging sound, she rose, stretched the stiff muscles in her back, and crossed to the windows. Rain, light yet steady, came down.

From upstairs she heard an occasional hammering. Quite the little builder, Aaron was. What was he doing up there? Whatever it was, she was glad he was keeping busy instead of shutting himself away in his room crying his eyes out. Aaron must have loved his mother very much to devote the past two years to her. She tried to imagine what it would be like to be eleven and lose your mother. To suddenly have no one, not knowing what the future held.

She turned away from the window, opened the linen drawer, and took out Caroline's diary. Leaning against the counter, she opened it and began to read.

The first entry was dated June 6, 1971. It began with Caroline meeting Richard Holt for the first time.

We were introduced by the Langfords at their barbecue on Sunday. I can't stop thinking about him.

Apparently it had been love at first sight for twenty-one-year-old Caroline. Flipping through, Roni saw the pages at the back of the book were blank, the last entry dated February 31, 1981—seven years after her husband was killed and six months before Roni and her family left town.

January 15: Everything about him is heaven. My knight in shining armor. So different from our southern boys. Celia says he's a damn yankee and I should go slow, that I'm too much the romantic with my head in the clouds. Yes, yes, she's right. But I don't care.

Another entry simply said: *My love.*

Roni skimmed through all of January's entries. Page after page of declared devotion and unequivocal love.

She closed the diary and rubbed her eyes. The entries, penned in handwriting so tiny, so elaborate, with loops and scrolls entwining one another and written with a fountain pen that at times had spattered or leaked, put a tremendous strain on her eyes. Once she got used to the ornate style, the journal would be easier to read. Until then, the going would be slow.

The diary went back into the drawer. She raised her arms over her head and stretched, sighing. Oh, to be so much in love. A blessing or a curse? She could only guess at the intensity. Mad, passionate

love, the kind in Caroline's journal, remained elusive
to most women. In Roni's twenty-eight years, crushes,
infatuations, deep feelings of caring had stirred
within her, but total, unrequited love . . .

Suddenly, like a whirlwind around her, she felt a
sense of claustrophobia. Accustomed to a nightly
walk, she desperately needed fresh air. She wondered
if Aaron would be all right alone. When Roni was
eleven she had pretty much been on her own, even
babysitting other children in the RV park. Aaron, she
realized, had been responsible for himself as well as
for his mother for the past year.

She went upstairs. At the landing to the attic she
called up to him. "Aaron, I'm going out for a walk.
Will you be okay alone? I can ask Mrs. Wiggins—"

"I'm not a baby!" he called back. The hammering
resumed with vigor.

The rain had stopped and the night air was cool,
yet mild. The stroll into town would be a breeze com-
pared to her nightly three-mile walks on the beach,
and she could use the quiet time to clear her head,
to think. There had to be a way to communicate with
Aaron. She felt another flash of anger at the sheriff.
That stupid, humiliating stunt of his that morning,
dragging Aaron out of bed in his underwear, telling
him she'd come to take him away, had probably cost
both of them valuable time in getting to know each
other.

With her hands in the pockets of her denim jacket,
she strode down the narrow lane, hardly conscious
of the blackness around her, the lights from town
drawing her forward.

On Main Street, country and western music from
the Eagle echoed along the wet, shiny streets. Roni
paused at the open door. The Eagle was divided into

two rooms. The tavern had a long oak bar with high-back stools and a couple of small tables. Slot machines, like painted soldiers with neon faces, lined the walls and she could see a pool table in the back area. The other room, which served as the dining room until nine, had its tables and chairs pushed back to form the large dance floor. A two-man band played a rock-a-billy tune. The place was crammed with denim-clad men and women in cowboy hats and billed caps, every table occupied, the bar and dance floor packed.

Roni spotted an empty barstool near the entrance. She slipped inside and quickly claimed it. Looking down the bar, the popular drink, hands down, was beer. Over the din, she shouted her order to the bartender. A petite woman with red pigtails and a T-shirt with "Arm wrestling champ of Jiggs Whistle '88," grabbed a long-necked bottle of Bud, twisted off the cap, and slapped it down in front of Roni.

A stack of coffee mugs stood within reach. Roni helped herself to one and poured beer into it. An old habit. Starting when she was just a kid, seven or eight, her father would come home from the mine and pour himself an icy stein of beer. Wanting to emulate him, Roni begged for a swallow or two in her own stein—a chipped coffee mug. With mugs raised high—hers mostly foam—they toasted to unicorns, the mother lode, and rising gold prices.

Back then, drinking with her father had made her feel grown up. Ironically, sipping the beer now made her feel the same way. With a smile she silently toasted herself: *here's to wanting to be grown up.* She drank, then licked the foam from her upper lip.

The barroom was warm. She removed her jacket, spread it flat on the stool, then sat on it. With her back against the wall, she looked around, thankful for the darkness and the crowd. No one seemed to take any special notice of her.

The band began a slow song by the Garth Man. Through the opening between the two rooms, Roni watched couples joining the circle that moved counter-clockwise around the dance floor. Other dance couples did their own thing at an area in the back.

To her immediate right she heard a loud clanking as a video poker machine spit quarters into a metal tray. Roni leaned forward to have a look. Four deuces. As the coins filled the tray the old woman playing the machine lit a cigarette, sucked at her beer, and appeared bored.

Turning back, Roni raised her mug to her lips and over the rim she saw James Glazer standing midway down the bar. This time there was no doubt in her mind that it was him.

Her pulse raced.

James, still in Eagleton after all this time? Or had he moved away, then returned, as she had? Was Larry here with him? A shiver of excitement ran through her. For some reason she felt that she wasn't so alone anymore, wasn't the only outsider. Another mine brat, the brother of her best friend.

He paid for a bottle of beer and a pack of thin cigars and, without looking her way, turned and went into the other room. She watched him wind his way through the tight-knit tables. When he squeezed into a chair at a table with the classy blonde in the expensive clothes, Roni felt a sinking sensation in her stomach.

She watched them rise and move to the smaller dance floor in the back. By the way the woman melded into him like liquid mercury, it was obvious his body was no stranger to hers. Any fool could see they were close—intimate. Years ago she had observed him in the arms of another pretty blonde, Jolie, at a dance in the high school auditorium. A very young Roni had watched her sister dancing and flirting outrageously with James and half a dozen other guys. It looked like the blondes had the edge where James was concerned.

Just as she rose to leave, the bartender smacked another Bud down in front of her.

"From Dean," she said, jerking her head toward the opposite end of the bar.

Through the swirl of cigarette and cigar smoke, she recognized Dean Scolli. He sat hunched forward, his head low.

She didn't want the second beer, yet to refuse it and leave would be rude. Settling back down, she gave Dean a thin smile and quickly lowered her gaze.

For the next few minutes she confined her attention to the narrow, smoky barroom. As the two-beat rhythm of the music had her feet tapping and her body swaying, she sipped her beer and made designs with her finger on the wet bar top.

A beefy hand wrapped around her wrist. "Hey, you can't dance sitting there on that stool," said the lawyer, Faddle Granville. Against her protests, she was lifted off the stool and propelled into the other room. She held back as they approached the dance floor, her heels digging in. "Faddle, I don't know how to dance this . . . this . . . whatever it's called."

"Two-step. Oh, sure you can," he shouted over the music. "Men lead, women follow. Don't come simpler. This here's a good one to learn to." He spoke rapid-fire, the sentences running together.

"No, really—" She was in the circle, a link, a weak link at that, blindly moving backward.

"Don't worry, I'll let you get the rhythm in your feet first 'fore we do anything fancy." He allowed some space between them. "Look down there at my feet. Fast, fast, slow, slow. See? Say, y'know, you got real interesting eyes. Like a doe."

Roni smiled self-consciously, moving stiff-legged like a robot. She looked down, trod on feet behind her, looked back at him, silently pleading. He only smiled and pointed downward.

Soon she found a pace of sorts. By no means as fluid as the others, but at least she was no longer trampling all over the feet around her. She risked a glance at her partner and grinned, suddenly pleased with herself.

Just when she thought it was safe to breathe, to raise her gaze from the floor, to release aching, petrified muscles, her partner spun her around—one, two, three dizzying spins. Then she was hauled back into his arms and stepping forward this time. She stumbled before finding the pace again.

"Slips don't count. You're doing fine, Roni, just fine."

She smiled again.

"Getting some air, are you? Gonna twirl you, ready?"

She nodded to both questions. He twirled her to the right, then the left, then they were stepping alongside each other, arms linked like a pair of ice skaters.

"Dang, this gal's a fast learner."

"It's the teacher."

"It's in the feet," he said as he threw back his head and laughed. "You're dancing country, little gal."

When the song ended he escorted her back to her place at the bar. She offered him the untouched beer.

"Never touch the stuff," he said. "Booze makes me act peculiar."

A moment later he was at a table in the other room pulling a lanky woman from her chair and leading her to the dance floor.

Roni tucked an unruly strand of hair behind her ear, lifted the mug, and swallowed deeply. She wondered if James had witnessed her stumbling act on the dance floor. She had been too preoccupied with her feet to notice anything else.

Leaning to the right, she looked for him. Strangers sat at his table. She scanned the dance floor. Gone. Both of them gone. Suddenly the beer tasted flat and the loud music grated on her nerves.

Pushing the mug away, she slid from the stool, lifted her jacket, and hugging it to her, headed for the exit.

A cool breeze caressed her flushed face as she stepped out onto the sidewalk. She closed her eyes and breathed in the sweet night air. To the right of her she heard a scratching sound. She caught a flash of a match. She turned to see a man leaning against the building lighting a thin cigar.

James Glazer looked over at her.

Eleven

Roni stared into James Glazer's clean-cut face.

"Hello," he said with that hint of an Aussie accent. She smiled.

He waved the cigar. "One nasty habit I can't give up. You headin' out so soon?"

"Yes, I was out walking and heard the music. I hadn't planned to stay long." It occurred to her that he may not remember her. Despite the fact that the sight of him had her heart racing, to him she may be just someone new to town who happened to be in the same bar at the same time.

He pushed away from the wall and came toward her.

The blonde stepped out of the doorway between them. "Oh, Jim, there you are," she said, slipping a hand in his. "I thought you had abandoned me,"

"Just having a smoke." He pulled the woman closer. "Linda, this is Roni Mayfield. Roni, Linda Shaw."

Naturally he knew her name. The outsider who was staying at the Holt house. News traveled fast in small towns. But did he remember her?

Roni turned to James and asked. "Are you working at one of the mines?"

"Saltzman. I'm one of two geologists there."

"Really? That's great. How's Larry? Is he in town?"

He stared at her a moment before saying, "No. I don't see him much these days. He bounces around a lot. Right now he's in Colorado, mining copper and zinc."

"Like father, like sons?"

Something flashed briefly in his eyes, a hard bitterness. But before she could dwell on it, Dean Scolli appeared in the doorway and asked Linda for a dance.

"Oh, sorry, Dean," Linda said. "I promised this dance to Jim." She looked at both Roni and Dean. "Last dance of the set. Will you excuse us?"

Roni caught the icy glare Dean directed at James before Dean stepped out the door and marched off down the street. If James saw it, he paid no attention. He turned to Roni and opened his mouth to say something.

Linda pulled at his hand.

Roni backed up. "Gotta go. Look, I'll see you around." She turned and headed in the direction opposite from Dean's.

Buttery light spiked from inside the tavern and guided her across the highway. She pulled on her jacket as she walked briskly toward the courthouse, her thoughts on James. He hadn't introduced Linda as his wife so they weren't married. But just how close were they, James and his citified girlfriend?

Roni laughed at herself. Who was she to pin labels on people? Yesterday when she rolled into town in her convertible with her laptop and array of other electronics, she'd been the citified one—out of place like glitter on tar paper. It took more than jeans and boots to make her one of them.

She had returned to Eagleton not knowing James would be in town. But, subconsciously, had she hoped to find him here? Over the years she often wondered how things would have worked out if she and James had had a chance to get to know each other. Well, here he was . . . in the flesh. What now?

Her boot heels sounded loud on the asphalt. Once off the main street the night suddenly closed in on her, opaque and bleak. The ground and trees still held moisture from the early-evening rain. She shivered, shoving her cold hands deep into the fleece-lined pockets. She hadn't realized just how dark the side streets were. Heading down, the bright lights of town had been a welcoming sight, a promise of adventure. Now there was nothing but the surrounding blackness.

An owl hooted, a cat screamed. The bushes rustled in the field to her right.

She spun around and saw lights—red, yellow, and blue reflected on the wet pavement. No sound of footsteps, no dark figure ducking in and out of shadows, yet she instinctively knew someone was behind her, watching her, gaining on her. She shivered again, picking up her pace. She turned the corner and moved toward the middle of the road, away from the dense foliage and the boarded-up structures on the block. Again she glanced over her shoulder and saw nothing. Whoever was behind her didn't have to stay on the road to track her. The overgrown lots on both sides of the street offered plenty of concealment.

Behind her, about a block away, she finally saw

movement. A tall hawthorn hedge shimmied and something glided out into the street. It stood still for a moment then came toward her at a brisk lope. A dog. A large dog, limping slightly on a front paw.

Roni felt her pulse quicken. Most of the dogs in town were fat, lazy, and harmless. Lord knows they had to be since they were allowed to run loose. Yet there was always the off chance that an ornery mutt was having a bad night and she just happened to be going his way.

She began walking backward, not wanting to expose her back to the animal. What if it attacked? There was no one on this end of the street to hear her if she screamed. No one, that is, except Mrs. Wiggins, who was deaf, and Aaron.

The dog continued to close the distance. She was about to shout at it to go home when it slowed, then stopped twenty feet away. It stood sideways in the street, watching her. Roni felt a strange tugging at her stomach. What was it about this dog that reminded her of something else? Acting high-strung, he went in a circle, whining softly before trotting forward several yards. Where had she seen this animal before? There was something feral, yet timid, about him.

She backed up. The dog kept pace with her.

Gathering enough moisture in her mouth, Roni whispered, "Go home, boy. Go home."

He whined again, bushy tail wagging irresolutely.

It came to her then. The bushy tail, the large golden eyes. This was the dog she had seen outside the cafe that morning. *Red*, half coyote and half mutt. ". . . Gentle as a kitten," Faddle Granville had said. And according to Faddle, unless you were a bitch in heat, you had nothing to fear from Red.

What did he want with her? Why was he following her?

"Red . . . ?"

The tail wagged enthusiastically at the mention of his name.

"Go home, Red. Now."

The dog trotted forward, tail at half-mast. When he got within a half-dozen feet of Roni he lowered his head and came to her cautiously, eyes gazing upward. He sat, making soft sounds in his throat.

"What's the matter, boy, are you lonely? Hungry? Looking for someone, maybe?" Gingerly, so as not to frighten him, she held out her hand for his inspection. He sniffed it, then gave it a hardy, wet lick, tail whipping back and forth. Then he started down the street in the direction of her house.

Roni followed. The house stood tall and dark in the deep shadows of the surrounding trees. With the dog marking her way, she felt safer, thankful now for his company. He was probably hungry, she thought. Perhaps he lived hand to mouth with no master of his own. The town dog. Faddle hadn't named anyone.

She found herself hurrying to keep up with him.

"You wanna race, huh, boy? Okay, I'm game." She broke into a run, passing the dog. He leaped into the air, spun around, then charged forward, catching up with her in seconds. He ran alongside, his wet, rust-colored nose nudging her hand. She had to slow down when her ankle, the one she'd broken from her fall down the shaft, began to ache. Running on the beach was not the same as running on hard asphalt. Red trotted at her side. Before she knew it, they had reached the Holt property. She turned down the driveway and jogged to the back door.

She was laughing, feeling giddy from the beer, the

exercise, and the dog's playfulness. Red stiffened and cocked his head. She stopped and listened.

Music was coming from the house.

Roni crept closer to the back door. Piano music. Sweet sounds of Brahms—a lullaby that Caroline used to play.

She unlocked the door. The dog ran around the back of the house. She could hear his paws rustling through the fallen leaves, hear him sniffing as though looking for someone.

She went in, leaving the door open as she went to the refrigerator, pulled the meat from a chicken breast, and returned to the door. Red loped toward her from the opposite direction. He had circled the entire house.

She held out the chicken. Red sniffed it, barked once, then gingerly took it from her hand. He turned and trotted down the gravel driveway with the meat in his mouth. At the street he veered left and headed back the way he had come.

Piano chords struck.

Roni listened. From the slightly-out-of-tune piano another beautiful melody emerged, filling the house with its sweet sounds.

After quietly closing and locking the back door, she made her way through the dark house, feeling along the wainscoting of the hallway, following the sounds to the music room. At the closed door the music stopped. In her head the resounding notes continued to play, beautiful and haunting.

She pushed on the door. It glided inward. Moonlight streamed into the room through the long, rectangular window. The piano bench sat empty.

Roni sighed, rubbing at her temples. How much longer did he intend to evade her? She started to turn away when something metallic glinted from the dark corner of the room. She turned back.

He sat Indian-fashion in an overstuffed chair. Moonlight danced along the metal edge of his large, round eyeglasses.

In the dim room they stared silently at each other.

He unfolded his legs and rose from the chair, walking across the room to her. Then he took her hand and pressed something cool into it. The metal of his glasses reflected the pale light. "My mother wanted you to have this," he said quietly. "She wanted you here."

"What do you want?"

"She wants you to find out what happened to him."

"Who? What happened to whom, Aaron?"

"The guy that belonged to." Then he went around her and left the room.

Roni crossed to the table, turned on the lamp, and held the bracelet close to the bulb. A medical alert bracelet. The chain, broken at the clasp, was made of a cheap alloy and badly tarnished. On the face of the bracelet, etched above the medical symbol of entwined twin snakes, was the word ASTHMA.

Twelve

Shortly after Roni Mayfield left the Eagle bar, James walked Linda back to Dr. Burke's house. Linda, a visiting therapist from Elko, only came to Eagleton when needed, which wasn't very often since people in small towns tended either to take pride in their eccentricities or hide them. Her last visit had been in late spring.

Eighteen months earlier Dr. Burke had introduced James and Linda. After several dates they began an affair that had lasted the better part of a year. The distance separating them and the infrequency of their time together, in addition to a mutual desire to remain free of personal commitment, ultimately recast their relationship into one of friendship.

On the way back to the doctor's house, however, she hinted several times about spending the night with him. They hadn't slept together in ages. He wondered why the renewed interest? Was it possible another attractive woman's presence in the bar earlier had stirred up a possessive jealousy in Linda? Possible, very possible. Thinking back, her friendliness had turned to flirtation just after she had spotted him with Roni outside the tavern. Whatever, he decided to let it pass; Linda would be back in Elko tomorrow and there was something important he had to do tonight.

She kissed him good night at the door of the doctor's house—a teasing, passionate kiss. He gave her a hug, kissed her temple, said good night, and quickly walked away before he could change his mind.

The doctor and his family lived on the north end of town and James lived on the south end, a pleasant, ten-minute stroll. As James neared his house, the moon slid out from behind a cloud and followed, reflecting in long puddles like a spotlight guiding him home. He whistled softly. Red came running. The dog danced around James, nudging and making greeting sounds in his throat.

"Did she get home okay, boy?"

Red chuffed, wagging his great tail.

"Good. What would I do without you?"

Red chuffed again.

They walked down the gravel path to the patio and entered at the back of the house.

In the bedroom James removed his boots and shirt and reclined on the bed. Needing no invitation, Red jumped up and flopped down alongside him. James crossed his arms behind his head and stared at the glossy redwood ceiling. The granite face of his father appeared in the wood grain. The last time James had seen him the sonofabitch was lying in a pool of blood in the driveway at the home of his latest whore where James had left him. The woman stood in the doorway in a loosely wrapped robe, yellow and purple bruises along the length of her arms, watching. As James walked away, his knuckles raw and bleeding, one finger dislocated, his ribs aching, he saw a look of sheer gratification in her cold, green eyes.

James willed the memory away. It was replaced by the dying face of his mother and the angry one of his sister.

He tightly squeezed his eyes shut. Soon an image of Roni Mayfield emerged—Roni dancing with Faddle in her snug jeans and knit turtleneck. This image he liked. His taut muscles relaxed. The girl from his youth had become quite a woman. Slender, long legs, a graceful neck. But it was her eyes, huge and a deep velvet brown, that attracted immediate attention. He thought of a tawny, long-legged doe.

His brother had been crazy about her. Larry and Roni had been practically inseparable. Because she was years younger than James, he doubted he would have noticed her, even in such a small town, if not for Larry's closeness to her. The other Mayfield sister, Jolie, was older, more James's age. But Jolie wasn't Roni.

And Larry wasn't Larry anymore.

Suddenly, Larry dominated his thoughts.

Hey, little brother, how's it going? Did you ever get that shit outta your blood? Ever conquer those mind demons? What the hell happened to you, Bro? What the hell happened?

Larry had been a good kid, a relatively normal kid considering the miserable life their old man put them through. But on the day Frank Scolli entered the widow's house something happened to change all that. *Larry* changed ... changed drastically. The nightmares came first. Then the mood swings. Soon he was failing in school, then drinking, dropping pills, and worse. The last time James had seen Larry had been five years earlier to sign him into a rehab center in Denver, a program he ducked out of after only a few weeks. Once or twice a year Larry got in touch: "Just thought I'd let you know you still got a little brother," Larry would inform him. "Gonna come visit you sometime . . . when I get my shit together." Not a word since James wrote him that he'd returned to Eagleton.

Dammit, there had to be a connection between Larry's problems and whatever happened that day at the Holt house. It was coming together, slow but sure. Roni was back in Eagleton, and not by mere chance. On his last visit to the widow, she'd revealed something quite confidential. He'd had a feeling she wanted to tell him more, yet he hadn't pressed, not then. The next time he saw her she was dead, being wheeled from her house to the waiting mortician's car.

James swung his legs off the bed and quickly stood. Red jumped up with a questioning look. "Down, boy."

James went into the tiny kitchen to the phone on the wall. He looked up a number and dialed, checking his watch at the same time. Ten-eighteen. As it rang he tried to figure out if Colorado was one or two hours later. Daylight savings time always messed him up. Someone on the other end picked up, then there was a clunking noise as if the receiver had been dropped. A husky voice said, "What?"

"Larry?"

"The number you have reached is no fucking longer in use. Please hang up and try—"

"Larry . . . it's me, Jim."

Pause. "Jim? Big bro Jim? Shiiit!"

"How you doing, guy?"

"Hey, great! Yeah, just great. How the hell you doing?" His words were slurred and his voice was too loud, with just a little too much gusto.

"I wake you up?" Or did I interrupt a good drunk? he wondered to himself.

"Yeah. Yeah, you did . . . the ringing did. It's okay, though, 'cause it's damn good to hear from ya. Christ, you sound close. You here in town?"

"No. I'm calling from Eagleton."

Larry's next words were said with wonder. "Eagleton. Man, what the fuck you doing there?"

"I put in for it. Our company had two mining operations starting at the same time, one in Nevada and the other in Oregon. I put in for this one."

Silence.

"Roni Mayfield—you remember Roni?—she's back, too, staying at the Holt place. The widow died."

James heard bedsprings creaking. "Bony Maroni," Larry said softly.

"She's not bony anymore." More silence. "Can you get some time off," James said, "come to Eagleton for a weekend? My treat. Hey, it'd be great. I'm sure Roni would love to see you again. She asked about you first thing."

"No. No, I can't," Larry said quickly. "We're running overtime as it is. Twelve-hour shifts. No can do. Maybe in a couple months. Hey, I'll let you know."

"I have some time coming—I might head up your way."

"Same deal, man. Love to see you, but got no time to hang out. It's gonna be a bitch till we get caught up around here."

"I see."

With nothing more to say, James signed off. He regretted calling. Aside from a sister in Australia whom he hardly knew, Larry was all the family he had. And Larry . . .

Larry never swore when he was sober.

Tom Mayfield leaned against a juniper and stared down solemnly at the two-story Victorian where his daughter was staying. Camped about a mile away at the fork of Ruby Creek, it was an easy hike for him across the Ruby range to Eagleton and this copse of trees above the house. Lights burned upstairs. Several minutes earlier he'd caught a glimspe of Roni as she passed the window. The sight of her in Eagleton, in the Holt house, did not please him. *Why did she have to come back?*

Roni lay awake in the big four-poster thinking about Aaron in the music room—frail, lost, dwarfed by the overstuffed chair.

She thought of the bracelet. What did Aaron know about Frank? What did he know about his mother's death? Tomorrow she'd get some answers.

Too keyed up to go to sleep, she opened the leather diary and began to read about Caroline's marriage to airman Richard Holt.

> *This is the happiest day of my life. It was a simple ceremony by a local Justice of the Peace—a funny-looking little man with tufts of red hair above his ears who giggled and kept forgetting my name. Tonight we honeymoon at the Clairemont Hilton. Tomorrow we*

leave on the plane for Reno, then bus to Eagleton. I
forwarded Grandmother's china, my dolls, and the
family photos on ahead. The piano was shipped last
week. I can't wait to see the house where Richard
was raised. Can't wait to meet all the people in his
hometown. I hope they like me.

According to the journal, the newlyweds had
arrived in Eagleton in the fall of 1971. Soon after,
the groom shipped out and the bride was left alone
in her husband's large house. Caroline made friends,
joined the few women's organizations in town, and
even took a part-time receptionist's job at the *Eagleton
Press.* She advertised to give piano lessons in her home
and acquired several pupils, all children except for
a crude miner who made a pass at her on his second
visit. For many months she worked on decorating the
room at the front of the house, the one with the
southeast exposure that caught the morning sun,
until it was the perfect nursery. She ended each day
by writing long letters to Richard—letters about children filling the rooms in the big Victorian house and
future plans for a full, happy life together in Eagleton.

Eight months later, at the age of twenty-two, when
notified by the war department of her husband's
downed aircraft over Laos, the stunned widow-bride
refused to acknowledge, to believe, her husband was
dead. With aching, empty arms she waited. Gradually
she withdrew from society, such as it was, when the
townspeople came forward to console her, to grieve
with her, to shatter the illusion that Richard was
alive—that he was merely missing in action. Time
passed agonizingly slowly. Entries in the diary for the
next five years were filled with desperate pleas and
prayers for Richard's safe return.

Please, God, send him home to me. We've had so little time together. There is so much to say and do. The nursery sits empty, waiting. It hardly seems fair that some have many children when Richard and I have none. There are nine children in the Westcott family and shiftless Harry Westcott can scarcely care for himself. The doctor and his wife have a beautiful son and daughter and Charlotte is pregnant again. The Scolli house is full—four boys about as healthy and spirited as they come.

Lord, you've taken all the family I have. You can't take Richard from me. You can't—

Though there was nothing or no one in Eagleton to keep her there, her only connection to Richard was the house. Without the children they had hoped to have, the empty rooms rang hollow. Yet she stayed. Waited.

Roni placed the diary on the nightstand, lifted the glass of brandy, and swallowed it down. Sleep was a long time coming.

He stood at the piano in the music room. Without making a sound he lifted the fall to expose the keyboard. Lightly, he pressed down a key and listened to the tiny ding. She had played so beautifully, he thought. He could never see or hear a piano without thinking of Caroline. There were so many other things—sights, sounds, smells that would forever remind him of her. She was beauty, desire. Just to be in her presence had made him feel unequivocally male. He had gone crazy with wanting her and she had turned him away. As unrealistic as it was, she had expected him to turn off his emotions like one turned off a water tap. Impossible.

He pressed down on the keys randomly. Tinny notes filled the air. He looked upward in the direction of the master bedroom where another now slept in Caroline's bed.

An anger, bordering on rage, burned in his chest. What was she doing here? Why had she come? He didn't believe in mere coincidence. His anger, charged by fear, grew. There were two of them in town now, the two who had been downstairs in the house that day. What did they want? What did they know?

He struck the piano keys with the flat of his hand once, twice, the sound reverberating like an eerie dirge in the room.

Roni dreamed. In the dream she was standing in the dim music room; behind her the billowing curtains gently caressed the back of her legs. The room was all cool blue light and shadows, flickering, waving like the sheer curtains at the window. The room, her head, the entire house, was filled with dulcet, melancholy music.

A slender Caroline sat at the piano, her hair down to her waist, dream shadows revolving mystically around her. Her hands moved gracefully above the keyboard. The keys pressed up and down, yet her fingers made no actual contact. *Is that you, my love?*

Caroline's hands dropped into her lap: she twisted around on the bench and stared toward Roni, through Roni, to someone or something beyond. The widow's delicate face was garish with makeup. Crimson lipstick was smeared over her mouth. Mascara was smudged under her eyes and black tear streaks ran down her bright scarlet cheeks.

Caroline rose, leaning on the keyboard, the keys beneath her hands continuing to move on their own. She glided toward Roni, her hand reaching out.

Roni felt a palpable presence at her back. From behind her a broad hand stretched and enclosed the widow's hand. Roni turned. Frank Scolli—his eyes seeming to penetrate through Roni to Caroline Holt—smiled a sad, tragic smile. The music played on. The two joined hands and moved together, trapping Roni within the circle of their arms. She moaned and struggled to be free.

Roni jerked awake, the sounds of fading piano chords still echoing throughout the house. Disoriented, hampered by a tangle of bedding, she flailed about. Her eyes flew open and saw only darkness. Aaron had been playing the piano. She held her breath, listening for more notes.

After a while, when even the notes in her head were no longer there, Roni left the bed, pulled on her robe, and went down the hall to Aaron's door. After knocking and getting no answer, she opened the door and looked in. His bed was empty. He was nowhere in the room.

She climbed the narrow stairway to the attic and finding the padlock in place, went through the house from room to room. The doors and windows were secure, safety chains engaged. Aaron was nowhere inside. Somehow he came and went without using the downstairs doors or windows.

She found herself in the music room.

Moonlight filtered in through the long windows as

she moved to the piano and sat down. Her fingers glided across the keys as she pressed one, then another, and listened to the faint notes.

A cool breeze passed over her, making her shiver. The lace curtains at the window rose, furling and unfurling. She crossed to the window and closed it, noticing again the wrought iron bars attached to it. What if there were a fire? With the bars, deadbolts, and safety chains, how difficult would it be to get out?

Below her, from inside the windowseat, she heard a faint scratching, then a faint meow. She reached down, took hold of the seat, and began to lift it. At the same moment, sensing movement across the room, Roni spun around and caught a glimpse of something dark, a shadow perhaps, passing through the door into the hallway. Startled, she dropped the seat. A shrill cat cry had her heart racing as she grabbed the seat again and threw it back. The black cat leaped up, clawing her arm as it jumped from its dark prison and ran off.

Streaks of fire burned her arm. She turned toward the door. "Aaron?" She stood there a moment, holding her arm, waiting. "Aaron?"

Nerves and the cold started her teeth chattering. She hugged herself and looked down curiously. How had the cat gotten into the windowseat? It had to be Aaron, but why would he put it there?

She returned upstairs. In the bathroom she carefully washed the cat scratches and sprayed them with an antiseptic.

She made one last visit to Aaron's room and this time found him in bed. She moved inside and stood over him. His eyes were closed. She bent down, gently sweeping his hair off his face. He looked so sweet, so angelic.

At her feet were his sneakers. She bent down and touched the canvas, darkly wet and crusted with mud. She turned and left the room, feeling his gaze follow her out the door.

Back in her room she climbed into bed and burrowed deep into the bedcovers. The moment she closed her eyes bits and pieces from the dream rushed back. The widow calling to her dead husband, and Frank, gone all these years, answering her. The dream, like most dreams, made no sense.

She glanced at the empty glass on the nightstand. Drinking brandy to relax her before turning in probably hadn't been such a good idea after all.

The man made his way through the tunnel, his steps sure-footed, his breathing tight. He moved quickly through the passageway without light. He knew the way. He had traveled it many times in the past.

Fear gnawed painfully at his gut, making him hurry.

Thirteen

Thursday

Roni awoke to the odor. The musty smell of age. Over the years the rooms had absorbed the odor—soaked it into the woodwork, the wallpaper, into the very fiber of the house.

After last night's nightmare, Roni had surprisingly fallen into a deep, drug-like slumber. If the house creaked, or a dog barked, or the shutter banged in the wind, she didn't hear it. And if the sheriff had come in the early morning hours, rattling the chain at the back door, she didn't hear that, either. She had slept like the dead.

She arose to another gray morning to find four cats in the room with her. The tortoiseshell and a white one with bright blue eyes lay curled at her feet. The tabby with the injured paw sat in the window watching her. High atop the armoire the black cat paced—the one in the windowseat last night. Roni stretched out her right arm and looked at the rows of angry scratches from elbow to wrist. One scratch in particular was deep and beginning to fester. The doctor would have a new patient today.

She scrutinized the large room in the cold morning light. Because of the passing of time and the absence of years of cleansing sunlight, a grunginess hung in the air; the once-gleaming whites were now dingy and depressing. The room could be restored to its pristine state, and should be. The entire house, for that matter. To see it in such disrepair saddened Roni. But Caroline was gone and soon Roni would have to leave, too. She could only take so much time away from the magazine.

Of course she could always freelance, but she'd worked too hard to get where she was at *Tempo* to throw it all away. After putting herself through school she'd gotten a foot in the door, tackled every crummy assignment, went after every lead, and worked on each piece late into the night until she collapsed in bed too exhausted to think. And for what? To prove that she could make a name for herself. Prove it to whom?

She got out of bed and stepped on the diary that had fallen from the nightstand. She picked it up and put it back. After a moment's hesitation, she retrieved it, glanced around, then slid it between the mattress and boxspring.

Downstairs several minutes later the cats pressed around her ankles, crying for breakfast. She fed them from a twenty pound bag of dry cat food on the back porch. The wastebasket lay on its side. Chicken bones, picked at by the cats, were scattered around the kitchen.

She closed the refrigerator door and leaned against

it. In the kitchen an empty can of beef stew, fork inside, lay in the sink. A bag of corn chips and a package of Oreos were missing. Aaron had eaten. The plate she'd made for him remained untouched in the refrigerator.

The telephone rang. The loud, jarring bell startled her. It was the first time she'd heard it ring. It took her a moment to mentally place its location. She stepped on a sharp chicken bone and, hopping on one foot and cussing like a trucker, she rushed into the dining room to answer.

"How's my little girl?"

"Dad?"

"That's right, unless you're now somebody else's little girl."

"Where are you?"

"In town. I'm calling from the Exxon station."

"Great. Come over."

"I thought maybe we could meet in town. I'm having some work done on the wagon and I have to get supplies. Honey, I'm just passing through, but I wanted to stop and say hello. Breakfast at the Eagle?"

She glanced at the clock and looked down at her nightshirt. "Sure. Give me an hour, okay? I have a few things to do here first."

"Perfect."

She hung up, smiling. So her father had come. She thought he would, but was somewhat surprised by his speediness.

She heard a creaking overhead. First things first.

After dressing, she knocked at Aaron's door.

"Aaron, we have to talk about . . . about the bracelet and Frank Scolli." No answer, but she heard him moving around inside. In a voice of authority, she said, "I'll be in the music room. Five minutes."

She went downstairs.

The piano bench was cool and hard. Roni closed her eyes, caressing the keys with her fingertips, and thought of Caroline. She had played so beautifully. Roni, unfortunately, wasn't cut out for music. Though she could sit for hours and listen to Caroline play, she couldn't sit long enough to practice on her own.

She poked a key. E-flat? B-minor? No idea. She poked at more keys. Notes filled the room. She began to play the only melody she vaguely remembered— "Chopsticks." It took her several tries to torture the keys into a recognizable facsimile. As she pecked on the white keys she glanced at her watch. It had been ten minutes. She slapped impatiently at the keys, swiveled around, and was taken aback to find Aaron in the large wing chair behind her.

He sat in a ball with his arms wrapped around his drawn-up legs. His feet were bare and so pale the blue-veined skin looked translucent. His hair was mussed, an Alfalfa cowlick standing straight up to give him a look of incredible vulnerability. Without the large, round glasses his dark brown eyes appeared smaller, wiser, the eyes of an old soul. The face of Caroline, Roni thought, as she might have looked as a child.

Again, the urge to reach out to him was overwhelming. Was she merely reacting to an emotional stimulus brought on by her affection for Caroline, or was it something more basic?

She studied his delicate features, looking for a resemblance to Frank. Aaron, in every respect, was the spitting image of his mother. Small boned, fair-skinned with brown hair and light brown eyes. Nothing of Frank.

She found herself leaning toward him, unaware that she was doing so, like someone in a trance.

"Aaron, I—I'm here to help. Really I am. I see no reason why we can't be friends, can you?"

He looked away.

"Okay." She rose and began to pace. "Your mother wrote to me. She asked for my help. Before I could respond, she called and left a message on my answering machine. She seemed pretty upset. I'd been out of town and by the time I was able to call back I learned she had . . . she was . . . I was too late."

He stared passively at her.

"Help me, Aaron. I think you know what this is all about."

His lips became a thin line.

She stopped pacing. "Aaron, can't you understand? I'm here to help. I cared very much for your mother. She was a wonderful person. Like a mother to me."

Those brown eyes seemed to bore into her like twin lasers.

"What do you know about the bracelet? Do you know that it belonged to a boy who lived in this town?"

Aaron tipped his head. She took that for a yes.

She worked her fingers together nervously. "Good. The more you know, the less handicapped we are." She clasped her fingers tightly. "Where did you get the medical bracelet?"

"My mother."

"Did she tell you to give it to me?"

He nodded.

It stood to reason Caroline had figured Roni would remember Frank's medical alert bracelet.

"Why did she want me to have it?" Would this whole conversation have to be conducted in this interrogative manner?

"She said . . ." He picked at the worn, frayed fabric of the chair.

"Go on."

"You . . . you'd want to know about Frank."

"I don't understand."

He turned his head and stared out the window.

Roni closed her eyes and pressed her fingers to the sides of her nose. "Aaron, wouldn't it be easier if you just told me everything you know?"

"Do you have kids?" he asked.

His question threw her. She shook her head. "I've never been married."

"You don't have to be married to have kids." His tone had hardened.

"Well, that's true, but—"

"My mother didn't have a husband but she had me."

"Your mother was married. Her husband was killed in the war."

"That man wasn't my father. My father's nothing but a shitty coward. He's the bastard, not me."

The obscene expletives from this angelic-looking child startled Roni. Santa Claus exposing himself would have been no less shocking. Roni bit her tongue, remained cool. The topic had shifted; now it had a more personal edge. She sensed they were about to tread on precarious ground. What did Aaron know? How much did he know regarding the circumstances of his own conception?

"Aaron, your mother—"

"No," he said, coming to his feet. "Don't talk about her. She was *my* mother, not yours. You went away and forgot about her. But she never forgot you. Never!" And he was out the door. A moment later

the sound of his bare feet could be heard padding
up the staircase. A door slammed.

Roni turned, leaned across the piano keyboard and,
with a sigh of frustration, buried her face in her arms.

The crispness of the morning swirled around her,
making the lightweight shirt cold against her skin.
To the east, behind yet another bank of storm clouds,
the sun struggled to come out. She hoped for an
improvement over yesterday's unseasonal weather.
September. Too damn early for winter. Winters here
were long and frigid. Nine months of winter followed
by three months of bad weather was the local motto.

The breakfast crowd at the Eagle Cafe had thinned
out. Roni spotted her father at a table along the
wall. Tall, lanky, with a gaunt but pleasant face. His
shoulder-length hair, caught in a leather strap at the
nape of his neck, had more silver than black. He
stood when she approached and gave her a hug. He
smelled of juniper and sage.

"Can't stay out of these dumpy mining towns,
huh?" he teased.

"Nope."

They sat. The waitress filled their coffee mugs, took
their order, and left.

A somberness came over his face and crept into
his voice, "Baby, what are you doing here?"

"Caroline died. I came to pay my respects."

"She was buried two days ago."

Roni looked at him. "How did you know?"

"No big secret. I asked the waitress."

Roni sighed and looked away. "Caroline didn't kill
herself."

"Roni, what difference does it make?"

"It makes a difference . . . to me."

"Are you suggesting someone killed her?"

"I don't know. I found a diary, and last night Aaron gave me something that belonged to Frank Scolli. Frank, in case you don't know, never came back to Eagleton."

"Can you blame him?"

Sensing she was not going to get help from her father, Roni changed the subject. She told him about Dennis Stemmer's rescue from the mine shaft and his remarkable recovery. The article, she said, would appear in the next issue of *Tempo*.

Their breakfast arrived—chicken fried steak, country gravy and biscuits. For the next half-hour they caught each other up on family and friends. After that the conversation turned to prospecting. Tom, excited about a new claim on the Nevada-Idaho border, was on his way to meet his partner to check it out. Everything he owned was loaded inside the Wagoneer that was being serviced across the street at the station.

"Does that mean you might be leaving Nevada and moving into Idaho?"

He nodded. "I've covered about as much of this state as I can. It's a little too dry here for me. Time to move along."

As Roni reached for the cream, her father's deeply tanned hand closed around her wrist, turning it over to expose the long, ragged scratch along the inside of her arm.

"What happened there?" he asked.

"Cat. We ran into each other in the dark last night."

"Better have that looked at. It might be infected."

She nodded.

With the check paid, both left the cafe and stood uncertain on the wooden sidewalk in front.

"Are you sure you can't stay the night?" Roni asked.

" 'Fraid not."

"The afternoon?"

"Sorry, honey, business takes me down the road. If you're still here when I come back through in about a week, I'll stay."

They hugged and kissed, then her father was running across the highway to the Exxon station and his dusty Wagoneer.

Dr. Burke's office and the examining room were located in the north wing of his recently remodeled homestead-style house on Sage Street, a block from Main. The clinic, a newly erected brick building, stood directly across the street, the front facing Main, the rear at Sage.

Bea, the doctor's nurse, showed her into the examining room, which seemed to have shrunk since she was a kid. A wave of nostalgia washed over her. The same Norman Rockwell prints on the walls. The same dangling life-size plastic skeleton, yellowed now and missing a foot. The same large apothecary jar with the seemingly endless rope of red licorice. She remembered how the doctor used to carry a rolled up length of it in his medical bag when he went on house calls—so much for hermetically sealed, germ-free standards—and at the end of his visit, he would reach into the bag and twist off a piece for his young patients. Proportions were determined by the severity of the patient's ailment.

Roni smiled. They didn't make doctors like that

anymore. She'd bet he still carried licorice in his bag and made house calls.

The door opened and Dr. Burke strode in. "Couldn't stay away, could you, Roni?"

"Guess not."

"Say, you still have trouble downing those iron tablets?"

She had forgotten that. As a teenager she had been slightly anemic and was placed on an iron program of liver, leafy vegetables, and green tablets the size of horse pills. Every morning she'd had to take one of the pills with V-8 juice, which she hated as much as the slimy liver. For hours she would swallow and swallow trying to dislodge it from somewhere deep down in her throat.

She smiled. "I don't take them anymore. That's the beauty of being an adult. I don't have to do anything I don't want to do."

"You and me both," he said with a wink, lightly pinching her elbow. "So you're not here for iron tablets?"

She held out her arm. "Cat clawed me. I was worried about infection."

In no time he deftly cleansed the wounds, applied an antiseptic, and filled a syringe. "Where do you want this?" he asked.

"I have a choice?"

"As an adult, yes, you do."

She pointed to her arm. The needle went in and she suddenly remembered why she hated to go to the doctor. Big or little, it still hurt. As he injected the tetanus serum, the door opened and a toddler waddled in. The boy child, diaperless, headed straight for the hanging skeleton and began to shake a leg.

"Mother!" Dr. Burke called out over his shoulder. "The baby is loose, he's indecent, and he's pestering ol' Jesse."

A moment later the doctor's wife, a blond woman in an advanced stage of pregnancy, hurried in, brushing hair from her forehead. She swept the little boy into her arms. In the doorway another child, a girl about twelve, stood wringing her hands.

"I'm sorry, Daddy," the girl said. "He ran off when I went to get a washcloth for his bottom."

"Teresa," Charlotte said, "I told you your father was busy with a patient. You can't let Johnboy run around." She turned to the doctor. "Paul, I'm sorry. I was helping Bette in the kitchen."

Dr. Burke pressed a cotton ball against the needle puncture on Roni's arm. He waved the other arm. "No harm done. We're about through."

The doctor's wife shooed the children out, then turned and grasped Roni's free hand in both of hers. Smiling, her attractive face aglow, she gave Roni a warm handshake. "Roni Mayfield. I heard you were in town."

"Hello, Mrs. Burke."

"It's Charlotte, dear. My heavens, I remember the last time you were in this office. Paul had put a couple tucks in that pretty little chin of yours."

Roni's fingertips automatically went to the raised flesh at the curve of her chin. She'd forgotten about that. The scar was a result of jumping off Caroline's porch the day Frank went inside. "And I remember you were pregnant then, too."

Charlotte laughed, a rich throaty sound that made Roni want to laugh with her. "Yes, I was, with Teresa. It seems I'm always pregnant."

"How many do you have?"

"Four."

Dr. Burke patted her stomach. "And baby makes five."

"Our two eldest are becoming a tad embarrassed," she went on merrily. "Seth is very active in politics. He has an image to maintain, you know. And Pam, who's engaged to be married this June, is afraid her first child will be older than her last sibling."

"Pam's getting married? That's great."

"To Eric Saltzman," the doctor said.

"Saltzman? Of the Saltzman mines?" Roni asked.

"That's the family," the doctor said proudly. "And very generous they are. Without them we wouldn't have the new clinic."

Charlotte changed the subject. "How's Aaron holding up?"

"I wish I knew. I haven't seen much of him yet."

"I hear he's quite shy. He needs a friend. Our Teresa is about his age. Why don't you bring him over and we'll get them together. She has Nintendo. It's sort of an ice breaker for children who aren't real outgoing. What do think, Paul?"

Dr. Burke was applying an adhesive patch to Roni's arm. He pressed it down, squeezing hard.

"Doctor?" Roni said, instinctively pulling her arm away.

His head jerked up. "Hmm? What? I'm sorry, Roni, did I press too hard?"

"It's okay."

The baby began to scream. Charlotte waved good-bye to Roni and hurried out.

"Okay, you're free to go," the doctor said, stepping to the sink. "No more cat fights. Promise?"

She nodded. "Dr. Burke, is it possible that Caroline Holt didn't commit suicide?"

With his back to her, his hands under the flowing water, she saw him pause. He turned his head slowly to give her an odd stare. "What are you suggesting?" he asked blankly.

"Could she have been murdered?"

"Murdered?"

"Yes, murdered."

"May I ask why you would entertain such a thought?"

"Before her death she tried to contact me. She was afraid for both Aaron and herself."

"You've told the sheriff about this?"

"Not yet."

Bea tapped on the open door. "Ernie's next up, Doc. He's grumbling about losing precious daylight."

The doctor squeezed her elbow again. "Talk to Lubben." He turned to leave. "Oh, almost forgot." He stepped to the apothecary jar, lifted the lid, twisted off about a foot of licorice, and handed it to her. Then he was gone.

Roni parked in front of Al's Tavern. As she rummaged in her deep handbag for her sunglasses, she looked down the street at the storefronts. There it was, on the corner a block away. James's office building. Putting on her sunglasses, she left the car and headed toward it.

When she wasn't watching for raised boards on the sidewalk, she studied the approaching faces for locals. As they passed her, some nodded, one or two even smiled. With school out for the summer, the park was filled with youngsters hanging and swinging on the gym equipment or playing games on the lawn.

The older ones were racing out of town on bikes to cast a line at Cutter's Creek or varmint hunt in the hills south of town, a fishing pole or small-caliber rifle braced across the handlebars. Two dogs warily circled each other in the middle of the highway, hackles rising menacingly.

She passed a bulletin board attached to the exterior of Coombs's market posted with weathered bills and events long past; yellowed index cards with outdated news items curled forlornly beneath rusty tacks: Baby-sitting—no housework; photographer with camcorder will videotape those special events; dog and cat show—common pets welcome.

The Goldenrod Mining Company was in an original building on Main; though renovated like so many others, it still bore a look of neglect. The interior was divided into two serviceable units, each filled with books, logs and maps, ore samples, and an odd assortment of mining tools, all coated with a fine layer of dust. Some archaic pieces—ax, pick, rusty-bottomed gold mining pans—hung on the walls along with the inevitable collection of deer and elk antlers. It was not the type of office that catered to clients nor encouraged them to linger.

Roni stepped in and removed her sunglasses. Just inside the door a young redheaded man looked up from a cumbersome chart unrolled in front of him.

"Help you?" He smiled and rose.

"Is James Glazer in?"

"Afraid you've missed him. He's left for the mine site. The Saltzman."

"Will he be back soon?"

"Hard to say. Depends on if he's at the mill or in the field. He could be gone as long as a week."

"I see. Well, thank you." Roni turned to leave.

"I'll tell him you were asking about him, Miss May-field."

Roni wasn't surprised that this stranger with the Gaelic accent knew who she was. In a town of less than two thousand, she doubted if there was a person here who didn't know about the new gal in town. They probably knew what she did for a living, her shoe size, the brand of coffee she drank, and who she was corresponding with. They just didn't know exactly why she was here or how long she intended to stay.

Disappointed that she'd missed James, she headed back the way she'd come. She had one more stop to make before going back to the house. At the door of Al's Tavern, she heard someone call her name.

A tall, white-haired woman with a mesh shopping bag approached. There was no mistaking her former teacher, Mrs. Anderson. The woman, though not as imposing as Roni remembered, still towered over her.

"Mrs. Anderson, you're back. How are you?"

"I'm in shock, that's how I am. I got in last night and heard the terrible news about Caroline. I can't believe it. My youngest daughter had a baby and naturally I had to go. Gone less than a week and everything comes crashing down."

"Mrs. Anderson—?"

"You can drop that Mrs. business. We're both out of school now, so call me Hazel. I can't believe it. Caroline was such a lovely person, far too young to die. And poor Aaron. He tells me you're staying at the house with him."

"You've seen him?"

"Yes, I've just come from there. He seems to be

managing all right for the time being. Is he eating? Sleeping?"

"He's eating. Junk food mostly."

"Well, it's better than nothing. How long will you be staying?"

"A week. Ten days."

"You're with your husband?"

Roni shook her head. "No husband."

Her brow crinkled. "That man I saw you in front of the cafe earlier . . . ?"

"Oh, you mean my father."

"Your father? Your father's back in town?"

"Briefly. Passing through on his way to a new claim."

"I would love to say hello to him. Is he still around?"

"No. We had breakfast and he was gone."

"Is he coming back?"

"Maybe, in about a week."

Roni moved away from the tavern door. "Hazel, what will become of Aaron? I mean, who will take care of him now?"

"I suppose I will. Caroline and I never discussed it at length. Nothing was committed to paper, but I'm the logical choice. Aaron and I are close. And since he can't be persuaded to move from that house, I guess there's nothing else to do. He's been housebound far too long. Not that I find caring for him a burden. I don't. Aaron is quite self-sufficient. Perhaps a little too shy and reserved for his own good, but very sweet."

She obviously hadn't heard him cuss.

The woman crossed her arms over her round belly. "Roni, why did you come?"

Roni looked past Hazel to see that Abby Cromwell had come out to sweep the walk in front of the post office next door. "Could we talk in private?" she said quietly.

Hazel caught her meaning. "Yes, of course. I want to talk with you, too. Listen, let me catch up on things here in town. Is tomorrow soon enough?"

"Tomorrow's fine."

"Come to my house. I'm still in the same place. Anytime after two." Hazel shifted her shopping bag. "If you're looking for Anna Scolli, she hasn't had anything to do with the bar in years. You'll find her at the RV park."

Roni returned to Caroline's house and went directly upstairs, hoping to catch Aaron. His door was slightly ajar. She peeked in. The twin bed was made, but otherwise the room looked like a normal kid's room. Books and magazines scattered about. A portable television turned on but without sound. An empty potato chip bag and a filmy glass with the dregs of orange juice sat on the floor. A hamper stood in the corner, clothes hanging over the rim and heaped at the base. Tacked to the wall above the bed was a poster of some rock group unfamiliar to Roni. On his dresser sat a framed picture.

Roni stepped into the room and moved to the dresser. She lifted the frame and stared at a color photograph of Aaron and his mother standing by the large lilac bush in the front of the house. Stuck with clear tape to the outside of the glass was a photograph of Arnold Schwarzenegger—clipped from a magazine and trimmed in such a way as to appear as though the man belonged in the picture—a happy, close-knit threesome.

Not wanting Aaron to find her snooping among

his private things, she quickly replaced the photograph and slipped from the room.

She stopped short when she entered the master bedroom.

On the neatly-made bed lay an untidy pile of odds and ends. Things she'd never laid eyes on before— or so she thought until she moved in for closer inspection. As she glanced at each item, moments from her past flashed before her eyes.

She leaned over and lightly touched a large, bare, wooden spool with four headless nails at one end. She closed her eyes and saw herself sitting in the kitchen of this very house holding the spool and working the needles, her awkward fingers guided by long, slender ones as the continuous rope of yarn fed down through the hole of the knitting spool.

Roni sank down on the soft mattress, her head slowly moving from side to side in wonder. A potholder, knitted on the spool. Paper dolls, the heavy cardboard figures, a mother and daughter, exquisitely drawn to resemble the artist and the child who had helped to design and cut out the various outfits. Samplers, unfinished samples, the material and embroidery floss rotting on wooden hoops. Needlepoint, petitpoint, delicate stitches that looked like rosebuds and stars. Skill, patience, and tenderness, made even harder by Caroline's left-handedness, had gone into the teaching of each craft. Roni remembered how her own mother hadn't the time, talent, and certainly not the patience for handiwork such as this.

Deep inside her, Roni felt a strange twisting. Among the assorted crafts she saw her first writing endeavor, a two-page story about a poodle named Pierre. After completing it, Roni had proudly offered it for a critique. At the top of the page in tiny, curlicue script: *A wonderful story of love and compassion. You will be a great writer one day.* Caroline had given Roni her first diary, had encouraged the young girl to write daily, to express her thoughts, experiences, and dreams.

Wave upon wave of nostalgia washed over Roni as she lifted one forgotten item after another, memories flooding back, so vivid they were almost painful. Clipped from *The Eagleton Tribune* was a yellowed photograph of herself when she'd won first place for an essay on "New Beginnings" and a Halloween ghost story she'd written in the eighth grade. Of all the fine things Caroline taught Roni, writing was the only one to take hold.

The mementos went beyond Eagleton. Scores of her magazine articles over the years were neatly preserved in a scrapbook.

Roni felt heartsick. A lonely woman and a lonely girl, close companions until the girl abruptly moved away.

Roni felt another stab. *Aaron.* Aaron, who had obviously put these things on her bed. Keepsakes of someone he did not know. Now he was alone, his mother gone forever. And showing up out of the blue was the stranger who'd had a place in his mother's heart long before he was born . . . *She's* my *mother, not yours . . .*

It was a little clearer now. No wonder he shied away from her. No wonder nothing had been finalized regarding Aaron's guardianship.

Roni began to absently gather everything together to return it to the cardboard carton at the side of the bed when she found the tiny white box. She lifted the lid. Inside on a bed of cotton was a perfect teardrop-shaped gold nugget.

With trembling fingers, Roni lifted it and placed it in the palm of her hand. Then she began to roll it between her fingers . . . the same way her father used to do all those years ago.

Fourteen

A late afternoon breeze rustled the leaves of the tall elm trees that lined the five-acre RV and trailer park. For the past hour, back at the house and now on the drive to the outskirts of town, Roni's mind remained occupied with Aaron and his feelings of resentment toward her. How deep-seated was the hurt? How destructive? Would he even try to be amiable?

And something else gnawed disconcertingly at her. Her father's gold nugget, his good luck charm; how had it gotten among Caroline's personal things?

As she neared the one-story house that sat far back on the Scolli property, a green and black VW Thing, painted with spray paint in a crude camouflage pattern, roared past, jolting her back to the present. She caught a glimpse of two teenagers inside.

More Scolli kids, she thought. How many were there? Dean had been the oldest, then Frank. Then, after a dozen years, two more had come along approximately a year apart. Four children, all boys.

Seeing Dean the day before prompted this visit. Twelve years ago the Mayfields had hooked up their trailer in space #18. On the first of every month Roni delivered the rent money. She arrived at the Scolli household with a white envelope and toted home an armload of fresh baked goods and garden vegetables. Frank's mother Anna would tease the Scolli boys: "If you hooligans don't act good, I trade all of you for this one little girl. She don't make no trouble."

The white wood frame house, a house that had grown with the addition of each child, had sprouted another unpainted wing, its asphalt shingled roof a variety of colors.

Roni left the car and headed for the front porch. At the drooping clothesline at the side of the house she saw a thin woman taking clothes off the line. A ripple of shock went through her. It wasn't possible. Surely that old, frail woman wasn't Anna Scolli. Frank's mother had been a tall, sturdy figure with dancing eyes, shiny black hair, and blushing cheeks.

The woman who lethargically dropped clothes into a plastic basket was stooped, gaunt, her once-dark, thick hair completely gray, the sparse strands pulled off her face.

As Roni walked toward her, the woman began to drag the basket along the weedy yard to the back porch, seemingly unaware of Roni's presence.

"Mrs. Scolli? Anna?"

"Shoo, go away," the woman whispered without looking at her.

"Anna, it's Roni Mayfield. Remember me? We used to rent—"

"Go home." Now the words were sharp, vehement. "Go away from Eagleton."

Roni stepped closer. "Anna, please . . . I—"

The woman spun around, stooped into the basket, grabbed a handful of clothes, and threw them at Roni. The wind caught the pieces and took them across the dusty yard.

Roni started to go after the clothes, but the woman screamed something in Italian and threw the basket. It bounced on the ground, hitting Roni's legs, scattering clothespins at her feet.

A man came out the back door. Alfonso Scolli. He put his arms around the woman and gently urged her up the steps, saying, "Enough. Enough, Mama."

"Mr. Scolli . . . ?"

He turned sad eyes to her. "You know where my boy is? You hear anything from him?"

Roni shook her head slowly. "No."

He helped his wife inside, then followed her, closing the door behind him.

Roni pivoted, watching helplessly as the clothes flew through the air or tumbled along the ground. A hundred yards in front of her, the same direction the clothes were headed, she saw a tall man, arms folded at his chest, leaning on the gas pump. Dean, the oldest of the Scolli boys, watched her.

Roni dropped her arms to her sides and returned to her car.

A strong wind pushed the clouds in. Thunderclouds. The distinct smell of approaching rain was heavy in the air. Fast-moving cloud images reflected in the dark windows of the house as Roni closed her car door and moved toward the back. She shivered from the unseasonable nip of early autumn and wondered if some of that bone-chilling coldness had anything to do with the fact that she was being spied upon from the attic window.

In the kitchen an empty fruit cocktail can and a knife coated with peanut butter and jelly told her Aaron had made lunch for himself. She hadn't eaten since breakfast with her father and suddenly she was ravenous.

She took down a jar of Ragu sauce and a package of vermicelli and put a pot of water on the stove. She opened the jar of spaghetti sauce and dumped it into a pan. In a large wooden bowl she shredded romaine, added slices of red onion, cut up tomato and black olives. Minutes later the water began to boil.

As she struggled to open the package of vermicelli, she looked through the rapidly misting windows and caught a flash of movement in the trees behind the house. The pasta slipped from her fingers and scattered like pickup sticks all over the floor.

She crossed the room, turned the lock on the door, and peered out through the squares of glass. Her own face looked back at her from the foggy pane—along with something else. She backed up and saw letters forming in the condensation: *Get out or die.*

She studied the words calmly, rationally. Aaron? How else could the words get on the inside of the window? But Aaron had only to tell her to leave the house and she would be out and checked into the hotel in no time. Why the games? What if it wasn't Aaron? Who else would try to scare her away? Who in this town had something to hide concerning Caroline, something they didn't want her to look into? And how did they get into the house? She thought of Sheriff Lubben and his key.

She swept up the pasta, dumped it into the waste-basket, then gathered the trash to throw out.

She unlocked the back door and was about to open it when she paused, again looking at the writing on the windows. In the utility closet she took out a can of Mace she'd noticed there the first night—Caroline probably kept it on hand to discourage dogs and raccoons from rummaging through the garbage—then she switched on the porch light and went out.

It was cold, dark, drizzling. At the metal can at the back of the shed she set the Mace on the ground, lifted the lid, and poured in the trash. A twig snapped in the trees behind her. She paused and listened. A raccoon or skunk. If she had a choice, she preferred the raccoon. When she picked up the lid she heard another branch snap. She stiffened, feeling the hair along her arms rise. She dropped the lid in place and grabbed the Mace—then she turned and ran into a tall, solid body. Instinctively she raised the can of Mace, but before she could press the button and shoot the burning mist into the intruder's face, her wrist was caught and forced down.

A scream froze in her throat.

Fifteen

Dean Scolli, his rugged features made harder by a scowl, stepped back to give Roni a measure of space, yet he held fast to her wrist. "I want to talk to you."

She smelled beer on his breath and remembered what Faddle Granville had said about Dean letting hops and malt do his talking for him. Men who needed booze to make a point, especially large men with an axe to grind, made her extremely nervous.

"You scared the hell out of me," she said. "What are doing out here creeping around?"

"I saw you out at my place today."

She wrenched out of his grasp. "That would have been the time to talk to me." She pushed past him and started walking again.

He followed.

At the back door Roni hesitated, then swung around to face him, blinking from the light drizzle. "Look, Dean, I'd love to talk to you. Why don't you come back when you haven't been drinking?"

He turned the knob and shoved the door open for her to enter.

"Dean, I don't think your coming in is a very good idea."

Ignoring her words, he brushed past her and strode inside.

"Hey, look—" What was it about this house that people around here thought they could just march right in whenever they felt like it? First the sheriff and now Frank's brother.

She stood on the porch, oblivious to the rain matting her hair to her forehead, and watched Dean pace the worn kitchen tiles.

He turned to stare at her. "Talk to me." Though his voice was gruff, there was a certain vulnerability in his eyes. "Please . . ."

Reluctantly she crossed the threshold, leaving the door partially open. "About what?"

"What happened to my brother?"

"I don't know."

"What do you *think* happened?"

Roni shrugged her shoulders helplessly.

"Do you think that kid upstairs is Frank's?" he asked.

"I don't know that either."

"Well, he isn't. And there's no one that can convince me or my family that he is."

He sank down on a kitchen chair, then dropped his head, breathing deeply. A large hand scraped across the back of his neck. "Why'd you come back? What do you want here?" His eyes met hers, imploring.

She closed the door, crossed to the table, and sat opposite him. "Is that your handiwork?" She pointed to the rapidly dissipating message on the window panes.

He read the message, his forehead furrowing in bewilderment. He looked at her. "Why would I write that? I don't want you dead. Least not till I get some answers."

"Thanks."

"So why're you here?"

Because answering his questions looked like the only way to get rid of him, she told him about Caroline's letter and the urgent phone message. Then, maybe because he still looked confused, she told him how close she and Caroline had been, how Caroline's son deserved a chance to stay in his own home, and how she felt she had unfinished business in Eagleton.

He took a moment to digest that information. "The way my Mama looked out there in the yard today shocked you, didn't it?"

"Yes."

"Mama used to be a strong, hell-fire woman. 'Member that?" Roni nodded. "Shit, when she'd grab that willow switch, me and my brothers would scatter. But she was a good woman. Had a good sense of humor, she did . . . a good mind."

"I remember." She cleared her throat. "Dean, why did she react that way to me today? At one time we were pretty close."

He chuckled ironically. "Yeah. My brothers and I almost believed her when she said she was gonna swap us for you." He looked up at Roni. "She don't have nothing against you. It's just that anymore she has a hard time separating the past from the present. You and Larry and the widow, the sheriff even, you're all a part of Frank. A dark part, maybe, 'cause you

were the last to see him. Try to imagine what it's like
to have a kid just up and vanish into thin air. Not a
word. Nothing. You wondering if he's dead or alive,
and if he *is* alive, is he suffering? You know about the
hippies?''

"Hippies?"

"Yeah, the sheriff claimed there'd been a report
that a van full of hippies dropped a kid who matched
Frank's description off somewhere in Reno. Me and
Papa went down there looking for him—Vegas, too.
Covered the whole damn state, practically. Even went
as far as Hollywood 'cause we'd heard lots of runaways
headed for Sunset Strip.

"We got letters from people—nuts mostly, knowing we were looking for him. Wild goose chases, all
of 'em. The worst was when Mama got this letter
about a year after he took off that said, 'Miss you.
Send money for fare home.' It had a P.O. Box in a
Mexican bordertown.''

"Was it Frank?"

"Naw. The letter was typed. Wasn't even signed.
But Mama sent the money. Said we had no choice.
Another letter came three, four months later. Same
thing. Papa tossed it out without showing it to her."

He fell silent, staring at the floor.

"Dean—" The phone rang. She excused herself
and went into the dining room to answer. It was Jolie.
Roni told her she'd call her back. When she returned
to the kitchen, Dean was gone.

The next hour was spent on the phone with her
sister—family, such as it was—and a link to another
world. As she spoke, she stroked the gray tabby curled
up on her lap, the tortoise shell content at her feet.

She munched on Gouda cheese, pickled herring, and rye bread. She told her sister that she'd seen both Dean Scolli and James Glazer that day.

"Dean was a loser. Always hanging around like some rutting buck. But Jim Glazer . . . *Jim* . . ." Jolie repeated reflectively, "now he was something different. He was nuts for me, y'know? I could've gone for him, too, if he hadn't been a mine brat. No way was I going to take the chance of falling in love with someone who'd only drag me around the country from one Dogpatch to another like Dad did to Mom."

She felt a heaviness in her chest at the mention of her father.

"So, tell me," Jolie said, "Jim is now this crude miner with a beer belly, thinning hair, and dirty fingernails, right?"

"Wrong."

"Oh? He can't still look like a cross between Mel Gibson and Kevin Costner."

Roni laughed lightly. "He looks like James."

"I'm surprised you remembered him," Jolie said. "You were just a kid."

A kid with a pretty wild crush.

"Hmmm," Jolie added, "maybe I'll have to make an exception and come for a visit."

Roni laughed again. Her sister would never change. Jolie remembered a good-looking guy and that was it. If she wanted someone or something, she took it, grew tired of it, then discarded it. A part of the facile, disposable world Roni had just left. To Jolie it wouldn't matter what lay under an attractive veneer; the man within meant little to her. It mattered to Roni.

"Speaking of Dad," Roni said, "we had breakfast together this morning."

"I'm not surprised. He called me the other day wanting to know what possessed you to return to Eagleton. He sounded upset. I had a feeling he'd show up soon. Is he still there?"

"No. But I think he'll be back." That morning when they parted, Roni hoped he would return quickly. He had always been the one person in this world she felt she could count on, trust. But now, after finding his gold nugget among Caroline's possessions, she didn't know what she felt.

Jolie began to tell Roni about the scorching LA heat wave and the rash of brushfires in the canyons when a car, its muffler coughing, cruised slowly past the house.

Very little traffic came this far down the street. The Holt house stood at the end of the paved road which dead-ended at the graveled Country Lane. Over the heavy idle of the car she heard shouting, which abruptly turned to laughter.

"Hold on a sec," she said into the phone. She laid the receiver down, rose warily, and made her way to the front of the house, her steps matching her accelerating heartbeat. By the time she entered the main hall she was running.

Her heart seemed to fill her entire chest. Through the frosted beveled panes in the front door she saw taillights coming at the gate. Whoever it was had passed the house and was now backing up at a good clip to the wire fence bordering the property. More laughing and whooping, then a series of wet, plopping sounds of something exploding on the porch.

Tires squealed, peeled rubber. When spinning wheels met the gravel road, the car fishtailed, spraying bits of rock as far as the front of the house, debris pelting the windows like hail.

With trembling fingers Roni unlocked the door and rushed out onto the porch. She got a good look at the camouflaged VW Thing before it disappeared behind a copse of red cedar trees and sped away, its exhaust backfiring in the still night.

Dean Scolli's little brothers and a few of their friends. Brothers who hadn't been potty-trained yet when Frank ran away.

The porch glistened with fresh black paint. Several of the paint-filled balloons, lobbed like grenades, had broken on the thorns of the wild rose bushes crawling over the porch's railing. Yellow roses now dripped black.

Sixteen

Friday

The next day, holding tall glasses of branch water spiked with Southern Comfort with a sprig of mint from Hazel Anderson's garden floating on top, the two women sat on the porch swing talking and reminiscing. No longer her student, Roni could now appreciate the large woman's warmth and wry sense of humor. She recalled a stern, imposing figure strolling up and down the rows of classroom desks, her eyes ever vigilant, a metal ruler tapping at her fist—ironically, a ruler she never had to utilize.

Within half an hour Roni knew she had a good friend and ally in Eagleton.

"Aaron doesn't quite know what to think of you," Hazel said when Roni told her about the memorabilia on the bed.

"I know. He seems to view me as a competitor."

Hazel patted her knee. "He's confused."

"Hazel, how can I get him to warm up to me?"

"Be yourself. You're a likeable person. He's bright, maybe too bright, so don't be condescending or fussbudgety. He can spot a phony a mile away."

"Hazel, did Caroline say anything to you about being afraid?"

The swing slowed, then moved faster. "Afraid? No, not afraid. Troubled, perhaps."

Roni told her about the letter and taped message.

"Of course, if something came up that frightened her, it may have happened after I left for Flagstaff to be with my daughter."

"What was she troubled about?"

"Her health. Aaron's welfare. What would become of him should she die before he turned legal age. That sort of thing."

"Did she mention anything about contacting me?"

Hazel tipped her head in thought. "Not really. I know she thought of you often. We spoke of you, wondered about you and how you were doing. The usual."

"Did she blame me?"

"For what?"

"For that day. For not having the courage to face her. For . . . well, for running away."

"Oh, Roni, Roni, how we torture ourselves. She never, ever blamed you for anything. Caroline was not the blaming type. She loved only three people in Eagleton. Her husband, her son, and you." Hazel sat back as the swing rocked. In a soft tone she asked, "Now that you opened the subject, do you think Frank really raped Caroline that day? Do you believe the rumors that he's Aaron's father?"

"I can't believe Frank could rape anyone. I knew him, he . . ."

Hazel pressed her lips together and nodded slowly. "I knew him, too."

"Caroline had his medical bracelet. Aaron gave it to me."

"That only means he was in the house. We already know that." She squeezed Roni's hand. "So, you're already working on it. Good. Good for you."

"Is that why Caroline contacted me? To see if I could expose some deep, dark secret?"

"Maybe. Partly."

"Give me something."

Hazel heaved herself out of the swing. She took Roni's empty glass. "First let me top these off."

With fresh drinks, the swing creaking again, Hazel began. "I promised Caroline that I wouldn't say anything about this to anyone in town, but you're not exactly from town and Caroline obviously wanted your help. And now she's dead—under rather dubious circumstances, I might add—so I think it'll be all right. About a month ago she asked me to drive her and Aaron to the clinic in Ely."

"Ely? Why not this clinic?"

"If you want to keep something a secret, you don't let anyone in town know about it."

"What sort of secret? Wasn't it common knowledge that she was ill?"

"Oh sure. Yet I had the feeling the trip was not for her, but for Aaron. He was very nervous. On the way home he seemed paler than usual, yet calmer, as though some dreaded ordeal was finally over."

"Which clinic?"

"The one on Baker Street. I can't remember the name. It's in the phone book."

Before Roni left Hazel's that afternoon, they agreed

that Roni would stay at the house with Aaron. Meanwhile Hazel would speak with the attorney regarding Aaron's guardianship. It would give Roni time to look into the situation as well as give her a chance to get acquainted with Aaron.

Roni was put on hold. Canned music, played too loud, came through the receiver. Sitting at the dining room table she doodled three-sided boxes, the only object she could draw with any precision. Caroline had taught her how to make faces proportionately—divide an oval in half, then again in half, and so on. But after all these years she was rusty. She drew a heavy-lidded eye with long, thick lashes and was starting a mouth with pouty lips when someone came on the line.

"White Pine Medical Group. This is Donna in billing."

Roni lied and identified herself as the trustee to the Holt account, explaining that she needed verification on a medical bill issued to Caroline Holt regarding treatment.

"They were for tests on a patient named Aaron Holt."

"What sort of tests?"

"You'll have to ask the administering doctor."

"Who is that?"

"Dr. Greene. I can transfer you."

A moment later a receptionist informed Roni that Dr. Greene was gone for the day and would be back at the clinic on Monday.

She hung up absently. Was Aaron sick? Was it possible he had inherited his mother's disorder? Active and robust or the epitome of good health he was not.

*   *   *

Red trotted ahead, favoring his forepaw and lifting his hind leg at every tree, pole, and post along the road. James wondered for the millionth time how the animal's bladder stored enough to mark every phallic-shaped object for half a mile. What if they went two miles, three miles? Would Red pace himself or eventually come up dry, only going through the motions?

Red ran back to James, again sniffing at the bag of venison steaks. When they neared Juniper Street, the dog leaped high into the air, twirled around happily, then shot forward. At the corner he stopped and stared in the direction of the big house, his tail wagging, before running back to James's side.

"You remember, huh? You like her? Did she scratch your belly?"

Red whined and danced about.

James liked her, too. Roni Mayfield, fellow mine brat. He was somewhat surprised that she had known he was Larry's older brother. In those few years their paths had crossed infrequently. The only time they'd had any sort of personal contact had been the day he pulled her out of the widow's house. He'd been somewhat rough and, he remembered, she'd cut her chin somewhere along the way.

He supposed he had changed little in twelve years. Some lines around the eyes, an additional inch or two here and there, but pretty much the same.

Naturally, she had changed. From lanky kid to well-proportioned adult. In the young girl he had seen the promise of something unique: graceful bone structure, the sensuous shape of her lips, depth in the eyes, the flawless skin, warm and rich. He wasn't the least bit disappointed.

She had come to the office looking for him today. Why?

There was something about twilight that got to Roni—a sense of loss and sadness, especially in the fall and winter months when night came too soon. Over the years, as she became more and more wrapped up in her busy schedule, the feeling had gradually dissipated. But since she'd returned to Eagleton it was back again. She wondered if this was where it originated?

If she turned on all the lights, then sat outside until dark, the transformation from day to night seemed less disturbing. The rickety front porch would have been an ideal twilight haven before last night's bombing with black paint.

Picking up fallen rose petals from the dining room table, roses she'd gathered alongside the road the day before, she decided to pass the time picking fresh ones. There was nothing like bowls and vases of sunny flowers to brighten things.

Locating scissors, a pair of canvas gloves, and an old towel to carry the flowers, Roni headed for the back of the property.

In addition to the roses, Roni came across two hardy bushes of pink and white primroses growing behind the shed. She went right to work, heedful of the tiny thorns biting into her wrists and forearms.

As she worked her mind whirled, trying to assimilate everything known or unknown. Once she knew all the questions, then she could find the answers. *Her father and Caroline.* Why hadn't she seen it sooner? Her mother's jealous rages. The divorce. Things she didn't want to believe then or now. Was that the only secret she was going to uncover here in Eagleton? So far it seemed she was the only one to think Caroline's death was suspect. If the sheriff, Dr. Burke, and even Caroline's closest friend bought the suicide theory, who was she to question it?

Flowers and sprigs of fern lay in a heap on the towel. Removing the gloves and tucking them in her waistband, she lifted the towel like a satchel and stood. From the corner of her eye she glimpsed movement in the lighted window of the attic. When she looked up no one was there.

As she came around the corner of the shed she saw a man and a dog coming up the driveway. James. She paused and watched him approach, feeling a nervous excitement. At the exact moment he raised his hand in greeting, she heard a loud ping—metal on metal—then a sharp crack. Something stung the side of her neck.

She spun around, reflexively following the sound. On the shed an old washbasin hung from a nail. Along one side was a shiny line, a trail blazed through the rust, ending at the splintered edge of the wooden shed.

Something rolled down her neck onto the ribbed collar of her T-shirt. Roni swiped at it. Blood. Her own blood. Her fingers touched the wound and she felt something jagged just under the skin.

She'd been shot.

Her mind reacted instinctively, associating her injury with the man coming up the driveway—his hand moving upward, the cracking sound, the sharp sting at her neck. Incredulously she looked at him, at his hands which held only a small bag.

She dropped the roses, pressed her palm to her neck, and looked up at the attic window. This time she saw the small figure before he stepped back out of sight.

James was close enough to see the confusion on Roni's face. He had heard the distant report and instantly recognized the sound of a rifle shot. He saw her drop the flowers and touch her neck.

Red growled. With his head cocked to one side, ears twitching and hackles rising, he turned a complete circle. Also no stranger to the sound—hightailing it over tall fences or hedges, a bitch's owner in hot pursuit—Red had heard more than his share of firearms.

James ran down the drive and grabbed Roni, propelling her out of the open into the tall hedges along the driveway, pulling her down and using his body to shield hers.

She pushed at him, struggling to stand.

He held onto her. "Were you hit?"

It took her a moment to calm down, to stop fighting him. With a disbelieving look she stared into his eyes and nodded.

He turned his head, scanning the area for a gunman. No one anywhere that he could see, no vehicles of any kind this side of Main Street. A shooter, however, with a long-range rifle equipped with a powerful scope could be miles away and completely undetectable.

He carefully pried her hand away from her neck. Blood oozed out at a steady clip—no spurting in sync with her heartbeat—which meant, to his great relief, that no major artery was involved. Despite the fair amount of blood, the wound looked superficial.

She reached for her neck again.

"No," he said gently yet firmly and held her hands. "Don't mess with it. Don't touch it."

She didn't protest when he lifted her in his arms and carried her to her car and sat her in the passenger seat. He ran inside the house, found the car keys in her purse, and, as he grabbed a clean dishtowel, noticed Aaron standing in the dining room doorway.

"Roni's hurt. I'm taking her to the doc. You gonna be okay here?"

Aaron nodded.

"Close and lock the doors. I'm leaving my dog behind. Keep an eye on him for me, will you?"

Again Aaron nodded.

Once behind the steering wheel he gently placed the towel over the wound. "Hold this, but don't press too hard."

She nodded and held the towel in a bloody hand, staring at him with an expression of bewilderment.

Leaving Red on the back porch looking concerned but in charge of the situation, James drove Roni to Dr. Burke's.

Seventeen

Roni sat on the table in the examining room at the back of Dr. Burke's house, the room with the red licorice and ol' danglin' Jesse. The stiff paper rustled under her as Dr. Burke leaned in and, with tweezers, extracted a small bloodied object in the shape of an arrowhead. He stanched the renewed flow of blood with a pad of sterile gauze.

"What is it?" James pushed himself away from the wall to have a look.

"A chunk of wood. Small, but deadly." The doctor held it up for both to see. "Look at that. Sharp as a blade's edge. A fraction of an inch farther back and it might have nicked the carotid artery. Lucky, darn lucky. Where in the heck did this come from?"

James told about hearing a shot. "The way it looked to me a bullet ricocheted off a washbasin, tore a chunk from the corner of the wood shed, and then one of the splinters hit Roni."

The doctor had injected a local anesthetic as soon

as he'd had a look at the wound. He irrigated the wound and gently probed for additional slivers and foreign bodies.

When Roni saw him readying a needle and suture thread, she asked, "Stitches? Is that necessary?"

"It makes for a nice, nearly invisible scar. You have a pretty neck and I want it to stay that way." Dr. Burke spoke to James. "Pot shot or what?"

"Hard to say. It was definitely a gunshot, Doc. High-power rifle. I've heard enough of them to know."

Roni looked at him. Their eyes met and she looked away self-consciously.

"Darn lucky," the doctor repeated.

She was damn lucky James had come along when he did. He had taken over when she needed a cool head. Shock and the sight of her own blood had disoriented her. In retrospect she remembered James's calloused hands holding hers tenderly, his strong arms carrying her to the car, the scent of his skin and shirt as she leaned against his chest.

Dr. Burke turned to Roni. "Who would want to shoot at you?"

"I wish I knew."

"Accident, I bet. But that's for the sheriff to look into. I'll get him on the phone soon as I close this up."

"Do you have to?" Roni asked anxiously. The less contact she had with Sheriff Lubben, the better; the man gave her the willies.

"I'm afraid so. I'm duty bound to report all injuries involving firearms. Hell, I wouldn't be surprised if the sheriff hasn't already gotten wind of it and is on his way over even as we speak."

Several minutes later, after tying off the last suture, Dr. Burke put an adhesive patch over the wound.

"One good thing, Roni, you don't have to have another shot for tetanus." He checked the cat scratches on her arm to be sure they were healing nicely. Somewhere in the back of the house a child began to wail. "All fixed. Now if you can just keep that pretty neck of yours out of trouble, and I don't mean that figuratively, it would save us both a lot of time. I'll drop by in a couple days and see how you're doing."

"A house call?"

"House calls are a luxury . . . for me," the doctor said, his voice rising over the wailing that seemed to be getting louder and nearer. "It's a pleasure now and then to go somewhere peaceful and quiet." He turned to James. "Jim, you'll drive her home?"

James jangled her car keys.

No red licorice this time.

Four minutes later when they pulled into her driveway the Chevy's headlights picked up the blue Bronco that sat in her driveway. Sheriff Lubben, holding a flashlight, was probing around in the pile of cut roses with a booted toe. When he saw them, he dropped his cigarette, ground it out with his heel, then slowly ambled over to the car as they climbed out.

"Doc called. Got problems already, I see." He turned to James. "And damned if Jimmy-boy don't get a chance to play hero to the new gal in town."

"Dumb luck, I guess."

Lubben chuckled. From him it sounded lewd. He held out a plastic grocery bag. "Who's this belong to?"

"It's venison for Roni and Aaron," James said, taking it from Lubben and handing it to Roni.

She thanked him.

"Okay, so who wants to go first?" Lubben said.

Roni began and James filled in the holes.

Afterward, Lubben strolled back to the shed, the flashlight beam bouncing off the weathered structure. He flicked at spiky bits of fractured wood. "The projectile just grazed that old washbasin and splintered the corner of the shed. Coulda been a bullet or pellet. Coulda been lead shot from a wrist rocket. Coulda been an arrow with a metal tip." He paused. "You hunt with a bow, don'tcha, Glazer?"

"I heard the report. It was a firearm," James said wearily.

"So you said." He turned to Roni. "What'd you hear?"

She looked at James. "I heard a ping, metal on metal."

"The projectile skimmin' along the washbasin. Do you know what gunfire sounds like?"

"I think so."

"Did you hear such a thing?"

Trying to mask her irritation, she said, "I can't be a hundred percent sure, but yes, I think I did. A cracking sound. If we can find the bullet, we'd know which direction it came from and we might have a little more to go on."

"When it cleared the shed it just kept right on a-goin', probably into that stand of trees and shrubs yonder. If you wanna traipse around out there lookin' for it, be my guest. Say, why don't the two of you just take over? Form some sorta task force, maybe."

James sighed with disgust and turned his back to Lubben.

"Yeah," Lubben went on. "Go on up there in those trees and find that itty bitty slug you're so sure about."

"Sheriff, if I'm a target for some—"

"Oh, hell, girl, you ain't no target," he cut in impatiently. "It's two weeks till the openin' of deer season. Someone up on that ridge was probably scopin' in a rifle. There's plenty of weekend hunters, goofy as all hell, don't have the foggiest notion how far a rifle projectile can travel. I seen this before. A window here and there gets shot out. A mangy mutt makes a convenient target and gets one. This is prime huntin' area, in case you don't know."

She'd have to be blind to miss that. Even the county library had an antler or two above the shelves. She'd also seen a man in hunter camouflage scoping down on her two days ago. Her stomach suddenly knotted.

"Now if you got reason to suspect someone . . ." Lubben turned and stared up at the attic window. He lurched forward, headed for the house, and disappeared into the kitchen.

Roni thrust the bag with venison at James and ran after Lubben. When she reached the second floor, she heard Lubben at the attic door, pounding.

"Hey, boy, open up! I know you know what's goin' on so I don't have to explain nothin'." He beat at the door. "Open up, now!"

The door to Aaron's bedroom opened. Aaron and Roni stared silently at each other.

The sheriff tramped down the stairs, saw Aaron, and with no preamble he strode to the boy and said, "You own a gun?"

"Sheriff, what are you doing?" Roni said.

"Stay outta this. A gun, you got one?"

Aaron, in an oversized sweatshirt, twill pants, and white socks, appeared even smaller, more frail with the large man towering over him. He looked at Roni, then back at Lubben. He shook his head.

"You got a wrist rocket or a bow an' arrow set?"

Again he shook his head.

"You fire somethin' at this woman when she was in the yard?"

In a feeble voice he said, "No."

"If I search your room and I find somethin' in there like I just asked you 'bout, you're in trouble . . . big trouble. You understand?"

Aaron pushed open his door, then stepped out into the hall, inviting the sheriff to enter.

Lubben poked his head inside and gave the room a cursory once-over. Over his shoulder he said to Roni, "You believe him?"

"Yes, of course."

"Straighten that room," he said gruffly to Aaron before marching back downstairs.

Again Roni's gaze met Aaron's. He broke eye contact first and returned to his room. The door closed softly behind him.

When Roni returned to the yard, Lubben was wandering around in the trees behind the house grumbling to himself. James sat on his haunches in the driveway smoking a slim cigar, the dog leaning against him.

She recognized the dog who'd escorted her home the night before. "Is he yours?"

"I guess you could say that. He sort of adopted me."

"Hi, Red. That's his name, isn't it?"

"Yeah, Red Dog. Red for short. Not very original, I know. We became acquainted when he was about half grown and a bit wild, undomesticated. I never thought he'd stick around, so I didn't bother to give him a name."

"Red Dog is a name."

"Well, yeah, only I didn't give it to him. People kept asking me where I got the red dog. See?"

"How long have you had him?"

"Four years. We hooked up in New Mexico."

Red loped to Roni and licked her hand. She squatted and got a sloppy tongue lapping at her ear.

"Faddle Granville said he was part coyote." She pushed at the dog, laughing.

"Shhh, don't let on that part of him may be considered an endangered species. He's paranoid enough as it is."

"He walked me home the other night. Checked out the house, too. Was that your doing?"

A corner of his mouth lifted. "How smart do you think he is?"

Before she could say *Pretty damn smart*, Lubben joined them.

"Nothing. But you two are welcome to look for yourself. Be a waste of time if you ask me. Ain't no reason anybody'd wanna shoot you." He squatted, then seemed to like towering over them better, and stood again, his legs spread-eagle, hands on his gun belt.

"Maybe it was me they were aiming at," James said.

Lubben turned to him, raising an eyebrow.

"Well, I wasn't more than forty feet from Roni, in what I consider to be the line of fire. I've had a couple of near misses lately. Accidents, supposedly."

"Yeah, like what?"

"Last week a tire blew on my Blazer as I was coming down Eagle Grade, right at that hairpin curve. I nearly rolled it. I didn't think much about it until two nights ago when someone tried to run over me on Country Lane."

"You get a look at the vehicle?"

"No, I was too busy diving into the ditch. Saw bright headlights and then a flash of taillights."

Lubben rubbed at his jaw. "Hmph. Well, you lemme know if either one of you has any more *accidents.*"

"So what now?" Roni asked Lubben, looking up as the man's mouth opened in a wide yawn. From the saffron light in the kitchen she saw that nearly all his upper molars were missing.

"I write a report. That's it unless there's something more you want me to do."

When she shook her head, he nodded, strode to his car, got in, and backed out.

"Damn pleasant fellow," James said.

"Always a favorite of mine."

He smiled. "Can I buy you a beer?"

She looked around at the house, thinking of Aaron.

"One beer. Red'll keep an eye on Aaron," James said. "He'll be okay."

They took a table in the back of the Eagle. It was early and only a handful of patrons were in the bar. Through the opening between the rooms, Roni watched as the dining room rapidly thinned out. The band was setting up and soon the tables would be pushed back to form the dance floor.

Roni settled into one of the oak chairs. She had changed the bloodied clothes for clean jeans and a long-sleeved top, telling Aaron she was going out for a short time and that Red Dog would guard the house.

The young waitress who had ignored her the morning she'd come in for coffee smiled and waved at James, her eyes flickering coolly over Roni.

In mining towns men outnumbered women at least two to one. A shortage of men was no problem, but a shortage of good-looking geologists was another matter. In a small town any new young woman constituted a threat.

"What are you drinking?" James asked.

"Beer is fine."

He went to the bar. A moment later he was back, depositing two dewy bottles of Bud on the table. He left again, headed for the coffee station in the corner of the dining room, hooked a finger through the handle of one of the brown coffee mugs, and brought it back to Roni.

She stared at him. "What's this?"

"For your beer. Isn't that how you like it?"

She smiled and nodded.

He smiled back.

She looked away from his steady gaze, tipped the mug, and poured the beer.

"So how've you been all these years?" he said. "How's your family?"

She smiled. He really wanted to know about Jolie.

"Good, real good. My sister—you remember Jolie?" When he nodded, she went on. "She's a casting director in Hollyweird. She went into film and I went into print."

"Never married?"

"Oh, yes. Twice. But she's separated now."

"Not her, you."

She shook her head. "Haven't found the time."

"You've found the man?"

"Haven't had time to look. And you?"

"Haven't been looking. I promised myself I wouldn't drag a family from one town to another. It was hard on me and Larry. It's hell on a woman. I saw too many marriages fall apart from the rotten living conditions, the day by day uncertainty, kids being pulled this way and that. Hey, I don't have to tell *you*."

"No, you don't."

"So how do you feel about moving around?"

She shrugged. "It's part of my job. Actually, I enjoy traveling as long as there's a home base. The coming home makes traveling that much easier."

"Where's home?"

"Southern California."

The last diner went out the door. The band finished warming up and began their first set of the evening. Normal conversation became impossible. They drank their beer and watched a handful of couples dance.

"Well, dang it, if it ain't my favorite dance pupil." Faddle Granville swept down on her, took hold of her hands, and pulled her from her chair. "Ready for lesson number two? James, settle down—I won't run off with her."

"She had a little accident, Faddle," James said. "She may not feel up to it."

Faddle looked at her inquiringly.

"It's okay. I'd love to."

"Have you been officially introduced to his honor, Mayor Granville?" James said.

"Mayor?" Roni turned to stare up at the attorney with the farmer's tan. "You didn't tell me you were the mayor."

"You didn't ask."

Again she found herself on the dance floor with the man with the two-toned arms and forehead. The mayor of Eagleton! Amazing, she thought. She liked this man. He was sweet and genuine. She wished everyone in town were as friendly as Faddle.

Without the competition and the crowd, Roni felt

more relaxed this time. She moved along with her partner, misstepping only once or twice. Near the end of the song, it all caught up with her. The beer, which had gone to her head right away, brought her down. Her feet became unwieldy, shuffling instead of stepping. The wound at her neck throbbed in sync with her pulse.

Her eyes closed. About to apologize for her sluggish feet and plead for a break, Roni felt herself being shifted around. Other hands moved over her. She opened her eyes. Faddle winked and moved away. Roni looked into the rust-flecked, hazel eyes of James, catching the scent of his aftershave as he pulled her close. He wasn't as tall as Faddle, but his frame conformed to hers; his body, warm and firm, melded smoothly along the length of her.

They danced slow, close, their bodies swaying to the rhythm of a cowboy love song. This was what she had wanted over a dozen years ago at the school dance. To have James hold her, his warm breath at her ear, the scent of him making her lightheaded, pulling at her insides. And now it was real.

Being so close to him, seeing him now, more mature, handsome, stirred up long-buried adolescent yearnings.

When the song ended, he whispered in her ear, "C'mon, let's get you home."

He held her around the waist, leading her toward the exit and through the door onto the sidewalk. Traffic was light as they hurried across the highway. The fresh air revitalized her.

On the walk home they took turns talking about their jobs. Roni was surprised when they reached the driveway—time had passed so quickly. Too quickly. What she had hoped to discuss with him had not been broached. Aaron, Caroline, Frank's medical bracelet, and what seemed to be a growing list of mysteries with Caroline at the heart of it all.

Red come out of nowhere to join them.

"He seems to have a habit of doing that," Roni said.

"It's the coyote blood. A stalker." James told her how he had freed the young animal from a game trap along a secluded stretch of the Rio Grande. "He wasn't wild, but he wasn't exactly a lapdog either. His leg was pretty badly mangled. The trap made him paranoid about any future confinement. There's no restraining him. He can jump any fence in town, squirm out of any collar or harness. He just won't be penned."

At the back door she took out the key and fitted it in the lock.

"You lock up?" James asked.

"Don't you?"

"Most people around here don't."

"Most people don't have balloons lobbed onto their porches, or graffiti scrawled across the side of their houses, or projectiles whizzing by their ears."

"Balloons?"

"Filled with black paint. The Scolli boys and a few of their pals paid us a visit last night. Redecorated the front porch."

"Damn them," James said, looking perplexed. "When the widow was alive the sheriff looked after her and the house. They wouldn't have tried anything like that. They're probably the ones who spray-painted the house. Other problems?"

"A few. But I'm afraid I'm not up to going into it right now. I have a pain in my neck, I'm coming down from an emotional high, and that beer has me dead on my feet.''

He put the back of his hand against her cheek, then moved it down to the side of her neck. ''You feel a little feverish. Take some aspirin and hit the sack.''

''Yes, doctor.''

He pulled out his wallet, took out a card, and wrote on the back. ''Office and home number, address, it's all there. Call me at either number.''

She stepped inside the kitchen.

''Just a minute.'' He turned to the dog. ''Red, run through and check it out.''

Red darted past Roni, sniffing at cabinets and the broom closet before disappearing into the house proper. The sound of cats hissing and spitting reached them.

''I forgot about all the cats,'' James said, laughing. ''Jeez, I hope he makes it out alive.''

Minutes later Red was back, tail low and business-like, a bloody scratch across his brick-colored nose. Looking from Roni to James, he made several *woofs* deep in his throat, then sat and waited.

''Good boy,'' James said as he patted his back.

''Thanks, Red. Sorry about the obstacles.'' Roni petted him. He licked her hand.

''He likes you despite the fact you're aiding and abetting the enemy.'' James stepped off the porch. '''Night,'' he said and walked off.

Roni locked up, took an aspirin, and went upstairs. She tapped on Aaron's door. He opened it right away this time. The TV was on behind him.

''I want you to know that I did not think you took a shot at me. Rushing up here and banging on the door was his idea. I'm sorry if he scared you.''

He looked down and nodded. "Does it hurt?"
She touched the bandage. "A little. I'll live."
"Who did it?"
"We don't know."
They stood there awkwardly.
"Well, good night," she said.
" 'Night."

Ready. Aim. Fire.
Roni heard the crack of a rifle, felt the bullet tear into her throat, saw the blood flying every which way.

She bolted upright in bed, her body drenched, her heart pounding, gasping for air. A cat on the bed beside her meowed, then rubbed against her and began to purr.

With trembling hands, she wiped her face. A nightmare. A horrible nightmare where she had stood in front of a firing squad of men, their heads covered in black leather masks, a half-dozen rifles pointing at her. One man had stepped forward and on the final directive, he and he alone pulled the trigger.

Two a.m. She lay back down, but something told her to get up and look in on Aaron. She put on a robe and went down the hall to his room, only to find it empty. She went from room to room. He was nowhere in the house. The doors and windows were secure, safety chains engaged. She continued to search, determined to locate his private egress. A short time later she found it.

It was in a place she'd avoided since her arrival—the windowless basement. Not a true basement, more like an antechamber for what was down another level. Beyond the open trapdoor the space yawned black and intimidating.

She directed the flashlight beam downward. A tunnel. She should have known. The entire town once consisted of a network of tunnels. She saw herself with Frank and Larry in the storeroom of Al's Tavern fourteen years ago. Frank had them convinced that Eagleton's main tunnels, condemned years before, were filled with a century of gold dust that had sifted through the floorboards of the saloons. They had pried open the rusty padlock and Frank and Larry had entered without her. There was no way they could talk Roni into going down there. From the day Frank had rescued her from the mine shaft, Roni harbored an unnatural fear of deep, dark places. Forty feet in, the boys came to a solid wall of silt, a cave-in from a flood years earlier, and were forced to turn back.

She had heard about tunnels in Eureka and Virginia City and she supposed they were common in many mining towns across the country. But a functional tunnel from the Holt residence was something Roni hadn't considered.

Six feet of wooden ladder went straight down to a floor of hard-packed earth.

Where did it go? Was it safe?

A chilling draft swept upward from the hole. Shivering, Roni lowered the trapdoor.

Aaron might be a creature of the night, but she wasn't. Shadows hid unpleasant things. Everything appeared a helluva lot saner in the light of day.

She returned to bed. Sleep took longer to come this time.

Eighteen

Saturday

Roni stood on the front porch with a steaming mug of coffee and breathed in the rose-scented air. Saturday morning had dawned warm and bright, a welcome change from the cold, stormy spell that had persisted since her arrival in Eagleton four days ago. Four days, and Roni was no closer to cracking any big secrets concerning Caroline's death. She had a medical bracelet, a diary, and a number of wounds to show for her trouble.

For a split second she felt apprehensive standing out in the open. Absently touching the bandage on her neck, she scanned the three blocks of town stretched out in front of her. Windows, rooftops, trees, the hillside backed up to the north. The bullet could have come from a number of locations or directions. Yes, even from the attic window.

No, she told herself, not Aaron. He was hurt, possibly angry, but something told her he was incapable of violence. Caroline had been gentle and refined—she would have raised her child accordingly. Twice now, the first night in the music room and again at his bedroom door last night, she had seen something in his eyes . . . a longing. Lost, yet wanting to be found.

You've come this far, Roni told herself, *don't throw in the towel yet.*

She sipped her coffee, letting her gaze sweep over the porch, grimacing at the ugly splotches of black paint and dead roses and wondering how many gallons of paint it would take for a fresh coat on the weathered wood. An hour later, after a quick trip to town, she was slapping white paint on the thirsty boards of the porch, working in time to country music from her portable radio. Time passed. Over the music she heard soft notes from a piano. She lowered the brush into the pail and went inside to the music room. Aaron sat at the piano, his hair still wet from the shower, the cowlick smoothed down. He played a classical piece she couldn't identify.

Quietly easing into the room, Roni leaned against the wall, scarcely breathing. He played exquisitely and with such profound feeling it made her heart ache.

"Beautiful," she said softly when he had finished. "Please, Aaron, play some more."

Without acknowledging her presence, he began with a Chopin waltz, moved smoothly into a dreamy nocturne, and ended with a Hungarian rhapsody by Liszt. At the close he lowered the piano lid, swiveled around, and faced her.

"You play even better than your mother."

Something flashed in his eyes at the mention of his mother—anger, jealousy, sadness, joy, a mixed bag that disappeared in an instant. They sat in silence for several long moments, then he rose and left the room.

Roni followed him out to the porch. He picked up a smaller brush and began painting the rail newel. She thought of Tom Sawyer whitewashing the picket fence and smiled inwardly—painting, like ironing, looked like fun and *was* fun for about two and a half minutes. She watched him from the corner of her eye. He worked with confidence, with a dexterity she found surprising. What did he do with his time? How did he fill the long hours? What was behind the locked doors of the attic?

She had so many questions. Little by little, Aaron was opening up and the last thing she wanted to do was drive him back into his shell. If they could just become friends, learn to trust each other. If they could just talk.

"Did your mother ever speak of me?" Roni asked without looking at him, the paintbrush dabbing at the weathered boards.

"It was 'Roni this' and 'Roni that,' over and over." The bitterness in his voice was unmistakable.

Roni turned to him. "Aaron, I had no idea she'd saved those things of mine. I didn't know how much she . . . she . . ."

"Loved you?"

". . . Cared about me." She absently dabbed paint on a knothole. "You weren't born then, you know, and she was very lonely. I guess I helped pass the time for a short while . . . until you came along."

He worked meticulously, his tongue at the side of his mouth in concentration.

"Aaron, was your mother good to you? I mean, did she . . ."

"She loved me, too," he said quietly.

Roni nodded, relieved that he hadn't been mistreated or neglected. He had known love.

"She wished I was a girl," he said. "A girl just like you."

"Did she tell you that?"

"No, but—"

"Then it wasn't true. Aaron, it just wasn't true."

Roni began to talk about Caroline, about how gentle and good she had been. "She wanted to fill this house with kids. Maybe she liked me because I was such a tomboy, which probably meant she liked boys better than—" Roni turned around to find herself alone on the porch.

To Roni's delight the temperature rose into the eighties. At three she ran out of paint. Aaron stayed out of sight. Sick of painting anyway, she decided to clean up, walk to town and wander around, maybe get a movie at the video store. When she went into the house she had no idea that instead of following through on her original plan she would wind up in the tiny basement, a lantern in one hand and a flashlight in the other. All afternoon she thought of the bracelet with its embedded chunks of dirt. Dirt. Buried. Tunnel.

The kerosene lamp glowed brightly at the edge of the open trapdoor, its light flickering along the barren walls of the tunnel's antechamber. The wooden staircase leading down from the storage room off the kitchen practically filled the entire area. Aside from a rolled-up rug and several cases of odd-colored canned fruits and vegetables, which Roni wouldn't touch if she were starving to death, the room was bare. A cat sat on the riser watching her with shiny copper eyes.

Although it was hot upstairs, the basement was incredibly cold and she'd bet it was even colder down below in the passageway. She shivered, remembering her fall into the shaft when she was a kid. The excruciating pain of her fractured ankle, the bitter cold, the many-legged things creeping over her, the fear that she would die down there all alone, now washed over her with profound clarity. Frank had finally shown up, standing above her, his face illuminated grotesquely by a flashlight. He looked like an angel of mercy, an angel who had threatened to leave her there, saying she was nothing but a mine brat and not worth his time and energy. But save her he did.

Forcing those thoughts away, she found a two-foot board under the stairs, used it to prop the trapdoor open, and with the flashlight in her left hand, started down the ladder. She counted the rungs—for no other reason than to distract herself, to keep from chickening out—eight in all.

The coldness of the ground seeped through the soles of her tennies. Her jaw tensed, her teeth on the verge of chattering. She sensed it was more than the temperature that made her so bitterly cold.

Taking a moment to steady her breathing, she surveyed the moldy-smelling area, probing along the passageway with the flashlight beam. For as far as she could see, the tunnel was lined with mortar and brick, the ground solidly packed dirt. It looked safe enough.

The light from the kerosene lamp in the basement above seemed to warm the top of her head and shoulders, like the sun to an underwater swimmer. The image encouraged her.

She advanced deeper into the tunnel—one yard, two, then three—until the light from the trapdoor narrowed to a silver. The thought of leaving that

opening sent a spasm through her. No longer thinking of it as the sun overhead, it had become a narrow
opening cut into the ice of a massive lake; if she lost
sight of it she was lost.

She turned back.

On the ground below the trapdoor the light caught
at something wedged between the ladder and wall,
almost completely buried in the dirt. She sat on her
heels and carefully dug the soil out from around a
hard, L-shaped object. It was made of plastic, yellowed
and cracked with age. Gently she tapped it against
the ladder to clear dirt from the hollow opening. A
breath inhaler.

Just like the one Frank had used for his asthma.

If it were Frank's, this could explain how he got
out of the house without being seen—with the sheriff
pounding on the door, Frank, in his haste to get
away, could have jumped down the ladder, his inhaler
falling from his shirt pocket. Frank would have known
about the tunnels because of the one in his father's
storeroom. It was possible this very passage led to Al's
Tavern.

A shadow slid over her from above. Roni looked
up at the cat as it watched her intently. Purring, the
cat began to rub against the board that propped the
trapdoor.

"No, cat! Get away from ther—" Roni blurted out
an instant before the board fell away and the door
slammed shut.

Roni started up the ladder, struggling with the
flashlight and inhaler. She crammed the inhaler into
her pocket and hastily scaled the rungs, banging her
shins. At the top she pushed on the door. It refused
to budge.

She had no voice to scream. She rammed the door

with her shoulder and back, her breathing coming in short, labored bursts. Through a haze of rising hysteria, she felt lightheaded.

A surge of adrenaline granted her the strength to push hard again. The door suddenly gave and flopped open with a bang, throwing her off balance. The flashlight flew from her hands, fell into the tunnel, and blinked out. She clutched at the ledge, sprang forward, and practically dove through the opening. Once off the ladder and onto solid ground, she twisted around and quickly scooted backward. She heard her own heavy breathing. She saw nothing. It was pitch black.

With trembling fingers she fumbled with the book of matches and struck one. The lantern lay on its side. She quickly relit it. She slammed the trapdoor shut, anxious to separate herself from the suffocating closeness of the tunnel. The light brought a measure of calm. After several deep breaths, she looked around. She was alone in the basement. The cat was gone.

Roni sat in the kitchen, her elbows on the table, her fingers buried deep into her hair at her temples, staring down at the medical bracelet and the breath inhaler. Frank's asthma had been acute. He couldn't have gone long without the medication. Even with it there had been times during a severe attack that he could have died. She knew what those attacks were like, the coughing and wheezing that led to his desperate struggles for air, struggles that had made her feel completely helpless.

The sensible thing to do was call Sheriff Lubben, hand over the bracelet and inhaler, and get the law

involved. Lubben, apart from being the sheriff, had been close to the widow. Something dark and ambiguous stirred deep in the folds of her mind. No, not the sheriff—not yet, anyway.

She groaned, flopped back in the chair, and stared at the ceiling. Okay, so who then? Dean Scolli? He and his family had never given up on finding Frank—alive or dead. But Dean was too intense, she told herself, too close to the situation. Dean or the sheriff, same difference.

Faddle Granville, the attorney? She remembered that he had commented on her vivid writer's imagination.

That left James Glazer. Funny how she had saved him for last when she knew all along he was the one.

Roni lifted the medical bracelet. There was someone else in this scenario. Aaron. He had handed over Frank's bracelet. This was his house and whatever secrets it held, Aaron had to be a part of them.

Roni cleaned up and changed into a tank top and a pair of jeans she'd cut off into shorts. She stopped at the open door of Aaron's room. He was sitting on his bed watching TV. "I thought I'd invite James Glazer to have dinner with us. Do you like venison?"

He nodded without taking his eyes from the set.

"Great. I'm going out for a bit."

He nodded again.

After her experience in the tunnel she needed fresh air, lots of it. She decided to walk to James's house and personally invite him. She took her time—it was too hot to hurry. As she leisurely strolled along she thought back to the day she had initially fallen for James. He was eighteen and a senior. She was thirteen. It was the time the sole on Larry's shoe had come apart at school. He'd taped and glued it, then tied it with string and rubberbands, but to his profound mortification nothing worked for long and the rubber sole flapped with each step. Throughout the day the other kids snickered and ragged at him unmercifully. After school that afternoon Larry approached his father for money to buy new shoes. Waiting outside of the Glazer's small travel trailer, Roni heard them arguing inside. "Make do with what you got," his father grumbled. "It ain't cold, go barefoot." But Larry persisted until the heated words turned to blows. Roni, wishing she was anywhere but where she was, hugged herself and waited, fearing for Larry. Then, a third voice, deadly calm, said, "Hit him one more time and I'll take you down, father or not. No more." A moment later Larry rushed out, his face scarlet, bearing marks of the blows he'd received, valiantly holding back his tears. James caught up with them a block away and took Larry aside. Roni watched James hand Larry several bills. Larry protested, saying James needed every cent for college. "Get the shoes," James said, then walked away.

Fifteen minutes later, on Euclid's tree-shaded lane, she came to two private residences, one in front of the other. Years ago both had been abandoned structures, a foundry and a liquor and smoke shop. James lived in the now converted smoke shop in back.

Again Red came out of nowhere to meet her. He executed his leaping dance, running ahead to indicate that she should follow. He led her to the back of the property where she heard a steady thwacking sound. Through the trees she saw a barechested James, target practicing with bow and arrows.

She stood quietly at a distance behind him. She

watched him set the arrow, pull back the bow string, the muscles on his tanned arms, shoulders, and back flexing. He released the string. On a target attached to a bale of hay, the arrow found its mark among a cluster of others, mid-chest on the picture of a mighty stag.

She applauded lightly.

He turned, then his cool gaze swept over her, starting at her feet and moving up to her face. He smiled.

"Very good," she said. "I assume that's a killshot."

"On paper it is." He motioned her to come close. "Here, try it."

She shook her head.

"Ever shoot one?"

"Tried it a couple times. With Larry, actually. I had trouble pulling back the bow. He said I was too puny, too weak."

"The tension was too much for you. C'mere. Try it."

"No, that's okay."

"C'mon, I'll help."

She came forward hesitantly, his eyes on her.

He showed her where to put her hands and how to pull back the string, testing the tension. He showed her how to insert the arrow, draw it back, sight in and release. His arrow joined the small grouping in the stag's chest.

He handed the bow to her and gave her an arrow. She fumbled it, nearly dropped it, fit the notch in the string, and pulled back—only to have the arrow tumble out again.

He caught it in midair as it dropped.

The sun beat down on her. She felt ridiculous, shook her head, and tried to hand it back to him. "I can't."

"Not so fast." He led her into the canopy of trees, closer to the target. It was cool, shady, the rich smell of loam heady. He turned her sideways, stepped behind her, fit the bow in her hands; then, with his arms around her, his hands covering hers, he inserted the arrow and took her through the motions. She shot. The arrow hit the back end of the stag.

"Not bad if you're playing pin the tail on the donkey," he said.

"James, really . . ."

"Again," he said.

This time he made her take careful aim. Still holding her, she felt his eyes on her, studying her profile. She glanced nervously at him.

"Don't look at me," he said, "look at the target."

His nearness unsettled her. She jerked, releasing the arrow hastily. It missed the target and the bale of hay entirely. She bent over, laughing.

He pulled her up, holding her tightly from behind. His knee slipped between her legs and nudged them apart until her stance was more steadfast. "Again."

She inhaled deeply and slowly stretched the bow.

He whispered in her ear, giving her instructions. "Breathe steadily, relax—not too relaxed, not too tense." He leaned into her, speaking slowly, softly. "You've all the time in the world. Concentrate. In your mind's eye, see the arrow soaring the distance from the bow to the target. See it hit its mark. Don't let go until I say."

She felt his arms around her, his hands over hers, his warm breath at her ear, the hair on his chest tickling her bare back above the scooped neckline of the tank top. She felt his heart beating at her shoulder blade, and lower, at her buttocks, she felt him becoming rigid. She felt the blood rise to the surface of her

skin, felt her own heart beating, her pulse pumping
madly.

James slowly eased his right hand from around her
hand and glided it along her arm to circle her waist.
"Concentrate," he whispered, his voice husky now.
"Don't let go yet." He bent his head, his lips grazed
her shoulder, her neck, along her jaw. His hand at
her side explored the curved indentation of her waist
and hip.

"James . . ."

"Shhh, concentrate," he whispered.

The tension in the bow radiated throughout her
body. Her arms began to tremble, then her legs. The
arrow tipped from the string and dropped to the
ground at their feet.

He brushed his mouth against the corner of hers,
his tongue tracing the moist contours. The bow
relaxed, then followed the arrow, landing with a rustling sound on the bright yellow leaves. She closed
her eyes, shifted, and melded fully into his arms. They
kissed, and it was exactly the way she imagined it
would be.

She was acutely aware of everything around her,
of James in particular. The texture of his skin, his
scent, the way his body fit against hers. All so familiar.
Yet, until a few days ago, she hadn't thought of him
in ages, his face no longer clear in her mind.

She wrapped her arms around his neck and
returned his kiss, her lips parting, her tongue meeting
his. It felt so good being in his arms, kissing him. *I
can get hurt*, she told herself. *Really hurt.* It occurred
to her that she had known him for the better part of
her life, but he had known her for only a few days;
physical contact between them had been limited to
one slow dance.

Time. They needed time to get to know each other. She had enough to think about without further complicating things.

With unimaginable strength of will she broke the kiss and pulled away abruptly. James reached for her. She stepped back, shaking her head. Confusion plainly showed in his eyes.

"We have to talk," she said in a shaky voice.

He dropped his hand. Waited.

"I wanted to talk . . . without Aaron." Inside the shade of the trees and with his arms no longer around her, Roni suddenly felt cold.

James bent down, picked up the bow and quiver of arrows, and was about to put his arm around her when he paused, glanced at her, then let his arm fall to his side. Instead he motioned with his head toward the house. "C'mon, we can talk inside."

James poured a cloudy apricot-colored liquid into two rock glasses. "It looks like hell, but it tastes great," he said, handing Roni one.

"What is it?"

"Crabapple wine. Homemade."

She sipped it. It was tart, thick and fruity, and took her breath away. "*Whooh*," she said when she got her breath back. "You make it?"

He shook his head. "A friend of mine, Effie Perkins. Her husband was killed at the mine a while back. Ed Perkins and I used to bow hunt together. Effie and I do a little trading every year. Wine and fruitcake for venison."

"What a coincidence—that's what we're having for dinner. Care to join us?"

"Wine and fruitcake?"

She smiled. "No, venison."

"Love to." He strode to the kitchen area, grabbed a wooden chair, brought it back to where she sat in a leather recliner. "I'll even help cook it." He straddled the chair and put his chin on his folded arms. He stared at her face, her bare legs, her face—then pulled in a deep breath and said, "Sooo, you wanted to talk?"

There was no point in beating around the bush. "I found a tunnel at the house."

He waited.

"In the tunnel I found a breath inhaler."

"A breath inhaler?"

"Frank had asthma. He didn't go anywhere without that atomizer."

"I see. So Frank was in the tunnel. He lost the atomizer."

"Maybe. Maybe not. Aaron gave me Frank's medical alert bracelet. Frank never took it off. Never."

She watched his eyes narrow.

"Where did Aaron get the bracelet?"

"From his mother."

"Go on."

"Someone is trying to scare me off."

"Aaron? Frank's little brothers?"

"I don't think so." She told him about the message on the mirror and the windows.

"That could be Aaron. He has the means. He lives there. Bar soap, candle wax, or paraffin on the mirror and windows, invisible until they get fogged up."

"No. He has his own reasons for not warming up to me right away, but his mother wanted my help and I have a feeling he does, too."

He rubbed the back of his neck. "Tell me what you're thinking."

She stared into his eyes. "I think Frank's dead."

"Have you talked to Lubben about any of this?"

"Are you kidding?"

His look told her he understood. "Anyone?"

"No."

"Why me?"

"I didn't know who else to talk to. I can't go to Frank's family. The sheriff . . . he'd be my last choice. Larry and I were involved—and in a way, so were you."

After a long pause, he said, "What did you see that day? I want you to tell me exactly what happened from the moment you met up with Larry and Frank until I came along."

She sipped the wine. It went down easier this time. "Larry and I found Frank spying on the widow with binoculars. He said she had a lover, that he'd seen her naked and with a man. He was curious, wanted to see who he was."

"Go on." A tightness had crept into his voice.

She told the story the way she remembered it. "Frank was inside. Larry was outside looking in." James's steady gaze was unreadable. "The next thing I knew, I was in the house."

"What did you expect to do inside?"

"I don't know. Warn Caroline, get Frank to leave. I was torn between the two of them. I didn't want to get Frank in trouble, yet I couldn't allow him to invade Caroline's privacy."

"And?"

"Then you were there."

"No," he said gruffly. "There's more, tell me."

"I don't know what—"

"Did you see anyone? Hear anyone?"

"I don't remember."

"Think."

Her pulse had picked up speed. Her heart thumped. "I thought I heard something—I remember I was scared—terrified, actually."

"Why? From what?"

"I don't know—" She squeezed her eyes shut, trying to see, to remember.

Suddenly her upper arms were gripped tightly. Her eyes flew open to see James standing in front of her, hauling her to her feet.

"You're not trying. *Try!*" he said brusquely.

She backed away, breaking his hold. "Why does everyone think I have the answers?"

"Who else thinks you do?"

"Dean Scolli."

"When did you talk to him?"

"Day before yesterday. He charged into the house insisting, like you are now, that I know something no one else knows. I didn't force Frank to go inside. I begged him not to. Dammit, James, you were there. You pulled me out of the house. You heard what I heard, saw what I saw. For Pete's sake, I can't remember something I didn't see."

"Maybe you didn't see anything, but you *know.*"

"What?" she said in exasperation. "What are you talking about?"

"Larry told you."

Roni glared back at James. *What the hell was going on here?*

"Larry saw something that night," James said. "I'd stake my life on it."

"And you think he told me?"

"Yes."

She shook her head, disbelieving.

"He was crazy about you. He would have told you."

"Why is what happened so important to you?" she asked. "What difference could it possibly make to you who saw what?"

"Because my brother's a psychological wreck. He's never been the same since that day. That's when he started to mess himself up with booze and drugs and God only knows what other shit. He saw Caroline struggling with Frank, but I think he saw more than that. He must have." He lifted the chair, then slammed it down again. "Larry's my kid brother, the only family I have. I want to help him, but I can't unless I know what's tearing him to pieces."

Roni felt a coldness inside her. James in Eagleton. His attentions, his conveniently being where she was, pretending not to know anything about her coming to town, even letting her make the first move. All along he only wanted what Dean wanted—*answers*.

She moved away. James reached for her. She jerked her arm away and backed up to the front door. "Your brother told me *nothing*. He never spoke to me again after that day. Not one word. Are you satisfied?" She rushed out the door, wanting only to be away from him.

Nearly a block from his house, Red caught up to her. She turned on the dog and shouted, "Go home!"

Roni banged around in the kitchen, trying not to think about James. When dinner was ready she called Aaron, then she sat down at the kitchen table. She was staring at the empty plate in front of her when Aaron quietly entered the room. He glanced at her, then got a plate and dished up food from the stove.

She watched, expecting him to take the plate and

go upstairs, but he sat down at the table. Between bits of venison steak and canned corn he glanced at her.

This was the first meal she'd cooked that he'd come down for. Was he here because James was supposed to eat with them? Did he know James? Did *she* know James? In a moment of weakness she allowed him to slip into her mind. Who was this man she'd had a crush on years ago? A guy she knew nothing about except that in a moment of compassion and generosity, he had defended his brother and given him money for new shoes. Big fucking deal.

She looked up to see Aaron staring curiously at her.

"Don't ask," she said, tears welling in her eyes.

Suddenly she was crying. Pushing the plate away, she buried her face in the circle of her arms and let go. What was she doing here? Why was she putting herself through this? She'd had an uncomplicated life before she came here. She had a good job and . . . and . . .

And that was it, she realized, there was nothing to look forward to beyond the job. She had been social, dating, an occasional affair, but not serious about anyone. And deep inside her, growing larger by the day was a damnable, empty hole.

For several minutes she cried quietly, her face in her arms. She felt a hand gently pat her shoulder. A moment later when she straightened, sniffing and wiping her face with her fingertips, the worst of it over, he was sitting across from her with his head bowed, solemnly watching her through his upper lashes.

He lifted a napkin and pushed it toward her. She took it, wiped her eyes and nose, then smiled weakly.

He smiled back.

Nineteen

"C'mon," Roni said, "let's go for a drive."

They had finished dinner. Roni had dried her eyes long ago and now felt silly for the outburst. Aaron was just a kid, a kid who had recently lost his mother, but she had yet to see him shed a single tear. If anyone needed to cry it was Aaron.

Aaron looked up in surprise.

"Grab a coat—it'll be cold once the sun sets."

"Where?" he said.

"You'll see."

She put the top down on the convertible. As she drove west, the air rushed at them, swirling their hair about their faces. At the junction five miles out of town, she turned right on a two-lane highway. With no traffic to contend with, the car raced north. Roni glanced at Aaron. His head rested on the back of the seat; his eyes were closed and his nostrils seemed to flare, taking in the rushing wind.

Twenty miles down the road Roni slowed, then

turned left on a narrower road, this one rough and badly potholed. After a couple of miles of dry, saffron-tinted landscape, an oasis of green appeared. She tapped Aaron's shoulder to get his attention and pointed to the left.

"A lake," he said.

"Well, not quite a lake. More like a pond. A big pond." She stopped the car, opened the door, and said, "You've never been out here?" He shook his head. "Then let's have a look."

She had crossed the road and was several yards into the meadow when she turned to see Aaron still sitting in the car watching her. "C'mon," she said, gesturing, "you can't see much from there."

She waited for him. He followed her out, carefully picking his way through the marshy meadow. Cattails and reedgrass grew along the banks of the pond. Dragonflies buzzed overhead and clouds of gnats blackened the air.

Roni lead him around to the far side of the pond where the ground was high and dry with fewer swarms of mosquitoes and gnats.

"Is there quicksand around here?" he asked.

"Quicksand?" She smiled and watched him tread tentatively through a muddy patch of ground, his tennis shoes darkening from the wetness. "You watch too much TV."

At the base of a large red cedar, she motioned for him to sit. "This is where we always came. It's the best place for skipping stones."

"You've been here before?"

"Millions of times. I used to come with my dad. Sometimes we'd fish for bluegill or trap crawdads, and sometimes we'd just sit here and skip stones."

"How do you trap crawdads?"

"There are several ways. My favorite was to tie a piece of ripe liver to a string and drop it to the bottom. They take hold of it and don't want to let go. Just haul them up."

Aaron picked up a stone, turned it in his fingers, and stared at it curiously.

"That one's too big for skipping." She pushed a few rocks around until she found what she was looking for—a flat, peachpit size stone. Wrapping her finger around the stone just so, she flung it. It hit the water with a flat sound and sank immediately. "I'm a little out of practice."

A stone hit the pond and skipped three times before disappearing underwater. "So am I," Aaron said.

Roni laughed. "Smartass, huh?" she said, searching for the perfect skipper. "Okay, I have to beat three, right?" She threw it. Three skips. Her next one made four.

Aaron stayed one ahead of her.

"Where'd you learn how to do that?" Roni asked.

"A friend of mine. He lived next door. He was older than me, but he liked to teach me things."

"Where'd you go?"

"There's a basin that fills with water every spring up by the old cemetery. Not big or deep like this one."

She nodded, knowing the spring. "Did he show you the tunnels?"

"No, that's something I showed him." He continued to toss stones, his large, brown eyes following the numerous leaps across the water, his face equally expressionless. He's very good at hiding his feelings, she thought. He's had practice.

"Where do they go, the tunnels?"

"All over. Some are blocked or completely caved-in, but if you know where the main entrances are, you can pretty much get around the whole town."

"Where does the one from your house end?"

"At this brewery on Sage that old man Holt owned. It's all boarded up, but I know how to get in."

"Is it safe?"

He shrugged. "I guess." He must have sensed a lecture coming, so he quickly changed the subject. "What was your dad like?"

Attempting to keep her tone flat, expressionless, she described her father. As she did, she furtively watched Aaron, wondering what his mother had told him about his own father, if anything. And then she found herself studying his features for a resemblance to her own family.

No, she told herself, *not my father. He wouldn't do that. Caroline wouldn't do that. He was not her* lover. *The nugget was payment of some kind. Payment for the piano lessons . . . payment for keeping me off the streets while they worked . . . payment for . . .* Yeah. Right.

They stayed until the sun was low in the sky. Before leaving, Aaron circled the pond picking cattails and pocketing tiny pebbles and bits of shale. On the way home he asked to go to the cemetery where his mother was buried.

"We'll have to see about getting her a headstone," Roni said, replacing dead roses from her last visit with the fresh ones she'd brought.

Dry-eyed, Aaron stood over his mother's grave. Roni laid a comforting hand on his thin shoulder.

"She didn't kill herself," he said. He stepped away, then turned and ran back down the hill.

Roni looked after him as he ran toward her car. A shrink would have said he was in denial—not unnatural for a survivor of a suicide victim. Denial against guilt, denial against the pain of abandonment. The survivor was left behind to sort out the ifs and whys. If she really loved me. If. If.

Roni believed him.

She looked down at the yellow rectangle of grass. "Caroline, he's a one-of-a-kind boy. You must have been very proud of him. I'll do the best I can for him . . . if he'll let me."

When they returned home at dusk, Roni was the first to notice the broken pane in the back door. The door was ajar.

She tried to hold Aaron back until she could decide what to do, whether or not it was safe to go in. But Aaron pushed past her and charged through the house.

"Aaron!" she screamed. "Get back here!" She heard him on the stairs and a moment later the creaking overhead told her he had gone up to the attic.

She grabbed the first thing she saw—a large butcher knife and just as quickly abandoned it for the can of Mace in the utility closet. Moving cautiously from the kitchen into the dining room, the Mace held in tremulous fingers, her eyes made a broad sweep around the room.

She tightened her grip on the can. The room was a mess. The drawers in the china cabinet were pulled out, the contents on the floor.

"Aaron," she called out softly, the tremor in her

voice adding to the tension. She moved from room to room to find the same disorder.

She climbed the stairs, quietly calling Aaron's name. Long shadows crossed the landing. Charcoal-gray twilight shone through the fanlight window at the end of the hall; the door to Aaron's bedroom was open. She whispered his name again, waited, then continued down the hall.

The master bedroom, on the east side of the house, was dark. The canister she held slipped in her sweaty palm as she crossed the room to the pull chain for the light. Downstairs the grandfather clock chimed. In the silence she swore she could hear it tick-tocking as the pendulum swung back and forth. Shadows stirred on the bleak walls.

She stepped on something soft and quickly jumped back. In the waning light she saw clothes from the wardrobe strewn about. She had stepped on a rolled up pair of socks.

Even without the overhead light she saw the room was like the rooms below, a shambles. She stayed far from the bed and its black space beneath as she grabbed the chain and pulled. Bright light blinded her at the same instant something touched the small of her back. Roni cried out and spun around, bumping someone. The Mace can flew from her hand.

"It's me," Aaron said, plucking at her shirt.

Roni's knees felt weak. She grabbed Aaron's hand and squeezed. They stood mute, surveying the room.

"Do you have any idea what this is about?" she asked.

He shook his head.

"As much as I hate to call in the sheriff, we have

to report this. Maybe, if we're very lucky, one of his deputies will respond.''

They crossed the threshold into the hallway, Roni in the lead. The air in the hall seemed charged. Sensing danger, Roni stopped, waving Aaron back. Someone was still in the house. On this floor. Watching. Waiting. A movement to her right. A shadow, human in shape, darted across the gray wall. Roni spun around. Too late. Whoever had rushed through the hall was already charging down the stairs. By the time she reached the banister and looked down, she caught only more shadows and the sound of retreating footsteps.

She called the sheriff's office. Their bad luck held.

Ten minutes later Lubben sauntered from room to room. There was something invasive about his presence. He asked his questions. How long were they gone? Did they see or hear anything when they entered the house? What was missing?

As far as they could tell, nothing had been taken.

"B and E with the intent to vandalize, that's what we got," Lubben said. "My guess would be one of the Scolli boys. Spiteful, mischievous little boogers. Maybe they was just curious . . . like some other kids a long time ago." He tipped his head, gave her a knowing look. "I'll take a run over to the house and have a talk with 'em."

"You don't think they—or someone else—might have been looking for something?"

"Looking for what?"

"I wish I knew." She told him first about the messages on the mirror and window, then about the man in camouflage clothing with the rifle.

"The messages sound like pranks—the Scollis again. The other one, the fella with the rifle . . .

poacher. One thing you don't want to do is stumble upon a poacher when he's working. Ruthless fellas, poachers are."

After Lubben left, she and Aaron straightened the place as best they could. She asked him to be alert to anything of his mother's that might be missing. Floyd Budner from the Trading Center replaced the window pane in the kitchen.

At ten o'clock, exhausted physically and emotionally from all that had happened that day, Roni slipped into bed, certain she would sleep like the dead. To unwind, she decided to read Caroline's diary.

She searched between the mattress and boxspring. The journal was gone.

She sat up. Had she moved it? Had it slipped beneath the covers? She reached under the sheet and felt around. Her hand passed over something smooth and cool. Something with hair.

Roni scrambled from the bed. With her heart pounding, she tossed back the bedding and stared in horror at the antique doll lying facedown. The doll with the dark hair and eyes, the one Caroline had named after Roni because it resembled her. Roni carefully turned it over. The entire porcelain face had been crushed in and the cloth body slashed open, its cotton batting spilling out.

Twenty

Sunday

The night before, after finding the doll in her bed, Roni had calmly disposed of it. Afterward she sat at the kitchen table sipping hot herbal tea heavily laced with brandy. At one o'clock she went upstairs, changed the sheets, and crawled under the covers. Shivering, she finally fell into a deep, exhausted sleep.

In the morning she felt like shit. Despite her hangover, she called the doctor and asked if he could spare a few minutes for some questions regarding Caroline. Time was growing short. She had been in Eagleton five days and, though it was apparent someone had something to hide, she was no closer to finding out who or what. Things between her and Aaron had improved immensely. Things between her and James had gone to hell. Not a word from him since she had stormed out of his house the day before. *Forget him,* she told herself. Just because Roni the "kid" had been nuts about him was no reason to moon over him now. She'd kissed him once. It wasn't as if they'd had a hot and heavy thing going.

While waiting for the doctor, she finished painting the porch, then took a roller and painted over the *Hell House* graffiti on the side of the house.

"Was an autopsy done on Caroline?"

Dr. Burke was inspecting the sutures in Roni's neck. He paused. "Autopsy?"

"Isn't it usual procedure to perform an autopsy on any questionable death, especially one of suicide?"

"I see you know your medical forensic." He applied a new bandage. "Yes, of course. I did it myself. I was her physician, after all. I found nothing suspicious or out of the ordinary, Roni."

"I'd heard it was difficult to bleed to death by cut wrists alone. The blood—"

"It clots. I know," he finished for her. "Unless it's a severed artery in the neck, arm, or leg, or the cuts are very deep, or the wounds are submerged in water to keep the blood flowing. Then normal coagulation tends to seal the veins after a while. You're right. With cut wrists it's difficult, but not impossible, especially if the victim had been taking an anticoagulant as Caroline had. She took Atophan to control the blood clots generated by the rheumatic heart disease. Bleeding, I assure you, would have been swift and steady."

"Was there evidence of lethal gas poisoning?"

"Roni, I'm impressed. You've given this a great deal of thought," he said. "If she had turned on the gas, then climbed into bed and cut her wrists, one would assume there would be such evidence. However, there was none, or I should say, only a trace."

"Then that means—"

"It means that by the time the fumes reached upstairs to her closed-off bedroom, she was so near death from loss of blood her breathing had become quite shallow. Remember, Aaron was merely groggy when the sheriff found him in his room down the hall."

"It still doesn't rule out foul play."

"No, it does not. Nor does it confirm it."

A light tapping at the door had both turning to see Hazel Anderson peeking through a pane and wriggling her fingers.

Roni waved her in.

"Hi, you two," Hazel said, stepping inside. "Goodness, what happened to you, Roni?"

Roni told her about being shot. Once started, she went on to tell of the break-in, the crushed, eviscerated doll, and the stolen diary.

"Good God, Roni, what's going on?" Dr. Burke said. "Break-ins, vandalism. Eagleton is a small, peaceful town, it's certainly no "Twin Peaks." And who would want to steal Caroline's diary, anyway?"

Hazel and Roni exchanged glances.

"Roni, take my advice and check into the hotel," the doctor said.

"What about Aaron?" Roni asked.

"He should leave, too. What about your place, Hazel?"

"I'm looking into it," she said. "These things take time."

The doctor closed his medical bag with a snap. "Well, on a lighter note, when Charlotte heard I was coming this way, she asked me to invite you to dinner this evening. Hazel, that includes you. I apologize to both of you for the short notice, but Stewart Saltzman,

our daughter's future father-in-law, popped in on us
and it's . . . well, it's one of those spur of the moment
things. Just a little gathering." Turning to Roni, he
added. "A few people Charlotte and I think you'll
enjoy meeting. Some you've already met. Say you'll
come. Charlotte won't take no for an answer."

"Roni will definitely attend," Hazel said. "As for
me, I hate social gatherings, little or otherwise. I'll
stay with Aaron. I've been dying to have some time
alone with him."

Put that way, Roni couldn't refuse.

"Oh, Roni, I saw your father this morning. I didn't
know he was back in town already."

"My father in town? Are you sure? Where did you
see him?"

"At the cemetery. He went over the hill and out
of sight before I had a chance to call out."

Her father was back in town and had not called?
"Well, I . . ."

Hazel patted Roni's hand. "Probably someone who
only looked like him. My mistake."

James rolled up his sleeping bag and tossed it into
the back of his Blazer among the assorted gear. He
and Sandy Watson had camped in a rocky section of
corporation land a hundred and eighty miles north-
west of the Saltzman Mine. It felt damn good to sleep
under the stars again. He'd been spending more time
in town and less in the field since Roni Mayfield
showed up.

For the past month, in an airplane owned by the
Goldenrod Mining Corporation, James and Sandy
had flown over thousands of acres of claim block
observing geologic formations. Last week they'd

located this site and yesterday they loaded up their gear and four-wheeled out to it. All day the pair of geologists collected samples of soil, rock, plants, and stream sediment, plotted on maps, made comparisons, and evaluated these samples with samples from other sites. They were ready to take their samples back to the mine for geochemistry and geophysics testing. Once done, then drilling, laboratory tests, assaying, computers, and more feasibility studies would follow to determine whether a site bore minable properties. At three o'clock, with their ground samples and photos, they headed back to civilization.

During the long, bumpy drive back to the mine, James sat quietly in the passenger seat and finally allowed himself to reflect on Roni Mayfield—the fine texture of her skin, the taste of her lips, her own special scent. He owed her an apology, and as soon as he got back to Eagleton he'd go to see her. When they reached the Saltzman site at seven p.m., she was still on his mind.

In the main office James found a message to call the doc. He picked up the phone and dialed.

Roni was the last to arrive at the Burke house. After complimenting Roni on her ivory silk dress, Charlotte escorted her through a house decorated with impressive antiques and original paintings and sculptures to the deck at the back where the other guests, in casual attire, sat in lawn chairs drinking cocktails from bright plastic glasses. A brick barbecue glowed red with briquettes.

Roni hesitated in the doorway, running her hands self-consciously over the soft material of her dress. "I didn't know it was an outdoor party."

"Leave it to a man to forget something like that," Charlotte said. "I should have called you myself, but I've been so busy putting this last-minute shindig together, and he was going to see you, so I—well, it's not a big deal. You look really great. I'd give anything to be in that dress of yours right now." She patted her pregnant belly.

As they moved through the doorway onto the deck, Roni removed her dangling earrings and slipped them in her pocket.

Charlotte introduced her to the group at the redwood table: Father Roberts, Pam Burke's fiancé, Eric, and Eric's father, the President and Chief Executive of Saltzman Mining, Stewart Saltzman.

Across the patio, in the gazebo, she greeted Doctor Burke and Faddle Granville. Faddle presented his mother, Elsa, and the woman sitting with her. Roni recognized the woman who had been with James the night at the Eagle bar. Linda Shaw, her smile cool and reserved, merely nodded.

Dr. Burke was pouring margaritas from a large pitcher into salt-rimmed glasses. "What can I get you, Roni?"

"Those look good."

He handed her one. "These aren't those sissy snow-cone kind. They pack quite a wallop."

"We're all here now," Charlotte said to Roni. "I'm afraid Jim Glazer won't be able to make dinner—something's come up at the mine. Roni, have you met Jim?"

"Yes. Years ago, as a matter of fact." Roni caught Linda's stark gaze before the pretty blonde looked away.

"Of course. I keep forgetting you and Jim knew each other as youngsters. Ironic, isn't it, that the two of you would leave Eagleton at the same time and return about the same time? It's a small world indeed."

Indeed. So James had been invited, too, Roni thought. As Linda's date? Had he learned Roni was coming and backed out? Well, whatever the reason, she was relieved he wasn't coming. The evening would have been endless with him there.

Doctor Burke excused himself. Several minutes later he emerged from the house with a platter of thick porterhouse steaks—the chicken and fish "eat healthy" craze had not reached central Nevada and probably never would. Red meat held supreme in these parts—the steaks sizzled when they hit the hot grill as the delicious odor of browning fat instantly replaced the sweet scent of evening jasmine in the air.

Faddle directed Roni to a chair next to his mother who, Roni now noticed, sat in a wheelchair. The rail-thin woman in black, from her tight curls to her ballet slippers, glared openly at Roni with beady black eyes. Linda sat opposite, her cool smile still in place.

"You got my Lifesavers, Fadius?" Elsa Granville asked.

He patted his pants pocket. "Got 'em right here, Mother."

"You know how I hate when you carry them in your trouser pocket. They get all fuzzy with lint."

"I don't give you the linty ones, Mother." To Roni he said, "Mother is diabetic. I carry candy in case her blood sugar needs a boost. She takes two shots of insulin a day."

"Don't be telling every living soul my business. Did

I go around telling everyone in town that you wet
your bed till you were twelve?"

"Yes, Mother, you did."

"Who are you?" Elsa Granville asked Roni in a
loud voice.

Roni looked for and saw twin hearing aids in the
woman's oversized ears. "Roni Mayfield," she said in
a strong voice, leaning forward.

"Don't holler. I can read your lips if you don't
mumble. Now, who are you really?"

Roni looked to Faddle for help.

"What she means is what do you do and why are
you here in Eagleton, stuff like that."

"I was a good friend to Caroline Holt. She died
recently."

"Yes, yes, I know all that," she said impatiently.
"So you're the one?"

"One what?"

"The one staying at the house. That widow was an
odd character. I'd have liked to be a fly on her wall
a time or two. Yessiree. Thank goodness Fadius had
the good sense to stay away from that one."

Linda Shaw, wearing a short, white split skirt and
aqua top, crossed her bare legs and leaned toward
Roni. "How is Aaron holding up? Is he having a
problem dealing with his mother's death? If so, I'd
be more than happy to counsel him."

"Counsel?"

"I'm a psychologist. Didn't James tell you?"

"No, he didn't. Thank you for the offer. I can't speak
for Aaron, but he seems to be handling it well. I will,
however, pass your message along to him, Dr. Shaw."

The woman smiled. Roni was aware that the doctor
hadn't suggested she drop the professional title.

"What'd those women say?" Elsa asked Faddle. "Who's handling what well?"

"They're talking about Aaron Holt, Mother."

"If you ask me, the boy needs discipline," Elsa went on in her loud, cracking voice. "Been allowed to do whatever the blazes he wants for far too long. Goes to school when it suits him. Prowls around the town all hours of the night. Looks like he don't eat nothin'. Never saw anyone so puny. The county people should get involved, see that he's put on the right track. You let 'em get control when they're little and you've lost 'em. There's no getting 'em back. That right, Fadius?"

Roni thought about Aaron being made a ward of the state. If the foster care system took over, Aaron would be forced to behave like a normal kid. Forced to leave the only home he knew, forced to go to school, to keep regular hours, to . . . to what? To give up his individuality, his independence? To be someone he wasn't meant to be?

Faddle nodded his head in agreement and said, "Yes, Mother," several times. Then, turning his back to her, he said with an apologetic grin, "Oh, Lordy, someone change the subject, quick."

Charlotte came to the rescue with a tray of stuffed mushrooms. The old woman held onto Charlotte's arm and ate directly from the tray until Faddle made up a plate for her.

From the barbecue pit the doctor clanged a ranch-house triangle and called out, "Soup's on. Who wants what? On the left we got 'em still kicking, shoe leather on the right, and anyone's guess in the middle."

Faddle wheeled his mother to the long redwood table.

"Don't put me on the end," Elsa complained. "Can't hear nothin' on the end. Put me in the middle next to Father Roberts. He don't ignore me like some of you others."

Faddle lifted the tiny woman from the wheelchair and deposited her on the bench in the middle of the table. The priest sat beside her, a brave smile on his face.

Roni was seated between Stewart Saltzman and Doctor Burke. It turned out the occasion was a sneak pre-announcement of Pam's engagement to Eric with a super bash planned at the end of the year.

During the meal of steak, pasta salad, garlic-toasted sheepherder bread, and baked potatoes with mounds of sour cream and chives, Roni watched and listened. The Burkes were wonderful hosts, casual and easygoing. When the doctor wasn't talking with Roni, he and Faddle, seated across from each other, talked of hunting and fishing. Whenever she could, Charlotte attempted to deliver Father Roberts from Elsa's clutches. Pam and Eric touched at every opportunity, obviously in love—a good catch for a country doctor's daughter, Roni noted. The Saltzman family, with active mines in eight states, had to be worth many millions. The senior Saltzman spoke of family-owned industries ranging from precious metal mining to drilling for geothermal energy.

Linda Shaw touched on the life of the small town therapist. When Roni asked Faddle, the three-term mayor, about Eagleton politics, he quickly changed the subject, saying he never mixed business with pleasure.

"He coulda been a doctor like young Paul here," Elsa piped in loudly, addressing Roni, "instead of a motormouth politician. He went more'n halfway through medical school, then gave it up. 'Bout broke his daddy's heart."

"It did no such thing. It was you who took it to heart, Mother. You just wanted your own doctor-in-residence."

"So what's wrong with that?"

"Nothing, 'cept I can't stomach the sight of blood."

"You don't have no trouble blowing those little birds and the rest of God's creatures to hell and back come hunting season."

"Now, Mother."

"So, Roni," Doc Burke jumped in, "what's it like being an investigative reporter in the big, corrupt city?"

"It's a job like any other. It has its ups and downs."

"What was your most exciting or dangerous assignment?" Stewart Saltzman asked.

"Well, it's always exciting when I get an interview with a celebrity. Several years ago on the set of *Cape Fear*, I interviewed Robert DiNiro, Nick Nolte, Gregory Peck, and Bob Mitchum. Today's superstars working with superstars of yesteryear—stars who, by the grace of God, have endured in this world of the fifteen-minute fame. I found myself overwhelmed by the magnitude of talent." She smiled. "But the most heartwarming was an assignment I had just last week." She told them about the rescue of Dennis Stemmer, the young boy who'd fallen down the mine shaft.

"And the most dangerous?" Charlotte asked.

"The most dangerous? Well, ah, that's not so easy. I've had more than my share of heartstopping experiences. Let's see . . . the LA riots were tense, a shootout and hostage situation at a savings and loan in La Jolla had its moments. But I think it was the '91 fire in the Oakland Hills that made me realize I was not invincible. Believe me, I now have the utmost respect for fire. We—a cameraman, three reporters, and me—found ourselves trapped when a wall of fire turned back on us. With a lot of luck and some powerful prayers, we were able to race down a ravine to a culvert and jump into it. The fire went over the top of us. A policeman trying to lead a small group of residents to safety got caught and . . . and I'm afraid they weren't, well, as lucky . . ." she let the words trail away.

Silence. Then the clearing of throats and adjusting of positions.

She had put a pall on the party with her story. "I'm sorry," Roni said, shredding a piece of garlic bread. "I . . ."

"Nonsense, don't be sorry," Charlotte said, smiling. "I think you were very brave. All your assignments can't be fun, exciting, and heartwarming."

"Are you still on the magazine?" Linda asked. "I mean, do you intend to go back to LA soon?"

Roni caught the doctor's eye. The look, though brief, told her not to let herself be trapped into disclosing what she didn't care to disclose.

"Enough about me," Roni said and, turning to Charlotte and Pam, she asked, "What about this wedding?"

Father Roberts spoke up first. With fingers steepled as though in prayer, he said proudly, "The youngsters have opted for a modest ceremony—modest by Catholic standards, that is. Two hundred guests, wasn't it, Charlotte?"

"It grows even as we speak, Father," Charlotte said.

"Then the wedding will be here in Eagleton?" Roni asked.

"Oh, yes," he responded, his pleasant face beaming. "At St. John's. The new organ arrives any day—a generous donation from our very own Mr. Saltzman—and we'll finally have the opportunity to show the church off properly. Fill it to the rafters. And there's no better way than a wedding. How I love a big wedding."

"You're a hopeless romantic," the doctor teased, excitement coloring his own cheeks.

It had grown dark during dinner. The mosquitoes descended. Those who made tasty meals for the bloodsuckers began to slap and scratch at themselves. The group moved into the house for after-dinner drinks.

Roni and Faddle chose coffee. The others gathered at the bar, helping themselves to brandy and cordials. She approached the priest as he stood gazing out the bay window. "Father, was Caroline Holt Catholic?"

His startled look was so fleeting, an instant later she wondered if she had imagined it. He turned back to the window. "Not to my knowledge, no. Why do you ask?"

"There was no service for her. I wondered why."

"I believe she was Southern Baptist. But she—I think . . . at one time she considered embracing the Catholic faith."

"But she didn't?"

"No. No, she didn't."

"Had she become disillusioned with her own faith?"

"I'm afraid I don't know why she considered converting."

"Was Aaron baptized?"

He turned to stare at her. "You're a journalist. It shows. Is this an interview?"

Roni laughed and shook her head. "I'm sorry, you're right. An interview? Hardly. Interrogation is more like it. It's just that I have so many questions and so little time."

Father Roberts squeezed her arm and smiled, softening his already kind, compassionate brown eyes. "We'll talk. Whenever you like. The doors at St. John's are always open."

The doc and Faddle joined them. Faddle said to Roni, "I hear you were victim to a random shooting a couple days ago, my dear."

"I hope it was random . . . the shooting, that is."

"Of course it was," Father Roberts said. "This town has more firearms than it has dogs and yellow roses. With irresponsible people at the triggers."

"I got shot at once myself," Faddle ventured. "Back in '55. Made it through the Korean War without a scratch, then nearly got my head blown off chukker hunting. Floyd Budner at the Trading Center, it was his boy, Sammy. Damn fool kid wasn't old enough to handle a gun, let alone be turned loose in the hills with one. Got so danged excited when the dog flushed that covey out of the sagebrush he just opened fire. Naturally, I dove for the rocks, but not before I caught a couple pellets in this ear." He bent to show Roni the scars.

Charlotte and Linda joined them.

"Jim tells me you and he were mine brats together in Eagleton during the last boom," Linda said to Roni.

"Yes, sort of. His brother Larry and I were good friends."

"Speaking of Jim," Charlotte said, glancing at her

watch, "he should be here any minute. He couldn't make dinner, but he promised he'd stop by for a nightcap."

Roni moaned inwardly. "What time is it?" she asked, holding Charlotte's wrist to look at her watch. "Oh, I've got to go."

"So early?" Charlotte frowned.

"Hazel's with Aaron. I wanted to visit with her before it got too late." Roni quickly said her goodbyes and Charlotte walked her to the door.

"Sure you can't wait and say hello to Jim?"

"No, I really should get back. We had some trouble with the Scolli boys the other night. And, well . . ."

"I understand. Frankly, I hope it turns out to be an early evening. Hot weather like today's makes me feel like a limp noodle. And this little guy," she said, rubbing her bulging stomach, "is gearing up to be a kick-boxer."

"Maybe twins again?"

"Paul says no. He's betting it's a boy."

"You don't know?"

"Oh, we're the old-fashioned sort of parents. Half the fun is guessing the sex, don't you think?"

Roni nodded.

In her car minutes later as she backed out of the driveway she wondered if she would ever be pregnant. Would she marry and have kids? So many women today were having babies without benefit of a husband and, with the exception of Dan Quayle and his attack on Murphy Brown, it had become almost commonplace.

As her Chevy turned the corner at the end of the street, Roni caught a glimpse of James's dark Blazer swinging into the Burke driveway.

Twenty-One

Monday

First thing that morning Roni had tried again to reach Dr. Greene at the clinic in Ely. The receptionist had taken her name and assured her the doctor would return her call as soon as possible. While waiting she dressed in shorts, T-shirt, and tennis shoes, then went out to the back of the house and chopped away the thick, woody vines that climbed the trellis and blocked the morning sun to the master bedroom. By mid-afternoon she was done.

Pulling off the garden gloves she stood in the rear yard admiring her handiwork. She looked from the tangled mound of vines to the now-naked trellis, her eyes following it up to the second-floor window of Caroline's room. Along the ledge that ran the length of the house, she saw a broken portion beneath the window apron. If she closed her eyes she could see

Larry standing on that ledge, could imagine it breaking away and dropping him to the ground.

What was it he had seen through that window?

After testing the strength of the trellis, she climbed it to the second floor just as Larry had done and, attempting to see from his vantage point, peered through a diamond-shaped section into the bedroom. The fireplace stood to the immediate right; to the left was the bed, nightstand, and the small closet.

A cloud passed in front of the sun, a cool gust of wind swirled around her. She shivered.

Her view of the right side of the room was blocked by the fireplace mantel. With her left foot she stepped on the ledge, holding tight to the trellis, and leaned to the side.

"Hey, look out!"

Startled, Roni's foot slipped and she lunged to the side. She cried out as her shin scraped along the rough edge of a shingle. Before she could reach the trellis with her free hand, she felt an arm around her waist pulling her back. She grabbed the trellis and clung desperately, her heart pumping.

James Glazer pressed against her back, holding her.

"I'm sorry," he said close to her ear. "I didn't mean to scare you. I was afraid you'd fall . . . like Larry. Are you okay?"

She inhaled a ragged breath and nodded.

"Good. Look, I'll get out of your way so you can get down. Something tells me I'm more hindrance than help." James eased his arm from around her, lowered himself down a couple feet, then jumped to the ground.

Roni descended carefully. Safely on the ground again, she turned back to the trellis, braced her foot on the bottom slat, and bent to inspect the scrape on her shin. "What do you want?" she asked flatly.

"To apologize. I don't blame you for being pissed." He leaned in. "How bad is it?"

"A scratch." She blew on it. "And it hurts like a sonofabitch."

He laughed. Before she could protest, he had her by the hand and was pulling her toward the back door. "We'll get you fixed up. While we do that I'll explain a few things. Things I should have told you from the beginning."

"Where's Red?" she asked as they climbed the back steps.

"When he's not with me he's off somewhere getting laid."

Remembering what Faddle said about Red's sexual prowess, she laughed.

"Amusing to you maybe, but try opening your door to find a litter of rednosed pups on your back porch— not once, but three times."

In the kitchen he asked, "Band-aids? Antiseptic?"

"Upstairs hall bath. Under the sink."

Roni found a pair of tweezers and began to pick at several slivers in her hand.

He returned with a box of Band-aids, a spray can of Solarcaine, and a damp washcloth.

He lifted her by the waist and settled her on the edge of the table. Then he sat in front of her, lifted her bare leg, removed her tennis shoe, and wedged her foot in the tight denim apex of his crotch. He dabbed at the scratches, blotting the thin columns of blood.

She sucked air through her teeth.

He glanced up at her. "Sorry. A couple of these

scratches are pretty deep. You might have the doc look at them."

"Uh-uh. Not unless gangrene sets in." As it was, she was turning out to be Dr. Burke's most recurrent patient. That tetanus shot was getting a workout.

"Look, I'm sorry about the other day. I was a real asshole." He sprayed the Solarcaine on her shin. "It's just that . . . it's this thing with Larry. I really care about the guy."

"I know. I wish I could help."

"You can."

"James, he didn't tell me anything."

"I believe you."

"Assuming he had seen something," she said, "wouldn't he tell you first? I mean, you were more like a father to him than . . . than his own father. He would've trusted you with anything."

"I agree. That's what makes it so hard to figure out." As he spoke he held her ankle absently.

"It isn't just Larry, is it? Nothing around here makes sense. Larry, Frank, Caroline, you and me, and now Aaron. I had no contact with Caroline in twelve years, absolutely none, yet she tried to reach me just before she died and I don't exactly know why."

"About a month ago I visited her. I had to hear her version of what happened that day," he said. "She was anything but comfortable talking about it. Yet, she had no problem discussing you. Something would come over her face, a look of pride, respect. You were still very much in her thoughts."

"But so much time passed. And she had Aaron."

Roni remembered that once she had come across the widow quietly sitting in the window seat, staring into space, tears rolling unchecked down her cheeks.

Roni had gone to her, held her hand. Caroline had told her never, ever to give her heart completely.

The scene was so vivid Roni could almost feel Caroline's hands tightly squeezing hers; smell her special scent of sweet gardenias and, sometimes, brandy; see the pain in her eyes.

She shook her head, trying to clear it. "The last year or so I'd sorta gotten involved with other things, other people, and I didn't visit as much. The piano lessons and ..." Roni lowered her head and shrugged.

"Guilt is a destructive emotion. Don't let it get to you," James said. "What she said was, 'If anything happens to me, I want Roni and Aaron to meet.'"

Roni looked up. "Did she say why that was important to her?"

"No."

"Did she sound like someone contemplating suicide?"

"Not at all. She sounded like someone who wanted answers, not death."

James lifted her foot, then rose. "Is Aaron here?"

"In the attic."

"Let's take a walk."

"You know about her heart, the rheumatic disease?"

"Yes," Roni said.

They walked down the driveway. James spoke in a low voice. "Every afternoon she took a nap. That particular day she was exceptionally tired and fell into a deep sleep. Some hours later she was roused by pain, a great deal of pain. Hands were on her, violating her.

She struggled, opened her eyes to shadowy shapes, and found herself on the floor beside her bed with a young man bending over her. She pushed at him, struggled, and then mercifully she lost consciousness once again. Later she learned the young man was Frank Scolli."

"So it's true—Frank did rape her," Roni said, disheartened by the news. "And he *is* Aaron's father."

"Frank may have raped her, but he wasn't the father. Caroline was already pregnant."

"So who was the father?" Roni asked. "She wasn't seeing anyone . . . at least not openly."

"I don't know. She wouldn't tell me."

"Is it possible she didn't know?" Roni was surprised by her own question. To ask it was to suggest that Caroline had been promiscuous, something Roni found difficult to imagine.

"Hard to say."

"But the time span from the assault to birth, that had to be considered."

"Apparently it was close enough. Besides, no one knew she was pregnant when Frank broke in, so there was no reason to think otherwise."

"Not even the doctor?"

"No one."

Suddenly she remembered the clinic in Ely. "Dr. Greene," she blurted out.

"What?"

"Hazel took Caroline and Aaron into Ely to a clinic. I've been waiting to hear from the doctor there about tests done on Aaron. I'll try again."

They went in. Roni made the call and was told the doctor was in surgery. For a small town doctor, reaching him was becoming quite a challenge. She left another message.

They moved into the kitchen where Roni told James about the break-in and stolen diary and—she shuddered again just thinking about it—the doll in her bed. "Looks like you and I aren't the only ones trying to get some answers. This isn't kid's play. He's serious and he wants me out of here," she said, absently picking at the slivers in her palm.

He took her hand and inspected it. "Those have to come out. They'll fester."

A few minutes later the slivers were lined up like wooden soldiers on a tissue. He continued to hold her hand as he lifted his gaze and stared into her eyes.

Roni felt her body flush warmly before she pulled her hand away.

An awkward silence filled the room.

He rose abruptly. "Got a flashlight?"

She gave him the one under the kitchen sink.

"Lead the way to the tunnel. Think I'll try a new way home."

She took him to the basement. As he climbed down the ladder he said, "I'll call when I get home." And he was gone.

Thirty minutes later he called.

"It came out at the old Holt Brewery. It went on, but I didn't. Unless you knew exactly where to look you'd have a helluva time finding the tunnel entrance in that old building. Aaron's got a pretty good thing going for him there."

"Why a tunnel from the house to the brewery?"

"Rumor has it that back in the 1800s several of the more prominent residents had tunnels dug from their homes to their businesses in town, simply to avoid going out in the inclement weather."

"Does it look safe?"

"Safe enough. There are a few off-shoots that I wouldn't want to be in during an earthquake—those I didn't investigate."

She told him she was still waiting to hear from the doctor. They said goodbye.

When the doctor hadn't returned her call by five, Roni set the answering machine, made a picnic meal of tuna salad sandwiches, chips, and fruit and, with some persuasion, coaxed Aaron out of the attic room. They followed a rainbow to the pond. The rainbow disappeared over the hill where the Saltzman Mine operated twenty-four hours a day. Roni bet there was more than a pot of gold at its end. They ate in the car with the top up, listening to the rain beat down on the canvas.

"What is it you do in the attic?" she asked.

"I have a project."

"What sort of project? May I see it?"

He looked at her. "You really want to?"

"Are you kidding? I'm dying to see what you're doing up there."

His smile was coy, mischievous. "Gimme a couple more days. I wanna finish something first."

She was about to tell him that a couple days was all she might have left here. She had a job, friends, family back in LA. Whatever she had hoped to expose stayed just out of reach like the mechanical rabbit at the dog track racing ahead of the greyhounds. There was no shortage of secrets, only a shortage of answers. If she could just convince the authorities that there was a case, she wouldn't feel so alone. James was involved, and that helped, but James was looking for twelve-year-old answers. Hers were more current.

"Okay, two days," she told Aaron.

After biting into an apple that was far from crisp,

she tossed it out the window for the squirrels. "Aaron, tell me about your visit to the clinic in Ely."

He ate the middle of his sandwich, leaving the crust. "Mom said it was a checkup."

"Why not go to the clinic in Eagleton?"

He shrugged.

"Describe what they did."

He told her. It sounded like a routine checkup to her, but it was the blood workup that interested her.

"Do you know your blood type?" she asked.

"It was either A or O. Mom said it was pretty common."

The rain had stopped and the sun burned through the clouds, warming the late afternoon. He leaned against the window sill on Hazel Anderson's front porch and waited for her to begin. Hazel, sitting on the porch swing, the seat listing to one side from the weight of her large-boned frame, looked uncomfortable. She cleared her throat, then said, "I was surprised to run into you at the cemetery today . . . at Caroline's grave."

He was silent.

"I think you know why I asked you here," she said.

"It's about Caroline Holt," he said, struggling to keep his voice even, without emotion. The constant squeaking of the chains in the swing as she moved back and forth grated on his nerves.

She nodded. "Not long before she died she confided in me, told me something quite confidential, something I suspect no one else knows." Hazel adjusted her position and the swing jerked spasmodically. "Perhaps it's none of my business, but I feel an obligation."

"Obligation?"

"To Aaron."

He leaned back, crossing one leg in front of the other. The picture of casualness; inside, his guts roiled.

The swing slowed. "Caroline felt it was time the truth were known about her son's . . . you know, parentage."

He watched her, his face expressionless. What did she actually know?

She went on. "There's a question regarding his biological father."

"She named me?"

"Not exactly. But I put two and two together. I understand a simple blood test could remedy the problem. Of course, I realize this is awkward and, for reasons known only to Caroline and perhaps the father, it has been kept secret all these years. If the question of Aaron's parentage were the only factor, I'd be hesitant to get involved, but now it seems that Caroline's death might be under investigation."

Hazel got the swing going again. "Roni is no dummy, as I'm sure you know. She's already asking questions. She doesn't seem to me to be the type who'd just let things slide. I'm sure Aaron wants answers, too. One's roots are hard to ignore." She sighed heavily. "Well, there, I've had my say, for whatever it's worth."

He stared at her for several moments. He pictured her dead, her head lying back on the floral cushion, a neat bullet hole in her forehead. Or better yet, her mottled throat slit from ear to ear, the blood vividly coloring her pastel blouse. He thought of Caroline's cut wrists, her lifeblood soaking into the snowy quilt.

He felt no qualms this time. Murder did indeed get easier with each wretched act.

Without a word he stood, crossed the porch, and descended the steps.

When Roni and Aaron returned to the house, Aaron again shut himself away in the attic room.

Roni pulled on a windbreaker and went for a walk. It was hour between sunset and darkness. Twilight, shadowtime. The rain had stopped. She decided to vary her usual route and walk down the rural Country Lane, a narrow gravel road lined with elm and poplar trees. The road was damp, though not muddy, and earth worms, brought out by the rain, twisted on the ground. An occasional puddle reflected her image as she passed.

In less than ten minutes she had descended the hill, crossed the main highway, and begun to ascend— Eagleton was nestled in a valley, with Main Street at the nadir. Three blocks up she turned left on a street mixed with private homes, businesses, and churches. Ahead loomed the grand spire of St. John's.

From the open porch of a house to her right, she saw the ultraviolet glow of a bug zapper and heard the snapping and cracking of hapless insects being incinerated against its seductive coils. She smelled steak grilling on a barbecue, heard the tortured sounds of a guitar as someone practiced. Sap and dew from the umbrella of trees overhead dripped down on her.

The light was nearly gone as she climbed the brick steps of the Catholic church. She tried one of the double doors, found it unlocked, and went inside.

The door eased shut behind her. The vestibule was cool and dim. At the font holding the holy water she hesitated a split second before moving on—when she was ten, out of curiosity, she had gone to church with a friend who was Catholic and although she wasn't of the faith, Roni went through the various rituals, emulating her friend, feeling both inspired and wicked for the small deception.

Moving down the central aisle she could understand the priest's pride in the church. In a town this size, the edifice was more than impressive. A cathedral ceiling, stained-glass windows, pillars, pews and rails polished to a high gloss, a main to altar to equal that of any city church. At the chancel rail she paused long enough to admire the altar and crucifix, then made her way to what she hoped was the office. She thought she might take Father Roberts up on his offer to talk.

Just as she pushed open the door she heard a door on the other side of the church close. She backtracked, following the sound. At the other door she quietly called out. "Father Roberts?" and tapped lightly.

She opened the door and stepped into a breezeway. At the end was another door and she realized it must be the rectory. After debating whether to go on or return to the church, she found herself moving toward the rectory door. Through long window panels she saw Father Roberts inside. He was slowly walking the floor, his head bent over an open book is his hands.

Roni rapped on the door. The priest looked up in surprise, saw her, and quickly closed the book—a leather bound book that looked very much like Caroline's diary. His smile was reflexive, a hand raised in greeting, then he came toward her. She lost sight of him behind a entry partition; then she heard him clear his throat several times and the door opened. With a warm, friendly smile he beckoned her inside the sparse living room.

"Roni Mayfield, what a pleasant surprise. Come in. Come in."

"Am I intruding? Were you preparing for Sunday Mass?" She looked for the book he'd been reading only moments ago. None was within sight.

"Of course you're not intruding. I was just about to brew tea. Will you join me?"

"Yes, thank you."

"Would you rather have something stronger?" he said, leading her to a small plaid sofa. "Mrs. McCracken makes a fine crabapple wine that packs quite a wallop."

She remembered it well. "Tea is fine, thanks."

He left the room. She heard water running, a cabinet open and close. She scanned the room for the book. A walnut coffee table held a collection of well-worn magazines on fly fishing and Indian artifacts. One wall held hundreds of books.

Roni stood, went to the bookshelves, and quickly searched for a brown leather volume.

"Are you interested in books?" Father Roberts asked behind her.

She pivoted, hit the shade of a floor lamp with the back of her hand, and laughed apologetically before saying, "I devour them. You know, like the potato chip commercial, 'Can't eat just one.' Who ever heard of a writer who's not a reader?" She was rambling. The book was nowhere in sight. Where could it have gone in the few seconds it took him to open the door?

The priest's salt and pepper hair was mussed in

front, as if he'd unconsciously raked fingers through it. A bell dinged in the kitchen and he was gone again. She heard him blow his nose.

She returned to the sofa and quickly lifted each cushion to look underneath before sitting. Across from her were two green club chairs and to her left was a blue tweed La-Z-boy. At the side of the recliner a magazine pocket bulged.

Roni was halfway off the sofa when Father Roberts entered the room with two steaming mugs. "Sugar, milk, lemon?"

"Just black." She eased back down.

He gave her the tea. She looked around for a coaster, saw none, and held onto the hot mug.

"Cold, Father?"

"Pardon?" He lowered himself onto the recliner.

"Do you have a cold?"

He rubbed the side of his nose. "Cold? No. I wish that's all it was. Allergies. There are so many things in the air. I suspect it's sagebrush this time around. I moved away from the bay area where I was plagued with earaches from the constant dampness. But here in the desert it's allergies. Hay fever, grass, juniper, there's always something making the rounds."

"Frank had asthma," she said.

"Frank? Oh, yes, Frank Scolli. Yes, I remember," he said pensively. "Suppose I shouldn't complain, huh? There's always someone, somewhere, worse off."

"Father, I'll get to the point. Do you think Caroline was suicidal?"

He stared at her before answering. "Yes, I do."

"Can you tell me why?"

"Because she told me she was."

Roni felt a sinking in her stomach. "When?"

"Some time ago. She was extremely depressed. She

would have surely died if not for outside intervention."

"When was that?"

He squinted his eyes, thinking. "Many years after her mate was killed. Grief and the phases of mourning differ greatly from person to person. As you know, Caroline went through a rather long period of denial regarding his death. Her suppressed grief was fueled by the fact that she was deeply in love; Richard was cut down in the prime of his life, the two still newly-weds. And of course there was an uncertainty, on Caroline's part anyway, as to whether he was dead or only missing in action—naturally she clung to the latter—hence the shrine. Added to that was the multiple loss of her entire family when she was a youngster. She must have asked herself how the Almighty God could be so cruel as to take everything from her again. Then she simply made up her mind that He couldn't. That He would surely return her husband to her."

She leaned in. "This was all before Aaron was born?"

He nodded slowly.

"Nothing was said regarding suicide after Aaron's birth?"

He shook his head. "Not to me. But as we discussed the other night, she was not of the Catholic faith. She didn't seek counsel from me."

"Yet you were friends?"

"Of course."

"She would have confided in you?"

"Not necessarily. Not unless she wanted help. If she truly wanted to die she wouldn't have told anyone, especially not me."

"Did she seem overly distraught just before she died?"

He seemed to ponder, then, "Now that you men-

tion it, she was acting rather strange. Not distraught
. . . different, out of character, you might say."

"Caroline kept a journal."

"Did she?" he said evenly. A muscle in his jaw
twitched. "Did she mention suicide in this journal?"

"I don't know. It was stolen before I'd had a chance
to finish it."

He looked genuinely shocked.

A buzzer sounded.

The priest glanced at the clock on the mantel.
He stood. "I'm afraid we'll have to continue this
conversation another time, Roni. I've a wedding
rehearsal. I do love a wedding." He smiled, then
walked her to the door.

She took Mill Crossing back, welcoming the occasional house along the way with its lights and human
activity. On the other side of Main where it was dark
and secluded, with only a deaf woman's house on the
way, she broke into a jog. This time Red didn't show
up to escort her home. And if anyone followed her
she was moving too fast to be aware of it.

That evening Roni drove into town, bought a frozen
pizza, a six-pack of Cokes, popcorn, and a Monopoly
game. And just in case Aaron didn't like to play games,
she rented a "Star Trek" movie. They sat at the
kitchen table and, long after the pizza had been
reduced to strips of greasy crust, waged a cutthroat
battle of real estate high financing. It was after midnight when Roni, too tired to go on, said good night
and turned in.

In Caroline Holt's bedroom, Roni struggled awake.
Someone had turned on the heat. The radiator sizzled

and wheezed. Despite the steady hissing of the steam, the room was icy, frigid.

Through a mind groggy with sleep, she could visualize the radiator under the south window, yet the wheezing seemed to come from the other side of the room.

Shivering with cold, she forced her eyes open. The room was inky black.

Then she heard it.

She strained to listen. The sound of breathing, scarcely discernible, came from the farthest corner. Inching upward, she stared hard into the blackness, the sound of her pulse raging in her ears.

A soft wheezing breath without a body.

She thought of Frank. Was it Frank? Had he come back? Had he ever left?

"Frank?" she whispered.

As her fingers searched for the base of the lamp on the nightstand the wheezing stopped and the room became deadly quiet. She paused, listened, turned her head and tried to see into the syrupy darkness. She found the lamp's switch and twisted it. Nothing.

The breathing resumed, and through it, somewhere in that sickening wheeze, Roni thought she heard a whisper of laughter. It closed in.

Roni pulled herself into a ball, her back pressed to the headboard.

If she searched for the chain of the overhead light she would be moving toward *it*. She couldn't do that. Nothing could make her do that.

Over the deafening sound of rushing blood in her ears she heard footsteps. The door swung open, hinges creaking. Still the room stayed black.

"Roni . . . ?"

Aaron. "Aaron . . ." she whispered, "someone's here . . . in this room. Quick, get help. Run."

Footsteps retreated, running, growing faint.

She sensed, rather than heard, a presence in the room, a measure of her space invaded. Roni clutched at the bedclothes, wanting to scream, praying for light.

After a full minute the footsteps came again. A beam of light swept around the room and hit her face, blinding her. She raised her hand to block the light.

The beam continued to sweep until it caught the glint of the chain of the overhead light fixture. Light flooded the room.

Aaron stood in the middle of the room, fully clothed, rain glistening on his hair and jacket, his pallid cheeks flushed crimson, holding the Mace. He blinked at her, his soft brown eyes behind the large round glasses confused and frightened.

Twenty-Two

"Did you see him?" Roni said in a hoarse whisper that sounded strange to her own ears.

Aaron stared at her, twisting the flashlight. "Who?"

"I don't know. Anybody. Did you see . . . hear . . . anything?"

"I heard you scream."

She had screamed? She recalled saying Frank's name, but she wasn't aware that she had screamed.

"Why did you come back? I told you to get help."

"I didn't know where to go or who to go to."

She quickly came to her knees and turned to the bedside lamp. After twisting the light bulb the lamp came on. Someone unscrewed the bulb. "Someone was here . . . standing where you are now. I heard him. I heard him breathing."

"Breathing?" Aaron blinked again.

"Yes, breathing, wheezing." Roni pushed trembling fingers through her thick tangle of hair, every nerve in her body alive and jumping. She inhaled deeply, let it out slowly. "Someone I knew a long time ago breathed like that. He had asthma."

"The one who wore the bracelet?"

"Yes. *Yes.* Have you heard it before? The breathing?"

He shook his head.

"What then?" she said in exasperation. "Dammit, Aaron, what *do* you know?"

"I'll show you."

She stared hard at him.

"Come on." He backed up.

As she climbed out of bed and reached for her robe, she saw the sheet had been pulled from the mattress in the same place where the diary had been. She shivered, hugging herself. Someone had been *that* close to her while she slept. Not finding what he wanted to find in the first diary, had he come back looking for another? "Oh, Christ."

"You better get dressed," Aaron said. "Shoes . . . and a jacket, too."

"What? Wher—" Roni glanced at the clock. Three-fifty. "It's still dark out."

"It's always dark in the tunnels." He turned and walked out the door.

At the mention of the tunnel, Roni's insides twisted painfully.

She dressed quickly in jeans, tucking the oversized nightshirt inside, and slipped on her running shoes without socks. When she came out of her room, putting on her jacket, Aaron was sitting on the top step.

Minutes later, in the tiny basement, each manned with a flashlight, Aaron started down the ladder to the tunnel. He motioned for her to follow.

Oh shit, she groaned inwardly. Why did it have to involve the tunnel? Anywhere but the tunnel.

She gripped the flashlight, stepped forward, and stopped when a spasm racked her. She hadn't even made it to the ladder and that suffocating sensation was closing in.

"Aaron, I can't. I . . . I just can't."

He paused. "The rats?"

Rats? Oh brother, she hadn't thought of rats. Another valid reason to dread the tunnels. "Did your mother ever go down there?"

He shook his head violently. "She was scared, scared shitless of mice and rats."

That explained all the cats, Roni thought.

Aaron kept going.

"Wait. I'm coming," Roni said. "Give me a second, okay?" She deep-breathed a couple times.

Aaron was already at the bottom of the ladder when she started down. When she reached the tunnel floor he was moving away. She had to hurry to catch up. Smart kid, she thought, to keep her hopping—no time to think, no time to panic.

"What is it you want me to see?" she called out.

He continued without answering.

"How about a tiny hint? A game of twenty questions to pass the time?"

Down here the cold seemed colder, the odors of damp earth and rot sharper, the indistinguishable sounds louder and more frightening.

As they moved along the passage, she felt an uncomfortable tightness in her chest. Don't look back, she told herself. To see that square of blessed light disappear would be more than she could stand. She tried to breathe deeply to avoid hyperventilating. Pinpricks of anxiety jabbed at her.

She sensed the downhill slant of the brick tunnel. They passed an off-shoot passage, narrower and not shored, that ended a dozen feet in. After following the main tunnel for hundreds of feet, Aaron turned left into one of the off-shoots. She shone her light into it—it seemed endless.

Roni stopped abruptly, fear stabbing at her in great, thrusting jabs. Everyone had their oddball quirks, their phobias—for Roni it was dark, confined places that smelled of earth. It was one thing to blindly follow a young boy hundreds of feet under the ground, a young boy she hardly knew well enough to trust with her life, but to stray off the beaten path in this underground maze was—well, it was insanely stupid.

Ahead of her Aaron slowed, then turned around when he sensed she was no longer following. He looked at her quizzically.

She pulled the fleeced-lined jacket tightly around her. "This is far enough," she said, her voice shaky. "I want to know where we're going and why."

The beam of his flashlight played over a pile of bones and a tiny skull the size of a newborn infant. By the form of the skeleton, she knew it was not human.

"Cat?"

He nodded.

"Is that what you wanted me to see?"

He pointed with the light, deeper into the passageway, then resumed walking.

She clenched her fists, filled her lungs with stale air, and warily followed, wishing she was back in her bed—her bed in California.

When he turned down yet another off-shoot, one that angled back the way they had come, Roni rebelled. "Now look here, Aaron, that's it. No more. Uh-uh. I'm going bac—"

"There," he said.

Hesitantly she stepped forward and looked around the corner. Ten feet in, the beam bounced off a wall of silt—black, fine, and glittering in the white light.

"A dead end?" she asked. "You brought me all this way in the middle of the night to see a dead cat and a dead end?" The beam lowered to the ground to illuminate an old tennis shoe.

Roni inched her way down the passage, her own beam playing along the wall of silt to the shoe. The closer she got, the more apprehensive she was. Silt. Cave-in. Somewhere in time this passage had become weak, releasing a couple of tons of sandy earth to close a portion of the tunnel. Roni looked upward. Silt fell into her eyes, making her blink.

Her heart thumped, once, twice, then pounded like a thing independent of her own body. She had come this far, maybe she could . . .

"This is where I found the bracelet," Aaron said.

"But you said your mother—"

"I gave it to her, she gave it back . . . later."

She squatted, poised to run if just a smidgen of that wall shifted or looked like it would move. She wrapped her fingers around the yellowed canvas shoe and lifted it. She felt resistance—the silt higher on the mound began to funnel down. Frightened, the shoe clutched in her hand, Roni pulled back and fell against the rough wall. Something inside the shoe rattled. Bones, tiny bones spilled from the shoe onto her lap.

God! Roni swiped at the small bones as if they were living creatures—slugs or maggots. She shuddered uncontrollably. Above her, sand and debris sprinkled down.

She panicked. Only one thought registered in her mind: she had to get out of there. It would all come down and she'd be crushed by a mountain of earth.

Scrambling to her feet, she ran blindly.

The beam bobbed and darted about on the walls. She turned at the first corner, ran, turned again, then once more, thinking only of getting out. When she reached the main tunnel she felt a tremendous relief.

Aaron. She had left him behind.

She stopped abruptly, gasping for air.

"Aaron!" she called hoarsely. The word reverberated off the walls. "Aaron, where are you? *Aaron?*" Before she could stop herself, she spun around and rushed back the way she had come. At the second off-shoot she turned again. Only a few feet in she stopped, certain now that she had turned too soon.

Listening, she heard sounds. Footsteps. The acoustics in the tunnel had a hollow quality. She couldn't tell where the footsteps were coming from—which direction. She stood uncertainly in the center of a T-shaped junction. With her flashlight, she twisted around, the beam catching the sameness of the walls.

"Aaron?" she said softly.

And then the sound was behind her, on top of her. Suddenly her head above her ear exploded in pain. The flashlight flew from her hand as she dropped to her knees. From the corner of her eye she glimpsed a dark boot. It hurt to lift her head. She heard a pounding, silt fell on her hands. Chunks of debris rained down on the top of her head and along her arched back.

She cried out when a blanket of dirt covered her. The footsteps thundered around her. Who was there? What were they doing? The pain in her head was unbearable. She forced herself to stay conscious. Struggled to rise. More debris fell.

She gasped, sucking in metallic-tasting silt. The wildest thought struck her. Accident prone. That's what she was, accident prone. Another trip to the doctor. More red licorice. Ropes and ropes of red licorice, and she didn't even like the crap.

Someone pulled on her arm. Too dazed to resist, she let herself be pulled to her feet and urged along, stumbling. A pale light bobbed at the ceiling. A moment later there was a whooshing roar. A powerful gust of air pushed stinging silt and chips of rock into her face. Roni covered her eyes with her arm.

She was sitting on the ground. Someone had her around the waist. She turned, groaning from the pain in her head, to find Aaron on his knees behind her. He looked as terrified as she felt.

With a light, gentle stroke, he brushed at the dirt coating her hair and shoulders.

She pulled him to her and hugged him tight. A moment later, hands clasped, they sat there in the shadowy, airless space, dust motes floating in the dim light like bits of fine glitter. He shone the flashlight beam into the passage. There was no passage. Where she had been seconds ago was now a wall of earth and jagged rocks.

Aaron helped her to her feet and led her out of the tunnel.

Twenty-Three

"You didn't just happen to stumble across this odd-ball find, now didya?" Sheriff Lubben asked Roni.

The electric coffee pot, perking madly, was in its final throes; a climactic serenade of sighs and moans. Predawn. They were gathered in the kitchen. Lubben, James, Aaron. The doctor, who had come over directly from a house call at the trailer park, was patching Roni's head.

After coming out of the tunnel, Roni had called James first, then the others. Aaron had led the sheriff, two deputies, and a miner experienced in mine shaft cave-ins to the skeletal remains in the tunnel. Roni couldn't bring herself to go back down that ladder.

A pair of cats chased each other around the kitchen. Lubben stomped his foot, clapped his hands, and they scattered. "You both out takin' a little tunnel stroll at four-oh-seven a.m.?" he asked, studying his digital watch.

Roni looked at Aaron. He sat on the floor leaning

against the broom closet with his knees drawn up and his chin tucked into his chest. He looked back at her through his upper lashes.

"Aaron stumbled upon it," she said.

Lubben turned to Aaron, glared down at him. "When was that, boy?"

"It had to be tonight," Roni rushed in. "He—"

"You—button it." Lubben waved a hand to silence her. Without taking his eyes from Aaron, he said, "Let *him*."

Roni saw James, who was sitting on the counter top, stiffen.

"When?" Lubben asked Aaron.

"T—Tonight." His voice was faint.

Lubben swung around to Roni and said, "Ever since you come to town things've been poppin'. You, girl, got enough cuts and scrapes on you to keep the doc busy without him havin' no other patients. You accident prone or what?"

Roni wanted to laugh, but didn't.

He swung back to Aaron. "So tonight was sight-seein' night? Did a little explorin', didya? Probably been traipsin' that passageway for years, but tonight was the big discovery."

Aaron looked down.

"I heard something," Roni said. "I woke up and . . . someone was in my bedroom. Aaron came when I screamed and he must have scared them off. We decided to look in the tunnel for . . . for whoever was in the house. Aaron was the first to find them . . . the bones."

The sheriff grunted, moved to the counter, lifted the coffeepot, and poured a cup.

Dr. Burke patted Roni's shoulder. "The laceration is superficial, but you got a dandy bump there, young lady. I'll want X-rays."

The younger of the two deputies entered the kitchen. "We've got the remains and we're ready to bring them out. You want to double-check the crime scene, Sheriff?"

"What the hell's to double-check, Deming?" Lubben growled. "The crime scene's a dozen years old. *If* it ever was a crime scene. Folks been stirrin' up dust down there for nearly an hour. Bring 'em up, for chrissake."

"Yes, sir."

"Crime scene, *Jesus*," Lubben said with a disgusted snort.

"You don't think there was foul play here?" Roni asked.

"Foul play?" He turned to her, holding the coffee mug like a beer stein. "Hell yes, I think there was foul play. Y'know what else I think? I think that Scolli boy did somethin' so terrible in this house that he made a run for it and in his panic to get away, he took a wrong turn down there and brought the place down around his head. *That's* what I think."

"So you're saying it's Frank?" James said.

"Who else we got missin' around here?"

Roni poured coffee, passed out the mugs, set sugar and milk on the table. At the sink she cooled her coffee with tap water, then turned and leaned on the counter next to James.

"How'd you get that goose egg?" Lubben asked Roni.

She touched the knot above her ear and winced. "Someone hit me."

All eyes turned toward her.

"I saw the body, I, ah . . . I guess I panicked. I'm not real comfortable in tight, dark places and the sight of the corpse . . . of Frank under all that—the silt shifted and, well, I sorta freaked out and ran. When I got to the main tunnel I realized that Aaron wasn't with me so I went back looking for him. I must have made a wrong turn." She cleared her throat. She felt James touch her, a light comforting touch at her lower back. "Someone clobbered me and the passage gave way. Aaron pulled me out." Her eyes caught his briefly before he looked away. He had risked his life to save her.

Lubben chuckled. "More likely a fallin' boulder clobbered you just before a section of that passage came down around you."

"This boulder was wearing black boots."

"Like mine?" Lubben said dryly. His boots, though dusty from moving around in the tunnel, were black. "Or, the doc's, or Mr. Glazer there?"

Everyone in the room except Aaron had on black footwear—even she wore black athletic shoes.

One of the two deputies, carrying the remains wrapped in plastic sheeting, its lack of weight apparent by the ease with which he toted it, came through the doorway into the kitchen. The miner followed. More black boots.

"I think we got all of him," Deputy Deming said. "We might've missed a few small bones. Cripes, I thought skeletons stayed all together like ol' Jesse in the doc's office."

"Would be nice if they did," the doctor mumbled.

"Well, we know where to look if anythin' comes up missin'," the sheriff added wryly.

In the dining room the phone rang. Lubben got it. "Yeah, yeah, appreciate it, doctor. I'll have one of my boys pick you up at the airfield. Couple hours? That give you enough time? Done, then."

"Pathologist?" Dr. Burke asked Lubben.

"Andrews. Elko's finest."

"That's a matter of opinion."

Lubben took a long look at the doctor. "Now, Doc, you didn't want this one for yourself, didya?"

"No, Sheriff. If there's any question of foul play, especially where the Scollis are concerned, I'll leave it to the experts. I'm content working with the living." He smiled at Roni.

The other deputy entered carrying a small plastic bag, the sort used for merchandise. "Found this in the basement, tossed in the corner by the ladder. Looks like someone's trash."

Lubben made a move toward it.

Before the sheriff could take it, Aaron scrambled to his feet and rushed to the deputy, grabbing the bag. "It's mine."

"Sez who?" Lubben got a hand around the bag. "Let's have a look."

Aaron's face contorted, his eyes behind the round glasses blazing with indignant outrage as he struggled to retrieve his property. "Let go . . . goddammit, it's mine. Let gooo!"

"Hey, now!" Lubben grasped the boy by the shoulder, his blunt fingers digging into the thin flesh and bones. "You just better cool yourself down, boy. An' watch that filthy mouth. Your mama mighta let you get away with murder, but I sure as hell don't have to."

Roni moved to side with Aaron.

James jumped from the counter and put an arm out, halting her. To Lubben he said, "Leave him alone. Whatever's in that bag has nothing to do with this." James nodded toward the plastic sheeting. "The kid's entitled to his privacy."

"I'm the law around here. This is my town, Mr. Travelin' Hotshot Geologist. It's me who'll decide what's got to do with what. Nothin's private in an alleged criminal investigation. That was near the crime scene."

"Crime scene? What crime scene?" James asked sarcastically.

"I never said there weren't no crime. It's Frank what committed the crime. Frank died by bringin' the tunnel down around hisself."

"Then there can't possibly be anything in that sack—"

Aaron had tried to yank the bag from Lubben's hand. The sheriff let go and the bag's contents spilled onto the floor.

Scattered about were bits of concrete, wood, plaster, paper, clumps of dirt, gravel, twigs, berries, scraps of soiled cloth, hair clippings in various shades, and even a dead rodent—road killed, by its desiccate, flat appearance.

The room was deadly quiet.

"Garbage," Lubben snorted in disgust. He poked at a pile with his boot. "A rag picker."

Aaron, his face crimson, turned and ran from the room.

"Aaron!" Roni called after him. She turned on Lubben. "Damn you. What is it with you and him?" Without waiting for an answer she knelt and began to stuff the things back into the bag.

"Look, you said he gave you the bracelet. That means he was diggin' around down there. How was I to know he didn't have more evidence in that bag?"

"You wouldn't know evidence if it grabbed you by the throat and shook you. For a dozen years Frank is buried right under your nose. You had to know the tunnel was there. Why wasn't it thoroughly searched when Frank disappeared?''

"You're the big *investigative reporter*. You tell me. Maybe I oughta turn this case over to you . . . let you solve it.''

"Maybe I will. Maybe that's what it'll take. Maybe that's why I'm here . . .'' The words spewed out. "Maybe—ah *shit!*'' She turned away, her hand covering her eyes.

"Let's get outta here,'' Lubben said to his deputies.

As the men crossed the kitchen with Deputy Deming in the lead carrying the remains, the door flew open and almost knocked Deming off his feet. Dean Scolli charged in. He looked from one person to another before his gaze dropped to the plastic sheeting, then said, "At the mine, one of the drillers said Crow was called out here to dig a corpse out of the tunnel. What the hell—'' His eyes swept from the miner to the bundle to the kitchen table where the breath inhaler, medical bracelet, and canvas shoe sat. Dean took it all in in one volatile moment.

He stepped in front of the man carrying the bundle. "Put it down.''

"I don't think you wanna see,'' the sheriff said quietly.

"Fuck what you think. Put it down, Deming!''

The doctor went to Dean and laid a hand on his rigid arm. "Dean, wait until—''

"What?!'' Dean said, his voice rising. "Wait for what? What's in there? A corpse? I've seen dead people before. Is my brother in there? If that's Frank then I've waited too fucking long already.''

The doctor looked to Lubben, who nodded and looked away.

"Let him see."

Deming laid the bundle on the worn tiles and tentatively began to unwrap it. Dean squatted, elbowed the deputy away, took a corner, and pulled it down. Roni saw a scrap of material and what she thought might be a portion of the skull—a brown, leathery orb, covered with patches of long, dark hair.

She looked away, bile rising in her throat. It was hard to believe that what was in that sheet of plastic, now reduced to bones, cloth, and hair, was once a friend of hers. For the past twelve years while she raced around the country, working, playing, living, Frank lay buried beneath the streets of the only town he'd ever known, a town he couldn't wait to leave.

Dean solemnly stared down at the grotesque remains of his younger brother, a brother whose life had ended at the tender age of sixteen.

Dr. Burke placed a consoling hand on Dean's shoulder. "You shouldn't be seeing him like this, son. You should remember him the way he was."

"Someone bashed his head in," Dean said in a voice barely controllable.

Twenty-Four

Dean rose to his feet, stumbling backward, batting away the doctor's arm. "Someone fuckin' bashed his face in!"

"What're you talking about?" Lubben moved in and stared down at the remains. "You can't know that for sure till the coroner's had a look. He was caught in a cave-in. Things ain't always what they appear to be."

"Doc?" With eyes wild and filling with tears, Dean spun around and pointed at the skull. "What's that look like to you?"

The doctor stared down. "Dean, the sheriff has a point. Until—"

"Either you don't know shit about bones and concussions, which makes you a quack, or you're trying to cover up something. Which is it, Doc?"

"Dammit, Dean, no one's trying to cover up anything. I admit there are signs of blunt trauma to the facial skeleton, to the temporal region in particular.

But one can't jump to conclusions without all the facts. A pathologist from Elko is flying in to examine your bro—"

"I want to be there."

"Forget it, Dean, this here's police—" the sheriff began.

Dean slammed a fist down on the table, then in a wild gesture he swept the sugar bowl onto the floor. He whirled around, fists clenched. "I got every right to be there," he said tightly to Lubben. "We believed you. You and your fucking reports about hippies, a van, and someone who looked like Frank getting dropped off in Reno that night. Shit, was you who claimed to see Frank running from this house."

"That wasn't no lie." The sheriff stood his ground. He cocked his head and pointed a finger at Dean. "You calm down, y'hear? You just better get a grip or, by God, Scolli, you'll be spending time in jail. We can take you in right now if that's what you want. That what you want, Scolli?"

The two men glared at each other. The seconds ticked away, the tension in the room palpable enough to taste. *Would this night never end?* Roni asked herself.

"He was my brother . . ." Dean said quietly.

"I know he was. And I'm sorry. We're all sorry. But acting up like this gets you nowhere. Your ma and pa gotta be told. Why don'tcha go on home and do that? 'Less, of course, you want me to be the one to . . ."

"Shit, if I leave it up to you, it could be another twelve years before the news reaches them." Dean lowered his head, his tone incredulous. "Twelve years. Frank . . . right here in Eagleton all the time."

Dean looked at Roni, an unreadable expression on his face. He opened his mouth as if to say something, then closed it and walked out. She knew he would be back to say whatever had been left unsaid.

No one moved for several moments, then the room came alive.

"Roni, I want you at the clinic today for X-rays," the doctor said as he left.

Lubben waved at the deputies to get going, then gathered Frank's personal items from the table. After his men had filed out with the body, Lubben paused at the door, lit a cigarette, and said, "If Frank *was* killed by someone's hand, me and the boys'll be back to sift through that dirt, so stay outta the tunnel. That goes double for the boy."

"I'll tell him," Roni said. Personally, she had no intention of going back down there—ever.

He started to leave, then turned back. "That kid ain't even a teen yet and he's out all hours of the night. We got curfew here the same as any other town. If he's up to no good . . ."

"Has he ever caused you any problems?" James asked.

Lubben glared at him, then went out, leaving the door open. Beyond the door the dawn sky to the east glowed several shades of pastel.

She and James were alone in the kitchen. Roni took two aspirins, then stood at the sink rubbing her temples.

"Headache?" James said.

"Ummm."

Strong fingers slid up her back and began to knead her neck and shoulders. His hands seemed to be always near, touching, caressing, almost an unconscious act. Was he this attentive, this demonstrative, to all women? She forced herself to relax, to let his skillful fingers work their magic on her bunched and knotted muscles. James was with her. His strength and cool-headedness would help guide her. He was an ally, a friend.

After several minutes of massage the tension began to slip away like the passing of darkness to dawn. She ached to be in his arms, to feel his strong, energizing hands comforting, caressing her, his lips . . .

Roni opened her eyes and stared at her dirt-smudged reflection in the window above the sink. Brushing at her chin, she said, "I look like a coalminer after a hard day."

James took a clean cloth from a drawer, dampened it, and began to gently sponge her cheek and nose. When he got to her chin he paused. "It did scar, didn't it? I thought it might."

"You remember that?"

He leaned down and put his lips to the fine, white line. Then his mouth covered hers.

She loved the way he kissed. Controlled, yet stirring; a hunger born from something deeper than mere passion. The heat of mingling tongues and moist, silky flesh blending liquid fire from one to the other, yet beneath his masterful lips, his secure embrace, she sensed a variable excitement rippling through his body.

With the counter at her back, he leaned into her. She felt him growing hard against the soft plane of her abdomen. His hand slid up the side of her T-shirt, brushing over a breast, the nipple taut and erect, aching to be caressed.

The turbulent air in the room changed again. Cooled.

They were not alone.

As difficult as being roused from a deep sleep, Roni broke the kiss, opened her eyes, and looked to the kitchen doorway. Aaron stood in the arch looking small and vulnerable. But as uncomfortable as he appeared, he refused to move away. His eyes seemed feverish, wounded.

Roni chewed at her lower lip. She glanced uneasily at James. They parted, self-consciously pulling at their clothes and brushing at their hair.

"Aaron, what is it?" Roni asked, going to him.

"Will I get in trouble for showing you the body?"

"In trouble with who?"

"Sheriff Lubben. Will he arrest me?"

"No, of course not."

"He scares me."

"Me, too," she whispered.

He stared at her with innocent, brown eyes. "Are you . . . okay?"

"I'm okay. Yeah, Aaron, I'm just fine."

He came into the room and sat at the table. "I'm hungry. Can we have breakfast now?"

James and Roni looked at each other.

Was Aaron afraid for her?

Roni turned to James, lifting her arms in a gesture of helplessness.

"Well, it looks like you're in good hands here . . ." James began.

"We'll be okay," Aaron said.

"Sure. Then I'll be going. I should have been at the mine half an hour ago."

Roni walked him out. On the back porch James pulled the door closed behind them and moved her to the side, away from the glass panes. Without Aaron's probing eyes, he slowly, gently pulled Roni into his arms. He held her to him; just held her, swaying slightly. She buried her face into the warm hollow at the side of his neck. And was afraid. Afraid because of her renewed feelings for him.

They separated, the brisk morning air chilling her instantly. As she reentered the kitchen, she heard his soles on the gravel drive, heard him greet Red.

Aaron sat watching her.

Roni hugged herself. "Aaron . . . thanks."

"What for?"

"You probably saved my life down there. I took off and left you, but you helped me and . . . well, I . . ."

"It's okay," he said, looking down modestly. "You got scared. You came back."

She smiled. "Breakfast, huh?" Looking around, she shoved her hands into the back pockets of her jeans and felt more fine grit. Everything about her felt gritty. "I have to jump in the shower. Can it wait a couple minutes?"

He nodded. But the tense way he held his body and the strange look in his eyes as he watched her leave the room made Roni wonder what he was thinking.

Over the smell of soap, shampoo, and the thick cloud of steam in the bathroom, Roni smelled bacon frying.

Several minutes later, dressed in a clean pair of jeans and a sweatshirt, her damp hair combed back, she entered the kitchen to find bacon, scrambled eggs, and toast on the table. The spilled sugar was gone.

Aaron poured hot water over tea bags. "The coffee-pot was empty and I only know how to make tea," he said.

She approached slowly, taking everything in. She grinned. "You've been holding out on me. I've only seen you eat out of boxes and cans."

"I didn't feel like cooking, and anyway, that's all there was. My mom didn't like to cook, so I taught myself. She said I was the best damned short-order cook in the state."

"She loved to bake though. Her shortbread cookies were not to be believed." The moment the words were out of her mouth, Roni was sorry, wondering if being reminded of those special days she spent with his mother would upset him.

The corner of his lips turned upward ever so slightly. "Did she ever make cream puffs for you? Those were the best."

"No," she said truthfully. "She never made me cream puffs."

"She taught me. Maybe I'll make them sometime."

"I'd like that."

They began to eat. Roni watched Aaron when she thought he wasn't looking. His manners were impeccable, the polite gestures making him appear even more waif-like. He was wasting his young, formidable years squirreled away in this enormous, dilapidated house. Precious years that should be spent playing outdoors in the sunlight with kids his own age. He should climb trees and swim in creeks and swipe fruit from neighboring orchards. He should have high color in his cheeks and scabs on his knees and tummy-aches from too much cotton candy and junk at the fair. He should hit a baseball out of the park, ride a bike with no hands, and wave a sparkler on a July night.

He should be a boy.

When he finished, Aaron lowered his fork and said

adamantly, "I'm not a rag picker. I don't go through people's trash because I get a kick out of it like that jerkoff sheriff said."

"It doesn't matter, Aaron."

"Yes, it does."

"I know you're not a rag picker."

He nodded and drank down his tea.

"He *is* a jerkoff, isn't he?" Roni said, delicately wiping her mouth. "A class A a-hole, too."

Aaron looked at her and smiled. He had a beautiful smile. He neatly smoothed out his paper napkin, the smile vanished, and he became somber. "He was my mother's friend. But I think she was afraid of him."

"Why was she afraid?"

Aaron began to toy with his fork, pushing on the tines and watching the handle rise. Roni sighed inwardly. Her years of journalistic training and interviewing did not prepare her for this young man's evasiveness. Though she was getting used to his habit of doling out information in minuscule bits, she still found it exasperating. *Don't push.*

Roni sat back, sighed in a satiated way, and said, "That was probably the best meal I've had in a long, long time. I've always had trouble cooking breakfast . . . y'know, getting it all to come out at the same time without something getting cold. Do you make the toast before the eggs?"

"At the same time."

"That's where I lose it. The eggs overcook, the toast gets cold, and the butter won't melt. This . . ." she pointed at her empty plate, "was perfection."

He looked pleased, but said nothing.

She rose, gathering her dishes to take to the sink.

"If Mom knew he was coming over, she'd get nervous," he said, as if there'd been no break in the conversation. "She'd drink the stuff she kept in that fancy glass thing."

Aaron was like a watched pot. "The decanter? Brandy?" Roni stood clutching the dishes, forgotten in her hands.

He nodded. "She would drink it down real fast before he came."

Roni eased back into her chair. "How did he treat her?"

"He was okay. Nice, I guess. Not like he treats everybody else."

"Do you think he was nice because he loved her?"

"I guess. Yeah, that was probably it." Aaron pushed on the bowl of the spoon; the handles of the utensils parried. "He watched all the time."

"Watched? I don't understand."

"The whole time he was here, he'd watch her. Watched everything she did. It really made her uptight. Her hands would shake, even. Funny, but he looked uptight, too. Wouldn't talk to her. Just watched her."

"What did they do . . . when they were together?"

"They had tea and most times she played the piano."

Not without a degree of difficulty could Roni picture Hank Lubben sitting on one of the delicate Queen Anne chairs listening to Brahms or Chopin with a teacup cradled in those crushing hands. She could only sustain the image for a moment before it was gone. *Beauty and the Beast.*

"And where were you during these rather inconceivable soirees?"

"She made me stay in the room with them till he left. Sometimes I had to play."

Roni wondered if Aaron's forced chaperoning

hadn't turned the sheriff against him. Had Caroline used her child to harness the attentions of her most ardent and unlikely suitor? How successful had she been? How determined had Lubben been? It was obvious the man disliked the boy.

Something Aaron just said abruptly brought Roni back to the present. She focused on his glasses. "What?"

"I said, I found the bones and then I told my mom about them."

Caroline's words came back to her: *Something has happened recently to compel me to write you . . . I don't know who I can trust in this town . . . I'm afraid . . . afraid for Aaron and myself.*

"So your mother knew? When? When did you find . . . Frank?"

"Not too long ago. It was the day after the Fourth of July. I remember because there was a lotta good stuff in the trash and still on the streets after the parade. I even found some fireworks that didn't go off."

"What made you go into that particular part of the tunnel?"

He looked sheepish and lowered his gaze. "I wanted to light the fireworks."

"You went that far back?"

"Well, no, I heard one of the cats meowing. I went to see if it was in trouble. It was Schumann, the big manx. He was digging around the shoe."

"Is that when you found the bracelet?"

"Uh-huh."

"So you showed it to your mother and told her where you found it. Did she call the sheriff?"

He shook his head vehemently.

"Did she tell anyone?"

"Not right away—she said she had to think. Then she hired this guy to find you and that's when she wrote you a letter."

Now they were getting somewhere.

Roni pushed the dishes away, put her elbows on the table, and buried her fingers into her damp hair.

Caroline didn't trust the sheriff with their discovery, yet she wanted someone she could trust to be privy to it. So many mysteries, old and new, surrounded this house, the town, and the people in it.

She raised her head and stared at Aaron. He must have felt the intensity of her gaze for he stopped playing with his utensils and looked at her quizzically.

"What is it I'm supposed to do?" she asked. "Am I supposed to solve Frank's murder?"

He nodded once. "And my mother's murder, too."

Twenty-Five

Tuesday

James piloted the small Cessna four-seater deftly despite the turbulence from the extreme weather. He'd had his pilot's license for five years and still experienced a certain thrill when in control of an aircraft. The mining company employed their own planes and James flew them often, but this was private business, so the expensive single-engine green and white Turbo belonged to his friend Faddle Granville, Eagleton's mayor, attorney, rancher, pilot, and most eligible bachelor. Landing in the storm wouldn't be much of a problem, but he suspected by the time he'd finished his business downtown, visibility at the small airport would be zero.

James was on his way to Colorado to check on his brother.

That morning he tried to reach Larry again at the boarding house where he had lived since coming out of rehab nearly five years ago. The phone, Larry's own private line, had been disconnected. James didn't know the landlady's number.

His brother and his father: whereabouts unknown. His brother he wanted to find. His father could rot in hell. What little there was between them died the day his father snatched him and Larry from the arms of their mother and fled with them to America. Once on U.S. soil they lived hand to mouth in one dismal mining town after another. From the time James was eight, care of his baby brother fell solely on his shoulders. They were left alone, sometimes for weeks on end, with a few dollars that James learned to stretch to buy food and necessities. On the freezing nights when there was little to eat and he huddled close to Larry's thin, icy body, he thought of his mother and her soft, loving embrace, and his hatred for his father flowed like liquid fire in his veins, warming him.

After landing in a small airfield outside of Boulder, James went straight to the boarding house on Barrel Street. A sign in the window read: ROOM FOR LET. The landlady, a large woman with a button nose and watery, red-rimmed eyes, a dishtowel draped over one shoulder, spoke to him in the vestibule.

"Larry moved out, let's see, two, three days ago."

"You evicted him?"

"Nope. Left on his own before I had to. Your brother's a nice boy, but he has that problem. It's such a shame, too."

"Problem?" James asked, already knowing the answer.

"The drinking. Got him fired from the mine. He could really tie one on when he set his mind to it. I found him right there one morning, passed out cold under the stairwell."

"Where did he go?"

"Somewhere in Nevada. Vegas or Reno."

"Do you have an address?"

"Just a phone number." She went inside her apartment, returned with a slip of paper, and gave it to him.

"What makes you think either Reno or Vegas?" James asked.

"It was a major city, so it had to be one or the other. I remember thinking how free-wheeling they are with drinks in those big gaming places, handing out tokes right and left. Thinking he should maybe go someplace like Utah, where it's dry."

"Why'd he give you his number?"

"He'd bought a second-hand car. The ownership certificate is coming here. He asked me to contact him soon as it arrived. Said he'd let me know where to mail it on." She clucked, shaking her head. "Personally, I doubt that old clunker even made it to the state line. Sorry piece of shit. Oops, pardon my grammar. It's being around these dang miners—mouths like truckers."

"How much did he owe you?"

"Owe me?—oh, you mean rent? Well, he was paying by the week and there was just that one week . . ."

"How much?" He opened his wallet.

"Forty should cover it. He was a good boarder, quiet most of the time and kept the room neat—'cept for the Miller cans. Tell you the truth, I hated to see him go. Liked to play rummy with me."

"Any idea why he left the state?"

"Said it was time he moved on. Something bad was catching up to him."

"Larry said that?"

She nodded solemnly. "I don't remember the exact

words, but that was pretty much the gist of it. Hope he's not in trouble with the police." She chuckled. "Y'know, I was watching one of those FBI shows one night and damned if I didn't see the fella that lived in 1B right there in living color on my Sony. He saw it, too, and got out quick. Left all his stuff behind . . ." She leaned in and whispered, "Dirty pictures and sex toys. Cops got it now."

James handed her the money. "Looks like the airport might be socked in. Got an extra room for the night?"

She took the money, counted it out, and gave him a wide smile. "Take your brother's room—2A, top of the stairs."

At a pay phone outside a convenience store a block away, James placed a call to the number in Nevada. An answering machine picked up and the voice of a woman repeated the number, then instructed the caller to leave a message. James left his name and number.

He dialed Roni's number, got her machine, but hung up without leaving a message.

Déjà-vu. She felt fifteen again, sitting in the cold, metal folding chair, the big, bad sheriff leaning over his desk, upper body braced on stiff arms, staring intently at her. The same office, the same mounted cutthroat trout and mule deer racks on the wall, the same roping and cutting trophies and local organization plaques. Even the subject was the same: the Holt place and Frank Scolli. The only difference was that Larry wasn't waiting on a bench in the hallway, and she, Roni Mayfield, was no longer a frightened teenager. Although, she had to admit, Lubben still had the ability to browbeat her.

"Until you showed up, everything was peaceful and quiet, not a licka trouble," Lubben said. "Now all hell's about to break loose. You have any idea what that body turning up this morning is gonna do to this town? The Scollis are respected business folks around here and a hot-headed bunch to boot. I don't envy you and the boy right now. Shit, I don't envy *me.* A lotta flack's gonna come my way, too."

"What was I supposed to do, keep quiet about what we found?"

He ignored her question. "You listen up, if you know anything, *anything*, by Jesus, I want to hear it."

"Let's level with each other. Was there an autopsy done on Caroline Holt?"

Lubben's head snapped up. He glared at her.

"Well, was there?"

"Doc took care of that," Lubben said.

"You know that for sure?"

"If I'd thought there was any question . . . 'specially of homicide, I'da looked into it."

"Isn't there always a question of reasonable doubt in cases of suicide?"

"Miss Mayfield," he said tightly, "don't let my manner of speaking and my hayseed appearance give you the impression I don't know how to conduct a proper investigation. Caroline killed herself."

"Convince me." Roni knew she was walking the razor's edge, but she couldn't stop herself.

After a moment of silence in which Lubben seemed to be collecting himself, he finally said, "Weren't no sign of forced entry. No signs of struggle. She lay in her bed, her arms crossed over her wedding picture, the weapon at her side. She was real peaceful-like. Murder victims, 'specially those been knifed, don't lay still waiting to bleed to death."

"What if she'd been drugged first?"

"Possible, but not likely."

"You could have her body exhumed and find out."

"Now look who ain't being so smart. And what if her body was full of drugs? Who's to say she didn't take them herself to relax before slicing her wrists? In fact, if we was to find barbiturates in her, the combination itself points to suicide. Case you ain't heard, it's called the *insurance factor*."

Roni hated to admit he was right. She'd once written an article on depression and suicide. Many victims, she learned, doubled up on methods of death. Booze and pills. Pills and carbon monoxide. One man had cut his wrists and throat, then jumped off an ocean pier where scavenger sharks were known to gather. The article had been titled, "Overkill."

"What convinced me was the hesitation marks," he was saying.

Roni looked at him and waited.

"When someone is gonna cut themselves, they make a couple test nicks . . . to see how sharp the knife is, to muster up courage, whatever. Hesitation marks."

"And she had these?"

"On her left wrist." He raised his own wrist and pointed. "Right there and there."

The phone on his desk rang. Lubben snatched at the receiver, his eyes remaining on her face. He grunted, then swiveled around with his back to her. She heard him mention Coggins Airfield which made her think of James. He had called that morning to say he had to fly out of town for a day or two on important business and he'd call when he returned.

Lubben swiveled back. "Yeah? Yeah. You're goddamn right I wanna be there. On my way." He hung up, stood, and put on his hat. "You're so big on autopsies, wanna go to one?"

It wasn't necessary to ask whose. She stood. "Yes."

The remains occupied a metal table in the embalming room of Crawford's Funeral Home adjacent to the clinic. The body, reduced to bones and bits of adhering leathery flesh, did not require a stainless steel table, for there would be no draining of bodily fluids, no Y-shape incision to the chest, no tissue, organs, or brain to remove and dissect. But protocol was protocol and this was the way it was done.

When Roni and Lubben entered the room they were met by Dr. Burke who then introduced them to Dr. Andrews. The pathologist, a tiny man in his sixties with a Gene Wilder head of dishwater-blond frizz, merely nodded. Roni sensed his annoyance.

"You should have mentioned the popularity of a post-mortem in Eagleton, Dr. Burke. We could have performed it on stage at the opera house."

"I had no idea . . ." Burke's gaze swept those entering and ended up staring solemnly into the corner where Dean Scolli leaned against a metal cabinet.

"Dean—" Lubben began.

"If she stays, I stay." Dean jerked his chin toward Roni.

"Jeez Christ," Lubben muttered as he turned to Dr. Andrews. "Doc, you want 'em out? It's up to you."

"Is anyone going to pass out?" The pathologist glanced from Dean to Roni. "If there are any faint hearts or weak stomachs, then leave now. There's no room in here to be stepping over bodies."

Roni and Dean stood their ground.

"Are you sure you're up to this, young lady?" Dr. Burke said to Roni. "We should be in X-ray getting pictures of that bump on your noggin."

"I'd like to stay," she said quietly.

A moment later she wondered if she hadn't made a mistake as a tremor rippled along her spine. In the harsh, glaring light of the embalming room the corpse looked grotesque. And if that weren't enough, her mind began to play tricks on her. Like a hologram, an image of the flesh-and-blood Frank, superimposed over the skeleton, flashed repeatedly. Her throat tightened and she found it difficult to swallow.

If she concentrated real hard she could pretend the remains on the table belonged to a stranger, not to someone she had known and cared about, someone who had saved her life and who she had kissed once during a game of spin the bottle in his father's storage room. If she concentrated real hard . . .

Get a grip, she told herself, bracing her feet and breathing deeply. A moment later her heartbeat began to steady and slow its wild thumping.

The pathologist had reconstructed the bones to form a full-length individual. Like a jigsaw puzzle, gaps indicated the many missing pieces. With a magnifying glass, he studied the skeleton. He spoke aloud, going through the examination procedure. Dr. Burke made notations on a clipboard. "Male, young adult . . . just under six feet."

The doctor's gloved hands skillfully poked and

prodded the skeleton, loosening more silt and scraps of rotten fabric. These particular bones were brown, he explained, due to the absence of light and weather elements. Aside from the canvas shoes and durable Levis which were both remarkably intact, all that remained of Frank's cotton T-shirt was the ribbed-neckline and, oddly enough, the air-brushed painting on the front.

The art work, a seventies fad of "muscle" cars and trucks with balloon tires and outrageous accessories, brought back instant memories. As a form of identification, that particular shirt was as good as a signature. It was Frank's favorite. It was taken off, washed, and put right back on. She closed her eyes and she could see Frank in the tree, the plastic straps of his binoculars swinging against the bright caricature of a monster-driven hotrod. With crystal clarity she saw his face close up, his mouth stretch into a wide grin.

Suddenly a profound wave of sadness washed over her. Someone moaned. She realized the sound had come from her when the pathologist looked up at her with a "don't you dare" glare.

"The dental records are on the way, Doc," Lubben said. "Gotta make sure everythin's done accordin' to Hoyle. How long you think this'll take?"

"Not long," Dr. Andrews said. "With a general autopsy there would've been plenty to do. Had there been internal organs, even preserved in a mummified state, I would have inspected the stomach contents for an approximate time of death. Soil from the recovery site in the lungs or oral cavity could have suggested he died after the shaft caved in. Lividity—that's the body's blood sinking to the lowest point—is essential in determining if the body had been moved after death. But alas, we have virtually no organs to speak

of, decomposition as it was, so I'm afraid this is it."
He gently lifted the skull.

He sighed dramatically. He had the audience and
the ball and he was running with it. "The skull—
what's left of it, that is—will have to do. And it certainly tells a story." He carefully turned it. "Of course,
I'm no forensic anthropologist, but in my opinion
the cause of death resulted from acute trauma to the
frontal and temporal region of the skull . . ." he said
as he pointed to the forehead and temple where
pieces of bone were missing. ". . . And not from
asphyxiation. These injuries are quite sufficient to
cause death."

"Could the tunnel comin' down on top of him,
with y'know, bricks and big rocks, cause head injuries
like that?" Lubben asked.

Dr. Andrews pushed out his bottom lip and shook
his head. "Not likely. These small pieces of the skull
were recovered." He lifted a plastic bag with several
quarter-to-half-dollar-sized bone fragments. "If we
had all the pieces they could be fitted together, very
much like a puzzle, to reconstruct the skull. But I
doubt it's necessary. By the size and number of the
recovered fragments, I feel confident saying that this
man was struck repeatedly. Look here," he pointed
to a crack in the ulna near the wrist. "a common
fracture sustained by someone attempting to ward off
a blow." He raised his arm to his face to demonstrate.
"The weapon was something heavy with a small base
. . . a hammer or wrench, or . . ."

"Fireplace poker?" Roni asked, feeling weak again.

"Ummm," he bobbed his head. "Yes, I'd say that'd
be consistent with this type of injury."

Roni turned to Dean. "The poker is missing from
the bedroom fireplace tools."

Lubben pulled Roni around to face him, his eyes flashing in anger. "Dammit, talk to *me*, not him. Who the hell's in charge around here?"

She stared at him, her own anger rising. That was a good question, a very good question. Who *was* in charge? So far she, James and Aaron—and Caroline, a dead woman—seemed to be doing most of the sheriff's job. How could he have been so blind to what now seemed so obvious?

Unless . . .

Lubben pressed. "What else do you know? The boy tell you somethin'? You find somethin' Caroline left behind? Somethin' she wrote down, maybe?" His fingers squeezed her upper arms.

She pulled away, saying tightly, "If I learn anything, if I find anything, I'll be sure to let you know."

They stared hard at each other.

Dr. Andrews broke the silence. "I'd say you have a criminal case here, Sheriff. I'd like to finish up, if I may . . . and without a host of bickering viewers. Dr. Burke, as soon as those dental records show up I'd like to see them."

They all filed out.

In the hall Dean turned on Lubben, his face a cold, stony mask. "What now, Sheriff? And, believe me, I use the title loosely."

"You look here, Mr. Scolli, I know that's kin in there an' I know you're hurtin', but I won't put up with no disrespect. No, sir. I'm gonna do whatever it takes to get to the bottom of this. We'll comb the tunnel for the weapon. If it's there we'll find it. But I don't want nobody buttin' in and gettin' folks riled or excited, not you or the rest of your hot-tempered bunch, y'hear?"

"You do your job—like you should've done twelve

years ago—and nobody will interfere. But if I think you're backstroking or treading water, I'm in it. And you'll be answering to somebody. Do *you* hear?''

"Don't threaten, Scolli."

The two men, equal in size and bulk, stood toe-to-toe like a pair of pit bulls about to go at it.

Dr. Burke gently separated them. "I've got enough patching up to do around here without taking on two more. Come on, fellas, give me a break." He turned to Dean, placed a consoling hand on his shoulder. "Son, Dr. Andrews will probably be done soon. That means your brother's remains will then be released. You and your family will want to start making arrangements for burial, if you haven't already."

Scolli broke eye contact with Lubben and lowered his head. He nodded, then turned and walked out.

The sheriff was left standing in the hall while Dr. Burke escorted Roni to the clinic across the street.

Ten minutes later, the X-rays taken, the doctor checked Roni's eyes and asked her about dizziness, double vision, nausea, or headache. "I'm worried about you, Roni. Three injuries in less than a week is somewhat excessive. Two of which were not your run-of-the-mill accidents."

"They say bad things happen in threes. Well, I've had my three."

He smiled and patted her knee.

"Doctor, apart from James and Hazel, you're one of the few people in this town who I feel I can talk freely to. When Frank . . ." She tipped back her head and inhaled deeply. "The day Frank was murdered I . . . I was right there . . . in that house. Oh God, I think way down in my gut I suspected as much." She looked into Burke's soft, blue eyes. "Maybe if I had—"

"Now stop. Don't you start thinking like that. There was nothing you could do. Nothing. Do you understand?" The doctor slowly sank down on the swivel stool. "I believe Frank was sixteen at the time. They're so full of life at that age, aren't they? So much to live for. If memory serves me, that boy was somewhat of a hell raiser like the rest of the Scollis, though more rambunctious than out-and-out bad."

"Under that large, bullish exterior he was incredibly sweet and gentle," she said. "Who would do it? And why?"

"Oh Lord, I couldn't venture to say. An aura of mystery has always surrounded that house. Richard Holt, Caroline's husband, couldn't wait to get out of this town. Packed up and left his father and grandmother, and as far as I know he never called or wrote. Couple years later the senior Holt had a massive stroke. His mother, Henrietta, in her early eighties by then, attended to him. Don't know how she managed with no one to help. The Holts owned half the town but they were never very social. As soon as he died, she collapsed and had to be put in a home. That house sat empty for five years. And no sooner had she passed on, then Richard surprised everyone by coming back to town with his young bride. Just plopped her down in that three-story monster and went off to war. Then—well, I believe you know the rest."

"Doctor, I knew Caroline was delicate," Roni said, "but I didn't know her heart was so weak."

"A bout of pneumonia and then the birth took its toll on it. Caroline Holt took care of herself and never whined. She was no stranger to hardship, I can tell you that much. The death of her husband, the rape and pregnancy, and . . . well, sad . . . sad.''

"She was pregnant before that day," Roni said quietly.

Dr. Burke stared at her curiously. "Impossible," he said. "What you're suggesting—no, Caroline Holt was . . . well, painfully old-fashioned. Almost puritanical in her beliefs and ideals. She wouldn't . . ." He paused, as if to form a mental picture. He shook his head, looking incredulous. "I'm afraid you must be mistaken. Small town gossip. Where did you get such a notion?''

The nurse poked her head in the door. "Dr. Andrews would like a word with you, Doctor.''

Burke lifted himself off the low stool. "This could take awhile," he said. "Go on home. If I find anything on the film, I'll call. If there's pain, or double vision, call me.''

He walked her to the door. "Roni, you look out now," he said before hurrying off down the hall.

She stared at the doctor's retreating back. Mysteries. Everywhere she turned there were mysteries.

She pushed through the glass doors of the clinic into the late afternoon sun. Her strides long and brisk, she made for home.

Roni found Aaron in his room lying on his stomach in bed watching TV. With chin in hand, he used the remote control to flip from one afternoon talk show to another. It seemed there was no age barrier, she thought, in the male fascination with the remote.

"That'll rot your brain," she said from the doorway.

He rolled to his side. "What?''

"Daytime TV.''

"It's interesting." He sat up, pushed up his glasses. "Can we talk a minute?"

He flipped off the TV, held onto the remote, and waited.

She crossed the room and sat on the bed, her hands in her lap. "Honey, what makes you think your mother was murdered?" she asked gently.

He twisted his fingers and looked down. "She wouldn't leave me . . . not like that . . . and not without saying goodbye."

"Aaron, your mother was very sick."

"She wasn't ready." His eyes welled. He opened them wider, refusing to let the tears spill. "She was going to tell me."

"Tell you what?"

"She was going to tell me who my father was. She was going to bring us together."

"Why now, after all these years?"

"Because I wanted it. At first I thought *he* was my dad." He pointed toward his mother's bedroom. "The one in the picture. The soldier. I thought that until the kids at school said I was a bastard. When I asked her about it she said I was her sole creation. She'd created me from all the love and goodness in the universe. When she started to get really sick, I think she was afraid she'd die and I'd be left all alone. She decided my father should know that he had a son. Maybe he wouldn't be too happy about it, but he should at least know."

He lifted large brown eyes to Roni. "You see, she wasn't ready. She hadn't worked it all out yet. She would never go without making sure there was someone to take care of me. Somebody killed her." His voice cracked on the last word, but he held fast.

He's trying to be so brave, Roni thought. The pain

was there in his eyes. If only he could cry. If only he could let it out, share it with her. He was much too young to hold all that grief inside.

Roni put her arm around him and felt his thin body stiffen. She gave him a brief hug, smoothed his hair down in back, then left the room.

Downstairs, speaking softly so Aaron wouldn't hear, she made another call to the clinic in Ely and finally was put through to Dr. Greene. When Roni explained the circumstances of Caroline's death and inquired about the tests, he offered to forward Aaron's medical record to Dr. Burke. She declined, saying that she and Aaron would be moving to LA soon and her GP there should have them.

"Then you are the boy's legal guardian?" the doctor asked.

"Yes," she lied without hesitation. "Doctor, is he in good health?"

"Generally speaking, yes. He's at the low end of the chart for weight and height, but some children just seem to spurt up all at once. I wouldn't worry at this point."

"What's his blood type?"

"A-positive."

"That's fairly common, isn't it?"

"Yes, it is."

She thanked him and hung up.

From the breezeway between the one-car garage and the house, he watched Hazel Anderson water the shrubs and flowers alongside her house. On the end of the hose a spray nozzle shaped like a gun sent out a fine mist that she waved back and forth, pink zoris flopping at her heels, humming and whistling as she worked. When she moved out of sight around the corner, he slipped into the house through the back door.

In the kitchen the table was set for one, with wine glass and a dusty bottle of Gamay Beaujolais. A Crock-Pot on the counter emitted ribbons of steam, the glass lid dewy with condensation. He crossed the kitchen, opened the door to the basement, and went through, closing the door behind him.

Hazel wiped her feet at the back door and entered the kitchen. In the thirty minutes it had taken her to water all the plants on her property, the ingredients in the slow cooker simmered nicely, the aroma making her mouth water.

She breathed deeply. The stew smelled divine as always, the scent of caraway permeating the room. Everyone said hers was the best stew in town. The recipe was an old one, handed down the line, but never given out to anyone outside the family. Once having tasted it, people had begged and cajoled and some, like the previous owners of the Eagle, for instance, even went so far as to offer her hard cash for it. The secret lay in the three different kinds of meat, caraway seeds, paprika, and that final dollop of sour cream.

It smelled too good to keep all to herself. Although she loved the leftovers, she felt like having company today. Roni Mayfield immediately came to mind. Roni and Aaron. Shoot, that might just be what they needed, she told herself, a mutual friend to pull them together. Roni seemed willing to meet him more than halfway, and if any two people were meant to be together, it was those two. Caroline, God rest her soul, was a very shrewd woman.

Hazel knew about jealousy and territorial rights and authority. She smiled, thinking back to the early days of her marriage to Logan Anderson. After the ceremony he had taken her home to his mother's house to live until they could afford their own place. The two Mrs. Andersons, both headstrong, had donned battle gear immediately. Territory being what it was, the elder Mrs. clearly stood to be the victor. Within four weeks Hazel moved out and Logan, bless his cotton socks, followed. They'd had forty-six lean but wonderful years together.

There was another reason Hazel wanted to have Roni and Aaron over—the matter of Aaron's alleged father. It was time Roni was apprised of the game rules and the players.

In the kitchen sink water ran over the colander of fresh spinach. When the last of the sand ran through the leaves, she turned off the faucet, took a terry towel and wiped her hands. She'd give Roni a call right now.

She paused and listened. She distinctly heard water rushing through pipes elsewhere in the house.

Frowning, she wandered through the house, checking each faucet and even the tap just outside the back door. Nothing. The basement? Earlier, before watering, she had put a load in the washer, but it should have gone through the cycles long ago.

She opened the door to the basement, poked her head through, and listened. Sure enough, the sound was coming from down there. She exchanged the zoris for the pair of knitted slippers that she kept near the door—the flip-flops made stair-climbing a bit too adventurous for a large-boned woman with a trick knee.

She flipped the light switch on the wall. Nothing happened. Bulb was probably burned out. In the graying light she made her way downstairs. The laundry area was located in the west corner and included a washer, dryer, and deep sink. Water ran into the sink and flowed over the edge onto the concrete floor.

"Now, how in blazes . . ." she muttered, hurrying to shut it off before the basement got completely flooded. Her wool slippers were soaked immediately. Bending at the waist, she reached over the full sink to the faucet. As she cranked the two metal spigots she heard a noise on the stairs and looked up. A man stood at the fusebox. Recognition hit at the exact instant he flipped a switch on the fuse panel.

Wet hands and feet provided a perfect contact for the washer's 110 volts to dance its dance of fibrillation with the elderly woman's heart.

Her last thought was not of her killer or even herself, but of the rubber-soled zoris at the top of the stairs.

Twenty-Six

Later that evening Roni began to go through the cabinets and drawers in the master bedroom. Since the break-in, one thing continued to gnaw at her. There had to be another journal. People who keep daily journals for years and years don't usually stop abruptly. It becomes a ritual, like brushing your teeth or reading the newspaper a certain way. Caroline had been a creature of habit. It was in Caroline's nature to keep a journal.

She looked up to see Aaron standing in the doorway, his expression inquisitive.

She motioned him in. "Aaron, whoever broke into the house stole a diary that belonged to your mother, a diary I found in the mattress in the shed. Did she keep any others?"

"Yes."

"Do you know where it is?"

"In the library. She wrote in one of those books from downstairs. Like that one." He pointed to a cloth bound volume of poetry on the nightstand.

"A published book? Are you sure?"

He nodded. "I thought it was weird because she would have had a tizzy if I tried to mark up a book. She was real fussy about that."

Roni rapidly thumbed through the book of poems. Nothing.

They hurried downstairs.

"Where?" she asked, as they stood in the doorway of the library.

"I don't know."

Her heart sank. She stood awe-struck, overwhelmed by the prospect of having to go though the hundreds of books lining the dusty wall-to-wall shelves from floor to ceiling in the high-domed room.

"We'll start low. Your mother was short and, for our sake, I hope she didn't like heights."

Dust filled the room as they rifled through one book after another. First Aaron coughed and sneezed, then Roni. After awhile neither bothered to return the books to the shelves, but tossed them on the floor in a heap. They'd sort it out later.

"Roni."

Roni turned toward Aaron. He sat on his haunches, a book open between his legs, a smile lighting up his face.

They met in the middle of the room. The book, a novel by an obscure nineteenth century author, was unmarked until page 100, at which point the very distinctive handwriting of Caroline Holt began. It was obviously a diary.

Again her heart sank. They had found what they were looking for, but the tiny, ornate script, squeezed in between the lines of the existing printed text, was nearly impossible to read.

"You say you saw her writing in more than one book?" Roni asked.

He nodded solemnly.
They continued to search.

This diary had no dates. The writing was in the form of a letter, each entry opened with *My darling Richard*.
The first:

> *The nursery, like our room, is done entirely in white. Depending on the sex of the baby, we can accent with the appropriate color, changing with each child. I sent a picture—let me know what you think.*

It was in this diary that Roni's name first appeared. Caroline must have had two diaries going at once. Roni hoped dates wouldn't be important; she was looking for a name, not a date.

> *A little girl of eleven or twelve came to the door today selling stationery and Christmas cards for school. I think she's one of the miner's daughters. She had a bloody stubbed toe, scabs on both knees, and the most beautiful brown eyes I've ever seen.*
>
> *I ordered one of each, little use I'll have for them, but I'd like to see her again. She refused my invitation to come inside. The poor thing looked scared to death. Probably thinks the house is haunted and I'm an ogre of some kind. I don't even know her name. Next time.*

Roni clearly remembered that day. With the box of samples in her hand, she knocked on the massive door. After a very long time Caroline Holt had answered. She wore not jeans or slacks like the other women in town, but a simple skirt and blouse. Her braided hair coiled neatly at the back of her head. Her only jewelry was a tiny pearl stud in each ear. She wore no makeup, and really didn't need any. Her lips were naturally rose-tinted and her lashes so thick and long, even a light application of mascara would have been too much. Her skin was fair, translucent, reminding Roni of the chunk of quartz her father had brought home from the hills: white, pure, yet cold to the touch. She was the most fascinating woman Roni had even seen.

I have no life outside of Eagleton, and only a thin veneer of a life within it. Without you, my love, the days are endless. This house, your house, is my lifeline. I hear the happy sounds of children running through the halls and sliding down that polished banister. Hurry home.

With a strong magnifying glass, she read while Aaron continued to look for more journals. She tried not to skim too lightly for fear of missing something vital. After several hours the strain of following the steep, back-slanted writing, typical of many left-handed people, brought on a dull, nagging headache behind her eyes.

Suddenly she stopped reading.

Left-handed people. Caroline had been left-handed.

Roni closed her eyes and brought up the image of Lubben sitting behind his desk telling her about Caroline's suicide. Hesitation marks. *On her left wrist,* he'd said, holding up his own arm and pointing. *Right there and there.*

Roni lifted an imaginary knife and pretended to cut herself. She was right-handed so she would have held the knife in that hand, making her cuts on the opposite hand. Right to left.

Whoever had placed the knife in Caroline's hand and made those hesitation marks was right-handed. Either he didn't know Caroline was left-handed or he'd overlooked it.

A piece of paper at the back of the book slipped out. An address in Caroline's handwriting. No name, just a P.O. Box in Nevada. Her father's box in Tonopah.

Roni shoved the slip of paper back into the book and slammed it shut. A sudden rush of blood through her veins caused the pain behind her eyes to throb.

About the same time Roni was reading Caroline's diary, Tom Mayfield, in his camp a mile from Eagleton, sat on a canvas stool poking a stick at the dying embers of his fire. His mind was filled with thoughts of Eagleton, of his daughter, and of things dark and disturbing. From his jacket pocket he removed the letter and unfolded it.

Her handwriting was difficult to decipher under the best of circumstances, but in the faint firelight it was impossible. It didn't matter—he had memorized the words.

He leaned forward, lowering the letter until a corner touched the white embers. Within seconds the paper was burning. When he could hold it no longer, he let it drop into the dying fire.

Two hundred miles away in Reno, Nevada, Larry Glazer also contemplated things dark and disturbing. He stood on rigid legs, his toes and fingers numb, six floors above Center Street on the top tier of the parking garage. Only minutes ago he had raced up the stairwell, hyper and disoriented, fueled by anger and anxiety. His brain was flying with Jack Daniel's and phencyclidine—better known on the street as PCP or angel dust.

Maybe he was loaded and wasn't thinking too clearly, but he knew damnfucking well that the news from his brother was not good news. The widow dead. Roni in Eagleton. It was like a conspiracy. Jim and Roni were about to join forces to blast him.

He couldn't take it anymore. It wasn't going to go away. The nightmares rode his back day and night like gargoyles from hell. Shadows and blood, black eyes pleading as liquid fire spurts from the third eye in Frank's head and swirls crazily around him.

The blood is everywhere. Everywhere. *Everywhere.*

Larry opened his mouth to scream, but no sound came out. The scream was locked in his throat—locked there forever—just as the nightmare was locked in his diseased and dying mind.

As he stared out at the kaleidoscope of lights from the casino marquees he felt a calmness wash over him, the sensation so unexpected that he made a sound in his throat like a whimper.

Absolute peace.

Completely together and focused like never before.

Below, the traffic flowed north, squiggly ribbons of taillights like bright red racer snakes. It made him dizzy to look at them. He looked up.

Above the building tops, above the lighted specks in the surrounding hills, his gaze continued upward to a cloudless expanse with a smattering of stars, their true brightness muted by the city lights. Twin spotlights panned across the sky, crossing at a point directly in front of him. The spotlights crossed once, twice, then merged to become one. A path to the heavens.

It silently beckoned.

A stairway to heaven.

My stairway to heaven, he thought. He began to hum the Zeppelin song. There'd be no blood up there, no nightmares—at least he hoped to God there wouldn't be. Frankie would be there, that much he knew for certain.

"Hey, Frankie, hey man, I'm sorry. When we meet up . . . I'm gonna tell you how . . . how really sorry I am. Shit, man, it's been hell, a fuckin' hell.

He climbed the parapet and squatted on the edge, his eyes on the stairway to heaven. *What if I go to the other place? Fuck. What if I never get to talk to you, Frank? No, God could never be that cruel, no way. God would want you to know how sorry I am. Yeah, sure, He'd do it for you, Frankie.*

He stood. A breeze came from nowhere to guide him.

Before he left the ledge he heard footsteps pounding on concrete. Someone yelled.

Larry stepped forward. The parapet was no longer under his feet.

Twenty-Seven

Wednesday

Most of the faces around Roni were familiar. The service for Frank Scolli had been held at St. John's and burial followed at the Catholic cemetery south of town—Eagleton, originally comprised of a blend of immigrants, at one time had seven cemeteries. Three were still in use and tended regularly.

Roni shivered. Her navy linen skirt and blazer offered little protection against the inclement weather. In the last twenty minutes the weather had turned from mild to bitter cold; a stiff wind played havoc with the flowered wreaths. The nylon canopy that stretched above the coffin cracked like a whip, and endless yellow rose petals swirled across the barren yard of the cemetery.

Ending with a prayer, the mourners began to disperse quietly. The Scolli family and Father Roberts hung back. Roni walked with Charlotte Burke. Charlotte leaned back, her round belly prominent in front of her. Then she duckwaddled down the slight incline to their late-model Suburban.

Roni opened the passenger door. Before climbing in she looked around one last time, hoping to see James. The day before he had mysteriously taken off—important business, he'd said. She wondered where he was and when he'd be back. Also absent was Hazel Anderson, which Roni found very peculiar, since Frank had been a student of hers.

"Lovely service," Charlotte said, settling herself in the driver's seat, her arms extended straight out to allow ample distance between belly and steering wheel. "Father Roberts did a remarkable job, considering the circumstances surrounding Frank's death. We're so lucky to have a priest of his caliber in a town this size. I wish Paul could've joined us."

"Who is it that went into labor?"

"Franchine Price, west of town in that trailer commune. Probably false labor. She's not due for another three weeks."

"And you?"

"It can't be long now. I'm getting my second wind. Just before labor starts I get this urge to move furniture and scrub down the walls. If it weren't for my ankles, I'd be doing the fall cleaning. Thank God Paul and I love kids and can afford them. I'm one of those women who feel best when she's pregnant. Paul says I'm fertile as a rabbit, strong as an ox, and healthy as a horse."

They pulled up to the Scolli tavern. The CLOSED sign was on in the front window, but the door was ajar. Inside, women hustled about, arranging casserole dishes, fruit molds, salads, and desserts along a buffet table. Behind the bar Dean Scolli drew pitchers of beer and carafes of hardy red wine. Within minutes the large room filled. Charlotte took a seat to take the pressure off her swollen ankles.

Henry Coombs pressed a mug of beer into Roni's hand and with a stern expression said, "Seeing you again reminds me of the time you, Frank, and Larry had to put in that stint at the store. The meat case ain't been that clean since."

"Oh, God." With a sheepish grin she added, "I don't think I've swiped anything since."

One summer the threesome had lifted a pack of menthol cigarettes from the market and had been snagged by ol' man Coombs. Instead of calling the sheriff or their parents, Coombs had struck a plea bargain with the novice thieves, and for the next week they cleaned and scoured the meat case, produce bins, and walk-in cold locker.

"You ever need a job, you got one at the store," he said and ambled off to the bar.

She took a sip of beer and felt the headache of the night before returning. Without James she felt out of place, an outsider. She wanted to offer her condolences to the family and go back to the house, yet she found herself stalling, hesitant to approach Mrs. Scolli. The memory of that dreadful afternoon at the Scolli house, Anna throwing clothes into the wind, worked painfully at Roni's stomach.

The balding, barrel-chested Floyd Budner of the Trading Center, along with a younger man of perhaps forty, strolled over to her, both grinning.

"Roni Mayfield, isn't it?" Budner's great, bushy mustache melded into his sideburns like a hairy "W" across his face. He squinted when he spoke.

"Hello, Mr. Budner."

"You remember my boy, Sammy? He repairs the small appliances in the TC."

She remembered. Not from the store but from Faddle's bird-hunting anecdote—the damn fool kid who shot up Faddle's ear and had him diving for the rocks.

"Sure. How are you, Sam?"

"Couldn't be better." He looked around guiltily. "Well, considering."

"You getting settled in, young lady? For a big-city girl with a career, coming back to Eagleton must be a real cultural shock," Floyd said. "But things have a way of working out for the best, now don't they?"

"Work out how, Mr. Budner?"

"Hell, a reporter couldn't ask for better material. And dumped right into her lap, too. The widow's suicide and now . . ." he went on under his breath in a conspiratorial tone, looking around, ". . . the boy finding Frank's remains in the tunnel right beneath her house. I'm told, by the looks of the skull, that he was bludgeoned. Lickety-split, young Frank goes from suspect to victim. 'Course, he could be both, couldn't he? Personally, I think he was up to no good and somebody did him in. Then there's still the widow's bastard to consider. Hell of a note. I'd be interested to know your thoughts on it, Miss Mayfield." He gave her a measuring look.

Roni matched him stare for stare, the headache pounding behind her eyes; then without uttering a word she turned and walked away. Had there been an exit nearby, she would have kept right on going, leaving the folks of Eagleton to speculate among themselves. Instead, she took momentary refuge in the restroom.

At the sink she shook out two aspirins from the bottle in her purse, poured her beer into the basin, filled the mug with water, and swallowed the tablets. As she patted cool water on her throat, the door behind her opened. A familiar face was reflected in the mirror.

Linda Shaw's shiny blond hair, tousled from the wind, gave her a sexy, daring look. Her long black skirt, matching western-cut jacket, and boots comprised the perfect outfit for a small town funeral.

As they exchanged cursory words of greeting, Roni wondered if James knew Linda was in town.

"I didn't see you at the funeral service, Dr. Shaw," Roni said.

"Only just arrived," she said, brushing at her hair. "I wanted to pay my respects to the family."

Roni dried her hands and left, the knot in her stomach constricting with each passing minute. Her head pounded, she felt sick, and she desperately wanted out. For the first time since coming to Eagleton, she couldn't wait to get back inside that old rundown Victorian house, the doors securely locked behind her. Aaron was there and she wanted to be with him.

Linda exited the restroom and brushed past her. Roni stared at the psychologist's slender back as she crossed the room, her posture exuding control and self-confidence. Beyond Linda, standing at the bar with his back to them, Roni saw James. Linda approached him and planted a kiss behind one ear. James turned, smiled, and opened a space for her.

Dean Scolli, tending bar, also watched. It was evident by the way he stared at Linda that he was infatuated with her. When he looked at James his eyes burned with indignation.

So that's where he's been . . . in Elko with her.

Dean caught Roni's eye and something that passed for empathy flashed across his face. Did she look as miserable as he did? If the situation hadn't been so pathetic, it would have been quite amusing. Dean wanted Linda and Linda and Roni wanted James and James wanted . . . ?

At the front door Roni found the bereaved parents conversing with Father Roberts. She took Anna Scolli's hand and mumbled words of sympathy, fully expecting some sort of rebuff or outright hostility, but Anna squeezed Roni's fingers and smiled sadly. Not a glimmer of recognition registered in the woman's red, swollen eyes. Disconcerted, yet relieved, Roni slipped out the door. The priest called to her, then joined her on the sidewalk.

"Roni, I'm glad I caught you. The diary of Caroline Holt's, the one that's missing . . . I have it."

Roni raised her eyebrows and waited.

"I found it in the trash receptacle behind the church. It seems to be intact and none the worse for the culprit's insensitivity to private property."

"*Stolen* private property," she corrected.

"So you said. Would you like me to drop it by the house?"

Roni thought of fingerprints. Maybe no one in this town believed in forensics, but they sure as hell did in LA. She'd send it to a friend of hers at the LAPD and see just how many prints they could lift. The less it was handled the better.

"Thank you, Father, but I'll pick it up." She was fairly certain now that the book she saw the priest reading in the rectory had been Caroline's diary. Of course, it was possible he had found it in the trash bin as he said, but he'd had a look through it first.

Father Roberts returned to the tavern.

The wind ruthlessly pushed at her back as she crossed the main highway and hurried past the courthouse. The wind also carried her name to her. She turned to see Dean Scolli, a bottle of beer in each hand, half a block behind. With his long-legged strides, he quickly caught up with her.

"I had enough of that," he gestured with a nod of his head toward the tavern. "I'll walk you home. Here," he said, offering a beer, "one for the road."

She shook her head.

Dean shrugged and staggered as he chugalugged one of the beers, then tossed the empty into a vacant lot. "Oops," he said. "Slipped. Hey, you won't turn me in for the hundred dollar litterbug reward, will ya?"

It was obvious Dean had skipped the graveside eulogy to open the bar, getting a good head start on the drinking. She crossed her arms in front of her and began walking again. Dean removed his sport coat and draped it over her shoulders.

They had crossed Sage and were approaching Juniper when Dean broke the silence, his speech thick and slurred, "I'm gonna find out who killed Frank if it's the last thing I do. I loved my brother. We were pretty tight at one time."

When? Roni wondered. Her recollection of Dean had been of a typical older sibling—mean and bullying, utilizing every opportunity to humiliate Frank in front of his friends. But time and tragedy had a way of clouding things unpleasant.

"Lubben's either too lazy to do his job, or he's hiding somethin'. Whichever it is, I'll be damned if I'll just sit around while he does some hall-ass investigation that'll fizzle out in no time," Dean said. "And that sonofabitch, the one who clubbed Frank to death, he must think his little secret is pretty safe after all these years, but believe you me, it ain't. No sir, it sure as hell ain't.''

"Dean, I'm sorry about—" She was interrupted by several loud whoops and the sound of a roaring car engine. The noise came from the end of the street where she and Aaron lived.

"What the hell?!" Dean said.

Roni caught a glimpse of the VW Thing before it drove off the road toward the house. The Scollis again.

Aaron was in the house alone!

Roni bolted forward, flinging Dean's jacket at him. She managed a half-dozen steps in her high heels before stopping to yank them off. In her stocking feet, oblivious to the sharp pebbles and broken asphalt, she ran toward her house. Dean sprinted ahead of her.

The boxy vehicle threw up dirt and leaves as it raced around the Holt property, dodging trees and boulders and narrowly missing the back corner of the shed.

As Roni drew near she saw Red Dog, his three good legs churning, coming up Country Lane in the opposite direction with James in close pursuit. Dean veered off to chase after the car.

The front door of the house flew open and two boys dragged Aaron, kicking and cursing, outdoors. A moment later Red leaped over the railing onto the porch, knocking one of the boys down. James vaulted the three steps and grabbed the other one.

Dean caught up with the car and leaped onto the driver's side. He shouted at the driver, cuffing him on the head. The car slid sideways on the loose dirt, then broadsided a pine tree. Dean reached in, shut down the engine, and pulled the boy out. He marched him up to the house.

James struggled with the young Scolli. Red ran back and forth from one boy to the other, growling and barking.

When Dean saw that James had a grip on his brother, he bounded up the steps and, with undue roughness, pulled him away from James. Grasping the boy by the back of the neck, he said under his breath, "You stupid little shit. What the hell's the matter with you?" He squeezed until the boy cried out.

Roni kneeled in front of Aaron and straightened his twisted shirt. "You okay, hon?"

He kept his eyes downcast, rubbing the places on his arms where the boys had gripped him, and nodded sharply. Red licked him in the face, then sat at his side as if to show his support. Aaron stroked his head.

Dean turned to Roni and asked, "You wan' me to kick their butts, huh? I'll kick their butts, no problem."

"No." She turned to Aaron. "Do you want to file a complaint with the police?"

Aaron looked from boy to boy, his mouth set. He shook his head.

Dean herded the three boys into a tight knot. Glaring at them, he said, "You jerks have anything to say?"

Looking contrite, they each muttered apologies, inching backward, away from their captors and toward the open yard.

Dean gave his brother a shove, then sent him on

his way with a kick in the pants that nearly made Dean lose his balance. "Get home. I'll deal with you later."

When the three boys had quickly disappeared, Dean turned a beery eye to James. "You got any complaints, Glazer?"

"Not if Roni and Aaron don't."

"Well, don't expect any thanks from me. I didn't need or especially want any help from you. Go back to your girlfriend. Roni and me, we're talkin', and this is one time you ain't buttin' in."

"Scolli, your brother just got buried and I realize you're upset—"

"And drunk, too, but that don't have nothing to do with nothing. I'm really sick of you, y'know. Ever since we were kids you've had to best me. In sports, jobs, with women, with . . . with every goddamn thing. Then off to college you go while I'm stuck in this hick town, spinnin' my wheels, goin' nowhere. You coulda gone a dozen places, but no, you gotta come back to Eagleton—a bigshot geologist. Good ol' Dean," he thumped his chest, "he's nothin' but a common miner, not good enough to keep the same company as Jimboy here."

James looked uncomfortably at Roni. "Dean, c'mon, this isn't the time or place."

Roni had put her arm around Aaron, feeling his frail body tremble. She looked from one man to the other. "Settle this somewhere else. We're going in." They crossed the threshold. Red tagged along.

"Roni," James said. "We gotta talk."

"Not now. Go home. Both of you." She eased the dog out of the way and closed the door.

Just inside the door Roni pulled Aaron to her. She stood behind him, her arms draped over his shoulders and across his chest. "You sure you're all right?" she asked softly.

He nodded.

"Where're your glasses?"

"I don't know."

"Let's find them."

The large wire-rimmed glasses were at the foot of the staircase, one metal temple broken at the hinge.

"You'll need new ones."

"I can fix them," he said.

"I don't think so."

"I can fix anything."

"Aaron, where did you get these glasses?"

"They're Mama's."

"Are they prescription?"

He shrugged.

"Honey, you should have your own glasses with lenses specifically made for you."

"I want these," he said flatly.

Roni knew it wouldn't do any good to argue with him now. They'd discuss it later. There were more important things to talk about. She removed her blazer and draped it over the banister. "How'd those boys get in?"

He shrugged again.

"I locked the doors when I left. Did you open them?"

He shook his head.

Roni pounded the edge of her fist against the newel post. Then with long, angry strides she marched down to the basement. Aaron followed.

The trapdoor stood wide open. She turned to look up at the entrance to the basement. The arched opening off the hallway had no door. From the basement, the house was totally accessible.

"Look, we've got to barricade this trapdoor. The way it is now, anyone in town can just pop up out of the floor and roam through the house. It's not safe. Hey, I know." She turned, grabbing his arms, adding, "why don't we pack a few things and go to the hotel? It'll be fun. Like we're on vacation." Without waiting for an answer she knelt, took his hands, and said, "Better yet, how would you like to take a real vacation? To LA? I have a place right on the ocean. Have you ever seen the ocean?"

He shook his head.

"Would you like to see it?"

He looked away and shrugged his shoulders. She took that for a sign of acquiescence.

"C'mon, let's pack a bag and go to the hotel. Then tomorrow I'll get it okayed with Faddle and Hazel and we'll jump in the car and take a nice little trip." She tried to pull him along.

He yanked his hands away, putting them behind his back out of her reach. He stepped back.

"All right, we don't have to leave right away. We can go in a couple of days. That'll give—"

"I'm not going. Not now or ever."

"Why not? Aaron, what's to keep you here?" When his only response was a defiant stare, she added, "Oh, I see. It's me. You don't want to go with *me*."

"Yes, I do. Roni, I do. It's . . . well, it's—what about my father?"

She felt immense relief. So that was it. The ties that bind. "Honey, going away for a while doesn't mean we can't try to find out who he is and where he is. There's a very good chance he doesn't even live in Eagleton."

He seemed to consider that.

She started up the stairs. "I'm going to make a few

phone calls—then we can think about what we want
to take with us."

A look of panic crossed his face. "No! I'm not
going," he screamed at her. "You go. Go on, go. I
can take care of myself. I did it before and I can do
it again. I'm not going to any shitty house by the
ocean! This is *my* house, and I'm not leaving!"

He pulled up the trapdoor and was down the first
two steps before Roni caught him and hauled him
out of the open space by one arm. "Aaron, for crying
out loud, be reasonable."

Aaron shook his head violently and pushed at her,
but she grabbed him and held tight. He struggled,
moaning and cursing.

"Go ahead and cuss up a blue streak. Fight me,
cry, do whatever you have to do, but I'm not letting
you go until you give me a good reason, a good solid
reason for not wanting to leave this house."

"I hate you! I wish you had never come!"

"Okay, you hate me. Now give me a reason."

His struggles seemed to go on forever. Several times
he managed to break away from her, but she caught
and held him. He continued to squirm and curse,
his language becoming more foul and increasingly
creative.

Then he went slack in her arms. Roni could feel
the anger and determination suddenly escape from
him like an airborne balloon. His rigid muscles
relaxed and he folded, limp and defeated. Tears
welled up in his eyes and spilled out. He began to
cry—great, gulping sobs that convulsed his body.
Roni pulled him down on the step and held him
tight, rocking and smoothing his silky brown hair.
He was so thin, she felt sharp, hard bones just beneath
the pale skin. His heart beat rapidly, like a frightened

bird. They stayed like that for an indeterminable amount of time.

These were not tears of anger, she thought, but tears of pain and grief. Roni, holding him tight, her own tears falling, shared both his pain and his grief. He still has so much crying to do. Tears for his mother, tears for the father he never knew, tears for his years of loneliness.

"I miss her," he said, his voice hoarse. *"I miss her so much."*

She pressed him closer to her.

"Roni, why did you come?"

"Because she wanted me to."

"Is that the only reason?"

She sighed, brushing away her own tears. "I'm not sure, Aaron."

"You're gonna go away, too, aren't you?"

"Not right away, not unless you want me to." She kissed the top of his head.

They sat huddled together on the bottom riser, his crying now merely tears and a soft sniffling. She spoke soothing words, her fingers tracing the washboard contour of his ribcage and spine.

How was it possible she could care so deeply for this odd little boy within such a short time? Was she only trying to recapture what she had shared and lost with Caroline? She had no way of knowing. But care for Aaron she did.

When his crying ceased altogether, Roni brushed at his tears with her fingers. "We have to fatten you up. You're much too skinny. I was skinny, too. The kids called me Bony Maroni." She poked between a rib and made him squirm and giggle. "Where did you learn to cuss like that?"

He sniffed. "Pay TV."

"I was right—you watch too much TV."

They were quiet again, content in each other's arms.

Finally Roni said, "Aaron, help me understand why you don't want to leave."

Aaron stood, lifted her hand by one finger, and tugged. She rose, then silently followed him up three flights of stairs to the attic door.

He reached inside his shirt and pulled out a key which hung from a string around his neck. He fitted the key into the padlock and turned it.

Twenty-Eight

The entire town of Eagleton was laid out before her. Light reflected off tin roofs, storefront windows, and the cobalt blue water of the community swimming pool. Patches of wild rose, yellow and sunny, melded with the dull-green trees, sandy soil, and rocks of the surrounding sanguine hills. To Roni, the view was breathtaking. A view not seen from the window, though she knew if she crossed the attic room and looked out, it would all be there for her to see—in *duplicate.*

Aaron's miniature town covered most of the irregular-shaped room; a foot-wide strip of hardwood floor around its perimeter allowed him to maneuver and work.

"It's not finished, of course, but I have it all laid out."

Roni carefully moved along the wall, taking it in. Such minute detail and precision. After going only a yard or two, it occurred to her that it would take her days—perhaps weeks—to see it all . . . really see it and appreciate the fine workmanship involved in his remarkable project.

"My God, Aaron, I'm speechless."

He smiled shyly, pride sparkling in his eyes.

Most prominent in the display was the red brick two-story courthouse. Roni recognized the other buildings surrounding it, great and small. Dozens of other structures, now vacant or boarded up, aligned either side of the main highway. The hills were complete with tailings, all seven cemeteries, the abandoned mine south of town, even Scolli's trailer park— it was all there.

"How long? How many years?" she asked, still moving around the room.

"Three."

She looked at him. "You started when you were eight?"

"Eight and a half."

"All this in just three years?" she said incredulously. "Impossible."

"My friend and I started it. Then after he moved away Mom helped."

On a table to one side of the room sat an assortment of odds and ends, clean and neatly sorted, ready to be added to the design. Another table held work instruments and materials. Roni opened a how-to book on lighting, then flipped through page after page of complicated symbols and diagrams.

"When I get older I want to learn all about electricity so I can wire Eaglcton. I want thc buildings and houses to light up at night. I don't know enough about that yet to do it."

Roni smiled. "You will."

She saw dogs, cats, horses, and various farm animals. She gently stroked a cow. Silkiness met her fingertips.

"The animals," she said, "How . . . ?"

"The ones that aren't made from pussy willows and cattails are from real animals. I carve their shapes out of wood, then I cover it with fur—animals killed on the road and scraps I find in the trash behind Mr. Johnstone's taxidermy place . . . things like that."

She remembered the stiff, dried, and unrecognizable critter in the bag of trash the deputy had found in the tunnel the night Frank's skeleton was unearthed.

She knelt to scrutinize a bush of wild roses. Real flowers, tiny dried ones, painted yellow, the stems comprised of thin electrical wires. The high school swimming pool was filled with water. On closer inspection she saw not water, but a clear resin.

He had taken no short-cuts, no easy ways. Three years' work. Hardly a typical project for a very young boy.

He told her all the materials that went into his project were collected by him personally. "Nothing store-bought. That'd be cheating. Since I get a lot of things out of the trash, I go out at night when no one's around."

Using the tunnels to come and go in extreme weather helped. In the dead of winter, with temperatures dropping to minus 30, he stayed inside, designing, constructing, and experimenting with various ways of duplicating one thing or another.

The Victorian house, his house, was nearly completed. Every gable, turret, and cornice, painstakingly accurate and exquisite, waiting to be a painted lady of distinction.

At the worktable she saw three small figures carved out of wood, painted and clothed. Man, woman, and child. The woman and child were completed. The man was not. *Mother, father, and son?* She lifted the male figure and turned it over in her fingers.

"I wanted to finish the house before showing it to you, but . . ." Turning, he stared down at his creation. "Roni, I can't leave it. Not until it's done."

"No," she said finally. "No, I don't suppose you can."

At four o'clock a student Hazel Anderson had been tutoring entered her back door to find stew in a Crock-Pot, cold, a layer of congealed fat across the top, the power in the entire house out. While calling her name he searched the house. Five minutes later he found her body on the concrete floor in the flooded basement.

Before dinner Roni and Aaron had lugged a heavy parlor settee down the cellar steps and placed it over the trapdoor. It would have to do until she could hire a carpenter to put up a door with a lock at the top of the stairs. As she was putting the dinner leftovers away, she heard Aaron at the piano. She followed the sounds of Schumann, or perhaps Liszt—classical music had never been a strong interest of hers—into the music room.

She sat on the edge of the wing chair, elbows on knees, chin cupped in her hands, and listened.

When finished he turned to her and asked, "Do you play?"

"Hardly. I'm afraid even 'Chopsticks' is out of my league."

He began to peck at the keys with a finger. "Chopsticks."

She smiled. He motioned for her to join him. A moment later, with a quick refresher course from Aaron, they were a duet, banging out "Chopsticks" on respective ends of the piano. Aaron turned to her and smiled, a merry glint making his eyes bright.

"I can teach you to play," he said.

She gently brushed hair from his forehead. "Honey, there are certain things that should never pair up. Mr. Piano and I were introduced many years ago and we were not the least bit compatible."

The phone rang. Roni hurried to the dining room to answer.

She hardly recognized Faddle Granville's voice, his tone somber, quiet. Dread inched up her spine.

"I've bad news, Roni. Hazel Anderson has passed on."

"Passed on?" Her throat tightened. *"Dead?"*

"She went real quick. Doubt she suffered much."

Roni sank to the floor and squeezed her eyes shut.

Twenty-Nine

Thursday

The next day news of Hazel Anderson's fatal accident quickly spread, rocking the small town. The school closed for the day and that afternoon at a memorial service held in the school auditorium the townspeople paid their final respects to one of Eagleton's esteemed citizens and beloved teachers. Hazel's daughter made arrangements to have the body taken from the mortuary in a hearse to Coggins Airfield and transported by plane to Flagstaff, Arizona, for burial.

The previous day, after the volunteer fire department had removed the body and pumped the basement dry, Floyd Budner, local merchant and part-time electrician, located a faulty wire in the washer. "Accidental electrocution" went on the police report and the death certificate. Estimated time of death: between 4:30 and 6:00 the previous day—Hazel

Anderson, a creature of habit, was known to water the shrubs at precisely 4:30 and sup at 6:00. The former had been done, but not the latter.

Roni attended the memorial alone. James was there, and except for a few words of condolences before the service, they went their separate ways. Roni mourned the loss of a good friend. In the short time she'd been in Eagleton she had become very close to her former teacher. If Hazel's death stunned and depressed Roni, it devastated Aaron.

Aaron waited until after the memorial began before moving the settee and going into the tunnel. With the flashlight in one hand and the shoebox in the other, he had made his way through the underground passage to the exit on Main, but instead of coming up through the condemned brewery, he turned right and followed the passageway another two blocks until it ended. He went up the concrete steps and through the door with the faded bomb shelter symbol on the front. A half-block further and he was inside the school grounds, running to the long, two-story brick building, avoiding the school auditorium where everyone was gathered.

The main doors of the library were locked. He made his way around the building until he came to the book depository cut into the brick wall. Aaron pulled open the metal door, reached a hand inside, and felt the canvas bag that kept the books from falling on the floor.

He sat on his haunches and lifted the shoebox lid. Attached to his memorial offering was a wood plaque with these words: *To Mrs. Anderson, the best teacher ever, from your friend Aaron.*

Aaron closed his eyes and whispered softly, "Good-bye, Mrs. Anderson. If you see my mother, tell her I miss her and . . . and I love her. Tell her I know she didn't kill herself and that Roni and I are going to find out who did. And . . . and tell her I like Roni, I like her a lot. She's cool. Tell her not to worry about me, I'll be okay."

He closed the lid, carefully fitted the box through the opening, and lowered it as far as his arm would reach before letting it go. It made a soft thump when it hit bottom.

He pulled his arm out, swiped impatiently at his eyes, and hurried away.

After the service that afternoon Mrs. Clancy, the school librarian, reached into the canvas chute of the book depository and lifted out a shoebox. She held it at arm's length as she carried it to one of the long reading tables and carefully laid it down.

From experience she knew anything could be inside that box. Anything at all. A leaping frog, a nest of slithering garter snakes, even a fresh pile of dog doodoo. Children loved their pranks and the depository doubled as a waste receptacle from time to time. With a Coombs Market yardstick, again held at arm's length, she loosened the top, then flipped it off onto the table.

She waited. Nothing leaped, crawled, or slithered out. She sniffed the air. "Hmmm," she said, inching closer. Over the lip of the box she saw what looked like a miniature house, roof, windows . . . a flag?

She moved closer.

"Oh, mercy me," she whispered, a thick-veined bony hand plucking at her throat. "Mercy, mercy."

Inside the box was a perfect replica of the Eagleton High School. And in a second-story window, in the room that had been Mrs. Anderson's before she retired, a painted figure that looked remarkably like her stood looking out.

For the second night in a row Roni suffered a dull headache from reading the nearly illegible handwriting of Caroline's diary. She couldn't prove it, but something told her there was more to Hazel's death than what Faddle and the authorities were willing to admit. Hazel knew something and now she was dead.

For hours that evening she and Aaron had gone over all possibilities, pitching motives and suspects at each other. Aaron racked his brain trying to remember anything his mother had said or done to help piece it together. Nothing.

Roni massaged her eyelids and wearily read on, sure that certain answers existed in Caroline's journal. Midway through the book, she came upon something. Initially she had passed over it, merely skimming the words, until she came to a passage regarding the "visitor."

Visitor? What visitor?

Backtracking several pages, she found the original reference. Four years after the fall of Saigon, Caroline got a visitor. He came in a specially equipped van, his seven-year-old son with him. They talked in the backyard, she on a blanket spread on the lawn and he in his wheelchair—pantlegs folded under his knees where both limbs had been blown away by a land mine. They stayed only a few hours. His name was Dale Oberbeck. He was an air force pal of Richard

Holt's on a long-overdue mission, a private mission he insisted on executing in person.

Dale came a thousand miles to hand-deliver a parcel entrusted to him. As we sat under the nectarine tree with a simple lunch of sandwiches and Pepsi, the boy brought me a tin box from the van—a box I once mailed to Richard filled with his favorite walnut cookies. Richard is not dead, I told Dale. He held out his hand until I finally took it. His eyes held that same awful sadness and pity which I saw in the eyes of those who came to offer condolences eight years ago.

Oh please . . . don't.
Two days after Richard gave him that parcel a mutual friend saw his plane go down in flames. There is no possible way he could have survived, Mrs. Holt. Your husband is dead. Rich is dead.

I wanted to cover my ears, to tell him to leave, to make this day not real. Instead, I sat there mute, the emptiness growing inside me and with greedy eyes I watched his young son play, wishing he was mine. Richard and I had planned to have children, lots of children. The patter of little feet . . . and voices soft and sweet . . .
Oh, Richard, what will I do now?

The tin box contained every letter Caroline had written to her husband, a snapshot of the newlyweds, and a small vial of her perfume. That night Caroline added these items to the mementos of Richard Holt. She knelt at the shrine on the nightstand and cried.

Grief and loneliness tore at her heart. She wrote of death. Her own.

Roni paused, closing her eyes. But Caroline didn't die. At least not then. Instead, she must have deliberately set out to have the child they had both wanted so badly. Her chosen lover would serve one purpose and one purpose only, to father this new life. Airman Richard Holt would remain constant in her heart, never to be replaced.

Roni began to read more carefully, searching eagerly for a name, a description, a clue to the identity of Aaron's biological father. There was nothing. Why the secrecy? She was a widow, entitled to see and date others. Unless her lover was married. That made sense. No commitments, no overt claims to the child should the affair produce one.

Roni's own father immediately came to mind. Certainly it was possible. Yet for some reason she just as quickly dismissed him. Her father may have been unfaithful, but he wasn't a murderer. Roni strongly felt that Frank's killer and Aaron's father were one in the same.

Sheriff Lubben? Not likely. The sheriff could be a murderer, he could be many things, but a lover to Caroline was not one of them.

Who then? Roni thought back to that year. Eagleton had been in a boom. Two major gold mines on opposite sides of town had brought in hundreds of contract mine workers, not to mention an influx of saloon and merchant proprietors and innkeepers who followed such strikes and made a quick profit before pulling up stakes and moving on to the next rainbow on the horizon. Aaron's father, whoever he was, could be mining in New Mexico or Alaska now.

But she knew better. She knew he was right here in Eagleton.

She sighed, put aside the book, turned out the light, and slid down beneath the covers. Caroline's written words cut to her heart . . . *The emptiness growing inside me . . . with greedy eyes I watched his young son play, wishing he was mine.* Emptiness. Wishing he was mine. Caroline's obsession for a child of her very own may have clouded her reasoning. If what Roni suspected was true, a lover was chosen, then discarded when she became pregnant. Her lover had to be the best-kept secret in town. No one ever suspected the widow of opening her arms to another.

No one but Frank Scolli.

He moved silently through the passageway, the gas in the can sloshing as he walked. Ahead, in the thin light of his penlight, he saw the ladder. He slowed, feeling a tightness in his gut. He had to do it, there was no other way. Once and for all he would rid himself of any and all threats—real or imagined.

He climbed to the top. When he pushed on the trapdoor it gave an inch, but refused to open. He lowered himself to the ground, put the gas can down, and returned to the top. With both hands now free, he pushed. The door groaned, moving upward several inches, then stubbornly resisted.

The sound of footsteps in the passage made the man on the ladder freeze. His heart began to race. Someone was coming.

Quickly he climbed down, pulling the claw-toothed hammer from the waistband of his pants. He sought the shadows, pressed his back flat against the wall.

He was trapped. He could go neither forward nor backward.

The heavy footsteps grew louder. A flashlight beam swallowed the darkness along the floor, coming closer.

He mustn't be found out. There was so much to lose.

Again, as it had a dozen years ago, sheer panic and desperation drove the man to attack. He charged, swinging the hammer with all his might.

Thirty

"Roni? Roni, wake up."

Roni turned away from the bright light. She tried to dislodge the persistent hand shaking her shoulder. "Tomorrow," she said.

"Goddammit, Roni, wake up."

"I'm gonna wash your mouth out with Comet," she mumbled, rolling away from Aaron. "I said *tomorrow*."

The covers flew off her. She groaned, trying to grab them back as an icy chill invaded the bare flesh of her arms and legs.

"C'mon, wake up."

She sat up abruptly, hugging herself. She glanced at the clock—2:01. She had been asleep a mere two hours. Rubbing her eyes, she said, "This better be good."

"I heard scratching coming from the trapdoor."

"What?"

"Someone's in the tunnel and he's scratching on the door."

"One of the cats, maybe?"

"There's a kind of knocking, too. Cats don't knock."

Roni stared into Aaron's brown eyes, huge behind the round glasses. He was young, frail-looking, but he was not an alarmist.

She quickly dressed.

As they made their way downstairs, Aaron told her that he couldn't sleep and had gone down to make sure the settee was in place when he heard the noises on the other side of the trapdoor.

At the door to the basement she hesitated. "We shouldn't go down there alone, Aaron."

"You're not thinking of calling the sheriff, are you?"

She didn't want to.

"Call James," he said matter-of-factly. "I know you like him and want him here. Tell him to bring Red. Red'd probably rip the throat out of anyone who tried to jump us."

"Lovely thought," she said, hurrying to the phone.

He answered on the first ring.

"James, it's Roni." She told him what Aaron had heard. "It could be nothing. I haven't gone down—"

"I'll be right there. Stay upstairs. Don't do anything until I get there. Do you have a gun?"

"No. Only Mace."

"Get it." The line disconnected.

"He's on his way," she said. "James said to— *Aaron!*" she called out to his retreating back, "Dammit, Aaron!" She rushed after him.

She found him in the basement on his knees, his ear pressed to the trapdoor. The light from the kerosene lantern cast eerie shadows over the walls.

He motioned for her to listen.

Roni sank to her knees on the cold floor and laid her ear against the door. Nothing.

She looked at Aaron and whispered, "Are you sure—"

He shushed her.

She listened again. They looked at each other, then both shrugged. Aaron gestured for her to help with the settee. They gingerly moved it aside.

Holding her breath, Roni lifted the door one inch, two inches, six inches. She saw movement from inside the black wedge but failed to react fast enough. Her wrist was caught in a vice-like grip. She screamed, struggling.

Aaron grasped the hand that held Roni's. Then, as if burned, he snatched his hand away. It was covered with blood.

Roni fell back with a sharp cry, but not before she caught a glimpse of the man in the tunnel. The door dropped shut on his bloody hand.

"Oh shit, it's Dean . . . he's hurt," she said to Aaron, pulling on the door again. "Help me with this."

Aaron threw the door open to reveal the large man, one arm looped around a rung on the ladder, the other hand clutching at air, looking for a solid hold.

"Dean . . . ?" she whispered. "God, there's blood—his head . . ."

Aaron and Roni tried to pull Dean Scolli up through the trapdoor. His left arm, wedged tightly through the rungs, held him fast to the ladder. He moaned, his eyes focusing momentarily on Roni before they rolled back in his head. His hair was matted and sticky. A black hole at his temple oozed blood.

"It's no good," Roni said, panting nervously. "We need help."

She heard pounding upstairs. A dog barked.

"Aaron, it's James. Let him in."

Roni turned her attention back to Dean. "Hold on . . . hold on. Who did this to you? Dean, can you hear me? Who hit you?"

Blood puddled in the cup of his ear and he made strange clicking sounds in his throat.

A moment later James was beside her. Together they freed Dean's arm and pulled him up.

"There's no time to waste," James said, lifting Dean under his arms. "Roni, call the doc and have him meet us at the clinic. Aaron, grab hold of his feet."

While Roni talked to Dr. Burke, James and Aaron carried Dean out to James's Blazer.

James and Aaron rode in the front. Roni sat in the back with Dean. She held his hand.

As they drove down the street, Roni watched Red running after them. Dean moaned and she turned back to him.

Thirty-One

Roni paced the clinic's small reception area while James leaned against the wall and silently watched her. Through the glassed vestibule she could see Aaron sitting on the front steps with Red. In a room down the hall Dr. Burke and a nurse tended to Dean Scolli.

With the brutal attack on Dean, Roni realized that these were no longer scare tactics. Frank's body had been uncovered. One secret was out. A killer was loose in town and it looked as if he would stop at nothing to keep his secret. Dean had been in the wrong place at the wrong time. Hazel had a secret and she was dead. It had to be tied to Frank's death, which put her and James in danger as well.

Dr. Burke entered. "He's conscious. X-rays have been taken. There's trauma to the temporal and frontal areas of the skull. Watch and monitor, that's the name of the game at this stage. I've got Care Flight on standby to airlift him to Reno if there's the slightest change. Right now, thank God, he's stable and responsive." He ran a hand across a face lined with concern and fatigue. "He asked me not to call his parents till morning, says they've been through enough today without having to worry about him. So unless there's a turn for the worse, I'll respect his wishes."

"It's impossible to keep anything quiet in a small town."

"If they find out, they find out, but it won't be from me or Nurse Petty."

"Can I—James and I, can we see him for a minute?"

"Afraid not. He needs absolute quiet."

"Doctor, did he say what happened?" James asked.

The doctor shook his head. "He's pretty disoriented. And frankly, I want him to rest right now. Tomorrow will be soon enough for questions and answers. Go on home now, both of you. Get some sleep."

James and Roni moved toward the exit. The door opened and Sheriff Lubben barged through.

"Not so fast," he said. "I got questions."

"Can't it wait until tomorrow?" James said.

"It could, but it ain't gonna. We're all here—now's a dandy time."

"Sheriff," the doctor said, "it's after three in the morning. At least let them take the boy home."

"It won't hurt him to—ah, hell, go on then." He moved aside for them to pass. "I won't be far behind you. Put coffee on."

On the way home, Roni and Aaron took turns filling James in on the events of the past two days: the autopsy; the stolen journal turning up in Father Roberts's trash; Dean's determination to find his brother's killer; Roni's suspicions regarding Hazel's death.

Back inside the house, Aaron and Red quickly disappeared upstairs amid a chorus of cat hisses and shrieks. Roni knew Aaron was uncomfortable around the sheriff and wouldn't hang around unless he had to.

Roni filled the coffeepot with water. "This hasn't been easy for Aaron. Up until his mother died his life was pretty simple—peculiar, to say the least—but relatively uncomplicated. I learned something about him today, James, something that explains some of his eccentric behavior."

"His project?"

She turned to him. "You've seen it?"

"No. His mother told me."

"The talent, musical as well as artistic, both beyond words." She started the coffee.

"The two of you are hitting it off pretty good, aren't you?" James asked.

"I think so. I hope so, anyway," she said, pausing to reflect on their relationship. "He's really a sweet kid. Mysterious as all hell, but sweet. Why does everything in his town have to be cloaked in mystery?"

With a half-grin, James said, "Guess it's just that kind of town."

"With those kinds of people."

"Right." He came up behind her as she took down coffee mugs. He tucked the tag on the collar of her T-shirt back in place. "A little mystery adds spice to life, don't you think?"

Though his fingers were warm, she shivered at his unexpected touch. She tried to cover it by shrugging nonchalantly. "A *little* mystery's okay. This is flatout ridiculous."

James touched her hair, wound a curl around one finger. She watched him in the window reflection. She turned, her breasts brushing across his chest, about to move into his arms when she heard footsteps on the stairs.

"Aaron," she said at the same time he said, "Lubben."

James turned and hoisted himself up on the counter.

Not bothering to knock, Lubben opened the back door and entered.

Aaron appeared at the opposite end of the room, and seeing the sheriff, he paused uncertainly in the kitchen doorway.

Red Dog, golden eyes focused on Lubben, growled deep in his throat. James wagged a finger at him and he quieted.

The sheriff nodded at them, picked up an empty mug, and headed for the coffeepot. When he saw the coffee wasn't ready, he let the mug swing from one finger, tapped a flashlight against his thigh, and turned to Roni. In a jovial tone saturated with sarcasm, he said, "My, my, my, but this here house seems to be the activity center of the entire town, its underground passage a regular Grand Central Station. And in the midst of all this action sits Miss Roni Mayfield and friends." He pivoted from Aaron to James, smiling, a fierceness in his eyes.

James matched his stare.

Lubben turned to Roni. "Is that java about done?"

Roni lifted the pot and, with it still perking, poured coffee into his outstretched mug. He ignored the hot liquid spitting out on the back of his hand.

"Whenever you're ready," Lubben said, blowing on the coffee.

As she filled two more mugs, Roni told the sheriff what had happened.

"Did he talk to you? Tell you who attacked him?"

"No."

Lubben turned to James, a black eyebrow raised quizzically. James shook his head. He turned to Aaron, who lowered his head and said nothing.

Setting down the mug and slapping the flashlight against his palm, he said, "Gonna check out the tunnel. Stick around, Jimmy Boy. You . . ." he pointed to Aaron, "hit the sack."

After the sheriff left the room, Aaron started out. Red trotted after him. At the doorway Aaron, his hand on the dog's head, turned to James, his eyes questioning.

"He'll hog the whole bed," James said.

"That's okay."

"Go ahead then."

Aaron's face broke into one of his rare smiles. "C'mon, Red, race you up the stairs." And they were off.

Ten minutes later Lubben marched back into the kitchen. Hitching a foot up on a wooden chair, he leaned over, bracing his arms on his thigh. "It's obvious there was a scuffle of some kind. And blood . . . lots of it. Looks like Scolli got jumped within a few yards of the trapdoor. There's a trial of blood to the ladder. The way it looks he was probably bushwhacked. I doubt anyone could get in those kinda licks if they was facin' Scolli eye to eye—he's too damn big." He lowered his head, scratched his chin, and glanced up at Roni. "Did ya know he was gonna be in the tunnel?"

"No."

"What'd'ya suppose he was doin' down there?"

"How would I know?"

Lubben stared at the floor for several long moments. He lifted his head and shifted his eyes toward James. "Heard you two got into a little tussle yesterday—*again*."

"We talked," James said. "I wouldn't call it a tussle."

"If I remember right, you two was always in competition with each other. Jobs, huntin' and fishin'—women . . ." He let the last hang in the air. He began to pace. "Now let's suppose one of you decides to take a shortcut to see Miss Mayfield in the wee hours of the mornin'. And the other one was already here and on his way home. The two of you meet up in the tunnel and . . . well, tempers flare. You're not as big as Scolli, but you're athletic. Could probably hold your own if the need arose. Especially if you got the jump on him."

"I was home. In bed."

"You got someone to vouch for you?"

"James wouldn't have to use the tunnel," Roni said. "He can come and go freely through the door . . . any hour of the day or night."

Lubben pursed his lips. "Is that so? A woman of the nineties right in this here teemin' metropolis of Eagleton."

"Sheriff," James said steadily. "You're out of line and I think you know it."

A dark look hardened Lubben's face, then abruptly it was gone. "I don't like outsiders comin' to my town and unsettlin' things. You two are outsiders. Seen it dozens a times. Your type come in, take what you can while you're here, and then it's *adios*, headin' out without a backward glance."

"What about Aaron?" Roni said. "He's not an outsider."

"Who you kiddin'? He's about as outside as they get. His mother didn't really belong, but at least she made an effort to join in, to mingle. But Aaron," his face darkened again, "Aaron is . . ."

Roni waited, but the sheriff clamped his mouth shut and offered no more. Instead, he pushed his empty coffee mug across the table and waggled it, indicating he wanted more.

James motioned to Roni to stay put as he dropped down from the counter. He snatched up the coffeepot and firmly set it down in front of Lubben. Lubben looked up at James, grinned, then reached for the pot.

"What did you see the day Frank disappeared?" James said to the sheriff.

"I think you got it ass backwards, Jimboy. I do the askin'."

"Humor me," James said. "We might both learn something."

Lubben took his time sipping his coffee. He swirled the liquid around, staring down inside the cup as though looking for something in its black depths.

"Okay. Sure, why not? I was passin' by that day when I saw someone runnin' from the house. He sprinted 'cross the lot to the trees in back like someone'd just set the hounds on him. Looked like Frank. Yeah, sure as shit looked like Frank. Guess . . . well, I guess maybe it was your brother, Larry. Anyway, wasn't nothin' to do but investigate. I had a choice to make . . . chase down the trespasser or check on the widda. I chose to look in on her and a good thing, too. I found her upstairs on the floor by her bed.

She was barely conscious and . . . and bleedin'. She'd
been assaulted.''

"Sexually?" James asked.

"It sure as hell looked like it. She had this clump
of black hair clutched in one hand . . ." He raised a
fist. "Hair she'd yanked out of her assailant's head.
And she even had skin under her fingernails. She'd
been fendin' off someone, I'd swear to that."

"No sign of Frank or anyone else when you got
there?" James said.

"None."

"Could someone have been hiding upstairs?"

"Well . . . yeah, sure."

"So you found Caroline. What did she say happened?"

"She was really out of it, confused. She didn't have
much to offer. But the one thing she did remember
was strugglin' with Frank. She couldn't recall him
turnin' up or leavin' . . . just the strugglin' on the
floor by the bed."

"Go on."

He paused a beat, then looked up. "That's it."

The sheriff was definitely holding something back.
"There were rumors that Caroline had been enter-
taining a lover . . . or lovers." True or not, Roni hated
herself for even voicing the rumor, but she saw no
other way to get Lubben to talk.

It backfired on her.

Lubben's grin was nasty. "Well now, why don't you
just ask your *daddy* about that."

Roni felt the blood rise to her face. What she had
suspected all along was true, and others knew about
it. *Her father and Caroline.*

The sheriff pushed his mug away and rose abruptly.

"Friggin' outsiders," he said in disgust, then crossed the room and slammed the door behind him.

Roni stared after him. When she felt a hand caress the back of her neck, she involuntarily stiffened. She turned to gaze at James. He kissed her lightly on the temple and enfolded her into his arms.

"How many knew?"

"Rumors, nothing more," he said quietly.

"Were there others . . . besides my dad?"

"Not that I know of. Your father, well, I took it he wasn't very good at that sort of thing . . . at cheating. Just the mention of her name and it was all there on his face, plain as a picture, the guilt and shame and . . . agony. He looked like a man turned inside out."

Yes, he would have been, Roni thought.

"Where is he now?"

"I'm not sure. He came through town last Thursday on his way to the Idaho border. Business. A new claim."

"Did he come to the house? Meet Aaron?"

"No. I met him at the cafe. He was in a hurry. He promised to stay longer on his way back. Why?"

"No reason."

She sighed. "My father and Caroline. How blind could I be?"

James gave her a light squeeze. "Don't think about it now. We better try to get a few hours' sleep. I have a feeling tomorrow is going to be an even longer day."

"You were awake when I called, weren't you?" she asked.

"Ummm."

"I'm sorry if I interrupted something."

He stared at her solemnly. "I was alone. Linda and I no longer share a bed. We decided a while back to be friends."

Somehow Roni doubted that, at least where Linda was concerned. She was too touchy-feely and desire still burned in her eyes when she looked at James. "But you went to Elko and brought her back with you."

"Says who?"

"Well . . . I . . ." she looked away.

"I was in Boulder. I went to see Larry, but got there too late. He took off without leaving a forwarding address."

"Not Elko?"

"Not unless it's moved to Colorado." James bent down and touched his lips lightly to hers. He drew back and stared into her eyes. She stood still, her arms at her side. Lifting her arms, he put them around his neck, then put his arms around her waist and pulled her to him. When he kissed her she leaned into him and gave herself fully to the heat of his mouth and body. His kiss both calmed and excited her. It felt so natural, so right.

On the floor above Roni heard laughter, then a dog chuffing and the sounds of roughhousing.

James broke the kiss, hugged her, and said, "Our chaperons are still awake. It's time we all turned in. I'll bed down on the sofa."

"The trapdoor?"

"I'll take care of it."

Roni went after the bedding, relieved that James would be close by. When she entered the parlor a few minutes later she found him stretched out on the sofa, the two parlor cats, proclaiming territorial rights, were curled at his feet.

"How's this for a fair trade? One dog for two cats," he said. "They're housebroken, aren't they?"

"Not all of them."

"Great."

As she spread the blanket over him a thought came to her. "James, that day . . . did you see my father here at the house? Is that why you were so determined I must have known something?"

"Roni, get some sleep. We'll get it all straightened out soon enough." He took her hand, kissed her fingertips. "Go on, get outta here."

Scolli's eyes were partially open, yet unseeing. His lips were parted and drool, blood-tinged, ran down the side of his face to form a wet, pink circle on the pillowcase. The head wounds, undressed, had stopped bleeding, the clotted blood matting the thick, black hair over his ear.

The other man in the room silently looked on. If not for the ever-so-slight rise and fall of the chest, the patient looked dead. Certainly brain-dead. No mortal man could take the blows to the head that this man had taken and live to talk about it; that he still continued to breathe was a miracle.

The man standing in the shadows of the room couldn't chance another miracle.

He crept forward. No one had seen him enter. The clinic was quiet, deserted, corridor lights reduced to half power. The job had to be finished. He'd come too far to stop now. If anyone tried, he'd kill them, too. There was everything to lose, much to gain. Anonymity. Freedom. Spending the rest of his life behind bars appealed little to him.

He approached the bed.

Thirty-Two

Something woke James. He couldn't have been asleep more than a few minutes when an intrusive sound brought him back. In a strange house, on an incredibly hard surface, a pair of cats crowding his feet, a light doze was the most he could have hoped for. He was wide awake again.

A cool, wet nose nudged him under the chin.

James slowly rose up on an elbow. "What is it, boy?"

Red whined low in this throat. One of the cats at James's feet arched slowly and hissed. The other one remained curled up, unruffled by the dog.

Red turned his head toward the back of the house and growled. James shushed him, left the settee, and quickly made his way through the house with Red at his side. When they reached the kitchen, James paused. The room was dark, but a bright moon clearly defined the figure on the back steps.

James quickly crossed to the door and flattened his body against the wall. He heard the doorknob turn.

James released the chain, unlocked the door then yanked it open, pulling the man inside. He threw an arm around his neck and grabbed his wrist, wrenching it high up on the broad back. The man grunted in surprised pain.

"Who are you?" James said.

The man struggled, trying to twist out of James's hold. "Who the hell are *you*?" he replied in a strangled voice.

Red growled.

"Don't piss off the dog," James said.

Suddenly the lights came on. James turned to see Aaron and Roni in the doorway. Roni held the can of Mace in front of her and Aaron wielded a sorry-looking mop.

"Dad . . . ?" Roni said.

"Hon, can you ask him to let go?" the man said through strained vocal cords.

James released him, putting a hand out to stay Red. To James, Roni's father had changed little over the years, a deeper tan, more gray in his dark, curly hair, but still the same. His brown eyes, like his daughter's, looked perplexed.

Tom Mayfield flexed his twisted arm and rubbed at his throat. He moved toward her. "Honey?"

Roni instinctively drew back. Her father stopped, his hand outstretched. Roni lowered the Mace, pulled her robe together in front, and gave her father a weak smile. "Funny, we were just talking about you a while ago," she said in a strange voice. "Your ears must have been burning."

"Roni . . . what's going on?"

Roni handed the Mace to Aaron, then closed the gap and went into her father's arms.

Tom hugged her, saying, "I didn't mean to barge

in. I knocked but no one answered." He looked from
Roni to James. "There's blood all over the place out
there. I got worried. Honey, what happened?"

"There was an accident—well, not quite an acci-
dent," she said, brushing her hair back from her face.
"It's a long story, Dad, too long to go into right now.
Aaron and I are okay."

He turned to James. "Yours is a familiar face, isn't
it?"

"Yes, sir. James Glazer," he said, extending his
hand. "My father and I worked with you at the Goldline Mine."

"I remember. And this is . . . ?" Tom nodded at
Red.

"Red. He lives with me."

"Coyote," Tom said flatly.

"Half, anyway."

She motioned for Aaron to come closer. "Dad, this
is Aaron Holt."

Her father extended a hand and Aaron tentatively
took it. "Pleased to meet you, Aaron."

Roni looked from her father to Aaron to James.
"I'll put coffee on."

Thirty-Three

Friday

The sun came up as they sipped coffee in the kitchen. Roni and James caught Tom up on everything. Aaron sat quietly, adding nothing, missing nothing. The talk mostly centered around the Scollis—Frank's remains and Dean's attack.

Aaron stuck close to Roni. Either he was afraid to be alone or afraid to leave her alone, she didn't know which. What she did know was that with Aaron present, talking to her father about Caroline was impossible.

At 6:00 a.m. James went home to shower, change, and send off an overdue ore deposit to the lab in Vegas for analysis.

Roni carried the mugs to the sink. "I'm going to run down to the clinic and see how Dean is doing."

"I'm going with you," Aaron said, jumping up.

She looked at him and smiled. "Okay. You feed

the cats while I jump in the shower. Dad, care to come?''

"No, you go ahead. I'll stay here and wait for Jim. Can't stand anything about hospitals."

She cleaned up, dressed in jeans, T-top, and a pair of sandals. The morning was crisp, yet mild with a promise of a true Indian summer day. As she and Aaron passed the gray stone house at the corner, Mrs. Wiggins, in a baggy sweater over a flannel nightgown, briskly swept her front porch. Her ears may have gone over, but there was nothing wrong with her eyes. The woman stopped sweeping to do some serious gawking.

Aaron waved.

Mrs. Wiggins broke into a big smile, flapped her sweater like a fledgling flapping its wings, and did a little marching in place step.

As Roni waved, she asked Aaron, "Is she all there?"

"Oh, no, she's nutty as a loon. But she's real nice. She can remember back when she was a kid. Her parents were clowns in the circus. She has some neat stories and she acts them out."

When they reached Mill Crossing they turned toward town and the clinic. Roni marveled at the clean air and fresh fragrance of nature. On days like this when the sun was shining, the wind a mere breeze carrying the scent of flowers, and the temperature mild, she remembered what a beautiful town Eagleton could be. The wild roses, at the end of their bloom, blanketed the streets and yards in petals of golden yellow. The recent rains painted the hills a mosaic of red, gold, and bright green. With only a little moisture, new growth sprang forth in abundance. For the first time she saw everything through Aaron's eyes.

She had assumed he disliked the town because he

rarely interacted with the people. But she realized there was more to a town than its inhabitants. Towns had their own personality, their own charm and beauty . . . evident in the mini-town in the attic. There was no denying Aaron was shy and not one to parade around. But since when did one need to perform in the production to play a major part in it?

Deeply absorbed in their own thoughts, they nearly passed the clinic. She pulled on Aaron's shirt to stop him and they backtracked to the concrete walkway. Once inside the front door, they walked down the short corridor to the reception desk.

She heard a baby's angry cry and a television, turned up loud, playing the theme song from "The Flintstones." At the vacant reception area the water in the Sparkletts cooler burped and gurgled.

They stood at the counter and looked around, waiting. After several minutes she decided people did things differently in small towns; they weren't as rigid with rules and regulations here. If she wanted to look in on Dean she should just do it. A quick glance at the clipboard on the desk told her Dean was in room 7.

"You want to come with me or wait here?"

"Wait here." Aaron flopped down in one of the molded plastic chairs, pulling his legs up. He picked up a magazine and opened it in front of his face. It was amazing how small—how imperceptible—he could make himself. Dammit, she thought, he was good-looking, talented, and sweet. He had too much going for him to remain stuck away unnoticed.

The corridor was dimly lit. Doors to vacant rooms were open. The aroma of cooking food became stronger as she approached the back of the clinic and Dean's room. The door to number 7 was closed. Roni paused with her hand on the door, wondering what to do. Go in? Knock? Find the nurse?

As she vacillated, she heard a noise beyond the door. A sound that made her heart race. The savage sound of rage, of violence.

She pushed the door open and looked in. Dean was not alone in the room. Leaning over him was the reddish blond head of Dr. Burke. He had a knee on the bed and seemed to be bearing down on Dean Scolli. Perspiration ran down the side of the doctor's harshly set, crimson face.

Roni was startled by the unexpected commotion. She'd imagined a quiet, somber scene, not this fierce struggle for life. A nurse, leaning over the patient from the other side of the bed, held a hand respirator to his mouth, squeezing the black bag to force air into his lungs. Both nurse and doctor worked frantically to revive the ashen, unresponsive patient. The priest, Father Roberts, stood at the foot of the bed, head bowed in prayer.

Roni stepped back into the hall, letting the door hiss shut. She turned around and leaned against the glossy beige wall. Cupping her hands over her nose and mouth, she breathed deeply. *This can't be happening,* she told herself. *Not another one. Not Dean.*

Minutes later the door opened and Dr. Burke stepped through, his face set, lined with fatigue. He stopped just beyond the doorway and rubbed his eyes with his fingertips. Roni heard him moan low in his throat.

"Doctor?" she said softly.

He turned, his eyes opening wide, surprised that she was there. "Oh, Roni, I didn't see you," he said in a weary voice.

"Did he . . . ? Is he . . . dead?"

He scrubbed at his drenched face, nodding.

"What happened?"

"There was nothing we could do. Nothing. Nurse Petty called as soon as it was apparent he'd stopped breathing. She started CPR, but . . ."

"His family . . . ? Where are they?"

Before he could respond she saw Dean's parents racing down the hall toward them. She heard the doctor sigh deeply.

"Doctor—our boy, where is our boy?" Al shouted.

"Al, Anna—" the doctor began, but they pushed him aside and rushed into the room.

Anna Scolli cried out, "Oh Mary, Mother of God!"

Dr. Burke turned to Roni. "Wait here a minute." He returned to the room.

A heartrending wail that seemed to come from the depths of despair followed, then trailed on and on.

Roni squeezed her eyes shut and moaned. With no strength left, she leaned against the wall again.

Several minutes later the doctor came out, took Roni by the elbow, and began to walk. "Father is with them—there's nothing more I can do. I need coffee. Join me?"

"Aaron's in the waiting room."

"He'll be all right."

They were silent until they were inside his office where the rich aroma of fresh-brewed coffee greeted them. He poured two cups, handed her one, then perched on the edge of his desk. He seemed smaller, his shoulders more bent.

"I . . . I chose to respect Dean's wishes and wait until this morning to call his parents. Oh, Lord, why didn't . . . if only I'd . . ."

"You didn't know," Roni said.

"Yes, of course I did. I'm a doctor. I've practiced

medicine long enough to know that a patient can be stable one minute, in code the next, then gone. Dammit. What in hell is happening around here?" he asked. "Frank murdered. Dean—it's no longer an assault case: now it's murder, plain and simple. The sheriff won't be happy." Dr. Burke lifted the phone's receiver, had it halfway to his ear, then returned it to the cradle.

"Roni, listen to me. Dean's attacker means business and I think you and Aaron are in grave danger. The way it looks, the one who killed Frank twelve years ago has resurfaced. If I'm right, he's killed twice and, who knows? It just might get easier each time."

She nodded. "My count is four, not two."

"Four?"

"Frank, Caroline, Hazel, and Dean."

"Have you told Lubben what—"

"Lubben is useless. For him to admit that Caroline was murdered is to admit that he blew it. He still has some soul-searching to do on Frank's death. The answer has to be right under my nose. All I need is to find—"

"It's not your job to flush out killers," the doctor cut in. "I'm sure you're an excellent reporter and that you've been in dangerous situations before, but you've got the boy to consider now."

"He won't leave."

"The choice is not his. He has no one but you now. You go, he goes. Speaking of Lubben . . ." He lifted the phone, dialed, and asked for the sheriff. "Nancy, when he checks in tell him his services are required once again. I'm at the clinic."

Roni stared silently into her coffee. After a moment she said, "Dr. Burke, may I ask you something?"

He waited.

"What made you so certain that Frank was Aaron's father?"

He rose, walked behind his desk, and sat down. "Caroline came to me afterward . . . after that day in question. She told me Frank raped her and she feared she was pregnant with his child. She did not want it. In fact, she asked me to abort it. Demanded, actually."

"You didn't examine her the day of the alleged rape?"

"No. Sheriff Lubben, as you know, was the one who found her. She refused to let him call me or anyone else. At the time I think she was too mortified by the experience. The typical emotions a victim goes through . . . guilt, shame, disbelief. She changed her mind, however, when she learned she was pregnant. She wanted an abortion. Wanted it on the spot."

"And?"

"I could sympathize, naturally. This is a small town and she was unmarried. To be forced to bear the child of her rapist . . . well, you can understand." Roni nodded. "Abortions were legal, had been legal for over a decade, but because of my religious faith I had to refuse. I asked her to reconsider. Personally, I felt the baby could be a great comfort to her. She was nearly thirty and all alone. And it wasn't as if Frank were some horrible fiend. He was a young man, with bursting hormones, in the wrong place at the wrong time."

"What about her health? You said the pregnancy and delivery weakened her already damaged heart."

"It did. Yes, it did. But I didn't know about the rheumatic fever until many years later. Caroline was not one to complain. Nor did she have annual medical exams."

"So what happened then?"

"When I refused the abortion, she left. I was certain she'd go somewhere else, to another doctor in a neighboring town. I guess she had second thoughts."

"You delivered Aaron?"

"No. A midwife. She never came back after that first exam. Didn't want to give me the satisfaction, I suppose. It's curious," he added, tapping a pen on the ink blotter, "you say she was already pregnant before that day?"

Roni nodded.

"Hmm, it doesn't make sense. Unless the abortion was—"

"What?"

"No, I have no right to . . ."

"Please, Doctor. Unless the abortion was what?"

"Lubben's idea. Lubben never did care for kids, but he sure was crazy for *her*. And he was practically the only one she could completely depend on. He'd have done anything for her."

"Kill for her?"

The doctor looked up—their eyes locked.

Thirty-Four

"Dean Scolli's dead, isn't he? I heard his mother crying," Aaron said when Roni returned to the reception room.

"C'mon, let's get out of here."

Once outside, Roni told Aaron about Dean and about her conversation with the doctor. "He thinks we should leave here. He's afraid for us."

"I'm not going. I already told you that. If you're scared, then you go."

"Is that what you want? For me to leave?"

"You're not responsible for me. You don't have to worry about me."

"But I do worry about you." As for being responsible for him, she could handle that. The thought of going away and leaving him behind gave her a profound sense of loss. Although she had known him only a short time, he had touched her heart and touched it deeply. It dawned on her that two men had suddenly come into her life, two men she cared for very much. James, of course, had more or less been on the fringe all along. Maybe Aaron had been there, too ... through Caroline. Roni felt she was being offered a second chance to do right by Caroline. Whatever the outcome, it was not something that could be decided hastily by either one of them.

When they turned on Mill Crossing, Aaron asked about her father. She told him he was a prospector.

"Why'd he come?" Aaron asked.

Roni shrugged. "He was passing through and I guess he wanted to see how I was doing." But she wondered if he had another reason for being here. A very specific reason. Again she found herself examining Aaron's features and wondering if this pale, underdeveloped boy was her brother.

Aaron's glasses slipped down his nose. He pushed them back up.

"We've got to do something about those glasses. Is there an optometrist in this town?"

He shrugged. "I like these glasses. I don't want another pair."

"I wouldn't dream of making you change, although it shouldn't be too difficult to have them adjusted to fit your face. What do you think?"

He grinned that sweet grin that had a way of lightly tugging at her heart.

When Roni and Aaron arrived back at the house, James was on his way out. An excited Red jumped up on Aaron's chest, nearly knocking the boy to the ground. Aaron laughed and hugged the dog. Red barked, grabbed a stick in his mouth, and dropped it at Aaron's feet. The two moved off toward the rear yard.

"You were leaving?" Roni said to James.

"I didn't know how long you'd be. I've already

talked with Faddle. His plane is fueled and ready to go.''

"Go? Go where?"

"To Reno. It's Larry. A friend of his called about an hour ago. I'd left my number on her answering machine. Larry's in Reno, in a hospital. He tried to kill himself two nights ago. Roni, I think it has something to do with both you and me returning to Eagleton. After talking to him, and then his landlady, I sort of expected something like this."

She felt sick. Larry ... suicide? Everything was crashing down around them.

"How long will you be gone?" she asked.

"If I can see him, talk to him, probably just today."

"Take us with you."

"What about your father?"

"What *about* me?" Tom said behind her.

"Dad, I want to go with James to Reno. His brother is there and ... well, it's kind of complicated. We should be back tonight."

Tom looked from James to Roni. "I know you wouldn't run off if there was any way it could be avoided."

She hugged her father, then turned to James. "Dean didn't make it. He's dead."

"Shit. Does Lubben know?"

"He should by now."

"Then we better get going before he tries to stop us."

"Aaron!" she called to the boy who was throwing sticks for the dog.

When he joined them inside, Roni told him an emergency had come up and they had to leave town. "You're coming, too."

"Let me stay here," he said.

"I can't do that. I can't leave you here alone."

"I'll be all right. Mrs. Wiggins can come at night."

"Look, we're flying in the mayor's private plane," she said forcing enthusiasm into her voice. "You'll love it." For Roni, private planes ranked right up there with abandoned mine shafts, fires, and riots.

He plopped down on a kitchen chair, pulled his legs in close to his body, and wrapped those thin arms around his knees. He wagged his head back and forth.

"*Aaron* . . ."

"I'll be happy to stay with him if he doesn't want to go," Tom said.

Aaron turned an eager face to Roni. "Roni? Please?"

Roni twisted her fingers. She turned to James. "Can I have a minute with my father, please?"

"C'mon, Aaron," James said. "Let's put Red through his paces. Did you know he can play dead when you pretend to shoot him?"

When the door closed behind them, she cleared her throat and looked at her father.

His eyes didn't meet hers. "Just because I cheated on your mother doesn't mean I can't be trusted with an eleven-year-old kid," he said.

"Then you and Caroline . . . ?"

"Yes. We had an affair."

She waited, saying nothing.

He paced the length of the kitchen before saying, "I want you to know that she was the only woman I cheated with. Honey, I loved your mother, but . . . but I loved Caroline more. I would have left your mother for her."

"Why didn't you?"

"Caroline wouldn't let me." He turned his back

to her and his voice became low, pensive. "There was something very special about her . . . tragic, vulnerable, incredibly feminine. I wanted to care for her, take away the pain and loneliness. At the same time I craved her gentle touch, her soft words, her . . . her love."

Roni thought back and realized that those were the same things she had wanted from Caroline, only in a different way. Anyone in close contact with her had no doubt felt the same; Lubben and, of course, Aaron's father, whoever he was. Caroline had so much love inside her with so few places to channel it.

"When did this happen?" Roni asked.

"You had just started the piano lessons. I took some sheet music back that she'd lent you."

Roni exhaled, shook her head, and turned away from him. "I can't believe she would do that."

"It wasn't what you think. We began as friends. I . . . we spent a lot of time together talking. Then it just happened. It wasn't vulgar or cheap. It wasn't like that. She wasn't like that."

"You were a married man. You were my father. *My* father. How could *she* do that knowing what it would do to our family, to me, if you were found out?"

"Maybe she sensed she was already losing you. You were nearly sixteen, Roni. We only had a few more months at the mine and then we would've moved on with all the others."

She thought about that, knowing he was right. "Dad, is . . ."

"Is Aaron my son? No. No, sweetheart, he is not." He again paced the length of the kitchen. "I didn't know the boy existed until Caroline sent me a letter asking if I'd submit to a blood test. And why."

"When was that?"

"A month or two ago."

"Did you? The test?"

"There was no point. I knew I wasn't the father. I had a vasectomy right after you were born."

"And Caroline didn't know that?"

"No."

"Then, as far as she knew, you could've been the father?"

Tom nodded. He looked at her, a sad smile pulling at the corners of his mouth. "I should have guessed what she was after. All she talked about was what a beautiful child you were, and how if she ever had a baby she wanted her to be just like you. It wasn't me she wanted, it was you, or someone like you."

"She wanted a baby. She wrote that in her diary. Dad, do you know of anyone else she was with . . . intimately?"

He shook his head.

"One more question. Were you here that day? The day Frank was killed?"

"God, Roni, you couldn't possibly think I'd hurt that boy . . . or anyone."

"I have to ask."

"She ended our affair weeks before. I never set foot in this house again . . . until today." He took her hand and held it in his tan, rough hands. "I'm sorry, honey. Sorry for whatever damage I've done to you and to your mother. It's not surprising that Caroline was so crazy about you. You're quite a gal, but then I've always known that."

She managed a smile.

"Her son . . . is he a good kid?"

"Yes," she said quietly. "Caroline must have been very proud of him."

She gave her father a quick hug, then called Aaron

and James in. She tried once again to persuade Aaron to go with them, but he was adamant. It was agreed Red Dog could stay with them.

Roni hurried upstairs to change clothes.

As she pulled on the navy blazer over jeans and a yellow silk blouse, she spotted Caroline's last journal on the nightstand. She slid it into her large handbag on the dresser.

"Roni?"

Roni looked into the mirror and saw Aaron standing in the doorway. "Come in."

He moved in tentatively. "You . . . you won't forget to come back, will you? You won't decide to go on to California without coming back here first?"

Roni paused, then slowly turned to face him. "Oh, Aaron, of course not."

"I know how much you hate it here."

"That's not true. You're here, right? So how bad can it be?"

"Really?"

"Really." She opened her arms and he rushed into them. "Aaron, honey, we'll work it out . . . some way."

Ten minutes earlier Roni had turned off Highway 50 onto the narrow two-lane road that would take them to Coggins Airfield. They had brought her car. Ahead and to the right she saw the row of sheetmetal structures that comprised the airport. As they neared the turnoff to the field, James pointed to a metal hangar on the left.

"That's the office."

She dropped him at the door and drove around the side to park. As she locked the car James joined her and pointed to a small green and white airplane.

They hurried across the tarmac. He helped her into the plane, sat her in the cockpit, then lowered himself into the pilot's seat. He started flipping switches and checking gauges.

"What are you doing? Where's Faddle?" she said, looking out the window toward the hangar.

"He's probably at his ranch or in town residing over a City Council meeting. I didn't ask. Did you want him along?"

"I thought—I didn't—can you fly this thing?" she asked incredulously.

"You be the judge," he said, starting the engine.

They hit an air pocket and the small plane went into a series of bumps and grinds. Roni glanced at James, trying not to show fear. He smiled without looking at her. She leaned over and looked out the window to see miles of barren, ocher land beneath them. A mountain range loomed ahead.

"There's usually some turbulence over the mountains," James explained.

"Ahhh," she answered, nodding lamely.

"Relax. I'd have thought flying would be second nature to you, Roni. Don't most investigative reporters travel a lot, and by plane?"

"These toy ones have always made me nervous, even with real pilots flying them."

"Would you like to see my pilot's license?"

"You know what I mean. It's like having Aaron tell me he's a dentist and I should try to relax while he gives me a root canal."

"You're comparing my piloting to a root canal?"

"No, I . . . I just didn't know. I guess there's a lot

I don't know about you." She turned toward him. "Tell me about your family."

"There's not much to tell. There are three of us. Me, Larry, and our little sister, Nell."

"Larry never mentioned a sister."

"No," James said pensively, "he wouldn't have."

"If it's something you'd rather not talk about . . ."

James looked out the window to his left, then let his gaze sweep over the gauges. Just when Roni thought he wasn't going to answer, he said, "She stayed behind with my mother."

"Your *mother*? Larry told me your mother was dead."

"That's what we were told to say. But, no, she was very much alive, living in Australia where my father left her." James squared his shoulders, inhaling deeply.

"Oh, James, I had no idea."

"No one did. That was the beauty of it—we almost believed it ourselves." James told her about coming to America and moving from town to town, about being left on their own, cold and hungry much of the time. The nearly buried Aussie accent became more distinct as he spoke of his early background.

"Why'd he do it?"

"Revenge. She tried to take us kids and leave him."

"Your sister?"

"She was newborn and sickly—he figured she'd be more trouble than she was worth. But Nell was his trump card. That's how he kept us from contacting Mum. He swore he'd go back there and take Nell— kill her if he had to."

"And you believed him?"

"Damn right we believed him. Claude Glazer was

a cold bastard,'' he said, as if the words tasted bad in his mouth, ''who didn't give a shit about anyone but himself.''

Roni remembered a man telling his son to go barefoot to school when his only pair of shoes had worn out, and using his fists to get the message across.

''Did your mother look for you?''

''She never stopped until she died.''

After a long pause he continued. ''Ten years ago he came to Reno where I was enrolled at Mackay, the mining school at UNR, and said he'd been wrong to take us from Mum and he was sorry for the hurt he'd caused. He'd been a mean, tough sonofabitch, he said, but age and a bad conscience had finally mellowed him, 'Go to her,' he said, 'let her see how good her son turned out.' Then he told me where she was.

''I found my Mum and sister in a little town outside of Melbourne. My mother was dying. A malignant brain tumor. In her diseased-infested mind, Larry and I were still little guys. She thought I was *him*, my father. She cursed me, then cried and begged to see her children one last time.

''The bastard knew. Before he sent me there, he knew. I wanted to kill him. And I tried. I tracked him down in Utah and with my bare hands I nearly killed him.''

Turbulence rocked the airplane, but Roni scarcely noticed.

''Nell hated me as much as I hated him. She blamed me. I was the oldest. It was my responsibility to have let them know where we were, that we were alive and well.''

''Does she still blame you?''

He shrugged. ''Maybe I blame myself. Maybe if I'd

taken a stand sooner, counter-threatened my father, physically forced . . . oh, Christ, I don't know. I could go crazy playing that game. I don't know. No one knows. What I do know is that I cherish the memory of my mother's love for me during those few years before he kidnapped us. Larry, poor guy, was too young when we left. He doesn't have those memories."

"Larry had you, James. He worshipped you, looked up to you. He was happy."

"Was," James said solemnly. "That seems to be the operative word. He's no longer happy and I have to find out why."

For the past ten minutes a smattering of small towns had appeared off to their left. Interstate 80 remained in view as the plane followed it west.

"Not much longer," James offered. "We just flew over Fernley a few miles back. Twenty-five miles or so to Reno."

"Why does Faddle own a plane?"

"Because he can afford one. But mainly because of his mother's health. Getting her to a major hospital fast could mean life or death for her."

"Has she ever gone into a diabetic coma?"

"No." He chuckled. "She'd never forgive Faddle if he let that happen. Even though he quit medical school, she's made him her personal doctor. He's responsible for her care. Her insulin shots twice a day come from him. She won't let anyone else do it, says he has a gentle touch."

"He's very good to his mother."

James grinned. "She keeps him in line with threats to leave all her millions to a charity for diabetes research."

The turbulence increased. For the next five minutes the plane shook, dropped suddenly, then recovered only to shake some more.

"Another mountain range?" Roni asked lightly as she gripped the edge of the seat.

"Reno's surrounded by mountains. It's nearly five thousand feet above sea level." He tapped a gauge. "Shit."

The softness in his voice made Roni's blood freeze. "What?"

He tapped again on the glass of a gauge. "We're losing fuel. There was plenty when I checked it just before the turbulence kicked up. With all this shimmying and shaking it's burning fast . . . or leaking. Damn, I thought this crate was sucking it up pretty quick."

"Could it be a faulty gauge?"

"It could, but doubtful."

"Will we run out?"

"Probably not."

"Can we land at a closer airport?"

"There isn't one. We've passed the point of no return. We're closer to Reno than Fernley or the one out by Stagecoach."

She watched him check the other gauges. He looked out the windows, as though getting his bearings or looking for a suitable place to put down.

"Can you land without fuel?"

He laid a hand on her thigh and squeezed it reassuringly. "Hey, don't worry. If necessary, I can put it down on the highway—395 runs right through town." He actually smiled. "We'll just taxi right up to Harrah's and get valet parking."

"You're a riot under pressure."

He made radio contact with Reno Tahoe International, apprising them of the situation. They were given clearance to land.

Roni couldn't keep her eyes off the fuel gauge. James tried to distract her by pointing out certain landmarks: farms, buildings, and highways. The Truckee River kept her occupied for about nine seconds. Every time the plane hit an air pocket and dipped, she was certain it would keep going down until they slammed into the ground.

The little plane cleared a rocky ridge and a city appeared before them. A gorgeous city. *The most beautiful city Roni had ever seen.*

At the exact moment the city came into view the engine coughed.

Roni sucked in her breath and held it. Her fingers dug into the cushion of her seat.

"That's the airport ahead of us," he said, and the engine went into another spasm. James clutched the stick back and the nose lowered measurably. The runway rushed at them. A moment later the wheels touched the ground, the instrument panel blurred, and she felt the vibrations clear to the marrow of her bones. It was a great feeling, better than the magic fingers of a vibrating bed. Better than a hundred-dollar massage. Her chattering teeth meant they had made contact with the ground—they wouldn't drop from the sky like a pellet-filled goose after all. The landscape whizzed by in a seething sea of brown, green, and gray: then they were slowing and soon everything was returning to normal again. The plane taxied down the runway and cruised to a stop at the edge of the tarmac. A sign read WELCOME TO RENO.

She turned and looked at James. He was staring at her, a curious smile on his face.

"We still have fuel. A fume or two. Wanna take her up again?"

Her response was to make a mock dive for his throat.

Thirty-Five

In the back seat of the taxi as it headed east through Reno, Roni noticed how drawn James's face had become in just the past few minutes. The landing had been ticklish, to say the least, but she sensed it wasn't what they were coming from as much as what they were going to that made him tense.

He smiled warmly at her.

At noon they had landed, called Faddle to inform him his plane was in a hangar being serviced, then hailed a cab to the Valley Center, a crisis and recovery clinic.

At the clinic, a nurse in Ward 19 consulted her register. "Larry Glazer? Yes, he's here, but you'll have to clear it with Dr. Lexington before you can visit."

"Could you get him for us, please?"

She made a call, then hung up. "He's in consultation. It shouldn't be long."

After taking a seat, Roni noticed a woman in a white uniform sitting on the other side of the nurse's station staring at them. The woman, in her mid-thirties with black hair, large brown eyes, and dark skin, stood and came toward them.

With a thick Hispanic accent she asked, "Are you Larry's brother, James?"

James stood. "Yes."

"My name is Dolores Mendez. I'm a good friend to Larry. I called you."

"Hello, Dolores. This is Roni Mayfield."

The woman nodded. She gave Roni a direct look. "You're the one he calls for when the liquor and the nightmares stir up the memories."

Roni felt a rush, a mixed bag of bittersweet emotions. She opened her mouth to speak, but found she had nothing to say.

"How is he?" James asked.

"I think he'll be okay. It's not the first time he has come to this kind of hospital, but it's the first time that he has tried to kill himself."

"What happened?"

"Come. We can talk in here." She led them into a small room with vending machines, tables, and chairs.

James fed in coins and got soft drinks. They sat at a table where James could see the desk in case Dr. Lexington called.

"Do you work here?" Roni asked.

"No, the VA hospital on Locust. I'm on my way to work now."

"How long have you known him, Dolores?" James asked.

"Four years. We lived together on and off. It is not easy, James, to live with your brother. I love him very much, but I could not watch him slowly kill himself. I moved away from Colorado. He followed me here."

"What happened the other night?"

"He got stoned and tried to jump from the top of a building downtown. A security guard caught him and pulled him back. It was very close. A matter of a split second or two and . . ." She allowed the words to die away as she looked from James to Roni ruefully.

The three were silent, each waiting for the other to speak.

"What was he on?" James asked finally.

"Booze, mostly. But that night he bought some street dope. Bad stuff. PCP mixed with God only knows. He was going to fly to heaven."

"Dolores, does Larry talk about . . . what bothers him? Why he's on this self-destructive kick?"

She shook her head. "Not to me, he doesn't. But whatever it is that haunts him, it will not go away. Not with liquor, not with drugs. A long time ago he told me he had turned against himself, but he didn't know why. I think now he finally knows, has come to remember, but he doesn't know what to do with . . . with . . ." She waved her hands helplessly, then tapped her forehead. "To remember is to suffer."

An icy chill caught Roni unexpectedly. She glanced at the air-conditioner vent with its fluttering streamers, but she sensed the chill came from deep within.

"It's good you're here," Dolores said.

"Post-traumatic stress syndrome," Dr. Lexington said. "Repression. Your brother's mind was literally crippled by a memory. He witnessed something very traumatic, something he couldn't deal with at the time, so he conveniently tucked the incident away." The doctor, with white cottony hair, bright blue eyes, and cheeks so rosy they appeared rouged, sat at his desk. Roni and James sat in matching club chairs on the other side.

"It's not an uncommon phenomenon. Unfortunately, these unpleasant memories don't stay tucked away. Sometimes they wait ten or twenty years and then *bam*, like long-lost relatives from hell, they suddenly pop up. Other times they have a way of creeping into the conscious mind through dreams and flashbacks. With your brother it seems to be the slower, more progressive method.

"This morning we had a regressive hypnosis session," the doctor said. "I think we accomplished quite a lot."

"Can you tell me anything about it?" James asked.

"I'm afraid that's confidential. Of course, there's nothing to stop Larry from telling you. I have a feeling he might just do that. I *can* say that he witnessed something that was remarkably traumatic, something he felt unable to handle; therefore, he repressed it— erased it, if you will. It's a defense mechanism, a totally unconscious act. In his mind *it* simply didn't happen."

"Larry's repression," James said, "was it instantaneous?"

"Hard to know. From what he's told me I'd say within several days of the incident."

"If we're talking about the same incident, and I believe we are, Larry was almost sixteen. He was no soft, coddled little kid. He was pretty damn tough. He'd been through plenty, seen plenty."

"Perhaps. But other factors can play a part in repression. Fear. Guilt. A certain sense of responsibility, however unfounded it may be."

In her mind's eye Roni saw Frank, moments before

entering Caroline's house, poking a finger into Larry's chest and saying, . . . *Signal me. Larry, I'm counting on you, hear?*

"Can we see him now?" James asked.

"I know you've come a long way, but I'm going to have to put you off for just a bit. We prefer to let our patients get acclimated somewhat before we allow visitors. Have you found a place to stay yet?"

"No, we were hoping to fly back to central Nevada tonight." James looked over at Roni.

He was concerned, she knew, about getting her back to Eagleton, to Aaron and her father. But they really had no choice anyway. A few minutes before their meeting with the doctor, James had made two calls: the first was to the mechanic at the Aero Service who informed him it would take another day to repair the faulty fuel line; the second was to Faddle to apprise him of the situation. She felt Aaron was in good hands with her father and Red. She wouldn't have left in the first place if she'd felt otherwise.

"If things continue to go smoothly, you can see him tonight. Come back around eight."

James nodded and rose. "Doctor, what's the prognosis?"

"I'd say quite good. He seems to be coming to terms with the memory now. Once that's underway, he has an excellent chance to shake any feelings of guilt and blame."

"It's all taken care of, Mr. Glazer," the hotel concierge said. "Compliments of Mr. Granville."

"What's taken care of?"

"Everything, sir."

"Faddle recommended the place," James said to

Roni, "but I had no idea he intended to pick up the tab."

"Your suite is ready," the man went on. "I've taken the liberty of making reservations for the headliner show should you decide to attend. I'll be happy to handle dinner reservations as well."

"We'll let you know."

"Fine, fine. No hurry. We always keep a booth available for Mr. Granville in any event. I'll be here to take your call when you're ready, sir. My name is Woodrow."

In the elevator James said, "So Faddle's a high-roller here in Reno."

"You didn't know?"

"Nope. Guess everyone's entitled to their little secrets."

"I wonder what his mother would have to say about that."

"I guarantee she wouldn't approve."

It was a large corner suite that consisted of two bedrooms and two baths with sunken tubs. A fruit basket and fresh flowers graced the living room. The wet bar was open, ready and waiting, with champagne chilling in a silver ice bucket. From one window the view was of the High Sierra. The other was of downtown Reno, complete with the flashing welcome arch: THE BIGGEST LITTLE CITY IN THE WORLD.

They ordered Japanese food from room service and ate sitting on the living room floor at the low coffee table. Roni realized she'd slept little more than two hours all night, her energy level sinking with each passing minute. When she could no longer stifle her yawns, James insisted she lie down before going back to the clinic. She didn't argue.

* * *

She awoke at 7:00 P.M.

She had fallen asleep fully clothed on top of the bedspread. Groggy from the too-long nap, she slipped off the bed and crossed to the bathroom, her bare feet sinking into the plush carpet. Arranged neatly on the sink top were various sundries: toothbrush and toothpaste, deodorant, a hairbrush. She smiled. James must have made a run to the hotel gift shop.

In the living room a baseball game, without sound, played on the large-screen TV. The drapes were open at the window with the mountain view. The setting sun glowed pink and orange at its jagged peak. From the bathroom on the other side of the suite she heard running water. The shower. She returned to her room, picked up the phone, and dialed. It rang a half-dozen times before she heard her father's voice.

"Dad, hi."

"Hey, honey, glad you called. Make it to Reno okay?"

She was about to tell him about their tense moments in the air and decided she had no strength to go into it. "Yes. How's Aaron? Has he eaten?"

"He's fine. I made him my famous chili/cheese/ onion dog. He loved it. So did the dog."

"Good. Listen, I'm afraid we won't be getting back until sometime tomorrow. You'll have to stay with Aaron overnight . . . until we get home."

"Sure. No problem."

"You can sleep in a real bed for a change."

He groaned. "I'll try. Is everything all right?"

"We'll know more tonight."

Silence.

"Yeah, well . . ." Tom said. "The sheriff stopped by. He was hopping mad about you and James *running out*—his words, not mine. He, ah, suggested I stick around until he had a chance to talk to me. He can be very persuasive. With lawmen like that around, who needs vigilantes, huh?"

"Talk to you? Why?"

"Everyone's a suspect. My early arrival this morning puts me in the running . . . proximity-wise. And he knows I know about the tunnel."

"I see."

"Where are you?" he asked.

She told him.

"Don't rush back on my account. Everything's under control here."

"Thanks." Roni cleared her throat, choosing her words carefully, "Dad, when the sheriff comes back, be careful what you say about Caroline, and how you say it. Lubben was in love with her, too, and . . ." The muscles in her neck felt tight and bunched. She rubbed at them.

After a long pause, her father said, "I know, honey."

"Where's Aaron?"

"Out in back with the dog. That dog hasn't left his side—it's the damnedest thing. Talk about duty bound."

"He's just what Aaron needs right now—something he can trust, something he can love unconditionally. Would you get him, Dad?"

A minute passed, then a small, tentative voice said, "Roni?"

"Hi. How's it going?"

"All right."

"My dad treating you okay?"

"Yeah, sure. He's been telling me about prospecting. He says that when you were my age you were tough as hardtack, whatever that is."

"I wasn't as tough as I thought I was."

"When you coming back?"

"Tomorrow. As soon as we can get out of here. Anything I can bring home for you?"

"I don't know. Just come back."

Roni swallowed. "I will."

"Aaron, maybe you and Red should stay inside now."

"Sure. Your dad wants to talk again."

"Aaron, do me a favor. Don't go out tonight and don't use the tunnel, okay?"

"Okay. I'll work on the model. I showed it to your dad and he said it was incredible. He wants to help."

They said goodbye, then her father was back on the line.

"Now you stop worrying. Pull a couple slot handles for me. Hit the *Megabucks*."

She gave him the number of the hotel, said goodbye, then went into the bathroom.

Hanging behind the door was a thick, white terry robe, the hotel's insignia stitched on the pocket. She turned on the shower, pulled her hair up and twisted it on top her head, stripped off her clothes, and stepped inside the steamy, oversized stall.

Fifteen minutes later, through the closed door, she heard the muffled pop of a champagne cork.

She closed the robe and tied the sash, then returned to the living room. The TV was off and the radio on. On the black lacquered bar sat two tall, fluted glasses filled with champagne, tiny bubbles racing to the top. Like a scene from a thirties movie, Roni thought. She smiled, lifted one, and sipped.

Halfway through the first glass she heard soft whistling and turned to see James walking into the room, his attention on the sleeve he was rolling up. He was dressed in his faded Wranglers and blue chambray shirt, his feet bare. He saw her and smiled.

His smile was contagious.

She grinned, then looked away self-consciously and sipped her champagne.

He crossed the room and lifted the other glass.

"I called Dolores and the clinic to tell them where we were, in case . . ." he let the words hang in the air.

Roni looked into his eyes. "James, I know how hard this is for you, having someone you love . . . well, falling apart like that. It's hard for me."

He nodded and refilled her glass. "To Larry." He touched his glass to hers. "To a full recovery."

"To Larry."

They drank, staring into each other's eyes.

The phone rang. James went to the end of the bar to answer it. "Yes, Dr. Lexington. *What?* Is he okay? When? Damn." James turned and looked at Roni. "Maybe I should be there. Yes, but . . . but . . . no, I'm coming over. You can't keep me from seeing him—dammit, he's my brother." A long pause, then, "All right, all right." He let the receiver drop into the cradle.

"What?"

"Larry had some sort of relapse this evening. Nothing serious, the doctor says, it's just that the drug he ingested takes a little time to work itself out of the system. He insists we wait till morning."

"He's the doctor, James. He knows best."

"He doesn't know shit," he said angrily. "If Larry manages to kill himself before I can see him, I'll personally wring the sonofabitch's neck."

"James, please, I know what you're going through—"

"How could you possibly know?" he said, slamming a fist down on the top of the bar. "You can't imagine what it's like to have your own flesh and blood, one who's like a son to you, pulling away, drifting, maybe lost to you forever."

"Larry is not lost. He is not gone. He's in a clinic five minutes from here and he's going to be all right. He knows you love him, James."

He turned away from her and leaned over the bar with his head lowered, his hands covering his face.

She went to him and ran her hands over his back. "We're so close, James. So close to the truth." She rested her head against his shoulder blade.

James swiveled around abruptly. When Roni stepped back he pulled her into his arms and brought his mouth down hard on hers. His embrace was tight, his kiss filled with anger, fear, frustration; yet she refused to pull away. Instead, she clung to him, more than willing to absorb some of his pain into her own body if possible.

As quickly as it came it was gone. Tenderness suddenly replaced the preceding roughness. James looked into her eyes and lightly touched her face with his fingertips. He kissed first one eyelid and then the other. He drew her back into his arms and kissed her throat, warm breath caressing her ear.

Her body conformed to his so naturally. She allowed herself to relax, to lose herself in his embrace. Champagne filled her head, helping to loosen any inhibitions she might have had. They swayed gently to background music—sweet, romantic music.

"James . . . ?"

"Shhhh. Our song."

She listened. The radio was playing Boggus and Greenwood's "Hopelessly Yours." The first time they had danced had been to this song. That night in the Eagle bar seemed like eons ago and though uptight and running on sheer tension from being shot at, she recalled how comfortable she'd felt in his arms.

Our song, she thought. Their movements were fluid—as one. Whenever he held her his body felt so familiar, yet each time it was as thrilling as a first encounter, as memorable as a first kiss. He was her first love, perhaps her only love, so what did she expect? She could stay this way forever, secure in his arms, his body moving sensually against hers. Knowing he was sexually stimulated excited her all the more.

As they moved with the music, he slowly opened her robe and slid his hands inside. His calloused palms on her bare back sent tingles down the length of her body. She pulled his shirt from his jeans, undid the buttons and pushed it open. Their bodies, feverish flesh on flesh, came together.

He kissed her again, his growing passion inflaming her. He pulled off his shirt as he backed up to the sofa, the rest of his clothes quickly following. She shrugged off her robe. James lay on his back, lowering Roni down on top of him, his hands gently stroking her buttocks. She sat up, straddling his slim hips. James ran those wonderfully coarse hands across her buttocks, over the deep curve of her waist, the flat of her stomach and finally found her breasts, which ached for his touch. He gazed at her, his hazel eyes bright with passion. *Beautiful*, he mouthed.

She felt his erection under her, wanted to feel it inside of her, wanted their bodies to fuse with the intense heat that radiated between them. Under heavy lids they gazed at each other. She shifted slightly and felt him enter her, slowly, sweetly, maddeningly and, looking into his half-closed eyes, heard him moan. They moved together as though they had shared each other's body for a lifetime—slow and lingering, wanton and reckless, teetering on the pinnacle. She closed her eyes, caught at her lower lip with her teeth and delivered herself to the pure, unadulterated bliss of James's lovemaking.

They lay in each other's arms in the king-size bed, a patina of sweat sheening their bodies, her pounding heart finally reaching a more normal pace. The second time, in the bedroom, had been even more wonderful than the first. James was a skilled, patient lover. Their lovemaking was everything she hoped it would be. Everything she'd imagined, and some she hadn't.

Roni took one of his slim cigars from the nightstand and lit it. They shared the cigar and sipped champagne.

"James . . ."

"I love the way you say that . . . *James*," he said softly. "James and not Jim—why?"

"It's the only name that suits you." She traced her fingers along his collarbone. "Once, long ago, while sitting on the steps of a trailer waiting for a friend, along comes this older guy, my friend's brother. He has these dark curls and hazel eyes all sprinkled with rust-colored flecks and in this sexy accent, he says: 'Hello, I'm James.'"

"Clever opening."

"I sat there like an idiot, staring, and this older guy stands there staring right back at me, smiling. Crazy, wonderful thoughts start going through my head, thoughts only a young, idiotic girl could entertain. Finally, he says, 'I'm James Glazer, I live here. If it wouldn't be too much trouble, could you move so I can get by?' " She laughed, embarrassed by the memory. "You probably don't remember any of that."

James smiled that same smile. "What I remember was that there on my broken-down steps sat this creature of unique beauty. All eyes and legs, with the most incredible golden-brown skin."

"I'm sure you thought those things."

"I probably shouldn't have. You were just a kid, jailbait for me. You were what . . . twelve?"

"Almost thirteen."

"At *almost* thirteen you were different from most girls with rare good looks. You weren't a flighty little tease, stuck on herself."

She rose up on one elbow. "You really did notice me?"

"I hoped I'd get the opportunity to see the girl all grown up, to see if Nature's promise had been fulfilled. I followed your career. I read your articles, your interviews, everything I could find. Your piece on that welfare case, the little Kincade boy, was the most moving thing I've ever read. Through your writing I felt close to you. You weren't just a mine brat with beautiful eyes and a cut on her chin who happened to live in the same town for a short time. You were Roni Mayfield, a woman I had to see again, to know . . . intimately."

As Roni moved into James's arms, an image of a weeping Caroline sitting in the windowseat came to her. And Caroline's words: "Roni, never, ever give your heart completely."

It was too late.

Thirty-Six

There was no resistance when he pushed the trap-door open. The settee sat to one side, dried blood streaked the satiny brocade fabric. He lifted the gas can—the one he'd hidden deep inside the passage the night before—through the opening, set it on the floor of the basement, and followed it up.

He would waste no more time. Fire would destroy any evidence, any information that could implicate him. It was important that he eliminate all risk factors: the house, another journal if one existed, but most importantly, the boy.

The dog came out of nowhere. Teeth bared, hackles raised, it growled menacingly, braced to pounce.

The man spoke to the dog in a soothing tone, calling it by name. The dog ceased growling, yet remained wary, alert. He had to disable Aaron's protector if he hoped to carry out his plan. The man's eyes darted about the tiny basement looking for something that would bring the animal down with one solid blow. Behind him he saw what he was looking for, a row of large canning jars filled with an unidentifiable matter.

"Here, Red, easy boy."

The dog stiffened, his teeth showing again. But before he could react the man lifted the quart jar and slammed it against the dog's head hard enough to break the thick glass. Red fell back with a yelp. The man kicked him in the side, sending him and the jar through the trapdoor opening. He heard both hit bottom.

Looking down into the tunnel, he saw Red on his side lying in a pool of blood, eyes and mouth open, tongue hanging out. There was no movement, the chest was still.

The dog was no longer a threat.

Roni gingerly lifted James's arm from across her body, his hand cupping a breast. He stirred, but didn't wake.

She and James had spent hours catching each other up on the years since leaving Eagleton. Then they'd made love once again before falling asleep. Concern for Aaron had her awake again. She wondered if Aaron had remembered to secure the trapdoor. Then she remembered that Red was there, not to mention her father, so everything would be all right.

She slid from the bed and quietly left the room. In the living room she took Caroline's journal from her purse, lifted her robe from the floor, slipped it on, then curled up in a wing chair. For several minutes she stared out at the glittering casino lights, thinking of James and their near-perfect lovemaking. Then, sighing with contentment, she switched on the table lamp, opened the book, and began to read.

Roni learned that after the "visitors," Caroline lost the will to live. She stopped eating, neglected to turn on the heat, and, with her resistance at its lowest, she soon contracted bacterial pneumonia.

The sheriff found her unconscious on the kitchen floor and called the doctor and the priest. Dr. Burke treated her at home with antibiotics and Lubben brought prepared meals from the cafe while Father Roberts prayed for her recovery. In the long days following her life-threatening episode the doctor, sheriff, lawyer, and the priest visited her often. Once she had regained her strength, she began to go out for long walks and played the piano for hours. When fully recovered, she volunteered to read to the children at the library three days a week and offered piano lessons again; several townspeople signed up, Roni among them.

Roni paused. Thinking back to that time, she recalled how the widow had seemed less melancholy, a less tragic figure, as if she had suddenly found a purpose in life. Even the tone of the writing had changed, and the pressure with which the pen met paper was steadier, more assertive. If Roni hadn't recognized the distinct loops and swirls, she would have sworn someone else had taken over the journal. The next entry may have explained it.

> *The nursery has been empty long enough. I think it's time to fill it with a baby's sounds. Without Richard I can't fill the house with children, I know that now, but the nursery . . .*
>
> *Mr. Granville came at noon, at my request, to dis-*

*cuss the possibility of my adopting a child. He was
not optimistic, however.*

Three unwritten pages and then these words:

*Today Fadius asked me to marry him. He doesn't
understand. I want a baby, not another husband.*

Roni read on, sure that Caroline would name her
lover. After many pages of musings and everyday
trivia, Roni came across the following entry.

*My darling Richard,
The little one is beginning to make himself known.
A flutter here and there. Feel it, darling? The baby
grows. Our baby . . . yours and mine. Oh, Richard,
I'll need you now more than ever. Please, my darling,
continue to guide me and help me to do what's right.
In the round-tower of my heart I keep you forever.*

The last entry read:

*I have broken it off with both without telling them
why. Neither seem to want to end it, though each knows
the affair could not go on indefinitely. They don't
know it but they have fulfilled their purpose (the baby
grows inside me, getting stronger day by day) and now
I return them to their own lives, to their own special
commitments.*

The lovers were not named, but the men in her
life at the time, Roni knew, had been the sheriff,
lawyer, doctor, and priest. All good, upstanding men
in the community. Of the four, two were committed—
doctor and priest—one to a loving wife and a passel

of children, and the other to God. The scandal of an illegitimate child could ruin either man. Not mentioned, but undeniably in the running, were Alfonso Scolli and Roni's own father. And what of Faddle? It was apparent Elsa Granville, whose fortune kept her son in line, had strongly disapproved of the widow. The sheriff, though unattached, in all likelihood had been more or less rejected. *Jealousy?*

The boy was in the attic.

The man came out of the shadows on the second floor and began to climb the narrow attic stairs. A padlock hung open on the doorknob.

From inside the room he heard the hissing sound of a propane torch. Through the slightly open door he saw the boy at a worktable against the far wall. The entire room was comprised of paper, cloth, dry wood, and flammable chemicals, all certain to flare up in an instant. After only a moment's hesitation he quietly closed the latch and slipped the padlock shackle through the eye.

With light steps he made his way back down to the second floor and entered the master bedroom. Enough light came through the window to see the bed and its lone occupant. As he approached the bed he took the syringe from his pocket and removed the sheath. He carefully inserted the needle into the relaxed tissue of the sleeping form and sent the insulin home. There was only a slight resistance to the prick of the needle. He knew about needles and painless shots—he'd had plenty of practice. He replaced the sheath, returned the syringe to his pocket, and backed away.

Hurrying now, he splashed gasoline around the

room, then backed out into the hall leaving a trail of gasoline across the landing and down the stairs where he emptied the can in the main hall and front parlor. He lit a match, dropped it, and in fascination, watched as the blue-white flame rushed along the floor and up the stairs.

Thirty-Seven

Saturday

"He's expecting you," Dr. Lexington said, walking down the clinic hallway with Roni and James. "He's quite calm this morning." He pushed open a door and they entered a ward with four beds. Two people were in the room.

Larry, in gray sweats, sat in a straight wooden chair. Dolores sat on the edge of a bed wearing shorts and a halter top. They held hands. Both turned when the three entered the room.

Roni paused in the doorway, shocked by the sight of Larry. With pasty complexion, face bloated and coarsely whiskered, eyes bloodshot and red-rimmed, he looked ravaged. Twelve years, she thought, only twelve years and look at him. She and Larry were the same age, yet he looked years older.

His gaze flickered over the doctor, lingered on James—the sight of his older brother produced a thin smile—then he was staring at Roni with a sadness that cut into her with an acute ache.

A flashback. She saw Larry and herself in a cave above Eagleton. Two twelve-year-olds. They sat half in sunlight and half in shade—she in the sun because she was afraid to go any deeper into the dim cave. It was summer and they wore bathing suits. Hers was a tie-dye two-piece, his was red with a little pocket for holding change. Both kneeled, bodies straight and tall. They had come to the cave for privacy, to play the age-old game of comparison. "On the count of three," she said. Larry counted and at three down went their suit bottoms. Almost immediately Roni's came back up. She stood. "Okay, let's go." Larry balked, claiming unfairness because she had kept her top on. "I'm not showing you any more than you showed me," she said. "But," he whined, "there was nothing there to see." She shrugged, laughed, and ran away.

They had shared something very private, very personal. For her it had been a highly-charged moment—intimate, yet sexless. A moment in time she would never forget.

In the large room with the stark walls, without taking his eyes from her, Larry reached for a pair of mirrored sunglasses on the table and slipped them on. It was like a curtain dropping over his soul. She swayed on her feet as if she'd been held against her will, then released abruptly.

Dolores stood, leaned down, kissed Larry's temple, and said something in his ear. He nodded, squeezed her arm, and raised his hand in a feeble attempt to wave.

She smiled at Roni and James as she left the room. The doctor followed her out.

"You're lookin' good, Big Jim." His voice was low and quiet. "But not as good as our li'l Bony Maroni. Hey, Maroni, never thought I'd see you again. So how's it going?"

"It goes okay, Larry."

"What happened to your tooth?" James said.

Larry ran his tongue along a chip at the corner of one front tooth. "Concrete floor jumped me."

The three fell silent.

Larry lit a cigarette and chuckled. "No point in asking how it goes for me, huh? The accommodations speak for themselves."

James stared at him, but remained quiet.

"Ahhh, Jim, there it is again, that concerned and somewhat disappointed look on your face. You'd think I'd shape up and spare you this crap, now wouldn't you? What a treat it'd be if just once you could drop in on me and find me sober and straight and maybe even working."

"Larry, the reason you're here, in this place, is the reason we're here."

"I don't recommend it. Room service is slow and there's some pretty freaked-out guests."

"Roni and I want to ask you some questions. Questions you may not want to answer."

"Questions, huh? Now what would possibly make the two of you team up after all these years? And what do the three of us have in common? Could it be something that happened in little ol' Eagleton, say, twelve years ago?" He didn't wait for an answer. "The shrink tell you about the hypnosis?"

"Only that he's convinced that years ago you repressed a memory that was too traumatic for you to cope with."

"Makes me sound like a real puss, don't it?"

"Larry—"

He inhaled deeply. "Okay, so why the fresh interest?"

"Frank's body was found in the Holt tunnel. And Dean Scolli was killed night before last trying to find out who did his brother in."

Larry mashed out the butt. The mirrored glasses reflected the far side of the room as Larry turned his head to look out the window. He looked back, pulled the glasses off, and rubbed at his red eyes with two yellow, nicotine-stained fingers. "Well, don't just stand there at the door. Come in, come in, gather 'round. Storytelling time."

Roni sat on the edge of the bed and James took the other wooden chair.

"So they found Frank." Larry slowly shook his head. "I have a feeling there's a whole lot more, but frankly, I don't have the strength for a full account just now."

"There's a whole lot more, yes. What do you remember, guy?"

Larry slipped the dark glasses back on.

"He was struggling with the widow," Larry said, and sipped water. "For years all I could remember was the sight of Frank trying to hold her wrists as she flailed about. She was sorta half on, half off the bed and she looked really out of it, y'know, spacey, like she was on something—and, hey, I should know. Anyway, that's what I told that hillbilly sheriff."

"Then what?" Roni asked when Larry paused.

"Then . . . I don't know if I remembered this part then or later, this is where it starts to get real muddled. I . . . I saw Frank turn toward me . . . where I was at the window. He had something in his hand. He looked puzzled, like he'd heard something and he was gonna check it out. He stood up and, cautious-like, moved toward the window. I thought for sure it was me he was coming toward—thought he knew I was out there looking in—and he was making sure, but . . ."

"But what?" James prompted when Larry paused again.

"Suddenly . . . something wet splattered across the window. A streak of blood. I thought to myself, now where'd that come from?. And through the blood I saw Frank standing there . . . staring right at me. There was a hole in his forehead. A perfectly round little hole . . . like a third eye. Blood began to trickle down into his eye. Then more blood splashed the window. But this time I caught a glimpse of something smashing into his face. Something long and thin, a fireplace poker. It came again . . . and again. And Frank just stood there. Now, how could he still be standing? It wasn't possible. His face, for chrissake, was caved in. Blood gushing out. And then what I saw next really freaked me out." Larry swallowed hard. "Frank stumbled forward, reaching out . . . finally making some kind of effort to run or protect himself, or to just grab hold of something for support. The venetian blinds spread apart where he clutched at them and his face . . . his *face*—this grotesque death mask of blood with eyes just beginning to register the horror of—Jesus Christ, man, it stared right at me. Right into my eyes."

Roni reached out and touched his hand. He made no move to return the touch, yet he didn't pull away.

"Who did it?" Roni asked.

He pulled off the glasses and rubbed hard at his eyes.

"Who, Larry?"

"I don't know. If I saw him, that part of my memory hasn't come back yet. The next thing I remember is I'm flat on my back on the ground. I took off running and I never wanted to stop."

Roni sat quietly, thinking. While Frank was being bludgeoned, Larry was looking through the window and she was downstairs in the music room about to meet up with James.

"What did Frank have in his hand?"

"I don't know. Something metal that looked like a weapon or a tool of some kind. I only caught a glimpse of it."

"A knife?"

"Maybe. I don't know."

"Larry, why didn't you come to me?" James said. "Why didn't you come to me with this when it happened?"

"Because you were there."

"What do you mean?"

"I saw you and Roni running away. You were *there*."

"And you thought . . . ?"

"I don't know what I thought," Larry said brusquely. "I just couldn't go to . . . to anyone. Not you, or Roni, and especially not that lovesick, dime-novel cop who claimed he saw Frank running from the house. If what I saw really happened, there was no way in hell Frank was running anywhere." He lit another cigarette. "And if Frank was murdered, then I . . . I was the one who killed him. Frank trusted me. He counted on me to signal him if I saw anyone. I let him down."

Roni squeezed his hand. "Larry, you can't blame yourself. You had no time to warn Frank. His attack was completely unexpected."

"The first blow, yeah, but after that I could have called out, screamed, broken the window, done something to make this guy stop clubbing Frank. Maybe if I'd done something, anything, he'd be alive today. Before Frank goes inside he says, 'Larry, I'm counting on you.' You heard him, Maroni. I can't forget that and I can't forget that look in his eyes when he was dying."

Roni and James exchanged pained looks.

Somewhere down the hall, loud, angry voices reached them. Someone, young and female, yelled, "Quit fucking with my stuff. Do I screw with your shit? You got cigs, smoke 'em."

Larry rose, crossed the room, and closed the door. "Although I managed to bury it pretty good, I see now it was there all along, cloudy with booze and dope and its own protective amnesia. It wouldn't stay buried, and the more it tried to surface, the crazier I thought I was. When I found out you'd gone back to that town, Jim, it almost drove me nuts. Then Roni. I knew it was all coming to a head and I couldn't handle it. I felt—it was like Frank was reaching out from the other side to me, saying, 'See? You couldn't hide it. It's your fault and you should be here with me.' So, hey, I decided to meet him halfway."

"Dolores said a guard pulled you back a split second after you jumped," Roni said. "Sounds to me like he isn't ready to meet you yet. I knew Frank as well as you did, and Larry, he would not blame you."

He returned to his chair, lifted her hand, and kissed the palm. "You ever think about becoming a shrink? You'd be good."

She cupped his hand with her other one.

"Frank was murdered and so was his brother," James said. "Aaron and Roni have been threatened.

The killer, whoever he is, is still in Eagleton and he doesn't want his secret known.''

"Caroline's lover?" Larry speculated.

"Yes, but we think she had more than one," Roni said.

"So we're no closer to a solution than before. Wait a minute." James's fingers fidgeted on the back of the chair. "Wait ... a ... minute." He turned to Roni, his eyes bright. "Lubben arrives in time to see someone running from the house. But instead of going after him, he decides to check on the widow, right?"

"Right."

"All he found was a dazed Caroline. No Frank, no body, no killer . . ."

"And no *blood*," Roni said.

"Not a word about blood."

They turned to Larry.

Larry leaned forward. "If he went into that bedroom when he said he did, he walked into a bloodbath. I mean, it had to be all over the place. The window, the blinds. Even if Frank had managed to leave the room, he would've left a bloody trail. Frank had to have been dead or dying when the sheriff entered. Unless . . ."

". . . unless the sheriff killed him," Roni answered for him.

"Which means he was probably there all along. If he saw me running away, he watched from inside the house, from the bedroom window."

"Who had a better motive?" James said. "He was crazy about her. He would have killed anyone he thought was trying to hurt her. The Scollis, however, had a little too much influence in town, making a cover-up necessary."

"But why would Frank struggle with her? He went inside because he thought her lover was with her and he wanted to see who it was."

James rose. "Maybe that's what he told you. Maybe rape was his objective from the start."

"No," Larry said. "He was my best friend. I knew him. He wouldn't do that. Frank didn't rape the widow."

They all fell silent. Roni played Larry's scenario through her head. She was back in the music room listening to a woman's soft whimpering, a commotion overhead, and running footsteps. If James hadn't pulled her out of the house they would have seen the killer come down the stairs.

Roni glanced at Larry. He was staring absently out the window, looking a million miles away. A single tear escaped the corner of his eye and got as far as the coarse whiskers.

"Larry?" Roni touched his shoulder.

Larry looked from Roni to James. He moistened his dry lips. "Do you know how good it feels to finally get this off my chest? To have the two of you here and us brainstorming? I'm not crazy. I saw a terrible thing, but it's out now. *It's finally out.*"

"And we're gonna find Frank's killer," James said.

"Look, you two get back to Eagleton and get that kid out of there. Maybe you ought to give the state police a call. You sure as hell don't want to butt heads with Lubben if your suspicions are correct. You're probably not in danger as long as he thinks his little secret is still safe."

James and Roni stood.

"Little Bony Maroni." When she grimaced, he chuckled. "You always hated that nickname, didn't you? That was to keep you from getting all conceited.

You grew up as beautiful as I thought you would. I had the hots for you," he said, taking her hand again. "But now I have Dolores, and you and James—Christ, funny how things turn out, isn't it?"

They both hugged Larry, promising to keep him informed. At the door, Larry called to Roni, and with a thin smile he said, "Hey, remember the time in the cave?" When she nodded, he added, "Thanks for *nothing*."

She smiled and felt tears spring to her eyes. She hadn't been the only one to flash back.

The phone was ringing when they entered the suite. James hurried to answer the one on the bar.

He said a few words, glanced at Roni, then looked away. Roni's heart skipped in her chest. He said yes and no a few more times, then hung up.

"That was Faddle. There was a fire at the house . . . Aaron and your father were inside . . ."

Thirty-Eight

"Aaron's at the clinic," James said over the din of the Cessna's engines. "According to Faddle, his condition is stable-to-good. First- and second-degree burns, mostly on his hands. Some smoke inhalation. Doc wants to keep an eye on him just in case."

"My father?"

"He's in a coma," he said quietly.

"From burns? From smoke? What?"

"I don't know, Roni."

The small plane rocked and dipped. Air turbulence on the flight back to Eagleton remained consistent. If Roni hadn't been preoccupied with the news of Aaron and her father and so anxious to get back, the relentless motion doubtless would have made her sick.

"Did Faddle say anything about the fire? How it started? How much of the house was burned?"

"Only that Mrs. Wiggins saw smoke, called the firehouse, and then stood in the street yelling her head off. The Scolli boys, who just happened to be in the neighborhood, broke in and got them both out.''

Happened to be in the neighborhood? Roni was certain they'd been up to no good, but torching an occupied house was a bit out of their league. Probably figuring they'd be the first ones suspected, they had no choice but to rescue them.

James frowned as he mulled something over. ''Where was Red? I can't believe he didn't try to warn Aaron and your dad.''

''I'm sure he did. Knowing Aaron, he ran straight up to the attic. I bet that's how he burned his hands, trying to save his models. Oh, the poor kid—he worked so long and hard on that project.''

''Aaron may not be safe at the clinic. Dean wasn't.''

''But Dean died from—'' She stopped, alarmed by his implication.

''He was alive when we took him there. He's dead now—that's all I know.''

James brought the nose of the plane up in search of a less turbulent patch of sky. He succeeded, for the plane vibrated only slightly now. ''Dammit,'' he said. ''I hoped we could sneak into town without the sheriff knowing. With the fire, he probably talked to Faddle and has a good idea where we were and when we're coming back. If he is our man, we'll have to play it cool, unsuspecting. I doubt he'll try anything with witnesses around, though I'd feel a lot better with some kind of protection . . . a weapon. We should have called the state police like Larry suggested.''

''We can call from the airfield.''

''If he's not there waiting for us.''

His talk of protection and weapons made Roni all

the more nervous. How did you protect yourself from the law in a small town? Sure, there were several deputies, but whose side would they be on? How easy was it for a top law enforcement officer to cover up his involvement in something illegal? Pretty damn easy, she thought; he skated for twelve years.

"Roni, if anything happens—"

"Nothing's going to happen."

"If anything docs happen I want you to know that I love you." He reached out and gently touched her face. "I've never said that to another woman. But then you're the first and only woman I've ever loved."

"And I hope the last." She took his hand, held it against her cheek. He gazed into her eyes, deep into her soul, and she felt strong and alive, ready to face what was ahead.

Twenty minutes later as they approached Coggins Airfield from the north, Roni looked for Lubben's Bronco along the highway and at the airfield and breathed easier when she didn't see it.

James put the Cessna down smoothly. They quickly deplaned. Midway to the office the blue Bronco pulled out of the shadows of the large hangar and headed straight for them.

"Shit," James said.

Roni grabbed his arm and pulled him to a stop.

"Stay cool," James said.

"How can I stay cool? What if he plans to kill us? It'd be so easy to shoot us and dump our bodies in one of a hundred abandoned mine shafts around here."

"Stay calm, hon, or we're in big trouble." He nudged her to get her moving again. "We're gonna get through this."

The police Bronco passed them before making a U-turn and pulling up alongside. Lubben cut the wheel and slid to a stop in front of them.

"Get in," he said flatly.

"We have a car." James took Roni's hand and squeezed lightly.

"Get in. *Now.*"

Roni realized there was nothing they could do. If they ran, he could mow them down before they reached either the airplane or her car—resisting arrest, he'd claim.

"Let me report in," James said, nodding toward the office.

"All taken care of. Let's go."

James reached for the rear door.

"No, Jimboy, you up front with me. She goes in back."

Roni got in and closed the door. The sheriff instructed her to move to the other side, behind the passenger seat. "I don't want to get no crick in my neck talking to you," he said.

Translated: *I want you where I can see you.*

James started around the front of the Bronco with a wary eye on Lubben. Just as he reached mid-bumper, Lubben popped the clutch and the vehicle lurched forward. James slammed a palm down on the hood and glared.

"Hey, careful there," Lubben called out. "That's government property."

When James was inside, Lubben said, "Fasten your seatbelt. It's the law."

He drove slowly, as if trying to figure out his next move.

From behind, Roni watched the muscles in Lubben's jaw twitch. He appeared tense, highly agitated.

Forget playing dumb with this man. She had always feared the sheriff, a fear she presumed was unfounded. Until now, when terror rushed at her with an explosive force. Play your hunches, listen to your gut—how many times in the past had she heeded those warnings?

Although no other cars were in sight, the sheriff flipped on his turn signal and came to a complete stop before turning onto the highway. He glanced in the rearview mirror, catching Roni's eye briefly.

"I wasn't too happy when you folks took outta here so suddenly. Guess you can imagine the flak I got over Dean's death. The Scollis got friends and the old man and that brood of his are raisin' holy hell." He looked from James to Roni, both remaining silent. "So where'd you go and why?"

"Reno," James said. "Had a night on the town, compliments of Faddle."

"You see your brother?"

James hesitated before saying, "Yeah, but he wasn't up to joining us."

Lubben's jaw seemed to saw back and forth. A vein in his temple swelled, beating visibly. He had been cruising down the two-lane highway well below the 55 limit. She saw his foot stomp down on the accelerator. Within seconds the Bronco picked up speed, the transmission whining as the tach needle on the gauge climbed toward the red.

Just as Roni thought the engine would blow, Lubben speed-shifted, simultaneously yanking the wheel sharply to the left. They crossed the highway and skidded off the asphalt onto a dirt road, the Bronco bouncing and pounding brutally. If not for the seatbelt holding her down, the top of Roni's head would have banged against the roof.

Lubben again slammed his foot down on the gas pedal. The Bronco raced down the road, hitting ruts and swerving erratically. Roni's shoulder repeatedly struck the window.

Each time James tried to grab the ignition keys or kick the sheriff's leg off the accelerator, Lubben swerved, throwing him off balance. There was a grim determination on Lubben's face, and his eyes in the rearview mirror reflected unrestrained rage. He doesn't give a shit what happens, Roni thought. It was in that deduction that she felt a profound hopelessness. They were *all* going to die.

Lubben slammed on the brakes and the Bronco skidded, then did a complete brody in the hard-packed dirt. In slow motion the vehicle tipped on two wheels, seeming to hang in the air for an endless time before teetering and finally dropping back to the ground on all four wheels.

Dust rose up all around them, holding them in a world of floating sienna. For a moment everything seemed to stand still. It was deathly quiet. Then a profusion of sound crashed in on Roni.

The horn was blaring. James lunged for the sheriff. Lubben quickly unholstered his gun and yelled at him to back off.

With the barrel of the gun pointing at his face, James halted, drew back, then turned to Roni with an apologetic look. She hoped the pleading in her own eyes would warn him off. James sat back against the door, a pulse in his neck throbbing.

The sheriff smashed a fist into the horn. The blaring stopped. "Don't touch those belts," he said harshly.

James opened his mouth to say something.

"Shut up!" Lubben shouted. "I gave you your

chance to talk and you blew it. There's just one thing
I want to hear from you now. No lies, no sidesteppin',
no bullshit.'' He unhooked his seatbelt and shifted
around. "Your brother told you he witnessed Scolli's
murder—''

"My brother—''

"Answer my question, otherwise keep your mouth
shut. Here's the question. Who'd he say did it?''

"He didn't.''

"You're lying.''

"No.''

"But he claimed he saw Frank gettin' it? Yeah?''
James stared at Lubben.

"We all saw Frank's skull,'' Lubben said. "Pretty
bashed in, it was. Head wounds like that bleed
somethin' fierce. Yeah, there would've been blood,
lots of it. And that bein' the case, it don't jibe with
what I said I saw, now does it?'' He waited, looking
from one to the other. "You two playin' it cool, huh?
Yeah, playin' it real cool. But you're curious, ain't
you? You think you got it all figured out. Jus' lookin'
for a confession, right?''

"No,'' Roni said too abruptly.

The sheriff laughed. "No? Well that's too bad,
'cause you're gonna get one. Settle back,'' he said,
waving the gun. "This might take a while.''

Aaron tried not to think about his ruined project.
The last he had seen of it the entire west side was
burning fiercely.

It had all happened so fast. He was using the small
torch on a thin sheet of tin, fusing the sides together,
when he heard a crackling sound near the door and
turned to see an entire block of his town in flames.

He rushed to put it out, peeling off his shirt and using it to slap at the fire, but soon the smoke overcame him. When he tried to leave the room he found the door stuck fast. Alternately trying to stomp out the fire and get the door open, he had called for Red over and over. The room filled with smoke, choking and blinding him. Minutes later when Vincent Scolli charged in and pulled him out, Red was nowhere around.

"I want to go home," Aaron said. "I gotta find Red."

Dr. Burke looked over at Faddle, who sat in a chair in the corner. "Red will turn up."

Aaron hadn't seen the dog since just before the fire broke out. Red, too big to move around inside the attic without stepping on some delicate structure, had been content to lie on the landing outside the door. Aaron knew with certainty that if Red had been anywhere near at the time he would have tried to save him. Aaron's concern for his project had quickly shifted to the missing dog.

"Something happened to him," Aaron said. "Something bad. He would have warned me about the fire. He would've tried to save me. But he couldn't because something bad happened to him." Aaron threw back the sheet and tried to get up.

The doctor held him down. "I'm the captain around here, son. Nobody leaves this ship until I say so."

"Look, I have to go home."

"Not to that soot-filled house, you won't. You've got both lungs full of smoke now."

"He can go home with me, Doc, till Jim and Roni get back," Faddle said.

"Let's just wait for them, shall we? In the meantime

we'll finish with his blood workup and get a little more oxygen in those lungs."

Father Roberts, clerical collar barely visible above the crew-neck of his black cashmere sweater, entered the room. He greeted the mayor and the doctor, strolled to Aaron's bed, and said, "Afternoon, son. Heard you had a bit of an accident last night. Fire, was it?"

"Yes, Father."

"You're a very lucky boy. Fires can be one of God's more treacherous offerings. My first church, right here in Eagleton, was destroyed by fire. Do you remember that, Faddle?"

The mayor nodded. "Like it was yesterday. Fall of '78, deer season and half the townsmen off hunting. Phoof! Went up like tissue paper. Hell, it wasn't much of a church, Father—a drafty, four-sided woodpile, no great loss to the town. If you ask me, that fire was a godsend."

"God works in mysterious ways," Father Roberts said with a teasing glint in his eye. "Thinking you'd be alone and bored to distraction, I dropped in for a visit. But I see you've a full house. Well, perhaps later? Do you play chess?"

"Yes, sir. A little."

"Good. We'll have a game."

As the priest was leaving, he said to the doctor, "Is it all right if I have a moment with Mr. Mayfield?"

"Of course, Father. He's right across the hall."

Dr. Burke turned to Faddle. "Why don't you go on home and get some rest, Fad? You've been here half the night and most of the morning. That chair must be molded to your backside."

"I promised I'd stay with the boy. Roni and James should be along any time."

"Suit yourself. Coffee?"

"Now you're talking."

"I'll have Bea bring it in. Aaron, how about you? Get you something? Juice? More ice for your water?"

Aaron shook his head.

A few minutes later a nurse brought coffee in a Styrofoam cup and handed it to Faddle. For Aaron she had a cup of orange sherbet. "Doc okayed this. It should cool that burning in your throat," she said to Aaron, then left.

The mayor sipped his coffee and stared out the window. He's not very talkative around me, Aaron thought. He must not be used to kids. But that was okay. Aaron didn't feel like being sociable either.

"You don't want that ice cream, son?"

Aaron shook his head.

Faddle stood, stepped to the lap table, and picked up the cup. "Mind?"

Aaron shook his head again.

Faddle smiled, backed up, and sat down. Two bites and the sherbet was gone.

Aaron stared out the window. A few minutes later he heard a series of snorts. He looked over to see the mayor, chin on his chest, fingers clasped across his belly, snort again in his sleep.

A dog barked outside. Aaron sighed, knowing by the sound that it wasn't Red. Where the hell was Red?

Never before had Aaron become so attached to an animal. He'd had pets before, a special cat here and there from the menagerie his mother had fostered for years. A manx, tough and independent—though not tough enough to escape the jaws of a coyote— had been his favorite. Cats were neat but a dog was cool, loyal. It would risk its life for its master. A dog was a boy's best friend.

He slipped the nasal cannula off, climbed from the bed, and went to the window. "Red," he called softly and gave a couple short whistles. "Hey, boy, you out there?"

Aaron slipped on his pants and, barefooted, sneaked down the hallway toward the front entrance. He had almost made it to the door when he heard one of the nurses greeting another at the desk in the main foyer.

Peeking around the corner, he saw the nurse who'd brought him the sherbet perched on the edge of the desk, a mug in her hand. The other nurse was stripping off a too-tight cardigan sweater.

The main door had glass insets in the upper half. Aaron rose on tiptoe and squinting, tried to see onto the front steps, hoping for a glimpse of Red. Without his glasses, everything was hazy. There was nothing wrong with his hearing, though.

"Any live ones left? Or did we kill them all?" the arriving nurse asked.

Chuckling, the other nurse said, "Bite yer tongue. The doc's around here somewhere and if he hears you talking like that he'll wash yer mouth out with Betadine. As a matter of fact, we got us not one, but two live ones. Though one's comatose."

"Aaron Holt and Roni Mayfield's father. I heard. Which one's comatose?"

"The father. He was looking after the kid while she and James Glazer flew off into the sunset for a little R & R."

Aaron drew back and flattened himself to the wall. The slick enamel felt cold against his bare skin where the gown opened down the back.

"La-De-Da Dr. Shaw won't like that. Contrary to what she says, she still has heavy-duty hots for Jim."

"My heart bleeds. Speaking of bleeding, you heard Dean Scolli died here night before last?"

" 'Course I heard—I was just over in Eureka, not on the moon. Got back this morning to find the whole town talking. With Dean being attacked at the widow's place, it's no surprise that old Victorian firetrap suddenly burst into flames. Everyone knows how mean and nasty those young Scolli boys can be."

"Wasn't them. They was the ones pulled the two outta the house."

"Change of heart, probably. So where's the boy?"

"In four. His Honor's been with him since he came in. Like he was keeping vigil. You know, the kid is really kinda sweet. Some people, I guess, just seem weird till you get to know them."

"Hmph." Silence. "Well, I better get to work. I'll look in."

Aaron backed up.

"You say the doctor is here now?"

"Yep." The first nurse chuckled. "Been here since the boy came in about midnight. Close your mouth, June, you'll catch a fly. Will wonders never cease? He's taken to the boy, too. Hovers around him like a mother hen. Even insisted on doing the blood workup himself."

"Drew it, too?"

"Everything."

"Very interesting," the second one said. "Next thing you know, he'll be emptying bedpans."

"Exactly. So I ask myself, what's so damn important about this kid's blood that he don't trust nobody else to do it?"

"Maybe, like some folks in town, he thinks the kid's got ice water running through his veins."

"Or maybe he was looking for a biological comparison," the first nurse said. "I snuck a look."

"And?"

"Aaron Holt has a rare blood type. AB. Now get this—someone else has that same blood type."

"No shit—who?"

"Dean Scolli."

"Sweet Rosie, you mean there's a possibility Dean is—was—Aaron Holt's father? That Dean and the widow . . . ?"

"With less than five percent of the population having that blood type, what'dya you think?"

"Could also be Frank. Same family, same blood."

"True. That could include Al, too. You know how hot-blooded those Eye-talians are?"

Lies. Aaron knew there was nothing rare about his blood. At home in his drawer was a blue card the clinic in Ely had given him stating his blood type as A-Positive. A and O, he knew, were common.

"When's the funeral for Dean?"

"Soon's the autopsy is done. Dr. Burke wants to do this one himself."

"The doc's been a busy beaver. Haven't had this much going on since that salmonella poisoning at the Fourth of July picnic three years ago."

"Funny thing about Dean," the first nurse said. "Not funny haha, but y'know, funny peculiar." Her voice lowered, became confidential, conspiratory. "Dean was bad hurt, comatose when they brought him in. Doc shoulda called Care Flight, but he didn't."

The second nurse lowered her voice. "That's not the story I heard. I heard Dean was somewhat lucid. Asked Doc Burke to hold off till morning before calling his folks."

"There's no way that man could ask for anything. I'm not a hundred percent sure, but I'd swear his skull had a depressed fracture, right here above his ear," her voice rose, then quickly lowered again, now barely audible. ". . . Pupils . . . fixed, dilated."

The linoleum under Aaron's bare feet suddenly felt unbearably cold. A violent shiver coursed through his thin body. He inched along the wall until he reached the turn in the corridor, then he ran the rest of the way back to his room.

Faddle slept on. And no amount of shaking could wake him. The man's breathing was shallow. Aaron found a long hair on the mayor's chest and yanked it out. He pulled another and another. The man didn't twitch.

"Shit," Aaron said. He coughed, his lungs ached. "Shit, shit, shit."

He ran to the closet, unwrapped the bandage from his right hand, tore off the hospital gown, then worked his T-shirt over his head, wincing at the pain in his burned hands. The shirt had burn holes and reeked of smoke. Parts of his running shoes had melted from the fire and intense heat, the synthetic laces welded to the rubber and plastic. He stepped into them and felt the warped lumps under his bare soles.

He hurried across the hall to the room where they'd taken Tom Mayfield. He looked very peaceful. After shaking the man several times and getting no response, he left the room and ran down the hallway to the rear door of the clinic. If he could just find Red, everything would be all right.

* * *

"It was no secret I loved the widow," Lubben began. "Any fool in town could tell. Even before she became a widow, when Holt was off servin' his country, I'd find reasons to come by, talk to her, just look at her, y'know? Then he got killed and, much as I felt sorry for her loss, secretly I was glad. Hardly nobody in town had paid her any mind, nobody but me, that is. But she waited and waited and kept sayin' he wasn't dead. That there'd been a terrible mistake and he'd be comin' home at the end of the war. Well, it ended, but he didn't come home. Still, she didn't give up hope.

"All those years went by. Eight, to be exact. She went about her business and kept to herself pretty much. But up in her bedroom was this little shrine she'd made. A lock of hair, their weddin' picture, letters, and—well, stuff like that."

Lubben drew up his leg and rested his arm on the top of his knee, the gun still pointed at James. "The first time I ever laid eyes on that shrine was a day I stopped by for . . . well, I had some lame excuse. It'd been a couple weeks since I'd seen or talked to her. I come around the back and find her passed out on the kitchen floor. She's ice cold and kinda blue. At first I think she's dead—she wasn't hardly breathing. But her chest is making this rattlin' noise. I get her into bed, call the doctor, and, 'cuz I don't know if she's Catholic, call the priest, too. Pneumonia and malnutrition," Lubben went on. "She'd just given up after all those years.

"When Doc asked me to see that she got regular meals and all, I couldn't'ta been happier. I came everyday after that, bringin' food, makin' a fire, seein' to her needs. She got better. That's when I told her my feelin's for her. She appreciated what I'd done, but bein' friends was all she wanted. After her husband, she said, there could never be anyone else." Lubben looked from James to Roni. "I believed her."

A golden eagle soared majestically across the horizon. Roni watched it, mesmerized.

"Okay, that's off my chest. Cut to the chase, Lubben," he said with a deep chuckle. "Months pass. The date is August 10. I'm cruisin' down her street. Didn't see no cars around. 'Course, I didn't think about the tunnel, not then anyway.

"I'd discovered the tunnel about a week before that when a cat got trapped down there and Caroline asked me to let it out. She'd've done it herself, 'cept she was scared to death of rats and wouldn't go near the place—I think that's why she had all those damn furballs clawin' up the furniture. So I get the cat out. At the time I don't think to ask how the damn thing got down there in the first place—but I'm gettin' off the track.

"Anyway, I'm cruisin' by her house when I see somethin' that gives me pause. The sun's goin' down, but clear as a bell I see someone runnin' across the back lot toward the ravine. I start after him, but change my mind. My first concern, naturally, is for Caroline, so I rush inside the house, tear up them stairs and walk into a . . . a goddamn *bloodbath*."

Roni felt an icy lump in her stomach. Larry had used that same analogy.

At first I don't see no one. It ain't till I cross the room to the far side of the bed that I find her. Caroline's lyin' crumpled on the floor with the fireplace poker in her hand, Frank Scolli's body within reach. I knew it was him by the medical bracelet. I could only assume that Frank had attacked Caroline and she'd managed to fend him off, killin' him in the process."

Roni felt a ton of pressure lifting from her. If what the sheriff was saying was true, he wasn't the one. This wasn't a confession of murder, but one of a cover-up.

"I carried Frank down to the tunnel and buried him in the loose silt. Then I cleaned up Caroline and the room. Even had to turn the mattress before I could put her back into bed. By then she was with it enough to ask what happened. I told her Frank had attacked her. I wanted to call the doctor, but she got hysterical and said she didn't want nobody but me to know what happened. She begged me not to arrest Frank. I figured then that she didn't realize she killed him. And I wasn't about to tell her. She had enough troubles without addin' more."

Lubben bowed his head, let his arm with the gun drop, the barrel pointing downward.

"What happened then?" Roni asked, no longer afraid.

"Nothin'. No more was ever said on the subject."

"She didn't do it," James said. "What Larry saw was Caroline passed out on the floor and Frank getting his head bashed in. He didn't see the killer, though."

The sheriff stared down into his lap and rubbed at the back of his neck. "I had to consider that," he said pensively. "I had to wonder where a itty bitty thing like her got the strength to club that young man to death. It happens, I know. Folks muster up strength to do what's gotta be done." He looked from James to Roni. "I said you was gonna get a confession and that's what you got. I covered up a murder to protect Caroline. Only now I see it wasn't her who done it, after all. The killer's still out there. He had twelve years to get real comfortable, to think he'd gotten away with somethin'. Only now he's scared, and he damn well better be, 'cause when I find out who hurt Caroline and who put me through this goddamn hell, I'm gonna kill the bastard with my own two hands."

"Any suspects?" James asked.

"Sure, at the time it was Larry. But when I hauled him in a couple hours later, he was wearin' the same clothes. They was dirty and sweaty and ripped where he'd caught them on a nail or somethin'. The one thing wasn't there was blood. There was no way that Frank's killer coulda come away from the scene of the crime without some blood on him."

Lubben holstered his gun. "Your turn. Whadd'ya got?"

Roni leaned forward, "Sheriff, my father and Aaron are in the hospital—get us back to town. On the way we'll tell you everything we know."

Lubben started the Bronco, cranked the wheel, and headed back the way they'd come. "That's another thing," he said. "That fire last night was intentional. I don't know what he expected to accomplish, or who he hoped would be in the house when he torched it; all I know for sure is he's gone over the edge. He's outta control."

Larry Glazer reclined on the bed, trying to doze. The experience of reliving his nightmare twice in as many days had him feeling drained and utterly exhausted, yet sleep wouldn't come. An image of the tool or weapon he'd tried to tell Jim and Roni about, the thing he'd seen in Frank's hand, kept intruding in his mind.

He propped himself on one elbow, took up pencil and paper, and began to sketch the thing. On his third attempt a shadow passed over him. He smelled Dolores's light perfume, sensed her standing at the side of the bed.

He turned his head and smiled at her. Instead of looking at him, she was staring at the drawing in his hand.

"Why did you draw that?"

"Do you know what it is?"

"You're not the best artist in the world, but it looks like a curette."

"A curette? This is something you're familiar with?"

"Sure. I'm a nurse, remember?"

"What is it?"

"It's a surgical instrument used to remove endometrial tissue."

"You're talking to a layman. No *comprende.*"

"It is used for scraping out the uterus and whatever grows there."

Something flashed across his eyes. A man. A man wielding a long, thin weapon, a poker. The man's face as he swung the weapon. Larry suddenly jolted back as if he, himself, had been clubbed.

Dolores was talking, explaining a surgical procedure. "What?" he grabbed her arm. "What did you just say?"

"Fetus . . . abortion."

"Oh, God," Larry said, jumping up and heading for the door. "I gotta warn them."

Thirty-Nine

The sheriff dropped Roni and James off at the clinic. At the front desk, the nurse told them Aaron was not in his room and that his clothes were gone.

"He couldn't have left more than ten, fifteen minutes ago," Bea said. "I brought him sherbet."

"Where's Faddle?"

"Sound asleep in a chair in Aaron's room. Poor thing—he was up half the night with the boy."

"And Dr. Burke?"

"He's out looking for Aaron. He feels kinda responsible. The little guy was hot to trot, worried sick about that dog. We think he went off to find him."

"My father? Can I see him?"

"Yes, of course."

Several minutes later Roni stood over the still form of her father. She held his hand and listened to the respirator that breathed for him. She felt numb, confused. Frank, Caroline, Dean, Hazel, all dead. And now this.

"I want my father flown to a Reno hospital as soon as possible," Roni said to the nurse who was checking an IV. "Let the doctor know and tell him I'll sign the necessary papers and take full responsibility." She turned to James, who stood at the door. "Let's find Aaron."

They walked to her house. James whistled for Red along the way.

Inside the kitchen Roni put her handbag on the table, then slowly moved through the house, calling for Aaron. The odor of smoke was strong. The fire seemed concentrated in the main hallway and up the center of the staircase. Patches of carpet burned through to the hardwood; it singed furniture, ruined drapes, but the majority of damage was due to smoke and water. Soot and ashes, airborne by their movement, floated listlessly about them, clinging with a greasy persistence to whatever they touched.

Upstairs in the master bedroom, Roni was saddened by the sight of Caroline's prized doll collection; the antique porcelain dolls now resembled war refugees with blackened faces, charred hair and clothes.

In the attic Aaron's project lay in ruins. Three years of tedious work, of painstaking labor and creativity. To see the devastation of those detailed structures made her heartsick.

Unable to look any longer, she quickly left and returned to the main level. In the music room she moved to the piano, stroked the keys, then brushed her hands together. "At least his piano was spared." She gripped the piano and lowered her head. "Oh, God, James, where is he?"

James, at her back, embraced her. Neither said a word. She wondered if he was feeling the same thing . . . time standing still. Had it been less than two weeks since she'd walked through that door into a dark, imposing house?

She leaned into James and squeezed his arm.

"James . . ." she turned in his arms and stared up at him. "Why did you pull me out of the house? I mean—who did you think was coming down those stairs that afternoon?"

"I think you already know."

She waited.

"I didn't want you to find your father with Caroline. You would have been confused, hurt . . ."

"But how did—was he here? Dammit, James, did you *see* him here?"

He shook his head. "Frank was overheard telling you and Larry about the man in the house."

"Overheard by who?"

"Someone I was meeting in the woods. Someone who didn't want it known we were going to be together."

A secret rendezvous. With who? It took Roni only a second to figure it out. *Jolie.* It had to be. Her sister, who only dated boys of well-off and influential families, would have made an exception with James, a miner's son, as long as the meeting was clandestine. "You blew a chance with the most popular girl in town to keep another girl from running into her cheating father?"

"It seemed more important at the time."

She hugged him. "Let's find Aaron."

"Listen, you stay here in case he shows up. I'll drive around and look for him. Lock the doors and don't open to anyone except Aaron or me."

* * *

At the bottom of the staircase, in the abandoned

building, Aaron turned south in the tunnel and headed uphill toward his house, running a bandaged hand along the wall. He had traveled most of the tunnels in Eagleton—this one was the last leg home and he knew it well. But with no flashlight to guide him the pitch-blackness closed around him with a palpable thickness, slowing him down. He had gone only a few yards when he heard a sound behind him.

He paused. Held his breath.

The sound was faint, a good distance away, but definitely identifiable. A dog whimpering.

Red!

Aaron whistled several sharp notes.

A bark, followed by more whimpering.

Aaron turned back and headed north, elation rushing through him, making his feet quick and sure.

Roni went into the dining room to use the phone. She thought she'd call the clinic to see if Aaron or the doctor had returned. The light on the answering machine blinked. She pressed the button. Larry's voice, high-pitched with excitement, said: "Roni, I *know* who it is. Call. I'll be waiting by the phone." She quickly jotted down the number, hung up, and began to dial.

She heard a noise behind her. She turned to see a man standing in the shadows of the dining room. Her heart dropped into her stomach. The man stepped into the light.

"Oh, God, Doctor, you scared me."

"Aaron's gone," he said quietly.

"I know. James is looking for him." She finished dialing the number. "Give me a sec, I have to make a very important call to—" she stopped abruptly. Fear caught at her again. She turned back to him. "How did you get in?" She had locked the house after James left.

"Hang up."

She slowly replaced the receiver.

"How much does the sheriff know?" he said, his features no longer pleasant.

Roni stared at him.

"No matter, I'll find out." His hand came out from behind him. He held a knife. She recognized it as one from the kitchen.

The doctor. The good Catholic doctor with the ideal wife, the ideal family, the ideal country life. The ideal choice for Caroline. He had strong, healthy children and divorce for him would be out of the question. Unfortunately for those involved, murder came easier than divorce.

"What are you doing?"

"You're leaving town. You and Aaron and probably Jim." His tone was soft, even, and it gave her a chill. Not an accident this time. They'd just disappear. An abandoned mine? If there was one thing Eureka County did not have a shortage of it was bottomless pits.

He pushed her down into a chair, pulled another one close, and sat, leaning forward. "We'll wait for Jim and Aaron."

"Doctor, have you thought of your family? They love you, they—"

"I am thinking of them. I have to protect them from scandal. I have to protect them. Frank Scolli, he saw what I was going to do. He would have told. I couldn't let him tell. I . . . I struck out before I could stop myself. It happened so fast there was no time to think. But he wouldn't go down. He just stood there and he wouldn't go down."

What did Frank see? Roni wondered.

His jaw twitched. His eyes glowed with remembrance. As though reading her mind he said, "I couldn't allow her to have that baby."

"Abortion," Roni whispered, unaware she'd spoken aloud.

"He intruded into something that was not his business and he got killed for it." He looked at her, his face passive. "I was going to turn myself in, but . . . but nothing came of it. No death report, no body, the sheriff claiming Frank ran off after raping Caroline. I couldn't believe it. I was spared. I'd made a terrible mistake, but God saw fit to absolve me from sin . . . to allow me to continue to serve Him by caring for the good people of Eagleton. To this day I have no idea why Lubben covered it up. In time the horror of that night faded, became nonexistent, until . . ." His voice became a growl, deep and fierce, "Until last month when *she* couldn't leave well enough alone.

"She said Aaron had a right to know who his father was. Not true. Not at my expense or the expense of my family. Neither of them had any rights, not after the way she deceived me . . . lied to me.

"I saved her life, you know? She'd fallen sick, pneumonia, and I treated her, nursed her back to health. Charlotte, whom I love dearly, was far along in her third pregnancy. Caroline, knowing how vulnerable I was, took full advantage. Once snared, I became obsessed. I was lost . . . totally *lost*, living for those few stolen moments with her. Caroline was . . . was . . ." He looked up, hatred blazing in his eyes. "She got pregnant and could not name the father. How was that possible? I thought she loved me. Thought I was the only . . ." He squeezed Roni's arm. "She used me. Used me and your father to give life to an illegitimate child."

James, for the love of God, where are you?

"I begged her to get rid of it and she refused. She had no right to . . ." He let the words hang in the air. With a sigh, he added, "It can't be turned around. At the time I was prepared to pay for my sins. But not now, not after all this time. A scandal like this would shatter the lives of my family. It would damage any chances for my son's political career . . . my daughter's marriage to young Saltzman. It was buried and it has to stay buried. Do you understand?" He pulled her to him and, within inches of her face, whispered harshly, *"It has to stay buried."*

Roni closed her eyes against the darting madness in his pale blue eyes. He had spent too much time mulling this over, too many years trying to protect his secret; many had died to cover up his crime. He had nothing to lose anymore. Where could he go? He was a small town doctor revered by all those in the community, existing in a glowing world of love, admiration, and contentment. Hazel had been a long-time friend of his. It occurred to her then that if he could kill Caroline and Hazel in cold blood, he was capable of killing anyone. *Kill any and all who would expose him*—it was as simple as that.

When had he gone mad? When he learned Caroline was pregnant? When she betrayed him? When he killed Frank? Caroline? Or slowly, over the years, like trickling water eroding a stone?

From the driveway came the sound of tires crunching on gravel.

The doctor paused, tilting his head to listen. "Jim?

Good. Might as well get this over with." He jerked her from the chair. "Let's go."

They moved into the kitchen. She watched not James, but Lubben, step up on the back stoop. He tapped on the glass.

Burke held the knife to the small of her back. She felt the sharp tip cutting into her skin. "We're going to let him in. No tricks or I'll kill you."

Roni's mind was whirling. The sheriff had a gun. She would open the door and, with a warning to Lubben, push her way outside.

She took one step and froze. The sheriff had the door open and was stepping in. He held up a key. "Guess I should give this back," Lubben said. "Hey, Doc. House call?"

"Aaron's gone AWOL," Burke said, grinning, once again the friendly country doctor. "Gotta find him and take him back."

"Good luck. That kid don't do much he don't want to do." Lubben turned to Roni. "Roni, I came for Caroline's diary. Evidence, y'know."

Roni saw a sudden spark in Burke's eyes. Lubben missed it.

The cloth bound book was visible inside her handbag on the table.

The sheriff lifted it out. "This it?"

Roni swallowed, glanced at Burke, then nodded when the point of the knife jabbed into her.

Lubben tucked the book under an arm and moved toward the door. "I'll drive around, see if I can spot the kid."

Roni held her breath.

Lubben's hand was turning the doorknob when the doctor stopped him. "Sheriff, while you're here I think there's something you should see."

"Oh?"

"In the passage."

"Yeah, what?"

"Could be more evidence. But you be the judge."

"My, ain't we the mysterious one." Lubben grinned again.

Obviously impatient to have it done with, he forged ahead, leading the way into the basement, then down into the tunnel itself.

With a jab from Burke, Roni went down the ladder. The doctor followed.

"Christ, it's cold in here," Lubben said. "Make this quick, will ya, Doc?"

"Over there." The doctor pointed to the dark corner where a broken mason jar lay.

Lubben directed his flashlight in the corner and moved toward it. "Hell, Doc, I seen this—"

Burke rushed at him.

"No!" Roni screamed.

The knife plunged deep into the middle of Lubben's back. The sheriff arched, trying to reach it with stiffening fingers.

Roni charged, attempting to grab the sheriff's gun and was knocked to the ground by Burke's powerful backhand.

With some effort Burke pulled the blade out. Lubben twisted around and was stabbed in the center of his chest. His hand, spastic, fingers twitching, fumbled for his holstered gun as he fell to his knees, a stunned look on his face. Then he toppled over, bright blood staining his tan shirt before darkening the earth beneath him.

The doctor bent down and lifted Caroline's book and the sheriff's gun. "C'mon," he said, yanking her to her feet and pushing her into the passageway, the faint beam from his penlight her only guide.

Forty

James had driven through the streets on Aaron's side of town, then decided to check at his house in case Red had gone there. Thirty minutes later when James pulled back into the Holt driveway, he saw Lubben's Bronco. The back door was unlocked. He entered cautiously.

He resisted the urge to call out. Instead, he moved quietly from room to room. When it was apparent she was nowhere in the house, he dialed the clinic and asked if she or Aaron had shown up. He was told they had not.

"Is the mayor still there?" he asked the nurse.

"Yep, and still out like a light. I've been trying to wake him, but no luck. Jim, I'm beginning to worry."

A knot formed in the pit of James's stomach. "Drugged?"

"That's what it looks like."

"Bea, call the sheriff's office and see if someone there can reach Lubben. His Bronco's here, but he's not. If you can't reach him, find Deming and tell them we have a situation here at the Holt place." He was about to hang up. "If Roni or Aaron shows up, keep them there. I'll check back."

James went to his truck. As he reached under the seat for the flashlight, his gaze fell on his bow stretched across the rack in the back window. He took it down and grabbed the quiver.

He returned to the house and made his way down into the tunnel. The first thing he saw was Lubben's body. The sheriff, face down in a pool of blood, was dead.

James saw Lubben's empty holster. He looked in the quiver—two arrows. *Shit.*

As he moved through the passage he had the bone-chilling suspicion that Red was already dead, and Roni and Aaron would soon be dead as well.

When Aaron ran out of wall, he knew he had reached the wide tunnel running east and west under Main Street.

He called softly.

From the west he heard low barking. He turned, heading toward the sound.

Red kept up a chorus of soft whimpers and throaty barks and finally, thirty feet or so in, Aaron came upon him. He knelt, wrapping his arms around him. The dog was sitting on one haunch, panting. When Aaron hugged him, Red cried out, licked Aaron's face, and began panting again.

"Hey, boy, what's the matter? Why're you sitting here? You okay?" Aaron gingerly patted down the dog. On one side of his head Aaron felt a warm, sticky substance he was sure had to be blood. A gash separated the fur.

"The dirty sonofabitch—he got you, didn't he?" Aaron said, wanting to hug the animal, but afraid he'd hurt him. "You were trying to protect me, huh, and the slimy bastard got you?"

Red licked Aaron's face again.

"Red, I gotta get help. I can't carry you, boy, so you'll have to wait here for me. Soon as I find Roni and James, I'll come back for you."

The mention of James brought Red to his feet.

"You sure, boy?" With a hand lightly holding onto Red's tail, Aaron followed the dog back the way he'd come.

With the doctor pulling Roni along by her arm, they made their way through the chilly tunnel. Her teeth chattered, as much from fear as from the cold. She was terrified of the man walking beside her, and terrified that the tunnel would cave in before he had a chance to kill her.

He dropped the diary. He stopped her with a yank on her arm. "Pick it up."

She did. "There's nothing . . . in this book. Caroline didn't name names. You killed the sheriff for nothing."

"He would have found out sooner or later and then he would have come after me. The damn fool was crazy about her. Granville wanted to marry her, but she kept them both at arm's length. Your father and I, now we were the perfect sacrificial lambs. Did your father think the kid was his?"

Roni refused to answer.

"She had the nerve to tell me not to worry because

she had no intention of naming the father, ever. *Don't worry!*" he spit out. "Christ, I pictured this freckled kid with blue eyes and red hair running around town asking every man, 'Are you my daddy?'" Burke laughed a dry, hard laugh. "I had to stop her. So the next day I got in through the tunnel and put a heavy dose of barbiturates in the brandy decanter. She always had a glass in the late afternoon before napping. I returned to the clinic to wait, but got detained by an emergency. It was nearly dusk before I could get back. She was in bed, out cold.

"The D&C is a relatively minor procedure. It was going to be so easy—a spontaneous abortion—and I'd be long gone when she woke up. Some blood, enough to suspect a natural miscarriage. It would have gone without a hitch except for two miscalculations. The drug was wearing off and that damn Scolli boy showed up.

"I barely had time to hide in the closet. Caroline was moaning. He heard her and made the stupid mistake of going to her. Caroline, still heavily drugged and confused, fought him. When he saw the curette and the blood he came toward the closet. He would have found me. He would have told."

Then it had turned his way again, Roni thought. The sheriff covers it up, Caroline is oblivious to it all, the Glazers and her family move out of town. The baby turns out to be a clone of its mother and, over the years, both become recluses. It was as if that night never happened.

"You can't kill everyone," Roni said.

"I'm beginning to think I can."

Those words, and the casual way they were said, sent a shudder through Roni. He had everything to lose and nothing to gain. She couldn't just meekly go along like a lamb to slaughter, waiting for all the victims to conveniently present themselves to him. He had a gun now. He could kill her, Aaron, and James without any difficulty. As long as he had her he had the means to draw in the others.

They approached an intersecting passageway.

"There's no point in going any further. Aaron will have to come by here. We'll just wait." He pulled at her.

At the mention of Aaron, Roni felt a surge of adrenaline. Moving quickly, she dropped down, throwing him off balance, then she rose and brought her knee up to Burke's crotch. She wasn't fast enough. He pivoted and caught her knee at the front of his thigh. She twisted away and tried to run. She felt her hair grabbed from behind, yanked hard, a torrent of pain shot into her scalp.

With all her might she drove the journal toward his face. The hard spine smashed against his nose. She heard a sickening crunch. He howled, released her arm, and grabbed at his face. Hot, sticky blood splashed across her chest and shoulder. She scrambled to her feet and began to run through the tunnel, back the way they'd come.

The deafening crack of a gun discharging sounded in the passageway, echoing over and over in Roni's ears.

James heard a man yowl, followed by a shot. He stopped, listened. It sounded at least a hundred feet away.

James flicked off the flashlight. No sense in announcing himself to the killer if he was coming back his way. There was a chance, a slim one, that

James might catch him off guard. He took an arrow from the quiver and readied his bow. Silently, in the dark, he hurried forward.

Roni ran blindly through the dark passageway, one hand extended in front of her and the other skimming along the wall, praying that the gunshot hadn't weakened the tunnel—her relief at getting away from the doctor was overshadowed by her deep-seated fear of a cave-in. Her weak ankle gave out—an agonizing pain shot through it. She lost her balance and felt herself pitching forward and slammed down, tumbling and sliding, onto the hard dirt floor. She tried to rise, gasping with the fiery streaks of crippling pain. Behind her she heard Burke grunting as he closed the distance.

She crawled on hands and knees, using the wall on her right to guide her. When she felt the open space of an off-shoot passage, Roni turned into it. Knowing how precarious the unshored passages were only increased her fear, but it was her only chance. If she could just hide.

Seven or eight feet in, she turned to see the faint light from Burke's penlight glowing on the walls of the main passage. She had to get far enough away to out-distance the weak beam. Another yard and she ran out of tunnel.

A moan of despair sounded in her dry throat. There was nowhere to go. Nowhere to hide. On unsteady legs, she came to her feet, ignoring the stabbing pains in her ankle, and felt along the wall. Eroded in the dirt and silt she found an alcove no more than three feet high and two feet deep and quickly worked herself into the tight space. For an instant she experienced the suffocating panic of the earth closing in

on her before the heavy footsteps of her assailant
drummed out all other thoughts or fears.

She heard his steps slow, then stop, his breathing
labored and wet. She imagined the blood gushing
from his nose. The beam of light swung all around
the passage she was hiding in. She held her breath,
trying to make herself small and invisible. The beam
crawled over the toe of her boot. She closed her eyes
and prayed.

A lifetime passed, her pounding heartbeat in a
deadly duet with Burke's ghastly breathing. And then
it was pitch black again and her heartbeat was the
only sound.

She listened carefully and was relieved to hear him
continuing down the main passage. She rested her
head on her raised knees and sobbed silently.

Several minutes later a dog's bark echoed in the
passageway.

Roni jerked her head up. Red was somewhere in
the tunnel. Was he alone? With James? With Aaron?

Her question was answered when she heard Aaron's
small voice call out to her.

Her racing heart filled her chest.

Aaron was coming. Aaron was returning to the
house and the doctor was not far away! Roni was
between the two.

She wanted to scream from sheer frustration.
Instead she crawled from the tiny cave, pulled herself
to her feet, and hobbled forward. She had to warn
Aaron.

As she neared the main passage she heard Aaron
again call her name.

Using the wall for support, she inched ahead. Suddenly, from out of the darkness she saw Burke rushing

in her direction, heading toward Aaron, the gun
raised.

A silent scream filled Roni's head. With no concern
for her own safety she lunged at the doctor as he
drew even with her, smashing into his left shoulder
and grabbing for the gun. She had to stop him . . .
she wanted to kill him, to turn the gun on him and
fire, to watch the life disappear from his eyes along
with the madness.

"Aaron, go back! Get out, run!"

Burke, with blood smeared over his face and pouring from his nose, spun around and slammed Roni
against the side of the passageway. The air exploded
from her lungs. He snatched her and held her in front
of him. Roni couldn't get a breath. She struggled
ineffectually.

Burke's light shone on Aaron.

Aaron, without glasses, looking smaller and more
vulnerable than ever, had hold of the dog's neck.
Even from this distance she saw the confusion and
indecision on his face.

The gun pointed at Aaron, the hammer came back
beneath Burke's thumb.

"Nooo!" Roni screamed.

"Paul!" James called out.

The doctor backed up to the wall and swiveled
around, pointing the light in the opposite direction.
Roni turned her head, wincing from the pain of
Burke's cruel fingers digging into her arm. Twenty
feet away, partially illuminated in the circle of light
from the flashlight at his feet, stood James. In an
archer's stance, the arrow in place and the bowstring
pulled taut to his right ear, he waited. Her eyes locked
on his. She realized that she and the doctor stood in

the middle with James on one side and Aaron on the other, the gun pointed at her head.

"Go ahead," the doctor said to James. "Shoot. Even if you hit me, I'll surely manage to get a round off into her temple." The doctor glanced at Aaron. "She's dead if that mutt so much as wags his tail."

Aaron tightened his grip on Red.

They stood that way, a three-way standoff. Silent. Minutes ticked away.

"Now this is ridiculous," Burke said. "This gun is very heavy. Of course, I don't imagine it's as heavy as your bow, Jim. Ease off the bowstring, then let it drop to the ground."

Roni watched James. His hands, so discernible that at first she thought she might be imagining it, began to tremble. Soon the vibrations traveled along his extended arm to his shoulder. A bead of sweat coursed down the side of his face.

"Look at you, Jimmy, you're shaking like a leaf. The pressure of that bow must be tremendous. How many pounds on that pull? Sixty? Seventy-five? To sustain so much weight for such a long time has to be excruciating. The way you're shaking, you don't dare release that arrow now. The chance of it striking Roni, the boy, or your dog have greatly increased. Do you want to take that chance?"

James worked his fingers on the grip. Another bead of sweat followed the first.

"Roni, talk to him," Burke said. "Tell him it's useless."

"James," she said evenly, "he's right, it's useless. Take your best shot, James. He's going to kill all of us anyway. He has nothing to—"

"Shut up!" Burke swung the gun around toward James.

James released the arrow.

It entered the doctor's wrist. The doctor screamed, his fingers locked, refusing to close.

Roni pushed away from him and ran to Aaron. Using her body to shield the boy, she hugged him to her. She heard the twang of the bowstring a second time, a split second before a gunshot exploded, echoing through the passage.

Roni spun around to see James fall against the wall of the tunnel, a hand pressed over the wound in his upper thigh.

With his back to her the doctor stood, an arrow sticking through his wrist, the gun, now in his other hand, pointed at James's chest.

Roni moaned. She wanted to look away but couldn't.

Then, as if in slow motion, the doctor twisted around, his profile to her. From the center of his chest an arrow stood straight out.

"Killshot," Aaron said quietly with reverence.

The doctor sank to the ground and toppled over, lifeless.

Roni and Red rushed to James's side. Aaron stopped to take the gun from the doctor's hand.

Leaning against the wall, James let the empty quiver drop from his shoulder.

"Oh, God, James," Roni said. She pulled off her sweater and tied it around his leg to stanch the flow of blood. "You goddamn better not bleed to death on me."

James took hold of her trembling hands. She looked into his eyes. He pulled her face to his, kissed her lightly on the lips.

She lifted James's arm over her shoulder to help support him. "Aaron, are you all right?"

"I'm okay. Red's hurt, but he can walk." Aaron got on James's other side to help.

"Then let's get the hell out of this place."

Forty-One

The three-story Victorian lady sat majestically within a square of green, orange, and yellow, the turning leaves of the surrounding trees giving the house color it did not in itself possess. Around several windows, the attic in particular, smoke stained the white shutters a charcoal gray. It was a warm, bright Indian summer day, two weeks after the fire and the tragic events that had followed.

The state police, with their own forensic experts, had come and gone along with a slew of reporters from a half-dozen states. Eagleton and the murders made national news, then were quickly forgotten.

It would take a long while for the people of Eagleton to forget. In less than one month a small town's population decreased by five. Three of those in less than twenty-four hours. All violent. The deaths would have been shocking enough, but to learn their dear and glorious physician had been the villain rocked them like nothing could.

After a private memorial for Paul Burke, Charlotte and the children, with the oldest son behind the wheel, drove away in their Suburban to her parents' ranch in Kingston, California, for a visit—length of time unspecified.

Alfonso and Anna Scolli buried a second son in nearly as many days. Anna locked herself in the room she shared with her husband and refused to come out. After four days Al and their two remaining sons broke down the door. In the old flatbed Chevy they took her to Elko to a sanatorium where a week later news of her paralyzing stroke further saddened the residents of Eagleton.

Mayor Fadius Granville appointed Vern Deming as acting sheriff to the delight of the other deputies. Deming, mild-mannered and soft-spoken, the opposite of Lubben, was a commander the men liked and respected.

Tom Mayfield went by Care Flight helicopter to a hospital in Reno. Still comatose, the doctors gave him a fifty-fifty chance to recover. Roni theorized that the doctor had used a drug that would throw suspicion on Faddle Granville—*insulin*, readily available to the son of a diabetic.

Roni and James sat in the Blazer at the fringe of trees above the house. James wore shorts, a bandage wrapped around his upper thigh. The bullet had gone through the leg cleanly, missing the bone. He got around with the aid of a crutch. He was young and strong and a full recovery without complications was expected.

They watched Aaron roughhouse with Red in the yard below. Except for a patch across the inside of

Aaron's wrist, the burns on his hands and arms were nearly healed.

"Aaron, not too rough," Roni called down to him. "You'll have Red's stitches coming open."

Aaron flopped down flat on his stomach in the grass and buried his face in his arms. Red jumped on him, trying to lick his face. Roni heard the boy laughing, a sound she was hearing more and more and eagerly looked forward to.

Roni had been named guardian to Aaron. Legal steps to adopt him had already begun. Her possessions and some of Aaron's were packed in the Chevy. Roni had declined James's offer to drive them. She and Aaron would make an adventure of his first time away from home. For the next several months they would live in Reno, near the hospital where her father had been admitted.

"I have at least another year here," James said to Roni, his fingers entwining hers. "Then I don't know where I'll go. I'd like you and Aaron, however, to be involved in that decision. I'd like you both with me . . . wherever."

She squeezed his hand and laid her head on his shoulder. "A year," she said, reflectively. "That will give Aaron and me a chance to work some things out, like whether I'll stay with the magazine or quit and freelance. By then Caroline's house will be renovated, ready for occupancy again. Faddle offered to buy it if that's what we want."

"I think getting Aaron out of Eagleton, giving him a chance to live a somewhat normal life will be the best thing for him," James said. "Having a dog will help."

"James, are you sure you can bear to part with Red?"

"I'm sure. I don't spend the time with him that I should. He needs someone to romp with, to watch over. Look at him," James tipped his head toward the dog and boy rolling on the lawn. "He's never been happier. Besides, I'll see him often." James planned to take Faddle up on his offer to use the plane as often as he liked.

"I talked to Larry this morning and he sounded good, real good," James said. "He has another three weeks in the rehab program, then group therapy for as long as he feels he needs it. He expects you to visit him."

"I intend to. I've already spoken with Dolores. She says for the first time the future looks good for Larry."

"And for the rest of us."

Roni smiled, leaned into James, and felt safe and secure. Across the valley atop the mountain range she saw a bank of storm clouds gathering. She thought back to the blustery day she had arrived in Eagleton. From above, like a scene on an inspirational card, luminous rays of light had fanned out of the clouds and pointed down into the little town. She'd wondered then if it was an omen. Good or bad? It had been both.

She and Aaron would be leaving that afternoon with the dark clouds behind them, heading into clear skies and a bright, promising future.

Roni looked down at the house again and thought of Caroline. Memories—warm, good memories were all she had now. Caroline may have been deceptive, but she was not the cold, selfish Jezebel the doctor had described. She had been merely a lonely woman obsessed with a memory and a desperate desire for a child, wholly unaware of the magnetism that drew the men in her life to her, a magnetism that ultimately cost her her life and nearly took the lives of those she loved.

Aaron, the child she had lived and died for, had given her eleven years of love and happiness. And now it was Roni's turn.

Goodbye, Caroline,

. . . and thank you.

*"MIND-BOGGLING . . . THE SUSPENSE IS UNBEARABLE . . .
DORIS MILES DISNEY WILL KEEP YOU
ON THE EDGE OF YOUR SEAT . . ."*

THE MYSTERIES OF DORIS MILES DISNEY